WEIGHING 1

Eileen Simkiss

© Eileen Simkiss 2016

This is a work of fiction. Certain real locations and public figures are mentioned but all other characters and events in the book are imaginary

Growing up during the grim, post-war years, our world was small and we had nothing with which to compare the quality of our lives. Like medieval villagers, many of us had never been more than ten miles from home. The only colour in our lives was provided by some of the characters living within our narrow boundaries.

Our playground was the cobbled streets and the nearest tree was ten minutes' walk away.

We had the radio, with its posh BBC voices, and regular trips to the pictures where we escaped into fantasy worlds of cowboys riding the range and glamorous ladies dancing and singing with handsome men. World events meant little or nothing to us. What we saw in the newsreels depicted a different world to the one we lived in.

There was little difference in the economic circumstances of the families who lived in the grey terraced streets. But then, as now, the family into which we were born, with a few exceptions, would be the dominant influence in our development.

***

1950

4,000 British troops are sent to Korea

Motor fuel and soap rationing come to an end

Sainsbury's open first purpose built self-service supermarket

First package holiday by Horizon Holidays, from Gatwick Airport to Calvi, Corsica

Published: 'The Third Man'– Graham Green
'The Lion, the Witch and the Wardrobe' – C S Lewis

Best Film Oscar: 'All About Eve' - Bette Davies and Anne Bancroft

Popular record: 'Goodnight Irene' - Frank Sinatra and Jo Stafford

Born in 1950: Jeremy Paxman, television presenter and author
Rowan Williams, Archbishop of Canterbury
Richard Branson, entrepreneur

Chapter 1

Maurice Marshall sat in the sunshine in the narrow confines of his backyard. Like a fat spider; he sat immobile, waiting for victims. Only his eyes, darting from the back gate to the notebook on the rickety table, and the fat fingers of his right hand moving rapidly to tot up gains and losses betrayed his alertness.

In well cut navy pin-striped trousers, matching waistcoat and white poplin shirt, collarless at present, he counted the afternoon's takings from illegal bets on the horses running at Aintree. There were still expenses to pay but takings were up.

Apart from the punters who slid into the backyard to place their bets, a couple of runners doubled backwards and forwards from the local pubs, delivering betting slips and cash. The last of the winnings had been collected and he was nearly done for the day.

'Fred, you still there? Get Clarkie and Charlie,' he shouted to the thin faced man loitering outside the back gate.

Fred waved at the watchers at the far end of the cobbled back entry and then opened the gate just wide enough to sidle in, followed by two other shabbily dressed men.

'Here you go, ten bob each. Any signs?'

Maurice paid the local bobby a couple of quid a week to turn a blind eye but it paid to be cautious. Spot checks were not unknown and he reckoned he'd stayed in business so long by watching his step – and watching his back.

These three were insurance. They kept a look out, one at each of the narrow entries nearest the house and the other at the far end with a view of the streets on either side.

Folding the rest of the notes, he stuck them in his back pocket.

'Same time next week?' asked Fred. 'All of us?'

Maurice nodded.

The three men nodded back and sidled out the way they'd come.

He sat back in the kitchen chair brought out every Saturday afternoon, weather permitting.

'Hettie, where's that beer?' he shouted.

His wife of fifteen years scuttled out of the kitchen carrying a jug and a heavy glass. Dressed in a nondescript jumper and a worn woollen skirt and enveloped in a floral, wraparound pinafore, she was clearly wary of him. No longer the pretty girl he'd married but now a worn out housewife, looking ten years older than she should.

She knew the drill, tea on the table in half an hour and woe betide the lads if they weren't on time. She'd fret until they came through the door. Though Maurice paid little attention to his sons, showed no interest in their activities or progress at school, he was a martinet where timekeeping was concerned.

Maurice drank his beer and enjoyed the sunshine while Hettie hurried round, checking the steak in the oven and peeling potatoes for chips; head cocked for the sound of the lads coming home. The back gate rattled, one pigeon home to roost.

'Hiya, Dad.'

Maurice grunted but she knew it was Harry. He came in and plonked himself at the kitchen table.

'You seen Johnny?' she asked. 'He's cutting it fine.'

'No, saw him earlier on but that was ages ago.'

At fourteen, Harry was filling out. Already as tall as his father, his shoulders were gaining breadth and there was the first faint sign of hair on his upper lip. He'd always been a scrapper, coming home with scratches and bruises after a bout with one of the other kids, but there was no malice in him. He'd settled down recently, smartened himself up and now spent hours up on the park with a gang. For the first time, girls were allowed to join the boys and the interest in the opposite sex was mutual.

Hettie lowered the basket of chips into the hot fat and gave it a shake; only a few minutes to go and no sign of Johnnie.

'That lad'll be the death of me,' she muttered. 'Where is he?'

The back gate rattled again.

'Hiya, Dad.'

Maurice fished his gold watch out of his waistcoat pocket.

'Just made it, another couple of minutes and you'd have copped it.'

'I'm here now though and I'm not late.'

'None of your cheek, get inside.'

Hettie had been beaten into submission years earlier and Harry kept his head down. Johnnie, three years younger than Harry, pushed his luck to the limit but never quite crossed the line.

Maurice would have come down on him hard but had a sneaking admiration for the lad, at least he showed some backbone. He looked across the table at the two of them; Johnnie, little and scruffy but with a certain set to the shoulders and a light in his eye and Harry, stocky and comparatively tidy, head down to avoid any prospect of confrontation.

The mismatched plates, loaded with golden chips and braised steak swimming in mouth-watering gravy went on the table and the three of them tucked. Idle conversation was discouraged

There was no sign of appreciation from Maurice as he nudged his empty plate away, just a grunt as he leaned on the table and pushed himself up. The routine never varied. He'd sleep in an armchair in the front room, expecting silence for an hour or so.

The lads sat looking at him, waiting. It had been a profitable day and it suited him to be magnanimous. He flipped a sixpence over the table to Johnnie and a shilling to Harry, the coins caught deftly by the boys.

'Thanks, Dad'. They pocketed the coins and disappeared. There'd be no sign of them until bedtime.

Hettie's turn; he took the roll of notes from his back pocket and peeled off a couple. This was a crucial time for Hettie, she was expected to make the cash he gave her last all week but she never knew exactly how much she'd get. Over the years, she'd learned to save a bit from the good weeks to tide her over the bad. On the other hand, he often came home with a parcel of black market sausages, extra bacon or a Sunday joint. He liked his grub and had contacts for things that "fell off lorries". She could never count on the extras though and a request for more cash halfway through the week would result in great displeasure or even a slap or two. Not daring to count them, she picked up the notes, but could feel it was a good week. Slipping them into her pinafore pocket, she muttered,

'Thanks, Maurice.'

He nodded and went into the front room. She heard him settle into his armchair; an hour's peace at last. Putting the chip pan back on the stove, she made her own tea. She never ate until everyone else was finished and was grateful the weather was fine. When the lads were forced to stay in the house, she was on pins. Any disturbance of Maurice's beauty sleep could have dire consequences.

She cleared away her plate and sat down again with a cup of tea and the "Evening News". Maurice's light snores wafted through the open door, he'd be good for another half hour at least. The packet of Players cigarettes lay temptingly on the kitchen table and she checked quickly. About fifteen left; he wouldn't miss one. Cigarette in one hand and tea in the other, she relaxed for the first time all day. She usually smoked Park Drive but was partial to something better. It made her day to get one over on Maurice, no matter how small the victory.

Her sister was coming down later, after Maurice had gone to the pub. What he didn't know wouldn't hurt him and those two hated the sight of each other.

She stubbed out her cigarette and downed the rest of her tea. She topped up the water in the sink and washed the pots, careful not to clatter anything.

Although the windows shone and the cooker and the fireplace were freshly black leaded, the air of shabbiness remained. The pre-war table and chairs had had their fair share of knocks and the worn oilcloth showed every mark no matter how often she wiped it; dust in the summer and mud in the winter.

Hettie sighed. As long as his meals were on the table on time and his shirts were clean and starched, Maurice couldn't care less how they lived.

He was stirring, so she went to get him a clean shirt and collar.

He stripped off his shirt and stood at the kitchen sink, his slight paunch hanging over his trousers. He wasn't a pretty sight. Hettie rubbed a duster over his shoes while he put on the clean shirt.

'Collar stud,' he muttered.

She passed it over and watched him knot his tie. She'd love to pull it *really* tight. She brushed the shoulders of his jacket and held it so he could slip his arms in the sleeves. Pulling the jacket straight, he squared his shoulders and left the house through the front door. He was the only one to use it. Everybody else came and went through the back.

The back gate rattled and there was a tap at the back door.

'Hett, it's me.'

'Come in Flo, am I glad to see you?'

Florence, in a shabby black coat and carrying a shopping bag, came through and pulled out a chair. She took off the headscarf, a permanent feature of her outer clothing, and stuffed it in her pocket.

'He's driving me mad again. He was in the pub all dinner time and he's already back there. There'll be nothing left by Monday and then he'll be on the scrounge.. He keeps me short and then complains about the grub on the table. Thinks I'm a flamin' magician.'

Flo's husband was a drinker. For weeks, he'd call in for a quick couple of pints but when the mood took him, he'd settle in for a full weekend's drinking. Unpredictable when full of ale, he could be handy with his fists and Flo had had more than one black eye. The kids kept out of his way, disappearing upstairs when he came falling through the front door at closing time.

He'd saddled her with five kids in seven years and, like Hettie, she looked old before her time.

'At least Maurice doesn't knock you about, at least not much.'

'No, just an odd slap and I know what riles him, so I watch my step. Never mind, look what I've got.'

She reached into the back of the kitchen cupboard and pulled out a half bottle of whisky, pouring two generous measures of golden, aromatic liquid.

Get that down you.'

Florence smiled, took a sip and savoured the taste.

'How'd you manage that, then?'

'Maurice always has a bottle of Scotch on the go. So when he's had a couple of tots, I top up my supply, just a bit so he won't miss it. Then when he has another couple, I top mine up again.'

'You're a wonder, our Hett. How you think of these things?'

'I do what I can. He's got loads of cash but we see little enough. It's hard to keep the lads in shoes, specially in the holidays when they're playing football all day. I'm just helping myself to what I'm entitled to and what he doesn't know won't hurt him.'

The sisters sat for an hour, making their drinks last and passing on the latest gossip.

Daughters of a domineering and brutal father and a downtrodden but God-fearing mother, they'd fallen into the same pattern, marrying men not unlike their father. They weren't treated any better than their mother had been. She'd bowed her head and said it was God's will but the girls, especially Hettie, had a bit more spirit.

Flo had pretty well had the fight knocked out of her but Hettie still had a spark of rebellion, kept carefully hidden from Maurice.

Flo stood up, buttoned her coat and tied the scarf firmly under her chin.

'I'd better get a move on. God only knows what the kids will have been up to and they need to be in bed before he comes home.'

'OK, I'll see you later in the week, Flo.' She leaned over and kissed her cheek. 'Take care of yourself.'

Johnnie came rattling through the door, late as usual. He came home only when all the other lads had disappeared.

'Anything to eat, Mum? I'm starving.'

With cocoa and a slab of bread and marge inside him, she sent him off to bed. Harry wouldn't be far behind so she put her feet up while she waited

Sally

Mickey Smith, a wimp of about ten, came round the corner, snivelling and wiping his eyes and nose on the sleeve of his jumper. It didn't make his face any cleaner, just moved the dirt around a bit.

'What's up, Mick?' asked one of the girls.

'It's that Johnnie Marshall. He's always thumping me,' he sobbed.

We crowded round him and I put an arm round his shoulders. He didn't smell too good.

'Never mind, Mick. When you grow up, you might be bigger than him and you can give him a good hiding.'

He snuffled, trying to control his tears.

'Yeah, I'd give him a real good bashin'.'

He smiled a watery smile and wandered off.

'Johnnie Marshall's a menace. He's always picking on someone. Someone'll sort him out one of these days.'

I'd heard it all before. The lads wouldn't start a scrap over Mickey Smith. Nobody cared about him and he had no big brothers.

Johnny Marshall's crowd played a couple of streets away and everybody knew he was trouble.

The lads kept the peace unless he pushed his luck and then there'd be a big fight and both sides would say they'd won. Then we'd all go back to normal until the next time.

It was the last week of the summer holidays and there were loads of kids out playing. Me and two other girls were throwing two balls each against the gable of the house at the end of the street. The boys were playing footie further down with rolled up jumpers for goal posts.

Alice Spencer was watching us from behind her mum's lace curtains. I gave her a wave and she smiled but looked fed up. Her dad thought he was better than the rest of us, except for my dad, who went to work in a suit too.

She was in my class at school but wasn't allowed to play out. She played in their backyard on her own. I felt sorry for her.

Someone's mum shouted from an open front door that tea was ready and, like magic, the kids started to disappear.

Apart from flowered curtains in some of the windows, there was no colour in the grim, grey street, not even a blade of grass.
Nothing grew here, except kids, of course.

Chapter 2

In the lounge of a city centre pub, Tom Phillips looked across the table at his companion, a clean cut thirty year old with clear grey eyes. The place was filling up with office workers released from a week of toil, looking forward to the first drink of the weekend. With Tom on a long seat against the wall and Nick on a stool with his back to the room, they had some measure of privacy.

'What do you think Nick, can we pull it off? I really want to make a go of this.'

Nick Metcalfe studied his pint for a moment and looked up.

'Not getting cold feet Tom - not you!'

'Not cold feet exactly, it's more I'm wondering what I've dragged you into. I know it's a step up for both of us in terms of money and status but the school's dreadfully run down. I don't mean the buildings but the general lethargy around the place.'

He looked worriedly over at Nick, his thick, greying hair bristling out of control and a frown on his intelligent face.

'Don't worry about me. I'm ready for a challenge. The pair of us would never have made the crossover to Head and Deputy in an affluent area, you know that. If we make a success of this, who knows what we'll be offered a few years down the line?'

Tom shook his head, as if trying to shake out the doubts.

'You're right. Kids are kids, aren't they? If they're a bit scruffier than we're used to, it doesn't make them thick. The eleven plus results have been shocking since the war but they're no worse than the other schools in the area.'

'Well, we won't know what were in for until we make a start,' said Nick. 'We'll be making it up as we go along. It'll take us a while to find our feet.'

'You were at the meeting with the other teachers, what did you make of them?'

'A pretty mixed bunch, I'd say. A couple of them looked keen and fired up but one or two of the older ones looked distinctly uncomfortable.'

'They're the ones who'll cut up rough. McFadden was happy to sit in his office doing heaven knows what and taking the occasional wander round the school to make his presence felt,' said Tom disapprovingly.

He'd met Mr McFadden, the retiring head, heard his views on corporal punishment and could guess the rest. There would often be a white faced boy outside his door waiting for punishment. Grey haired and distinguished, he dressed in a suit, waistcoat, white shirt and regimental tie. Still strong of arm, he'd carefully hang his jacket behind the door before wielding the strap.

In every school Tom had worked, it was a point of honour with the boys not to cry after strapping. They'd leave the headmaster's office blowing on scarlet palms, shaking their hands to cool in the draught and then tucking them into their armpits to try to relieve the pain.

McFadden had been a constant threat held over the heads of unruly boys.

Tom frowned again.

'He was a bit too handy with the strap, as though he almost enjoyed it; always a bit suspect.

Some of the teachers have made little attempt at discipline, apart from holding the threat of a thrashing over the lads' heads.'

Nick nodded in agreement and sipped at his pint.

'Not any longer, I'll be making it clear that everyone will be responsible for the discipline in their own classroom. I don't agree with thrashing as a standard punishment. I'd be reluctant to use it except in the worse of cases.'

He drained his pint.

'Time for another?'

Nick raised his wrist and looked at his watch.

'Yes, but make it a half. I'm taking Heather to the flicks tonight.'

'A half it is. I'll drop you off. I'm going your way and Margaret will be glad to see me home early, we're expecting visitors.'

Tom made his way to the bar and came back with two half pints. Raising his glass, he made a toast.

'Here's to it. Good luck to both of us.'

'I'll drink to that,' said Nick and they grinned at each other like school boys.

Tom pushed open the gate of his semi-detached house in Didsbury. The tiny square front lawn was neatly mown and the scent of the roses in the borders floated on the still air.

His heart sank at the prospect of an evening with his in-laws but there was no escape, it had to be done.

A racket erupted at the sound of his key in the door and as he walked into the hall, delicious smells assaulted him from the kitchen, the only benefit of the in-laws' visits. His young sons hurtled down the stairs, yelling 'Daddy, Daddy' and he hugged the boys to him, savouring the joy of coming home.

'I'm in here,' came a voice from the kitchen.

He released the children, whispering 'Wait there, I'll be back in a minute,' and walked through.

'Smells good, what are we having?'

Margaret looked harassed. She always was when her parents were due, struggling to meet her mother's exacting standards. There was a smudge of flour on her nose, her sleeves were rolled up and her hair was escaping in tendrils around her face, a far cry from her usual immaculate self.

'I've made a celery soup and, thanks to flattery, wheedling and self-abasement, managed to get a chicken. There are roast potatoes and veg and an apple pie for later.'

Though things had eased considerably since the end of the war, meat supplies were still difficult. Like most families, they'd eaten their share of Spam.

'It'll be marvellous, is there anything I can do?'

She was always taut as a wire when her parents were visiting.

'You could get the boys ready for bed.'

'Righto, won't be long.'
He called to the boys,
'Come on, you two. Let's have you up the stairs.'
The boys came at a rush. Bedtime was always fun when dad was in charge.
Tom ran the bath while the two boys got undressed. Michael, at just three, needed a lift with some of his buttons but he could fold his clothes and lay them on a chair for the next morning. Peter, at four and a bit, managed by himself and the two boys were soon in the water.
Out of the bath, they scrambled into cotton pyjamas and Tom pulled a comb through their unruly hair.
'Right, lads. Play in your bedroom quietly until Grandma and Grandpa arrive. You're to come downstairs as soon as I call, not before, and don't run.
Mummy will be up in a minute so keep out of her way until she's ready.?'
'OK, Dad.'
They pattered back into their own bedroom and pulled out a box of toys from under Michael's bed.
Order had been restored in the kitchen. Everything was under control, with fifteen minutes to spare.
'Take it easy, love. There's plenty of time. Why don't you go up and change and I'll finish setting the table.'
She smiled tremulously.
'I don't know why you let it get to you,' he said. 'Try and relax, even your mother won't bite.'
She looked a little huffy but he saw a glimmer of amusement in her eyes as she turned to leave the kitchen.

The spartan furnishings of the early years had been augmented and the house was now a comfortable home. Margaret's maiden aunt had bequeathed her a houseful of furniture and they now had several good antiques dotted around the place.
He checked the dining room, breathing in the echo of the scent from the garden in the bouquet in the middle of the dining table. After

casting his eye over the table, nicely set with a white damask cloth and the best cutlery, he filled a crystal jug with water and brought in the glasses. Margaret's father usually brought a bottle of wine but they couldn't be seen to be expecting it so no wine glasses would be produced until the bottle was on the table. Tom would have been reluctant to splash out for wine and Margaret's father would certainly have seen it as living beyond their means while depriving him of an opportunity to play the patriarch.

The food smelled wonderful. Despite the company, he was looking forward to his dinner.

The doorbell rang as Margaret came down the stairs.

'I'll get it,' he said as he opened the front door.

'Good evening, Elizabeth, good evening George, do come in.'

Coats were removed, the wine ceremoniously handed over and then they were all in the sitting room nursing glasses of sherry. Tom would rather have had a glass of beer but he went along with the formality. No more than one small glass would be offered or accepted.

George Richards, silver haired and lean, stood with one hand in his trouser pocket and his back to the fireplace. Elizabeth, a heavy woman with what Tom thought of as a large bay front, was ensconced regally on the settee, daintily holding her sherry with one hand and smoothing the skirt of her dark green dress with the other.

'How are the boys?' asked George. He had a soft spot for his two grandsons.

'They're fine, they're looking forward to seeing you. Shall I get them?'

George nodded and Tom went to the foot of the stairs.

'Peter, Michael, please come down and say hello.'

They came slowly down the stairs, one after the other.

'Good boys,' Tom whispered. 'Go on in.'

They liked Grandpa, he smiled and generally gave them sixpence each but Grandma was a bit frightening - and they always had to kiss her.

They looked like little angels and Michael was holding on to Peter's hand for courage.

'Go and give Grandma a kiss.'

The boys dutifully kissed Elizabeth's cheek. She hardly ever smiled and smelled a bit funny when you got up close but the worst was over.

Grandpa held out his hand. The boys knew the form and, in turn, shook hands solemnly with their grandfather, glancing at each other in glee at the sixpenny piece pressed into each of their palms.

'Well, Peter, how are you?'

'I'm very well, thank you, Granpa. How are you?'

'I'm very well too. How about you, young Michael?'

'Fine, sir,' he managed.

Tom stood, leaning against the door. He decided to rescue them.

'Come on, boys. Say goodnight.'

Margaret bent to kiss them in turn. 'Sleep tight,' she whispered, brushing her hand over their shiny, sweet smelling hair.

'Goodnight, Grandma, Good night, Grandpa,' they chorused and Tom chivvied them towards the stairs. This rigmarole was a complete fiasco. They were little boys not royal envoys; what a carry on.

'I'll get them settled. Be down in a minute.'

He tucked the boys into bed, gave them each a kiss and said as he was leaving the room,

'You did really well, both of you. If the weather's fine, we'll take the football to the park tomorrow. Settle down now.'

He glanced at his watch on the way downstairs and thought wryly, even a sixpence wouldn't make me look forward to the next couple of hours.

Dinner went smoothly. Even Margaret's mother had no complaints.

Elizabeth was an appalling snob and judgemental to boot and had plenty of gossip about various neighbours, local shopkeepers and church members.

Margaret listened patiently, with an odd comment to keep her going.

The two men talked about the cricket scores and the state of the country although they kept carefully away from politics. There'd been disputes in the past, the elder being a staunch Conservative and Tom a Labour voter of some conviction.

The meal finished, Tom helped Margaret clear the dishes into the kitchen.

'Why don't you go into the sitting room?' she said, 'I'll be just a minute with the coffee.'

Sally

I loved Saturday nights. Dad came home early and sometimes I went round to the bus stop to wait for him. He looked so smart in his suit and trilby and always had a big smile for me as he stepped off the bus. It didn't matter if a couple of buses came and went. I was happy sitting on a wall, watching the traffic.

Even though I was nine, I didn't mind holding his hand all the way home. Nobody ever made fun of me. Well, he looked like someone special, like a doctor or a teacher or something.

Saturdays and Sundays were the only days we sat down to eat together. The rest of the week, Mum fed us kids about half past five and then she and Dad sat down together when he got home. We were better off than a lot of the other kids. We never had to make do with bread and jam for tea.

Saturday was payday and Dad handed Mum a small brown envelope which we knew contained the housekeeping money for the week. I got sixpence and my brother, David, got a shilling to spend or save; it was up to us.

There was always a clean table cloth on Saturday night and I'd set the table neatly with matching flowered cups and saucers so it all looked nice.

We were lucky, our mum and dad talked to us, me and my brother, David. Some kids had to be seen and not heard and some kids' dads never noticed them except to shout.

'Back at school on Monday, Sally. How do you feel about that?' asked Dad.

'OK, I don't mind school. Anyway, some of it's interesting'

I'd have suffered thumbscrews before admitting it to anyone outside our front door, especially the other kids. I wanted to be like everybody else. It was bad enough our David was a brain box.

'What about you, David?' asked Dad, settling back in his armchair and accepting a cup of tea.

'I'm looking forward to it. It's boring hanging around all summer and I've missed my mates. At least at school, I see them every day and not just an odd weekend.'

David was in the third year at Manchester Central High School for Boys, commonly known as Whitworth Street. He was the only boy in the junior school to have passed the eleven plus in his year. He was learning all sorts of new things, like French and chemistry. Some of his homework looked really complicated. The other lads came from all over Manchester and some of their dads were posh, like doctors and shop managers but David could hold his own with anyone. He was big and strong and looked after me. No-one ever pushed me around. I was David Steadman's little sister.

***

As Sally disappeared, Eva Steadman looked across at her son. He was almost a young man now.

'What about you, David, what are you up to?'

'I might go to the pictures. There's a good western on with Alan Ladd.'

'Make sure you come straight home. Your dad and I are going to the pub and we need you to be here with Sal.'

'OK, I'll be back,' he said over his shoulder as he left the house.

Eva's family lived five minutes' walk away and most them went for a drink on a Saturday night. Arthur got on well with them although they sometimes exchanged surreptitious grins when they thought he was being toffee-nosed.

Finally, the two of them were alone and for a while, they sat in companionable silence, Eva engrossed in an Agatha Christie and

Arthur checking his pools against the "Football Pink", the radio playing in the background.

Arthur looked at Eva over his newspaper.

'By the way, Michael Grey was in the shop yesterday. You remember, the rep for that big jewellery company in London.'

'Yes, I remember you telling me about him.'

'Well, he dropped a bit of a bombshell.'

'How's that?'

'I've always got on well with him and we managed to get fifteen minutes in the office for a bit of a natter.'

'Well, and?'

'Turns out he's retiring towards the middle of next year and says I should apply for his job; said he'd put in a good word.'

'It's a big step. Would you want to take a chance when you already have a good job?'

'There's no rush but it would mean more money as basic and they pay a good rate of commission. I'd be covering the whole of the North West so they'd give me a company car. You'd like that, wouldn't you?" he smiled.

'I can't say I wouldn't. Imagine being able to jump in a car and go to the seaside or over to Yorkshire to see your Uncle George.'

'I'd also get Saturday off, have a proper weekend; even go to the match.'

One of the penalties of working Saturday was that he never got a chance to watch his beloved United in action.

'It's tempting, Arthur, but please don't rush into anything. You've got a safe job where you are. Do you want to risk it?'

'Yes, it's safe, but I won't go any further until Mr Simon retires and that's years away. I won't do anything unless you agree, just let the idea settle. In the meantime, we'll keep it to ourselves'

She frowned and nodded. After the uncertainty and upheaval of the war years, she wasn't keen on change and liked the feeling of being safe. This was a risk but the thought of a car was very tempting.

Times had been hard when Arthur was in the army. Struggling on army pay, she'd made ends meet but hated the scrimping and saving. Before she married, she'd worked in Lewis's department store in the city centre and when she'd approached them for part time work, they'd been glad to have her back. She worked Friday afternoons and Saturdays until four. Although it didn't pay a fortune, it made a big difference to a wartime budget. The children were taken to Grandma's on her way to work and collected on her way home.

The arrangement had worked well. The children settled happily at Grandma's for a few hours a week and Eva slipped her mother a few shillings to help stretch her widow's pension.

All her earnings had gone into the household budget and when Arthur was demobbed, things were pretty hairy for a while. He'd said once he was back at work, she'd be giving up her job to stay at home with the children but she'd had a taste of freedom and independence and liked it.

She was saved by circumstances. Arthur had worked in insurance before the war and he was reluctant to go back. After his years in the army, she couldn't see him stuck behind a desk all day.

Alice Spencer's father worked for the same firm and he'd been unfit for the services so he'd stayed with the company through the war. As he'd been promoted a couple of times, Arthur would have had to start back as his subordinate. That wouldn't suit at all. He liked Jack Spencer well enough but it stuck in his craw to be a step behind him.

Arthur was a personable young man, smart and willing, and had made sergeant in record time. One of the senior officers had taken a shine to him and on the day Arthur left his unit, had given him a business card.

'Call in and see me when you get home. If you're interested in working in the jewellery trade, I'm sure I can fix you up.'

Arthur had put the card away safely and only after hearing about Jack Spencer's promotion did he bring it out again.

'Should I go down and see him?'

'Yes you should, there's nothing to lose. Now's the time to start something new.'

Although she didn't have Arthur's grammar school education, she was clever in her own way and had a knack of bringing him round to her way of thinking.

'Go and see him this week and see what he's got to offer. Maybe I'd better stay on at Lewis's until you're fixed up with something permanent.'

She played down her eagerness. Although the alterations workshop was tucked away on the top floor, she was often called down to the ladies department to pin up hems and measure alterations. Always smartly dressed, she was patient and polite and the customers liked her.

Now her earnings were her own and she was building up a little nest egg. A talented dressmaker in her own right and, coupons permitting, she made clothes for herself and Sally. Before the war and while David was a baby, she'd made a bit extra sewing for other women but clothes rationing put paid to that. Arthur wouldn't have minded her sewing at home but she loved her job and loved the escape, even if it were only for a few hours a week.

'After all, it's only a few hours a week and my mother's only too happy to have the kids. She's glad of the extra few shillings and it could help to tide us over until you're properly settled.'

Arthur reluctantly agreed and Eva thanked her lucky stars. It would be easy to string out her leaving until he'd become used to the *fait accompli.*

'OK, I'll go on Friday. If your mother will give the kids their tea, I'll meet you from work and we'll go for a bite to eat in town. We haven't done that since before the war.'

'I'm sure it won't be a problem. It'll be lovely to be out, just the two of us.'

Keep him sweet, let him have his way and things will work out.

She looked at him roguishly.

'We'll feel like we're courting again.'

Chapter 3

George Richards was the senior partner in one of the largest firms of solicitors in Manchester. A wealthy, influential member of the business community, he thought his darling Margaret had married beneath her. Neither threats nor entreaties had failed to sway her from her intention to marry Tom Phillips. His wife had tried blackmail and bombast, pointing out her luxurious life would be over. She'd have to cook and clean for herself. That hadn't worked either. It was complete surprise when his meek and mild daughter finally dug her heels in.

'It doesn't matter what you say, Daddy. I'm going to marry Tom. I'm over twenty one and don't need your consent. I love him. You can cut me off without a penny and it won't matter. We'll get married in the Registry Office and find digs somewhere until we get settled.'

She fled upstairs to her pretty, well-furnished bedroom, even then realising this sort of luxury would disappear if she married Tom. There'd be no spare cash for fripperies.

Elizabeth, who'd been listening outside the door, blanched.

No, never; a Registry Office wedding in their family, she'd never hold up her head again.

She stormed into George's study.

'The ungrateful wretch, what are we going to do?' she screeched. 'Think of it, our daughter in digs. It can't be tolerated.'

'She's got us over a barrel. Either we consent and foot the bill for the wedding or she'll elope, leaving us looking complete fools.'

'I blame the war. These girls had too much freedom. When I was a girl, I did as I was told.'

George seriously doubted it but addressed the matter in hand.

'That's as may be but she's made up her mind and we either agree or we'll lose her altogether. I wouldn't want that, even at the price of Tom Phillips as a son-in-law. He's a decent enough chap but he'll never make any real money, not in education.'

'Well can't we get him out of education? Why don't you offer him a job, a well-paid job?'

'I've tried. There are plenty of openings for go-ahead young men and he has a fine war record. I could fix him up. There are plenty of people who owe me favours,' George responded, shaking his head.

'What did he say?'

'He's as pig-headed as she is. His heart's set on a career in education, wants to make a difference, whatever that means. Money doesn't mean much as long as he earns enough to live decently.'

'Margaret has no idea what life will be like on a budget, she's not been brought up to it.'

George was truly concerned about his daughter and her future. Elizabeth's concern was her standing and reputation and what people would say.

In the end they'd capitulated. They'd had no choice.

Tom and Margaret were married in the church where she'd worshipped since she was a child. She wore a beautiful white gown remodelled from her mother's wedding dress. He wore his navy demob suit.

The church was filled with well-wishers; Margaret's parents on one side and aunts and uncles she hadn't seen for years. There was no family on Tom's side but there was a respectable turnout of friends from his job and from his army service.

They looked delirious with happiness, gazing into each other's eyes during the vows.Even Elizabeth's eyes filled with tears.

She clutched at George's arm, seeking reassurance.

'Perhaps it will work out. They make a lovely couple.'

The reception went well. The food at the Midland was always up to scratch and it was amazing what a little goodwill in the shape of folded pound notes could produce. All the aunties sighed over the young couple, with only a few whispers about Tom's lack of standing in the community. The uncles leaned on the bar and drank their fill of the plentiful supply of whisky.

'This must have cost him a fortune," said one of them. "But she *is* his only daughter. I'd have thought she'd have done better for herself than a school teacher but these young things today, they will have their own way.'

The happy couple were ready to leave and a room had been taken for Margaret to change after the reception. Elizabeth had begged and borrowed enough coupons for Margaret to have a new going-away suit and she looked lovely in pale grey. Tom didn't have another 'good suit' and had resolutely refused all offers to arrange something.
There would be little compromise with this stiff-necked young man; anything smacking of charity would be instantly rejected.
There'd been trouble enough about the house. George had wanted to buy them a house as a wedding present but Tom was having none of it. In the end, George bought the house, a decent sized semi in Didsbury, and they were to pay a nominal rent until they were in a position to buy it from him. Even that concession had taken all George's powers of persuasion. Pleas for Margaret to have somewhere decent to live had finally won the day. The furniture, sparse and utilitarian, was in place and they were to move straight in after the honeymoon.
An old friend had generously offered the loan of a cottage in Bournemouth and Tom couldn't wait to get away. When Margaret appeared, he shook George's hand and kissed Elizabeth on the cheek.
'Ready?' he asked his new wife.
In a surge of real affection, her mother hugged Margaret, speechless for once. Then George held her tight for a minute.
'Never forget how much we love you,' he said, looking Tom straight in the eye. 'Take care of her, I'm relying on you.'

That was then, this was now and accommodations had had to be made.
They'd come to a working arrangement. Margaret's parents came for a meal once a month and though it always left Margaret like a wrung-out dishcloth, he could hardly object. Margaret agreed with practically everything her mother said in order to keep the peace and the two men talked only in the most general of terms; politics was a strictly no-go area.

Over the years, relations had become easier, softened by the arrival of the grandchildren, and although Tom regarded his in-laws' views with disbelief sometimes, he'd learned some restraint. George still thought Tom was stiff necked but made allowances, wanting to avoid discord at any cost.

Margaret pushed open the door to the sitting room, carrying a tray with cups and saucers and milk and sugar.

'Perhaps you'd bring in the coffee, Tom. It's all ready.'

Tom was pouring the coffee when George remarked,

'I hear you have a new job, Tom. Promotion, isn't it?' He sounded pleased.

'Yes it is. I'm to be headmaster and Nick Metcalfe, you met him here at Christmas, is moving with me as deputy head.'

For once, Elizabeth beamed.

Headmaster? It was certainly a step up, something to drop into conversations at social gatherings.

'That *is* good news. I suppose it will mean more money,' George beamed.

'Yes it will. Give me twelve months to put a bit more capital together and we can maybe talk about paying for the house at last.'

'No hurry, my boy.'

George still liked having some control although he knew it galled Tom to be in his debt.

'Where's the school?'

'It's down in West Gorton. The area's pretty run down and overcrowded but the job is a step up.'

Elizabeth couldn't contain herself.

'West Gorton? It's almost a slum. How could you think of mixing with those people and then coming home to Margaret and the boys? Heaven only knows what you'll bring with you.'

Even George looked a bit uncomfortable. He knew he shouldn't interfere but couldn't help adding.

'She has a point, you know.'

Margaret could see Tom was on the verge of exploding. The last thing she wanted was a real row. She stepped in,

'Tom has worked hard for this promotion. As a step on the ladder, it could lead to much better things. I've no doubt he'll turn things around in no time.'

She looked pointedly at her parents.

George knew that look. He'd only seen it once before when he'd tried to stop the marriage but here it was again. Her darling Tom was under attack and she wouldn't have it.

Tom struggled to keep his temper, not wanting to be the cause of a rift between parents and daughter. He took a breath and remarked casually,

'You know, even those children deserve an education. Heaven knows they've little to look forward to without it.'

George and Elizabeth exchanged looks; time for a strategic retreat.

'Perhaps Elizabeth spoke without thinking, Tom. We're glad you've got the promotion and, with a bit of luck, you won't have to stay there too long.'

It was an olive branch of sorts and Tom accepted it.

'It will be a challenge,' he said. 'I've no doubt of that. Let's wait and see.'

Aware a problem had been narrowly avoided, George spoke,

'Come on, Elizabeth, It's time we made a move. I've an early start in the morning. Thank you both for a lovely dinner.' Better not overdo the compliments and claim a lovely evening.

They took their leave and Tom and Margaret stood at the front door watching until they reached the car.

"Phew, that was a close one,' said Tom. 'Thank you for saving me from an outburst but they can drive me crazy.'

'I know, love. I'm proud of you for keeping the lid on. I know it wasn't easy.'

'Well, it's over now for another month. Let's have another drink. I'll open the bottle your dad gave me for Christmas and we'll have a tot before we go to bed.'

'Good idea. You go and sort the drinks and I'll finish in the kitchen. I won't be a minute.'

***

Maurice pushed open the door of The Queens and nodded at the landlord who pulled a pint and placed it on the bar. This was a working man's pub, a little shabby but clean enough, the smell of beer sharp in the air. Men in overalls and those playing darts or dominoes drank in the vault where no women were allowed. Maurice usually propped up the bar but couples went into the lounge where upholstered benches lined the walls and chairs were placed neatly at round tables.

'You having one, John?'

'It's a bit early for me, mind if I leave it in the pump 'til later?'

'Not at all, take it out of that,' he said expansively, dropping a pound note on the bar.

He looked across into the vault and nodded at a couple of his runners propping up the bar in there. The money he'd paid them a couple of hours ago would end up in the landlord's pocket before the night was out.

Arthur and Eva Steadman walked in. It was Saturday night, their one night out and they were smartly dressed, Arthur in a dark blue suit and Eva in a red and white polka dot dress, pulled in at the waist with a white belt.

My God, she's a good looking woman. Wouldn't mind a couple of handfuls of that.

He looked at her speculatively, caught her eye and gave her a wink. She flushed and looked away, putting her hand on Arthur's arm and whispering in his ear.

Better watch my step. Arthur boxed a bit in the army and she's got all those brothers.

Maurice had lost interest in his wife years earlier although he still had an eye for the ladies and took his chances where he found them.

On Sunday nights he often went into Manchester to drink with other bookmakers and their ladies but Saturday was a hard day and he preferred to stay nearer home.

A couple of Eva's brothers and their wives came in, all dressed up too, and went into the lounge bar to settle round one of the big tables. When her youngest sister arrived with their mother, the tribe was complete.

He stood at the bar drinking steadily and chatting to the landlord, who was keeping a watchful eye on the bar staff. He ran a tight ship and was the only one in the pub Maurice regarded with any respect. After all, he too, was in the business of taking money off the punters.

About half past nine, the singing started to float in from the lounge bar, started by Eva's lot but soon joined by the rest of the customers. They all loved a sing song and it was the same every week.

Maurice watched the door. He glanced at his watch, she was late tonight. Perhaps she wouldn't come.

The door swung open and the McGuire sisters walked in. Only two years apart but Doris, the youngest, was a real looker. The hair was a little brassy and the dress a little tight but she had a glint in her eye and gave him a sneaky look under her lashes. Mavis sat down at a corner table and Doris came to the bar.

'Two port and lemon, please.'

'Coming up.'

Derek, the landlord stirred himself to serve her and passed the glasses over the bar.

'Allow me," said Maurice, passing the money over.

"Thank you kindly, sir," she said and, taking the glasses, wiggled across the bar to sit with her sister.

The two men watched with interest.

'A sight for sore eyes, Maurice.'

'You can say that again.'

When Arthur came into the bar, crossing over to the gents' toilets, Maurice nodded.

Evening, Arthur.'

'Evening, Maurice,' said Arthur giving him a hard look.
Better watch my step. I'm too old for fisticuffs.
Maurice sent a couple more drinks over to the McGuire girls and they smiled and waved their thanks.

He glanced at his watch as the landlord shouted
'"Time, gentlemen, please.'
The customers would get ten minutes to drink up and then the pub would empty.

Doris McGuire sidled past him on her way out.
'You comin' round?'
'See you in half an hour. Got the whisky?'
'Yeah, see you soon.'
Derek locked the front door behind her. One of the barmaids was clearing tables and the other washing glasses.
'You manage another, Maurice?'
'You know me, Derek. I'll have a scotch. Join me?'
The landlord never bought a drink, particularly after time. The extra takings could be a nice little bonus but tonight there was only Maurice. Never mind, an early night wouldn't hurt.

As Maurice left the pub by the back door, he heard the bolts being slid behind him and walked along the main road. The last bus had gone and the streets were deserted.

Taking the first turning on the left, he walked along to number five, the only house in the street still showing a light. He tapped on the door, which opened quickly, and he stepped inside. The door closed sharply behind him and Doris pulled him into the front room.

'Mavis has gone up to bed, shall we have a little drink?'
Maurice gave Doris cash on a regular basis to make sure she always had whisky in the house. She had a good source and never gave him rubbish.

A heavy drinker for years, Maurice could hold his liquor. He picked up the bottle and gestured towards the stairs.

'Ooh, you *are* a naughty boy.'

He followed her up the stairs and into the front bedroom, the smell of face powder and cosmetics heavy in the air. Same procedure every time; he sat down on the bed and watched.

She knew what he wanted and performed a slow strip, humming as though she were alone. Bits of clothing slid to the floor until she was standing in just her pants.

'Your turn now, lovey. Come on.'

Maurice stood while she pulled the shiny satin eiderdown off the bed and pushed the jacket off his shoulders. She hung it on a chair back while he kicked off his shoes and unfastened his trousers. Pushing the braces off his shoulders, she pulled his trousers down to his ankles.

'Step out of them, lovey.'

She took off his shirt, pushed him back onto the bed and pulled off his underpants.

'There now, isn't that better?'

Maurice lay back while she straddled him. He was a big man and slightly overweight and he loved it when she did all the work. It wasn't long until he was gasping and groaning, gripping her hard around the waist. She grinned.

'Better?'

Catching his breath, he muttered,

'You'll do me in. Where's the scotch?'

With his head against the padded headboard, pink like the eiderdown, he nursed a sizeable scotch while she nestled on his shoulder.

He downed the whisky.

'I'd better get a move on. It's nearly two o'clock.'

The evening's boozing was catching up with him.

He pulled on his clothes, fished in his pocket and pulled out his wallet.

'Here's a fiver. I don't care how you spend it, just make sure there's plenty of scotch when I come again.'

Five pounds was a fortune; more than many working men earned in a week. Smiling, she unfolded the large white five pound note, so much more impressive than five ones. She'd make it go a long way. As well as the scotch, there was a pair of navy shoes she had her eye on.

A little unsteady now, Maurice left the house and wandered home. He'd have a long lie in tomorrow.

Silence reigned in the Marshall household until Maurice came stumbling home. Hettie heard him coming down the hall and finally, creaking his way up the stairs.

He was unlikely to bother her but she lay still, listening to him dropping his clothes on the floor and finally falling into bed beside her. From the scent of cheap perfume wafting off him, she knew exactly where he'd been.

She waited and in seconds, he was snoring. When she was sure he was asleep, she crept silently out of bed and picked up the clothes lying on the floor. There'd be murder if they were all creased in the morning so the jacket went on a hanger behind the door. Giving the trousers a good shake, she folded them carefully over the back of a chair. As usual, he was asleep in his shirt. She fished the wallet out of his inside pocket and checked. There was a fortune in there.

The lock box in the front room was untouchable. The cash was counted and bundled, but he'd been drinking all night and by morning would have only a vague idea how much he'd spent. She ruffled the notes, about thirty five pounds and after considering for a minute, took out two pounds and put the wallet carefully back in the jacket. No point being greedy, that way led disaster. Pulling out a drawer full of pillowcases and taking great care not to wake him, she slid the notes inside one near the bottom. They'd be moved to somewhere safe in the morning. He didn't stir when she crept back into bed and she managed to fall asleep despite the racket. God knew, she was used to it by now and could have slept through gunfire.

***

The holidays were over and the children were back at school. At nine, Sally was still in the junior school on the ground floor.

When Johnnie had moved to the senior school upstairs, the younger children had breathed a sigh of relief. Playtimes were split and they no longer suffered him running riot through the playground.

Sweets were hard to come by as the coupons didn't go far and toys were few and far between. The few things that did appear were frequently confiscated and shared among Johnnie's gang. None of the children would ever 'shop' Johnnie so he generally got away with murder.

Though he was amongst the younger of the boys in the upper school, he had some measure of protection from the older lads. Everybody knew if you messed with Johnnie Marshall, you'd have Harry to deal with and nobody was keen to walk that route.

The girls were more or less exempt from bullying, they made too much fuss. There was an occasional push or shove and the odd flick of the heel to trip them.

Sally was lucky, she had a big brother too. He was now at a different school but his reputation still protected her. Even though he now wore a school uniform, nobody called him a swot or a snob, at least not to his face. He'd taken on Harry Marshall the summer before and the scrap had been declared a draw at two bloodied noses and a few bruises. Although they didn't finish up the best of pals, they showed mutual respect and greeted each other in a friendly fashion when they passed in the street.

Lined up in the playground, facing the looming, smoke-blackened building, the children waited. Some were inwardly groaning at the loss of their freedom, some resigned to their renewed incarceration but few, just a few, were glad to be back. There were two new faces, pleasant enough but watchful, giving them the once over. At the shrill sound of the whistle, they marched raggedly into school, the infants through the entrance at one end of the building and the rest clattered up the staircase at the other end to the hall on the first floor.

There was some jostling and, as usual, most of it around Johnnie Marshall. From nowhere, a hand reached out and grabbed him by the arm, pulling him out of line. Who was this man? The rest of the children were waved on their way.

'Keep moving, stand in classes with your teachers in the hall. Go on, keep moving.'

He looked at Johnnie and gave him a little shake.

'Name?'

Johnnie looked at him belligerently.

'Marshall.'

'Which Marshall?'

'John Marshall.'

'John Marshall what?'

Another shake, this time a little more vigorous.

'John Marshall, sir.'

'That's better. Wait until everybody's inside and then go and stand outside my office.'

This was the new headmaster and Johnnie had fallen foul of him before school had even started.

Daylight came through the large windows at either end of the hall and filtered through the glass partitions of the classrooms on either side.

The children stood, grouped in classes, with those who had moved up from the lower school right at the front, looking overawed and a little anxious. Although the layout was identical to the ground floor and the youngest children knew the teachers by sight, they shuffled closer together for protection. Downstairs, they'd been the oldest and now they were the youngest; the pecking order had been reversed.

The door at the far end of the hall opened. All heads turned and all eyes followed Tom Phillips as he made his way down the hall to the platform and climbed the three steps. He took his time looking over the sea of faces and then, putting both hands on the lectern, spoke in a deep, clear voice.

'Good morning, children.'

'Good morning, sir,' came back in unison.

'My name is Phillips, Mr Phillips or sir to you and I'm your new headmaster. The gentleman over there,' he gestured with his head at the other new face, 'is Mr Metcalfe and he's taken over from Mr Jones.'

He spoke briefly about changes in the school but the children paid scant attention, their thoughts mainly on bagging the coveted back row seats. There was a rude awakening to come.

A short reading and a prayer and they were dismissed.

In Mr Metcalfe's classroom, Johnnie's pals had bagged three seats at the back, one each side of an empty desk for Johnnie.

Mr Metcalfe rapped on his desk with the wooden board cleaner.

'Right, settle down.'

Gradually, silence fell.

'There's a different seating arrangement this year. I decide who sits where. I'm going to take the register and then I'll move you."

He started the call, 'John Anderson.'

'Here, sir.'

'Right John, I want you to change places with this boy here.'

He pointed to the desk at the extreme left of the front row. The children started to mutter.

'That's enough, silence now.'

'Mavis Brown.'

'Here, sir.'

'You sit there, next to John Anderson.'

On he went, placing the children in alphabetical order and splitting up friends, putting boys next to girls and vice versa.

They didn't like it but there was nothing they could do. The same procedure was going on in every classroom.

For Nick Metcalfe, it was a godsend. He had a plan of the classroom with each child's name inked in and he'd know who was who from day one.

Tom Phillips walked along the short corridor to his office, jingling the coins in his pocket. Johnnie Marshall stood outside the door, shuffling his feet, fully expecting to get 'six of the best'.

Tom unlocked the door and walked in, gesturing Johnnie to enter.

'When you come in here, you stand there, you stand straight and you don't speak until you're spoken to,' he pointed to a place directly in front of his desk.

'Have you got that?'

'Yes, sir.'

Tom sat down behind the desk and spoke.

'Right.'

Johnnie, who'd been looking at his feet, looked up. He'd been in here a time or two and the place looked different. Instead of an empty, polished surface, the desk was piled with books and files and the tattered old posters had been replaced with brightly coloured pictures. The strap which had hung on a hook behind the desk was gone. The place even smelled different. There was still the pervading air of furniture polish but the musty, old man smell had gone.

'You and I had better understand each other. I'll take no nonsense and you'll behave properly whilst on school premises. Have you got that?'

'Yes, sir.'

'Now let me tell you something. I won't be strapping anyone except for the most serious offences. Anybody who breaks the rules or is sent to my office by a teacher will be punished a different way. They'll tell their mothers they'll be late the following day, when they'll be kept behind after school. They'll sit over there at the table in the corner and do some extra school work.

How long I keep them will depend on what they've done. It could be anywhere between half an hour and an hour. In certain circumstances, the punishment could be carried over for a second day or even a third.'

Relieved as he was the strap hadn't materialised, Johnnie was horrified.

'Have I made myself clear?'

'Yes, sir.'

'Right, well off you go to your classroom.'

Yes, sir.'

Johnnie made his way across the hall. At least his mates would have saved him a good seat. However, he wasn't a fool and knew he'd been singled out. Both the headmaster and his new teacher knew exactly who he was and would be keeping an eye on him. He wasn't sure what to make of these new ideas so he'd keep his head down for a couple of days and see which way the wind was blowing. He went into his new classroom.

'Ah, John Marshall, at last. Where have you been until now?'

'In Mr Phillips' office, sir.'

'Well I hope you had a pleasant chat.'

Some of the others sniggered and he squirmed, giving one or two of them looks to kill. His eyes went straight to the back row. Where were his mates?

'That's your desk there.'

Mr Metcalfe pointed towards an empty seat in the middle of the third row.

He had no choice. He made his way along the row and sat down. He was furious. His desk was between two girls and his mates were split up too. The coveted back row was occupied by people who had no right to be there.

Nick Metcalfe had volunteered for the first playground duty and was in the school yard with a whistle on a cord round his neck, watching the children and soaking up the September sun.

The staffroom would be buzzing with comments about the new headmaster and the new procedures and he knew he'd only cramp their style.

As a newcomer, he needed to tread carefully. Some of them would assume he'd go running to Tom Phillips with every bit of gossip and every adverse comment. Although as deputy head, he was Tom's right hand man, the support of the other teachers was crucial. He'd be walking a tightrope until things settled down. A poor performance from a deputy could be as damaging to morale as an ineffectual headmaster.

He leaned back against a wall where there was a clear view of the whole playground and watched the children who'd gathered in their self-selected groups. He was keeping an eye out for potential trouble makers and particularly for any sign of bullying.

The children played with other children in their class, the boys with boys and the girls with the girls. Johnnie Marshall and his followers were tearing around in a game of tag in one corner and the other children were giving them a wide berth. The game was fast moving with some grabbing of arms and jumpers but it wasn't rough enough to warrant intervention.

The girls were in groups. Some of them, pigtails swinging, were hopping gracefully from square to square on a hopscotch chalked on the concrete. Others stood in groups of three or four, arms folded like little old ladies nattering.

Only at the top end of the school, the fourteen year olds, was there any sign of the sexes mixing and there were a few of them, gathered in the corner furthest away from Johnnie and his crowd. One of them was Marshall's older brother but there was no obvious family likeness.

Apart from his own class, he knew none of the children by name but within a short time, he'd know them all. After the first few minutes, he'd become part of the scenery and all but a wary few had forgotten he was there.

Like most staffrooms, there was a collection of odd chairs and a cooker in the corner on which sat a fat-bellied aluminium kettle. Cups and saucers of various sizes and patterns were assembled on a tray at one end of the lino covered table and an ashtray in the centre.

Each teacher poured their tea into their own cup and saucer. Heaven help the new teacher who used somebody else's. Milk was appropriated from the children's daily allowance of a third of a pint. There was never a hundred percent attendance and there were invariably a few bottles over.

The five members of staff were split into two camps. Miss Marsden, the youngest, who taught the children who'd moved upstairs this year and Mr Jackson, the oldest, who taught those who'd be leaving at the end of the year, were provisionally well disposed to the new head and his ideas.

Mr Royle and Mrs Cooper were set against change of any kind. Neither of them far off retirement, they wanted an easy life. They'd been at the school for years, right through the war, and had been firm supporters of Mr McFadden's methods.

Mr Royle, pompously, spoke up first.

'I can't see the point. By the time they're in our class, we know them anyway, know which are trouble makers and know their brothers and sisters. Good heavens, I even taught most of their parents. All this alphabetical nonsense is just disrupting a working system."

'I know exactly what you mean,' chirped in Mrs Cooper, rattling her beads in sympathy.

Miss Marsden felt quite strongly about this.

'Well, I thoroughly approve. It splits up the trouble-makers and puts well behaved children between them. It's bound to be easier to keep discipline."

Mr Royle pulled back his shoulders.

'I've never had trouble keeping discipline. Heaven knows, I've been teaching for nearly forty years and I've seen these new-fangled ideas come and go.'

'Don't forget, we won't be sending the boys down the corridor for a thrashing. That'll be a thing of the past," sniffed Mrs Cooper.

'What's the world coming to? A good thrashing is all most of them understand. This place will be bedlam in six months.'

Miss Marsden, colour rising in her fair complexion, clearly disagreed. Qualified for only two years, she always treated the older teachers with respect although she thought these two were dreadfully old fashioned. On the other hand, she often talked over problems with Mr Jackson, the eldest of the three. In her view, he was the best teacher in the school and the one least likely to send a child to the headmaster.

He stepped in, ever the diplomat, in an effort to keep the peace. The last thing he wanted was a row on the first day of term. Smoothing back his thinning grey hair, he spoke quietly. An old hand at classroom psychology, he knew if people had to strain to hear, they paid better attention and it took their minds off other things.

'Let's not get all hot headed here. We all knew things would change when Mr McFadden retired. It's only natural for a new headmaster to want to run things his own way. Understandable enough.'

'Starting with an upheaval is hardly likely to endear him to the staff. It's his first post as head and he's brought a deputy with him. We'll have to watch our step with him too, no doubt,' sniffed Mrs Cooper.

'It was hardly his fault Mr Jones was forced to retire so suddenly. His heart had been playing him up for years but no-one guessed it was quite so bad.'

'I should have thought a promotion from within the school would have been more appropriate,' said Mr Royle, who'd half fancied his chances.

'It was never going to happen. Look at us, we're none of us far from retirement apart from Miss Marsden and even she'd agree it's a little early for her to be taken on as deputy head," he said, trying to lighten the atmosphere. 'You know, and I know, the authorities never promote anybody this close to retirement.'

Mr Royle grudgingly conceded the point with a slow nod.

Mr Martin was sitting on the fence as usual, confining his comments to 'hmm' and 'ah' without committing himself one way or the other.

Though it was difficult, Miss Marsden held her tongue during these exchanges. They thought she was too young and too inexperienced to have an opinion that counted and the last thing she wanted was to aggravate unrest in the staffroom.

She liked the look of the new head, and his deputy, and thought they'd bring a breath of fresh air to the school.

'Why don't we give them a chance? See what happens? We might as well accept the inevitable and make the best of it.'

Mrs Cooper sniffed again.

'Anyway, for the time being, I'm going to watch what I say around Mr Metcalfe in case he goes carrying tales.'

As usual, she'd had the final word.

Tea drunk and biscuits eaten, they straggled out of the staffroom towards the final lesson of the morning.

'Don't worry too much,' said Mr Jackson in Miss Marsden's ear.

'It'll all come out in the wash and I'm confident those two will be good for the school, and the children, in the long run.'

Tom Phillips and Nick Metcalfe sat in the headmaster's office. It was a quarter to four and the teachers and children had left for the day. The caretaker was moving in and out of classrooms, emptying waste bins and tidying up but otherwise, the school was in a state of peace.

'Well, Nick, how did it go for you?'

'To be honest, better than expected. You helped a lot by sorting out young Marshall at the outset. It gave me a chance to get the others settled.'

'As a rule, I wouldn't make judgements based on other people's opinions but I'd heard so many rumbles about the Marshall boys I couldn't help but give them some credence. As it happens, he played straight into my hands and now he knows I've got his card marked. Any other thoughts?'

Nick paused a moment to consider.

'There are one or two kids in the class with real potential. Miss Marsden, young as she is, has done a good job and they're up to snuff as far as the curriculum is concerned.'

'That's good. By Christmas we'll have a better idea of where we stand. What about the staffroom, any problems there?" Tom asked.

'Just as I expected; two for and two against and you can understand Mr Royle and Mrs Cooper in a way. They've had their boat rocked and would have been resistant to change of any kind. I don't know what to make of Mr Martin though, he's very non-committal.'

"I suppose you're right. Mr Jackson's older than the pair of them and he's wide open to innovation. If it hadn't been for the war, he'd have made headmaster himself although he seems happy enough. He's a good man and I'm glad to have him on board."

Tom sat back and stretched.

'Shall we call it a day then?'

'Good idea, we've got the first day behind us. Let's see what tomorrow brings.'

They left the office together, Tom locking the door behind him, and walked down the stairs and out of the school, parting company to go their separate ways.

Chapter 4

Sally

Christmas was getting closer. Christmas Eve was a Sunday so Mum and Dad would be at home and have Monday and Tuesday off. They worked late on Saturday and left me and David to fetch the shopping Mum had ordered earlier in the week. We had to make two trips to collect everything; the greengrocery, the bread and the chicken for Christmas dinner. Although it was cold out, we noticed Johnny Marshall hanging around the corner as we came and went.
'I wonder what he's up to.' David said.
I looked up at him. He'd got taller in the last twelve months.
'You know, David, I really don't like him. He's creepy and he's dead sly.'
'He needs watching. keep out of his way.'
'Don't worry, I keep as far away from him as I can.'
On our last trip back from the shops, we saw Miss Pritchard at her front door. She and her sister lived next door and as Mum would say, they kept themselves to themselves.
They were nice old ladies, even if they were old fashioned and they always smiled and nodded when you passed them in the street.
This Miss Pritchard was the one we saw out and about, going to the shops and running errands. The other Miss Pritchard didn't go out much except to church on Sunday, walking slowly and leaning on a silver topped stick. Always dressed in dark colours with neat, shiny shoes, they never left the house without a hat and a handbag.
'Is something the matter, Miss Pritchard?' asked David.
She looked a bit upset, fidgeting with her hair and pulling her dark blue cardigan around her.
'Someone keeps knocking on the front door and when I get here, there's nobody there. This is the third time in half an hour. I suppose its only children but it's making my sister nervous.'

David looked at me. I knew what he was thinking.

'Don't worry, Miss Pritchard. Go back inside, it's too cold to be standing on the step. I'll sort it out.'

He opened the front door and put the shopping bags down in the hall.

'You stay here, Sal. I won't be long.'

I went into the front room. It was pretty cold as there was no fire but there was a good view of the street from the front window.

David slipped into the space between the bay windows further along and waited.

Sure enough, Johnnie Marshall came sneaking round the corner with two other lads. Sniggering and nudging each other, they crept towards Miss Pritchard's front door. David stepped out and grabbed Johnnie by the scruff of the neck.

'What you up to then, young Marshall?'

'What's it got to do with you? Let me go, I'll tell our Harry.'

David gave him a shake.

'Tell him, and *I'll* tell him you spend your time tormenting old ladies. Knock and run's only a game and I've played it myself but this is past a joke.'

The other two lads were looking sheepish. Where Johnnie led they usually followed but they'd been caught red handed and didn't like it.

Johnnie was squirming in David's grip and he gave him another shake.

'Right, you,' he said to Johnnie, 'and you two,' staring at the other lads, 'if I hear any more of this, I'll come looking for you. D'you hear me?"

With a final shake, he gave Johnnie a shove.

'Clear off. I don't want to see you round here again.'

I was still watching from the front window and as David came back, Miss Pritchard opened her front door. She'd been watching from their parlour too.

'Thank you, David. I really appreciate it. We've had problems with them before and that boy seems to be the ringleader.'

'Let me know if you have any more trouble and I'll have another word.'

She gave him a lovely smile; you could tell she was grateful.
'Thank you again, David. You're quite a hero.'
David blushed to the roots of his hair, came into our hall and picked up the shopping to take it into the kitchen.
I was sorry he hadn't thumped Johnnie Marshall but I'd known he wouldn't. He'd never hit somebody smaller than him but Marshall didn't know that.

After tea on Christmas Eve, David went out carol singing with some people from church. Mum said I could go with them next year but I was glad to be inside this year. It was cold out there.
'Before we settle down, Sal, take these mince pies next door to Miss Pritchard.'
Mum looked at Dad.
'Well Arthur, I don't expect there's much Christmas cheer next door. I get the feeling they're a bit tight for cash and they like our Sal. They'd accept something from her when something from me might offend. Put your coat on, Sal, before you go. It's cold out there."
I stood on next door's step and knocked firmly with the knocker. I could hear Miss Pritchard coming down the hall. She looked a bit anxious as the door opened but smiled when she saw it was me. I could hear music pouring down the hall, wonderful music, like nothing I'd ever heard before. I think it was the kind Mum called classical.
Miss Pritchard took one look at my face.
'Don't stand there on the doorstep Sally, come in for a minute.'
She ushered me down the hall and into the parlour and there was the other Miss Pritchard, the older one, at the piano. She looked lovely, back straight and her hair caught up in a bun with a few wisps falling out over her lace collar. The piano had been polished until it shone and a small lamp threw a puddle of light over her hands while her fingers danced over the keys. She didn't see me so I stood still, holding the plate with the mince pies until she'd finished. I didn't want it to end.

'Constance, look who's come to see us. I thought it might be those nasty boys again but it's Sally from next door and she's brought us something.'

'Mum thought you might like some mince pies and she's made such a lot.'

'How very kind of her, I'm sure we'll enjoy them. Please thank her, such a kind thought."

My head was still full of the music and something must have shown in my face.

'Did you like the music, Sally?' she asked gently.

'Oh yes, I thought it was lovely.'

I knew one of the Miss Pritchards played the piano because we could sometimes hear it next door but you could never hear it clearly.

'I don't play as often as I used to but would you like to hear it again. I don't mean tonight, we wouldn't want to keep you on Christmas Eve but if you could come one afternoon during the holidays, I'll play for you again.'

'Yes, please. Could you tell me what it was called so I can tell Mum and Dad?'

'It was "The Dream of Olwyn" and I'm glad you liked it. If you'd like to come round on Wednesday about four o'clock, I'll play some more.'

'I'll have to ask my Mum but I'd really like to.'

'I'm sure your mother won't mind. Tell her it's a little thank you for the mince pies.'

'I will, I'll tell her. Goodnight Miss Pritchard,' I nodded to the lady at the piano 'and Merry Christmas.'

The other Miss Pritchard came down the hall with me and let me out.

'Goodnight Sally and thank you again.'

'Merry Christmas.'

When I went in, Mum was coming down the hall.

'That took you a long time.'

She took one look at my glowing face and leaned over to give me a hug.

'Come back into the warm and take your coat off. What happened?'

It all came out in a rush, how pleased they were with the mince pies and the lovely music and how Miss Pritchard looked sitting at the piano and how she'd asked me if I wanted to go again. Mum and Dad couldn't get a word in.

'Can I go again, Mum, Dad? Can I?'

'It won't do her any harm,' said Mum. 'Look at her face, she's all lit up.'

"I don't see why she shouldn't. She might cheer them up a bit and I'd like to think she was getting a taste for the finer things in life.'

'You heard your Dad. Yes, you can go on Wednesday.'

Great, I thought, I can't wait.

Dad had stoked up the fire and Mum had put three candles on the mantelpiece. She lit them with a taper and turned off the light and we all sat together, watching the flickering of the fire and the candle flames, just Mum and Dad and me.

***

Round at the Marshall's, Hettie heard the front door slam behind Maurice with relief. There'd been the usual song and dance about the shirt and collar, the shine on the shoes and the clothes brush on the shoulders of the jacket. Then on with the overcoat and a final brush over the Homburg hat but at last he was gone.

She hadn't a clue as to his destination but smiled at the thought of the plump chicken sitting in state in the pantry. Maurice could be relied upon where his stomach was concerned. Small blessings, she thought, small blessings.

There was no Christmas tree but the fire was stoked up and she'd put up a few decorations. A couple of candles threw a gentle light across the table and for once, the place looked cosy. The lads were at the kitchen table playing cards and she sat down with them, sharing out a box of matches to bet with.

'Come on, you two. Let's see what you're made of.'

She shuffled the cards, a fancy shuffle, and dealt a hand. Maurice had taught her to play poker but after she'd pasted him a time or two and he couldn't shrug it off as beginner's luck, he hadn't wanted to play anymore.

She'd taught the boys to play and they'd caught on quickly, especially Johnnie. He wasn't above a tricky shuffle himself and Harry had given him a crack or two for cheating. She wouldn't normally stand by and watch Harry push his brother around but this was different. He had to learn and she'd confiscated the cards more than once when there was rough stuff going on. Johnnie had come to terms with the fact that if he wanted to play, he'd have to use his wits to win. He couldn't get anything over on either his Mum or Harry, they watched him like hawks.

He'd been touchy since he walked through the door and Hettie wondered what had happened. She'd never get it out of him but no doubt he'd get over it.

Johnnie was still smarting from his encounter with David Steadman. If he told Harry what had happened, he'd say it had served him right. He wouldn't fight David again over this. Strong though Harry was, there was no guarantee he'd come off best. Harry had his own reputation to think of and David Steadman was tougher than he looked.

Maybe he could get at Sally, she was an easier target; a trip in the street or a crafty push in the park. Then he thought again. If anything happened to Sally and he was within a hundred yards, retribution would be swift. Pity though, she was such a cocky little beggar, he'd love to have a go at her.

Mickey Smith, that snivelling red-headed little rat, would cop it next time Johnnie caught him. A Chinese burn or a twisted pinch always reduced him to a quivering mass. Trouble was, he was fast on his feet these days but that made it more of a challenge.

Hettie looked at her two boys. She wasn't a sentimental woman but she worried about them. Harry was pretty steady now. He'd been a scrapper up to a few months ago and had often come in looking a bit battered but he was settling down.

Johnnie was another matter. He sometimes had a crafty look and although she couldn't be certain, she suspected him of helping himself to coppers out of her purse, not much, but enough to make her uneasy. Her purse was now kept in her apron pocket and under her pillow at night. She could hardly face him with it. She was doing the same thing to his father, just on a grander scale.

It had been a constant problem to keep the boys from under their father's feet. They'd learned early on to treat him with caution and keep out of his way.
It wasn't too bad when they were at school but the Christmas holidays in particular were a nightmare. The weather often confined the boys to the house and this year there had been frequent snowfalls. They played out for hours but then came in frozen and hungry, clothes wet through, so the rack hanging from the kitchen ceiling was constantly draped in steaming, damp clothes. She'd be glad when the holidays were over and they were back at school.
At nine o'clock she sent Johnnie up to bed and she and Harry sat watching the fire.
'Any idea what's up with Johnnie?' she asked.
'Who ever knows what's up with Johnnie? It's probably some falling out with the lads.'
'I worry about him sometimes. You never know what's going on in his head.'
'You worry too much. Johnnie will always fall on his feet. Anyway, I'm off to bed. Should I put some more coal on the fire?'
'No, go on up, I'll see to it.'
Harry kissed her cheek and she stroked his hair quickly.
'Good night, son.'
'Good night, Mum.'

Her turn now and she reached into the back of the cupboard, pulling out the hidden whisky and poured herself a tot. Settled in the old armchair in front of the fire, she nursed the glass and stared into the flames, silently calculating. Her plans were vague but whatever she decided, she'd need some cash and the more the better.

***

Christmas was a happy time in the Phillips' household. With two young children in the house, there was a constant buzz of excitement.

Margaret's father had arrived on Saturday with a real Christmas tree and the scent from the pine needles filled the sitting room.

Tom had never been happy about contributions from her father but Margaret was glad he'd accepted the tree with good grace. He'd be less than pleased if he knew about the turkey and the extra bacon. As he had no idea what groceries cost, he never questioned the quality of food on the table.

On Christmas morning, Tom lay in bed with his arm around his wife, listening to the boys whispering on the landing. He looked at his watch; seven o'clock, not too bad.

'We'd better get on with it,' he said, leaning over to kiss Margaret, and then in a mock stern voice,

'What's going on out there?'

A high pitched, excited little voice squeaked out,

'Daddy, Mummy, we think he's been. Can we go down?'

'Wait there, don't move.'

Tom and Margaret got out of bed, pulled on dressing gowns and joined the boys on the landing.

'Mummy and I will go first to check.'

He wanted to be downstairs before the boys. Which parent's heart wouldn't delight at the sight of two happy faces, ripping open presents and squealing with pleasure, mouths smeared with chocolate surreptitiously extracted from the nets of chocolate money amongst their presents?

After lunch, during which the boys had laughed giddily at the paper hats perched on Mum's and Dad's head, they settled in to listen to the King's speech, Peter on Tom's lap and Michael on Margaret's.

Comfortable in his armchair, Tom drifted off, the aroma of Christmas dinner still in the air. The whole family snoozed together. Even Margaret had no thought of things still to be done in the kitchen, she dozed comfortably under the warm weight of her youngest son.

1951

The Festival of Britain – promoting the best of British art, design and industry.

Winston Churchill, aged 77, was back in power after six years of Labour government.

The Cold War was in full swing.

Zebra crossings introduced

Austin A30 put on the market

First commercially available electronic computer delivered to Manchester University.

First BBC broadcast of 'The Archers'.

Rationing still in force

Published:	'The Day of the Triffids' - John Wyndham 'The Catcher in the Rye - J D Salinger
Best Film Oscar:	'An American in Paris' - Gene Kelly and Lesley Caron
Popular record:	'Too Young' - Jimmy Young and Nat King Cole
Born in 1951:	Sting Bill Bryson Peter May

Chapter 5

Sally

I didn't realise this was the point at which things began to change. It's easy with hindsight to say, 'it started then' but the changes came so slowly and imperceptibly I didn't recognise how far reaching they were to be.

The Wednesday after Christmas, I tapped on Miss Pritchard's front door and stood freezing on the step, listening to the slow footsteps coming down the hall.

'Sally, there you are. I wondered if you'd remember.'

Remember? I'd been on pins for days, humming the tune I'd liked so much under my breath and falling asleep with it running through my head.

'Come in, dear. Take off your coat and go into the parlour.'

The lamp on the piano was already lit. At four o'clock it was dark and gloomy outside but Miss Pritchard sat in a pool of warm light. I knew she was old but she really was lovely, like someone out of one of those old fashioned pictures. The room smelled of lavender polish, I recognised it. My gran used it too.

She turned on her piano stool and smiled.

'Hello, Sally. Come over here and have a look at the music and decide what you'd like to hear.'

I knew I had to be on my best behaviour and talk properly. My hands and face had been washed and a duster wiped over my shoes. I wasn't a timid child but I was out of my depth.

I stood next to Miss Pritchard and looked at the pile of sheet music while she turned each piece over. I couldn't tell anything from the titles or even from the pictures on the front.

'What do you fancy?'

I was stumped.

'Sorry, Miss Pritchard, I don't know any of these names. I don't know what I'd like. I did like what you played last time.'

'We'll start with that. Bring over one of those chairs and put it here next to me.'

I sat, entranced, while her fingers flew over the keys and the music poured out of the piano. This was the best thing I'd ever heard. No other thoughts in my mind, only the melody filling my head.

Sighing as the music drew to a close, I could barely speak.

'That was smashin', Miss Pritchard.'

Her lips twitched as if she were trying not to laugh and I felt my face go red. 'Smashing' wasn't the right word.

With a twinkle in her eye, she said.

'I think it's smashing too.'

I'd been unaware the other Miss Pritchard had come into the room and was sitting behind me at the dining table.

'Why don't you play some Chopin, Constance?'

Miss Pritchard placed a new piece on the carved stand fixed to the piano.

'Good idea. Let's see what you make of this.'

She played for an hour, piece after piece, each one as wonderful as the last and I read the names carefully so I'd know them again.

The other Miss Pritchard coughed a little.

'Yes, you're right, Muriel. It's enough for one day. I don't have to ask if you enjoyed that. I can see it in your face.'

I nodded, lost for words.

'Would you like to come again?'

'Oh, yes please. I'd love to but I have to ask my Dad.'

'Yes do, and if he says yes, we'll see you at the same time next week.'

I ran into the kitchen, shouting for Mum.

'It was great, Mum. It was like magic. They've asked me to go again but I said I'd have to ask Dad.'

She pulled me into her arms and gave me a hug.

'We'll see, my love. I'll have a word,' and that usually meant she could wangle it.

I told Dad all about it when he came home but he had something else on his mind and wasn't listening properly. It was no use pushing. He'd get to me in his own good time.

'It's time you were in bed now, Sal. Give your Dad a kiss and go on up. I'll be up in a minute.'

I'd been shuffled off a bit early but I didn't mind. The music filled my head and I lay there, reciting the names of the tunes I'd heard and the people who'd written them.

Eva placed a cup of tea on the arm of Arthur's chair and laid her hand gently on his shoulder.

'Come on, let's have it.'

'How did you know there was something on my mind?'

'Arthur, how long have we been married? It's not like you to shrug Sal off. What's up?'

'Michael Grey was in the shop again today. He tipped me the wink and I met him in the pub at lunchtime. He's under doctor's orders and has to retire early. It won't be in June but before the end of the month. He didn't look well but it puts us in a bit of a spot. He's making calls to his oldest customers and then he'll be gone. He said if I wanted to apply for his job, I should do it while he's still there so he can put in a good word for me. I need make my mind up within a day or two?'

'It's been on my mind since you first mentioned it. It must be your decision.'

'That doesn't help much. This is a real chance to move up in the world. If I stay where I am, there'll be promotion when Mr Simon retires but that's years away.

The thought of more money and a company car is very attractive but it's the challenge as much as anything. I'm ready to try something new.'

Eva thought for a moment.

'If Michael Grey hadn't come along, you might have stayed where you are until *you* retired and been quite happy. Now you have to make a decision.'

'What *do* you think?'

'You'd better have a go at it. You could regret playing safe for the rest of your life. There's nothing worse than 'if only'.'

'That's it then,' he said. 'I'll set the ball rolling tomorrow. I can't afford to lose any time and don't know what the competition will be like. I might not even get the job.'

'You'll get the job, I know it.'

'You're one in a million Eva. Thank you.'

'Now that's sorted, I want to talk to you about our Sal. Go over there and settle down.'

'What about her? I heard her at teatime. It's the music thing again isn't it?'

'Yes, it's the music thing again. I don't know where she got her highbrow taste from, certainly not from you or me, but she loves it. She was next door for an hour this afternoon and Miss Pritchard's asked her if she would like to go again next week.'

Arthur frowned.

'I wouldn't want her making a nuisance of herself.'

'How about I have a quiet word with them before we say yes or no to Sally?'

'Good idea. You can find out how the land lies.'

They heard the back gate close and then the kitchen door.

'Is it so late already? Is that you David?'

'Who else would it be? What's up, you two are looking a bit serious?'

They didn't tell him Arthur's news but they did tell him about Sal and her visit next door.

He thought for a minute.

'She's sure to pass her eleven plus and go to grammar school. They do all sorts of stuff like music and drama. If she manages to learn something about music, it will be one thing she knows something about, not just another new subject to tackle.'

'That's a thought, Arthur. Anyway, we'll think on it.'

***

Nick Metcalfe was early the first day back after the Christmas holidays. The weather was still bitterly cold and the roads icy but he'd made good time.

He came through the door of the staffroom to find Miss Marsden balanced on a chair trying to reach something out of a top cupboard.

'Hang on a minute; I'll give you a lift.'

Stuffing his gloves into one pocket and his scarf into the other, he shrugged off his coat.

Miss Marsden wobbled a bit and he put out a hand to steady her. She took his hand. Hers was soft and warm against his cold fingers. When her feet were firmly on the floor, she pulled away, looked up at him and flushed slightly.

'Thanks. Still, you could get me down that box right at the top. It's a word game I used with my class last year, something to cheer them up. They can be a bit down in the dumps after the holidays.'

He climbed on the chair and retrieved the box, passing it down to her.

'Anything else while I'm up here?'

'No, that's all for the moment.'

He hung up his coat and rubbed his hands.

'We're pretty early; I reckon we've got time for a quick cup of tea before we start the day.'

They sat holding mugs, facing each other across the staff room table.

'Have a good Christmas?' he asked.

'Yes, it was lovely. I went to Chester with my mum and dad. We have family over there and it was party after party. Christmas Day was great. My brother was on leave from the Navy. Altogether, eight of us sat down to Christmas dinner. It was a bit of a squash, but good fun. You?'

'Yes, very pleasant but it's over now and it's back to work.'

Nick's parents had died in a bombing raid and his only sister had married a GI and gone to live in New York. To all intents and purposes, he was alone in the world.

He had spent Christmas Day uncomfortably at Heather's house. Her mother was a poor cook - underdone chicken and overdone potatoes served with watery vegetables and matching gravy. Glad of the invitation initially, on the day, he caught Heather's mother looking at him in a particularly suspicious fashion. Her father had been a bit curt too. Heather had tried to smooth things over, chattering about nothing to fill the silences.

He suspected they had expected him to give Heather an engagement ring instead of the pretty locket he'd bought. Heather's face had lit up when he presented her with the box from the jewellers.

'How exciting,' she'd said as she ripped off the paper, saw the box, and lifted the padded lid. Clearly disappointed, she covered it quickly and pulled the locket out.

'Just what I've always wanted.'

She held it out and asked,

'Will you fasten it for me?'

Turning her back, she lifted her hair while he fumbled with the clasp. Her perfume became more noticeable as he bent towards her and he breathed in her sweet scent. As the locket settled against her skin, she went look at it in the mirror.

'It looks lovely. Thank you, Nick.'

The time had come to make a decision. He either had to ask her to marry him or let her go. The last thing he wanted was to hurt her. She would be devastated but it was unfair to keep her hanging on when his intentions weren't honourable. Funny how those old phrases sprang to mind.

He had decided to wait until after the holidays. Why spoil Christmas for her? Maybe it was a bit cowardly but he suspected this was going to be agonizing all round.

She's a lovely girl, he thought. For both our sakes, I need to be honest. I can't see myself twenty years down the line, living in the suburbs with her and a couple of kids.

Even with the decision made, he still fancied her like mad he often noticed envious glances from other men.

Their courtship had progressed from chaste kisses to passionate embraces and she was, if anything, more passionate than him.

He always managed to bring himself up short. Though they had talked about going all the way, he had never taken the final step, feeling he would have committed himself irrevocably.

This often left him frustrated. They'd thrash around on his settee, the breathing getting heavier until he had to disentangle himself to go and throw cold water over his head. A normal man, with normal instincts, it would have been easy to let nature take its course but something ticking in the back of his head held him back.

Invariably, after seeing her home, he would resort to the single man's consolation and it didn't make him feel much better. It was just a physical relief.

She had little to talk about except what happened at the salon. Her only other interest was in films; the great escape to Hollywood and depictions of a life so very different to her own. She showed no interest in what was happening in the real world.

What would they talk about once the physical had become the mundane? She listened attentively when he talked about his work but he believed she saw the future through rose coloured glasses and longed fervently for wedded bliss.

Cornered, it was time he did the decent thing. He had watched Tom and Margaret Phillips together and saw the kind of marriage he wanted; mutual understanding and support. That would never happen with Heather.

He had begun to hold back or even evade the passionate embraces. That hurt her too. The deed would have to be done, and soon, before he inflicted any more damage.

***

John Marshall was a bright boy, very bright indeed. As a result of being separated from his friends, he had little opportunity to muck about in the classroom. It was no use talking to the girls next to him, they never played up. They were too scared of getting into trouble.

Despite himself, over a period of a few weeks, he found he was interested in the lessons. It was less boring to listen to the teacher than to stare at the wall. He'd managed to pass a couple of notes to one of his pals along the row but Metcalfe had eyes like a hawk.

His school work improved and so did his marks and he'd discovered a previously unsuspected talent for arithmetic. They progressed to difficult problems and fractions and percentages and he realised his father must be pretty quick with a pencil when it came to working out odds on the horses.

He didn't turn into an angel. His behaviour outside school was the same as ever. He still led his little clique and still ruled the street he regarded as his territory. He did, however, show some caution in the playground and whilst on school premises. It was one thing to show bravado about a strapping but he wasn't too keen to be under the close scrutiny of Tom Phillips in his office.

Mr Metcalfe handed out the English exercise books and everyone looked to see what marks they'd got. Johnnie had a dismal six out of ten and was furious. As if that wasn't enough, there was a note underneath.

See me after school.

It was the last lesson of the day and all the other kids clattered out. His lieutenant, Jimmy Gill, gestured with his head towards the door.

'He wants to see me,' mouthed Johnnie.

'I'll be at the gate,' came the response and Jimmy followed the other kids through the classroom door.

The room seemed bigger with only the two of them in it and Mr Metcalfe came and perched on a desk at the front.

'You're not in trouble. I just wanted to have a word. You know your work's improving and you're keeping up easily.'

'But you only gave me a measly six for that composition and I tried really hard.'

'Do you know why?'

'No, Sir,' half belligerently and on the verge of saying it wasn't worth trying.

'Because I couldn't read much more than half of it. You can write the best story in the class but if I can't read it, you'll never get a decent mark. I'll tell you something. If you buckle down and work hard, you've got a very good chance of passing the eleven plus.'

Surprised, Johnnie looked up into his teacher's eyes.

'Yes – I mean it. But you won't pass with the state your work's in at the moment. Those examiners have hundreds of papers to mark and won't be bothered to struggle with something they can't read. They'll mark you down and that'll be the end of it.

You don't have to say anything now. I want you to think about it. Will you do that?'

'Yes, Sir.'

'If you decide you want to try for it, you need to practise your handwriting and figure work. Look, here's a notebook. Practise writing numbers and keeping them neat and one below the other; the same for letters. Pick a sentence out of a newspaper or magazine and copy it out until you can write it neatly and quickly.

Then do another one. If you keep at it on a regular basis, not just five minutes now and then, by the time the exam comes round, you'll be ready. You'll be able to spend the time allocated for the exam on the answers and not struggle with the writing. Do you follow?'

Johnnie's habitually sullen look in the face of authority had softened. He looked pleased and a little scared.

'Could I do it, Sir?' and he looked up into Nick's serious blue eyes.

'It's up to you. This is my last word. If you work, you work. If you mess around, that's up to you. Off you go now.'

He watched Johnnie leave the classroom, pushing the notebook inside the back of his pants and under his jumper so his pals wouldn't see it.

Nick Metcalfe looked after him speculatively.

We'll see. He's clever enough if he can buckle down. It's a shame the child who looks to make the most improvement in the class is so unlikeable. He's a bit of a thug but he deserves a chance. Maybe we can put him on the straight and narrow.

Jimmy and the gang were hanging around the school gate when he swaggered up.

'In trouble again, Johnnie?'

'Just the usual stuff; must try harder, could do better, yak, yak, yak. Never mind, let's go to the park. Call for your football on the way. Jimmy. Come on,' and the gang trouped off with Johnnie in the lead.

There was no way he could tell the lads what Metcalfe had said. No way could he tell them he was even thinking about grammar school. None of this lot had it in them anyway. He would leave them behind without a thought but for the moment, he was still in charge.

Nipping through his own back door on his way to the park, he stashed the notebook under the cushions on his mum's armchair. As he lay in bed that night, he worried at the problem until he fell asleep.

Though he was only eleven, like his mother, he had an eye on the long chance. He had a sneaking respect for Mr Metcalfe and an even greater respect for Mr Phillips. Though their primary interest was in the education of their pupils, they came down heavily on bad behaviour and it was practically impossible to get anything past them. They were definitely in charge.

Johnnie respected few adults. He knew how far he could go with his mother. She couldn't be pushed and now had caught on to his petty thieving. Nothing was said but she had stopped it. His father, who could be heavy handed, was treated with caution. He admired him because he had more money than anyone else for seemingly little effort. While other fathers left the house for work every morning, his dad could lie in bed until lunchtime if he felt like it.

He wanted to be somebody and the somebodies he knew were Metcalfe and Phillips. People, even parents, looked up to them and listened to them. They had authority and control. True, his dad was somebody too but he wasn't quite respectable and Johnnie wanted above all else to be admired and respected.

Perhaps there was something in this education lark. He loathed the sight of David Spencer but knew he was smart, not just a swot, but really clever. *He* wouldn't spend the rest of his life in the back streets of West Gorton. Johnnie wanted something better too and if the price was working hard at school, he'd pay it. He'd claw his way up the ladder any way he could.

The following evening he came in early, leaving his pals playing football and in the street. His mum was in the kitchen washing up after tea and his dad was asleep in the front room. He pulled the notebook from under the cushion, found a pencil in a jar in the kitchen cupboard and sat down at the kitchen table. Hettie was watching him out of the corner of her eye and he flushed, looking a bit shame faced.

'What you up to? It's not like you to be in early,' she said, wiping her hands on a tea cloth.

'Mr Metcalfe said I should practice my letters and figures. He said I might have a chance to pass the eleven plus.'

'What, you?' She stopped what she was doing and stared at him.

He flushed again.

'Why not? Don't you think I can do it?'

She could see he was hurt and struggled to retrieve the situation.

'It's not that. I'm surprised you're interested but it's great. What have you got to do?'

He explained about his writing and she took the notebook from him. It was new and clean and she turned to the first page. Her own handwriting was beautiful, almost copperplate, and she wrote down a simple sentence at the top of the first page.

'There you go, copy that. Try to keep the letters even and the words spaced like mine and do half a page. Then we'll have another look.'

He took the book and started to copy, pencil poised and tongue sticking out of the corner of his mouth. He paused.

'Mum, you won't tell Dad, will you?'

'Not if you don't want me to.'

'Or our Harry?'

'Not a word to a soul.'

Reassured, he carried on, struggling to keep the letters straight.

'Done, Mum.'

'Let's have a look. Look now, you can see the last line is better than the first but you'll need to practice a lot, half an hour a night if you want to make real progress. Now let's do some numbers.'

Carefully, she wrote from one to ten across the book.

'There, copy that and keep the numbers one under the other.'

He put his head down and started again. She could hardly believe her eyes. She didn't expect this to last but would help and encourage him, pleased he wanted to make the effort.

He finished a half page and pushed the book towards her.

'The same applies, son. You can do it but you'll have to keep at it.'

'Mum, suppose, I do pass. What will Dad say?'

'Let's wait and see. You haven't passed yet.'

'Yes, but if I do, it will cost a fortune. There's the uniform and gym kit and all sorts of stuff.'

'We'll face that when we get to it. If you pass, I'll sort it out somehow.'

Hettie generally meant what she said and he felt a bit safer.

'You won't tell anyone will you?'

'No son, it's between us. Now get off to bed. You've got school in the morning.'

She watched him go, touched he'd confided in her. Normally such a cocky little beggar, he'd looked so vulnerable. She suspected his newfound enthusiasm wouldn't last. If it did, she would help him all she could. If it fizzled out, she would say no more about it.

Nick Metcalfe was an inspired teacher. He presented lessons in clear, easy to understand terms. Coloured posters appeared on the walls, a map of the world had pride of place and gold stars were introduced. Johnnie was as keen as anyone. Although he pretended he didn't care, he was inwardly delighted when a coveted sticker appeared in one of his exercise books.

With very few exceptions, the children in Nick's class were making great strides forward.

He genuinely liked children and took pride in their progress, even if some of them niffed a bit at close quarters, especially on wet mornings.

For the last half hour on Fridays, he read aloud to the children, adventure stories mainly, and they sat in complete silence, hanging on every word. One of the boys was heard to remark,

'It's as good as the pictures,' which gratified Nick no end.

After Christmas, he pushed the brighter kids a little harder, impressing upon them the idea there really was a possibility some of them could pass the eleven plus. Johnnie was one of them. He had taken Nick's words to heart and it wasn't a complete surprise when his written work began to improve. His marks were steadily improving too and though Johnnie tried to hide his satisfaction, he was pleased.

Nick wondered how he squared his sudden interest in school work with the other lads. He'd never stand being laughed at and would thump anyone who even looked at him funny.

Nobody knew Johnnie's weak spot. He thought the world of Alice Spencer. There was something about her; she looked so fragile, as though she were made of china. Always so clean, her blonde hair in neat plaits, he thought dirt would slide off her and never stick.

She was unaware she was safe at school on his say-so.

'Leave her alone,' he said. "She's more trouble than she's worth. You mess with her and her dad will be round at school causing trouble. It's not worth it.'

She was under his protection and the rougher kids left her alone.

***

Alice's first memory was of sitting on her Daddy's knee while he sang to her. While his tuneful tenor held the melody, she could feel his chest vibrating against her ear. She attached no significance to the words, she only knew her name was in it and she liked that.

'Sing it again, Daddy,' and he would, a song about a girl in a blue dress.

She was a quiet, shy child. She played happily with her dollies and her doll's house and followed her mother round the house, dusting and sweeping with a tiny brush and dustpan. Sometimes her mother would play 'Snap' or 'Happy Families'. They had the wireless and she loved

"Workers' Playtime" and "Housewives' Choice" and the stories on "Woman's Hour."

Alice didn't notice her father was one of the few fathers around. Most of the others were off in the army. At the time of the call-up, Jack had been dismayed to discover he wasn't fit enough to go into the forces but came to count his blessings as the other men in the street started to leave. He just wished the reason for his rejection had been something a bit more dramatic than fallen arches

Brenda Spencer and Eva Steadman gave birth within two days of each other, both safely delivered of girls.

Brenda had a complicated delivery and the doctor had come out of the delivery room to have a word with Jack who had been pacing the floor. The doctor looked pale and harassed and he motioned to Jack to sit down.

"What's the matter, doctor, is it the baby? Is something wrong?'

"No, the baby's fine. A bouncing seven-pound girl and she's doing well. It's your wife I'm concerned about.'

'Why, what's the matter?

'Your wife's had a hard time and she's lost a lot of blood. There were complications. It would be a mistake for her to try for another child. You understand what I'm saying.'

'Yes, I understand,' he said, impatiently. 'When can I see the baby?'

'She'll be taken to the nursery as soon as we get her cleaned up. You can go along and see her there. Your wife will be back on the ward soon but she won't be very responsive. We had to give her a general anaesthetic."'

'I'll go along to the nursery now. I want to see my daughter.'

The doctor watched him go, walking briskly along the gloomy corridor, almost running in his eagerness to see the child. Had what he'd said about the wife really registered?

Jack stood in the corridor looking through the glass into the nursery when the nurse brought his daughter in. He managed to catch her eye and she mouthed at him,

'Baby Spencer?'

He nodded vigorously and she brought the blanket wrapped bundle over to the window and held up the baby so he could see her. Her face looked a bit crumpled but he could see a tiny waving fist and perfectly formed tiny fingernails. He was entranced, unaware of the tears rolling down his cheeks.

My daughter, my beautiful, beautiful daughter.

The nurse placed the baby, tightly wrapped in a soft white blanket, in a crib by the window. She was lying on her side but he could see her face. He could have gazed at her for hours, watching her breathe.

Finally, he dragged himself away and glanced up at the clock. He had better go along and see Brenda; she would be back on the ward by now.

It was visiting time and people were wandering along the corridors, carrying flowers and carrier bags. The smell peculiar to hospitals, a mixture of cabbage and disinfectant, hung in the air. When he reached the ward, the heavy doors were closed and visitors were milling around, looking at their watches and muttering.

The door opened and was fastened back by one of the nurses. The visitors streamed through, looking towards the beds which held their relations. Jack halted by the matron's office and tapped on the door. She looked up from her paperwork.

'Mrs Spencer, Brenda Spencer? She's just come from surgery.'

'Ah yes, she's in the first bed on the right. She's still asleep I'm afraid.'

'Is it all right if I go through?'

"Yes, yes, of course but don't stay long. She'll be feeling poorly when she does wake up. Have a quick look and then you can come back at visiting time tomorrow.'

Jack walked towards the bed with the curtains drawn around it. He pulled the drab green curtain aside and stepped in.

Brenda had never been a pretty woman but she looked dreadful now, her face so drained of colour she looked almost grey. Propped on a couple of pillows, moist snores escaped from her half open mouth, damp hair clinging to her scalp and fingers twitching.

There was no point hanging about. She would have her hands full when she got home so she'd better get all the rest she could. He would come back tomorrow; bring her some flowers to cheer her up.

Chapter 6

After an anxious ten days, Arthur received a letter inviting him to an interview at the Midland Hotel.

His best suit had been dry cleaned and his shoes polished to a high shine. The interview was set for Wednesday afternoon, half-day closing.

David and Sal were to go to their gran's for tea and Eva and Arthur travelled into town together by bus. Eva was also dressed in her best and they were a fine looking couple as they walked through Piccadilly Gardens and down Mosley Street. They parted company outside the Midland Hotel.

'Are you sure you'll be all right? I don't know how long this is going to take.'

'Arthur, I'll be fine. I've got my library book and I'll either be on a bench in Albert Square or I'll be in the Kardomah on the corner. Take it easy. They'd be fools not to want you.'

'I wish I had your confidence,' he said nervously.

He turned and walked up the steps but looked behind him.

'Wish me luck.'

'Good luck, love. You'll be fine.'

Eva walked into Albert Square and found a seat. It was pleasant in the January sunshine and she was warmly dressed. Taking her book out of her bag, she opened it with gloved hands at the bookmark and tried to read. She couldn't concentrate so she idly watched the passersby and the folk going in and out of the town hall.

Its dark grandeur appealed to her although she supposed it must have been white once, not the murky grey standing against the blue sky. She looked up at the clock and was surprised to find half an hour had passed. The light was going and it was becoming chilly. Pushing her book back into her bag, she strolled across the square and down the steps of the Kardomah where the smell of freshly ground coffee rose to meet her.

With a milky coffee in front of her, she tried again with the book but her thoughts wandered and her fingers drummed on the table. If it came off, this would mean a considerable change in their lives. She looked at her watch again, almost an hour now, surely a good sign. She folded and unfolded the paper napkin, looking repeatedly at the stairs, stirring the coffee grown cold in the half-empty cup.

Footsteps rattled down the stairs and she looked up. It was Arthur, looking non-committal. He leaned over and kissed her cheek.

'Want another coffee, love?' he said.

There would be no rushing him. He would tell the story in his own good time.

'Yes, please.'

She watched him cross to the counter and walk back with a tray bearing two cups.

'Well, what happened?'

'It went pretty well. They asked me about my experience in the shop, how used I was to paperwork, what sort of customers and so on and they were pleased I could drive.'

'You don't look all that cheerful though, Arthur. Is there a snag?'

'A big one. Michael Grey came down with me to hotel reception and told me what was going on. Since the job came open, one of the directors' nephews has applied and Michael thinks he'll get it. The other director, Mr Samuels, doesn't seem so keen and insisted my interview went ahead. I don't know whether I'm glad or not. Apparently, this other chap has tried his hand at a few things and his uncle's anxious to give his sister's boy a chance.'

'Oh Arthur, I'm so sorry. You must be disappointed.'

'I was sorry for Michael. He was mortified. He said he knew I was the best man for the job and was sorry he'd led me to believe I had such a good chance. He couldn't have known this would happen and, as they say, blood is thicker than water. I could see Mr Samuels liked me but I'd be surprised if he went against his partner.'

Eva put her hand and over his and squeezed it gently.

"At least your job is still safe. Nobody knows you were looking around for something else.'

'I'm glad we didn't tell anybody else. Eva, you didn't, did you?'

'Certainly not. I said I wouldn't. What will you do now?'

She looked at him across the table and saw the disappointment in his eyes.

This wasn't like one of the kids, she couldn't kiss it better.

'It's a funny thing. I was happy until this came up and now I'm unsettled. I'd been looking forward to the challenge and the thought of carrying on as before makes me go cold.'

'I know I was a bit lukewarm to start with but I can see you'd set your heart on a change. There must be other jobs, why don't you start looking around. You've plenty of contacts in the trade. If not a rep's job, you could try at management level in one of the big chains or even go for a job outside the trade. You'd be a star on the road, you could sell anything.'

She'd said enough. Arthur would make up his own mind but the seeds had been sown.

'Never mind, at least we've got the evening to ourselves. What do you fancy?'

"Let's go and have a bite to eat and then decide.'

***

Sally

I started going to Miss Pritchard's once a week. Every week they asked me if I'd like to come again and I always said yes. Always the same, Miss Pritchard, the younger one, would open the door and say,
　'Good afternoon, Sally. Do come in.'
　I'd walk down the hall, take off my coat and sit next to the other Miss Pritchard at the piano. I could fit names to some of the tunes now and was beginning to have favourites. The speed with which her fingers flew over the keys was amazing and the room filled with music.
　Occasionally, I'd wondered about the printed music at school and at Sunday school but watching Miss Pritchard running her hands up and down the keyboard, gaze fixed on the sheet music in front of her, I became intrigued. The final notes rang out.
　'What is it Sally? You look puzzled.'
　I felt a bit of a fool trying to put my thoughts into words.
　'You know the music you have in front of you?'
　'Yes,' she prompted gently.
　'I've been thinking about it. You're reading it aren't you?'
　'Yes, I am. I know some pieces by heart but for ones I don't play so often, I need to read the music.'
　'And do the notes on the page tell you which notes to play on the piano?'
　'Yes, they do. That's exactly it.'
　'It's like a language then but instead of words, sounds come out?'
　'You're a clever girl, Sally, to work it out.'
　'Can anyone learn?'
　'If they want to but it's hard work, like learning a new language.'
　'Our David's learning French and I've had a look at his books. The letters are all the same but the words they make up don't make sense because it's French. I suppose it's a bit like that.'
　'Would you like to know how it works?'

I nodded and Miss Pritchard picked up a sheet of music with a few blank lines at the end. The other Miss Pritchard brought a pencil over so the notes could be lightly written in at the bottom of the page.

"See, Sally. This is what we call a scale. The note there represents this key on the piano and the next note up gives you the next key."

I knew I had a big grin on my face.

'So the third note is that key there and the fourth note that key there.'

'Correct. You have it. It's much more complicated, of course, if you want to play a tune.'

'I can see how it works. Wait 'til I tell my mum.'

On Saturday afternoon, Sally invariably went to the children's matinee, coming back with stories of cartoons and what kind of a mess Flash Gordon was in; hanging off a cliff, falling into a bottomless pit or something similarly hazardous..

Everyone was out and Eva took the opportunity to have a word with Miss Prichard. She tapped on the front door and heard footsteps coming along the hall. The door opened slightly while Miss Pritchard peeped through and then much wider when she saw who was there.

'Oh, Mrs Steadman, it's you. Sorry to be so wary but since we had a problem with those boys, I'm always careful opening the door.'

'I'm glad David was able to help. Would it be possible to have a word with your sister? It's about Sally.'

She opened the door wider.

'Do come in, she's in here,' gesturing toward the front room.

Eva followed her and noticed the lino in the hall was highly buffed and several black and white ink drawings hung on the walls.

The front sitting room was in similar good order. The piano was polished to a high gloss and a dark maroon chenille tablecloth covered the circular table. Several floral pictures hung on the back wall and a beautiful mirror over the mantelpiece. Eva had a good eye and had walked through the furniture and china department at work often enough to know quality when she saw it.

Miss Pritchard fluttered a little in the doorway. Whipping off her apron and folding it neatly, she asked

'Can I offer you a cup of tea?'

Eva hadn't expected this much formality but was delighted.

'That would be lovely, thank you.'

The younger Miss Pritchard bustled off to the kitchen and Eva turned to look at her sister.

There was no doubt she was looking a little frailer but the back was straight, the hair in perfect order and the clothes brushed and neat.

The blue eyes looked at Eva a little anxiously.

'Is there a problem, Mrs Steadman, something to do with Sally?'

'In a way. We're concerned she might be wearing out her welcome. She came back on Wednesday and had our heads spinning with her stories of notes on paper and keys on the piano. We were wondering if it might be too much for you.'

'Let's sit down with a cup of tea and talk about it,' said the older of the two ladies.

A fragile china tea set on a silver tray was carried in and placed on the table; sugar lumps in the crystal bowl and even a pair of silver tongs. Eva looked on appreciatively; this really was gracious living. The tea was poured and passed round.

'Mrs Steadman, she isn't wearing out her welcome, quite the reverse. She's like a breath of spring, especially if the weather's bad and we can't get out of the house. It's a pleasure to play for her; she picks things up so quickly. I enjoy picking out things she might like. It's so long since I played some of them and am rediscovering pieces I haven't played for years.'

Eva smiled broadly. She was proud of Sal, who was obviously giving these two elderly ladies a great deal of pleasure.

'If you're sure she's not too much trouble.'

'She's no trouble at all. Mrs Steadman, I hesitate to broach the subject but I'm sure she'd love to take lessons.'

She raised her hand gently before Eva could speak.

'I know what this entails. I would be happy to teach her but she would need an instrument to practice on and I don't know how practical that is. May I suggest you talk it over with your husband? I won't say a word to Sally but I'd be obliged if you would let her come as usual next Wednesday.'

Eva sat silently for a moment.

'You've given me something to think about. Leave it with me, will you, Miss Pritchard.'

She smiled and nodded and offered more tea.

'No thanks, I must get on. Thank you so much for the tea and the chat. I'll let you know what we decide.'

The younger sister led the way down the hall and opened the front door for her.

'Thanks again,' she murmured and then hurried to her own front door.

***

For Hettie too, things were changing. Her eldest was now almost a young man and had steadied down from his former, scrappier self. She found the cash to buy him a new pair of trousers, a shirt and a sweater so he'd look decent at the weekend. He'd all but filled up when he found the new clothes laid out on his bed and he came downstairs and gave Hettie a hug, murmuring,

'Thanks, Mum' into her neck.

'That's all right, son. Get along with you now.'

She had asked Maurice a couple of times about work for Harry but she daren't push him. Last time she'd asked, he'd fixed her with his gaze.

'Leave it alone. I'll sort him out. Anyway, as of this weekend, he can take his turn as lookout. I'll tell him at teatime.'

This wasn't the result Hettie had been looking for. She tried again, knowing she was on thin ice.

'You know he's leaving school when they break up?'

He responded dismissively.

'Course I know. I'll get him a job on the wagons at the brewery. It'll do until he's called up. In the meantime, he can give me a hand on race days. I'll even pay him a couple of bob. What's the face for?'

Hettie quickly made her expression as impassive as she could manage. He hadn't clouted her for ages but that didn't mean he wouldn't.

Maybe it wasn't so bad. Maurice would find Harry a job. He'd never stand for him hanging about the house after he left school. Although the crafty devil wouldn't pay Harry as much as the other lookouts, Harry would still have a couple of bob in his pocket for the weekend.

He wouldn't be asked, he'd be told and that would be the end of it. He'd be working within weeks and Hettie was grateful there'd be more cash coming into the house. If Johnny did pass the exam, there'd be an enormous amount to find.

Johnny had surprised her. Always single minded when he was after something, he'd stuck at his practice. His handwriting had improved and his columns of figures were now legible and neat. This last week she'd read out a simple piece from a magazine and he'd taken it down in dictation. It was perfect, legible and neat.

'Our Johnny, that's marvellous. I'm proud of you. You've worked hard and must be able to see it's paid off.'

He squirmed a bit under the praise but glowed.

'Do you really think so?'

'I do, what does your teacher say?'

'Not much but my marks have been going up. He says I can write a good story now he can read my writing. He even read one out to the class last week.'

Hettie smiled. It wasn't often Johnnie confided in her.

'Well, you can't afford to let up now. It's not long to the exam and you need to be as good as you can be.'

'I'll keep practising Mum. I know it's not long.'

'Are you sure you want to go if you pass? There'll be a lot more work than if you stay where you are, homework every night and not as much time to be out with your mates.'

'I'm sure. I want to get on. I don't want to be stuck here, doing some rotten job Dad finds me. I don't fancy our Harry's chances. Dad'll have him shovelling horse shit 'til he goes in the army.'

Hettie tutted at the language but he was unrepentant. She let it go. She'd had no idea he was looking so far ahead but the look in his eyes made her uneasy. It wasn't normal for a lad his age to be so set on the future. He wasn't thinking of a couple of weeks ahead but several years.

'Best get up them stairs now; it's school in the morning.'

He stashed his notebook and ran upstairs, shouting 'night Mum' as he went. Not a word of thanks but she hadn't expected any. He and Harry were like chalk and cheese.

***

The end of term was only a couple of days away and Tom Phillips and Nick Metcalfe were in Tom's office, reflecting on the year that had passed. Tom ran his hands through his wiry hair, put his feet on his desk and looked across at Nick.

'How would you assess the year as a whole, Nick?'

'It's gone better than I expected. My class has made good progress and I'm delighted with the eleven plus passes. The increase from the one or two in previous years to five is encouraging. We'll do even better next year."

'I'd agree. But let's not count our chickens,' Tom said. 'What I *am* pleased with is the general atmosphere. Everyone was so apathetic when we arrived and now when I walk down the hall, there's a buzz. The kids look happier, more settled.'

We'll be losing two major trouble makers as well, the Marshall brothers.'

After a full school year, Tom had a good idea about the backgrounds of many of the children. Maurice Marshall's reputation had come to his attention early on.

'Who knows what kind of job Harry will end up in. His father's fixing him up and I hope he doesn't end up in the family business. I'd hate to see him in court for taking illegal bets.'

Nick nodded his agreement and back on the subject of his own class, he added,

'I won't be sorry to see the back of Johnnie either. I've rarely seen a kid improve at the rate he has. He's worked so hard, he'd have been inconsolable if he hadn't passed. Heaven knows what kind of problems we'd have had if he'd had to come back next year."

Tom summed it up.

'It's amazing that two boys from exactly the same background can be so different. Harry's a bit of a rough diamond but there isn't a malicious bone in his body. Johnnie's still the ringleader of that little gang and not above shoving the other kids around but he's crafty enough not to get caught. Let's hope the change of school sorts him out. Changing the subject, he asked,

'I don't want you to betray any confidences but how's the general feeling in the staffroom now?'

'I had my doubts early on but they've mainly come round to your way of thinking. Discipline has improved. The kids dread a stint in your office even more than six of the best.'

'What about Janet? She seems to have her head screwed on.'

Nick tried to be objective in the light of his changing feelings towards her.

'She's a good teacher. She lacks experience but she's learning and isn't afraid to ask for advice. More often than not, she turns to Martin Jackson. He has more experience than anyone else and he keeps that class of leavers in order when most of them are losing interest. In my opinion, he's the best teacher in the school.'

'You're not bad yourself, Nick, but I know what you mean.'

'The first year is almost behind us and next year should be easier.'

Any plans for the summer?'

'We're taking the kids to Blackpool for a couple of weeks. I'm looking forward to the break.'

He knew Nick had had a painful breakup with Heather. Viewed from the outside, there could have been no future in the relationship and he thought Nick had done the right thing. He asked Nick,

'What about you?'

'I'm going walking. France, with just a rucksack and a pair of good boots. The ferry's cheap enough and I'll go where the fancy takes me.'

'Good idea,' said Tom, maybe the break would cool Heather down.

'It won't do any harm to brush up my French, it's slipping away and I want a change of scenery.'

Tom nodded sympathetically.

'Let's make a move, shall we?'

He pushed himself to his feet, picked up his shabby old briefcase, and they left the school together.

At the time of the break up with Heather in January, Nick had hoped that was the end of it. He was not to escape so easily. She had waited for him outside school a couple of times on her half day and he'd hustled her off before she made a scene. She'd knocked on his door on a Sunday morning and been on his step on a Saturday afternoon when he came home from the match. No matter how calmly he talked to her and how many times he said he wouldn't change his mind, she turned up again.

He was constantly looking over his shoulder and, as well as the aggravation and mounting irritation, the guilt persisted.

He reproached himself with thoughts he should have ended it sooner. This was no clean break; it was heartbreak for her and heartache for him.

He felt trapped and though it galled him, he decided to run away. Pounding along the streets yet again, his thoughts were becoming clearer. He was too accessible, she lived only twenty minutes' walk away. He couldn't do anything about school but he could look for another flat. He was earning more and could afford something better. He would start looking, sort it out, then go off to France for the holidays. If she couldn't get to him at all for several weeks, maybe she would cool down. Having made the decision, he felt a little easier.

Chapter 7

Alice was dreading the holidays. Five whole weeks of captivity loomed before her. She would be stuck with her mum, escaping the confines of her home only to go to the shops and the library. If the weather were fine at the weekend, her daddy would take them for a walk or out on the bus. No matter how many times she asked, he wouldn't let her play out with the other children.

The last time she had asked Jack had looked so stern; her eyes had filled with tears. Only a little contrite, he'd said gently,

'I've told you and told you. You're too good for the likes of them.'

So desperate was she, she'd made a final anxious plea.

'Even Sally Steadman? I thought you liked her and you like her daddy, she's not like the others.'

'Not even Sally Steadman. Now don't ask again.'

Brenda dare not interfere. She and Alice were almost under house arrest and couldn't stir without Jack's approval. There was no physical abuse but he could be very cruel, especially if he'd been to the pub.

If he was out, Brenda could listen to the radio in peace without him chipping in with some sarcastic remark but these days, she never went to bed until he was home. She'd woken up twice and found him sitting by Alice's bed, with eyes full of maudlin tears and it made her uneasy.

She liked the Steadmans, all of them. Arthur smiled and waved when he saw them, Sally and David were polite children and Eva always stopped for a chat if they met at the shops.

She and Eva had been in hospital together and Eva had come to sit by her bed several times. After they came out of hospital, she had knocked on the door to check on Brenda, who was pale and harassed. When she mentioned it to Jack, he was tight lipped and disapproving.

'Don't encourage her. Before you know it, she'll be in and out of the house, interfering and snooping. You have to learn to manage on your own. This is my house and my family and we keep ourselves to ourselves.'

Unlike most fathers, Jack soon learned to bottle feed and change his daughter's nappy. In the early days, he even got up in the night to see to her. He wasn't like other men in that respect and Brenda wasn't sure it was a good thing. It was odd, unnatural even.

He'd married her on the rebound and under duress. His heart had been set on Mary Jenkins but she'd had bigger ideas. She wanted more than a two up and two down in a terraced street.

She had turned him down flat and even laughed at him.

'Think I'd marry you? Whatever gave you that idea? Just because we've had a bit of a kiss and a cuddle on the back row doesn't mean I want to settle down. I'm going places.'

He'd gone out to get drunk, on his own, in a pub fifteen minutes' walk away where he knew no-one. The pints had gone down swiftly but he couldn't reach the oblivion he sought. He left the pub, half-angry and half-disgusted, knowing there would be trouble if he hung around much longer. He had been belligerent and rude and it was only a matter of time until one of the regulars thumped him.

Brenda had just been convenient. She had been walking home from the cinema with her friend when they bumped into him. He'd never given her a second glance. She wasn't much to look at after all.

Tonight she was thrilled he had stopped to talk. She could tell he'd been drinking but he didn't look drunk. He walked along with them until her friend reached her front door.

'You be all right, Brenda?' she whispered as she turned to go in.

'Yeh, fine, go on now. See you tomorrow. 'Night.'

''Night, Brenda, 'night Jack.'

They carried on walking, silent at first. Unexpectedly, Jack started to cry, great heaving sobs.

'Jack, Jack, what's the matter?'

He couldn't speak but he pulled her quickly into an entry. He didn't want anyone to see him.

His sobs were subsiding and she rummaged through her pockets and found a not too grubby hanky.

'Here, Jack, take this. Give us a good blow.'

He blew his nose, still weeping slightly and she did what came naturally, she put her arms around him.

He hung on to her as though his life depended on it. It was a dream come true. Her and Jack Spencer, there were stars in her eyes.

She suddenly realized he was holding on too tight. He swung her round so her back was against the wall and kissed her hard, very hard. She was frightened and broke off.

'Jack, stop it Jack. That's enough.'

He was oblivious, pushing himself against her and fumbling with his trousers.

'Jack, stop it, stop it.'

He was pushing her skirt up and she tried to fight him off. He had her pinned against the wall, holding one wrist tightly while her other hand beat ineffectually against him. She could hear him mumbling,

'Bitches, you're all bitches, all the same in the end, like cats in the dark.'

With one great heave, he was inside her. The pain was excruciating and when she screamed, he put his mouth over hers to shut her up. It was over in a minute and he pushed himself away, leaving her shaking and frightened.

Leaning against the wall, he fastened up his trousers and pulled down her skirt. He couldn't look at her and stumbled away leaving her crumpled against the backyard wall.

***

Brown envelopes bearing the legend 'Manchester Education Authority' were falling on the doormats of the parents whose children had been selected to sit the eleven plus. There were a few disappointments, some jubilation and in one house, great trepidation.

Hettie had intercepted the letter. There would be no mention of it if Johnny hadn't passed.

She picked it up and stuffed it in her apron pocket where it would burn a hole until she got five minutes on her own. Johnny was watching her from the top of the stairs. She shook her head and put her finger over her lips. He nodded.

Maurice was at the kitchen table, bleary eyed and unshaven. Very little post arrived in these streets. This was a strictly cash culture; the rent man called every Friday, gas and electricity was paid by coins in a meter and groceries paid for on the nail.

'Was that the postman?'

'No, Maurice, only was kids messing about.'

He grunted 'more bread' and continued ploughing through the great plate of egg and sausage.

Hettie cut another doorstep from the loaf on the kitchen table and, catching Johnnie's eye, nodded towards the back door, indicating he should make himself scarce. He took the hint and disappeared though she could see the strain on his face.

The morning ritual got underway as Maurice prepared for the day's business. There was racing this afternoon so he would be around most of the day.

She scurried out to the lavatory, practically the only place she would get a couple of minutes on her own today. Heart pounding, she ripped open the envelope and gasped.

He'd done it. The little beggar had done it. There it was in black and white, Manchester Central High School for Boys. Now all I have to do is make Maurice think it's all his idea.

She smiled grimly. This was not going to be easy but for once, she would get what *she* wanted. She would keep him sweet until she had a plan.

It was a fine day and Maurice would be taking bets in the back yard. She wiped over the table in the yard and brought out a kitchen chair. Maurice puffed and panted and brought out his cash box and ledger.

Business was always brisker when the sun shone. It made no sense. His punters never went to the races but they definitely placed more bets when the weather was good. Perhaps the sun made them more optimistic.

Johnnie had hung around in the street for ages. He was waiting for the runners so his dad would be too busy to notice him.

His mates were waiting but he was on pins, a knot the size of a fist in the centre of his chest.

'What? What did you say?' he snarled at Jimmy Gill, his main partner in crime.

'You goin' deaf or somethin'? I've asked you twice if we're playing footie in the park.'

'Yeh, get the ball and I'll meet you there. I've got to nip back home.'

Jimmy looked at him questioningly. Johnnie could be moody at the best of times and from the look on his face, it would be better not to cross him this morning.

Johnnie slipped through the back gate and into the kitchen, barely noticed by his father. He closed the door behind him.

'Mum?'

He was so strung out, he couldn't speak. His anguished face said everything.

Hettie broke into a wide grin, pulled the letter from her pocket and waved it under his nose.

'You've passed, Whitworth Street for you. Well done, son. You deserve it.'

Johnnie snatched the letter and scanned it. Then he read it again.

'It's true isn't it? There couldn't be a mistake could there?'

'No, no mistake. Now I've got your father to deal with.'

Johnnie blanched. He had been so caught up in waiting for the results; he'd pushed this problem to the back of his mind. All the kit he was bound to need would cost a fortune. What would his dad say? Would he shell out for uniforms and the like?

Johnnie suddenly looked like the little boy he really was. His face crumpled and he looked beseechingly at his mother.

'What'll you do, Mum? What if he says no? I'll have done all that work for nothing.'

'Don't you worry. I'll deal with your father.'

Slightly reassured, he nodded. He could only trust her although it went against the grain to trust anybody.

'Go on, get along now. Go and find your pals, '

He went out the back door, passing his father who was entering betting slips into his ledger and working out odds. He didn't lift his head as his son passed.

Johnnie fluctuated between elation and despair. After all, he'd passed - but he couldn't tell anybody. All his mates knew he had taken the exam and he'd seen the look of disdain in their eyes. They thought he was a traitor to the gang. He knew he would have to fight a couple of them to regain their respect and it would all have been for nothing if his dad said he couldn't go. Time enough to put the cat among the pigeons when he knew which way the wind blew.

He was so preoccupied; he didn't even notice young Mickey Smith scuttling round a corner out of his way. For once, Johnnie's perpetual victim, had escaped the blows which usually followed an encounter with Johnnie Marshall.

Meanwhile, Hettie was at Maurice's beck and call for the afternoon. When things got hectic out in the yard, with runners coming in at frequent intervals and the radio giving results of various races, she would get a respite.

Maurice had a mug of tea. That should keep him quiet for a bit. Her thoughts skittered right and left. Maurice would need careful handling. An inkling he was being 'managed' and things would go badly for her - and for Johnnie too.

This was her greatest challenge yet.

***

Sally

I'd been at my gran's all morning and, a bit fed up, decided to go and meet my dad off the bus. Early closing in Manchester meant he'd be home early. Mum was working and David had gone to see one of his friends from school. It didn't happen often and I liked having Dad to myself for a while.

I watched as the bus turned the corner. He might not be on this one but I had nothing better to do. If I went home with Dad, I could go out and play and wouldn't have to wait until Mum collected me.

As the bus pulled up, I could see him on the platform. He hadn't seen me but his face looked serious and a bit sad. When he did see me, he shook his head and grinned.

'Hello, Sal. This is a nice surprise.'

'Hiya, Dad. Thought I'd come and meet you. Our David's out so there's just the two of us.'

'Does your gran know where you are?'

'Course she does. She knows I'll be going home with you.'

'It's such a lovely day and I've been cooped up at work. Why don't we walk the long way round and maybe I'll treat us to an ice cream at Sivori's.'

I held his hand as we walked and smiled when we met Alice Spencer and her mum and he raised his hat as they passed.

I could sense something was bothering him so I told him about gran's run-in with the milkman and how she'd ticked him off and by the time we'd got our ice cream, he'd cheered up..

When we got home, he took off his jacket and tie and rolled up his sleeves. The sun was shining through the kitchen window and he opened the back door and breathed in.

'I'm going to sit out for a while,' he said, picking up a kitchen chair. 'You coming?'

'Maybe I'll go and see if there's anyone playing ball round the corner. D'you mind?'

'Course not, sweetheart. Off you go, I'll have a ten minute snooze in the sun.'

I looked at the kitchen clock. There was time to play out before I'd have to wash my hands and face and comb my hair. Miss Pritchard was expecting me at four and I wouldn't miss that for the world.

Arthur had been pleased Sally had come to meet him. Her chatter distracted him from his pre-occupation and entertained him no end.

She's a good lass. I'm a lucky man. David is doing well at school and I've got a wife to be proud of.

Unsettled since the fiasco with Stein & Company, he was trying to count his blessings. There had been a good chance of a better job but it had slipped through his fingers. Leaning back, he closed his eyes. The sunshine felt good on his face but still his mind raced.

He was still looking, checking the trade magazines and discreetly asking around. Standards were kept up at work but his enthusiasm lagged. He had been marking time too long. A relatively young man, there was still time for him to make his mark in the world.

He woke with a start. He'd dropped off after all and could hear Eva calling from the kitchen.

'Out here, love.'

Eva came smiling through the kitchen door. She looked lovely in her working clothes, white blouse with a black skirt and shoes; a little severe, but the look suited her.

'It's all right for some, sleeping in the sunshine while the rest of us work. I'll put the kettle on, shall I?'

Arthur nodded and Eva went inside, only to come out again with an envelope in her hand.

'There's a letter for you, must have come by the lunchtime post.'

'Give it here and let's have a look.'

Eva handed it over and watched him look at the typed address on the front and then turn it to look at the back.

'It's from Stein and Company,' and he held it out so she could see the printed name. 'Wonder what they want?'

'For crying out loud, open the perishing thing. You've not got X-ray eyes.'

He carefully opened the envelope.

'Come on, come on. It won't bite you.'

Arthur unfolded the letter and slowly, a smile tweaked the corners of his mouth. He passed it to Eva, who scanned it quickly.

'I know what it looks like. That other chap, the nephew, didn't work out and they want to give you the job,' she said.

'Maybe you're right. They want me to ring them to make an appointment.'

Despite himself, Arthur's spirits lifted. He reached out and took her hand, pulling her against him.

'Come here, you.'

He pulled her on to his lap and she rested her head against him.

'We still won't say anything. Let's not tempt fate.'

'Not a word.'

She cuddled closer and rubbed her palm up and down his back. He lifted her chin and looked into her eyes, then leaned in to kiss her. In seconds, her breathing deepened and his own matched hers. His hand was on her breast and began a slow, circular motion. She moaned a little beneath his kiss.

Suddenly, from the kitchen,

'Mum, Dad are you out there?'

Eva jumped up and smoothed her hair.

'Here, love.'

Sally came galloping into the yard and Eva gave her a hug.

'Come on, Sal. Get yourself ready. Don't keep Miss Pritchard waiting.'

Over Sally's head she mouthed at Arthur.

'Later' and gave him a slow, languorous wink.

Arthur smiled and nodded.

***

Eva had knocked on Miss Pritchard's door two weeks after her first visit and again, been invited in and given tea in the beautiful china.

'Arthur and I have talked it over and we're prepared to buy a piano for Sally, provided the cost isn't exorbitant.'

'I'm happy to hear that, Mrs Steadman, have you told Sally?'

'I won't tell her until we're sure. Who knows how long it will take to find something suitable. Naturally, we couldn't consider buying new but sometimes, you hear of second hand pianos coming up for sale. Could you give me some advice on what to look for and whether you've any idea of what it might cost?'

'As to cost, it's impossible to predict. It depends on the instrument and its age and condition. Sorry I can't be of more help but you'll have to play it by ear.'

They both smiled at her little joke and she went on,

'Let's hope it doesn't take too long. It would be marvelous if we could get her started during the school holidays. She's keen and constantly asking questions.'

Eva glowed at the praise for her youngest child and left the house ten minutes later with a rough idea what to look for.

She put up notices in a couple of local newsagents and spread the word in the pub. It would be easier if she could find something locally, she didn't want huge delivery charges on top of the cost of the piano.

A couple of weeks had passed and nothing had turned up and then, one Friday evening in the pub, Jimmy Gill had come over to Arthur.

'You still looking for a piano, Arthur?'

'Yes, heard something?'

'The wife's mother passed away last week and there's a nice piano in her front room. We don't have room for it and any road, none of our lot is interested. The wife learned as a kid but never kept it up. It was only the old lady who played.'

Eva had caught the tail end of the conversation and asked,

'Any idea what make it is?'

'No, but it is in good condition. If the polish on it is anything to go by, it must be a good 'un. My missus is fretting about it going to a good home. The rest of the furniture isn't worth much and we've got to get the house cleared by next weekend. You interested?'

'How soon can we have a look at it?' Eva asked.

'I'll tell the missus when I get home. Maybe you could come round in the morning, eleven o'clock suit you?'

'We'll be there.'

Maurice, standing at the bar, rolled his eyes at the landlord. What next? The Steadman's were getting above themselves, again.

The house was only two streets away and prompt at eleven the following morning, Arthur knocked on the front door.

Jimmy's wife answered, wrapped in a flowered overall, a scarf wrapped round her head to keep out the dust.

'You'll have to excuse the state of me. It's breaking my heart to clear this stuff out, as though I'm packing mother's life into boxes,' she said tearfully.

Eva reached out and put a hand on her shoulder.

'I was so sorry to hear about your mother. I know how much you'll miss her.'

'We grew up in this house, me and my brother. He lives in Preston now and though he came up for the funeral, the rest of it is left to me. Enough of my troubles. There's the piano, have a look.'

It stood against the back wall, polished to a high shine with a padded stool in front of it. Eva lifted the lid and was thrilled to see the name inside was one of those on Miss Pritchard's list. She'd feared a hulking great chunk of furniture but this was relatively small with smooth, clean lines. It would easily fit in their front room.

Arthur reached out tentatively and struck a couple of keys. It sounded fine.

'It's been tuned regular, that was one thing mum never skimped on. It was her pride and joy. I want it to go to a good home. Is it for you, Arthur?'

'Oh no, lass, it's for our Sally. She's that keen to learn and we've found someone to give her lessons.'

'Mother would love that, somebody starting from scratch, learning to play on her piano.'

Arthur looked at Eva enquiringly. She smiled

'We'd love to have it, wouldn't we Eva? Our Sally will be thrilled. Now then,' he asked gently, 'of course I have to ask you what you want for it.'

'If you can take it away in the next couple of days, you can have it for twenty pounds. It's worth a lot more but I couldn't bear it to go into a second hand shop or be hammered at in a pub.'

Though he had to be seen to be paying, the cash had come from Eva's savings though she'd winced at the price.

'Me and our David could come for it this afternoon. Eva's brother will lend us his van for an hour and I reckon the two of us could shift it. Would that suit you?'

'The sooner the better. If you come about four o'clock, I'll make sure Jimmy's here to give you a lift.'

Arthur discreetly took out his wallet and passed over four large white fivers, which disappeared instantly into an overall pocket.

As they left the house, Eva turned and said.

'I'll look after it and I can tell you, you've made a little girl very happy.'

Jimmy's wife's red-rimmed eyes filled again. Unable to speak, she gave a half smile and nodded.

Sally was ecstatic. She ran her fingers up and down the keys. It sounded lovely, even though there was no tune at all. Then she started at middle C and played up the scale, *doh ray me so fah lah tee doh*, she knew that much.

Arthur stood in the doorway with his arm round Eva, watching his little daughter indulgently.

'Worth every penny,' he whispered and Eva grinned back.

'Have you told Miss Pritchard?'

'Not yet. I'll call round in the morning and see if she can spare five minutes to have a look at it. I'll have to warn her she'll be giving lessons from this Wednesday on. Hope it won't be too much for her.'

The following morning, Eva gave the furniture in the front room, especially the piano, an extra polish and ran the carpet sweeper round and along the hall before she knocked on the Pritchards' door.

The younger Miss Pritchard opened the door.

'Could I have a word with your sister?'

The door opened wide so she could step inside and Miss Pritchard nodded towards the front room.

The elder Miss Pritchard was at the table, neat and elegant as ever, but with a broad smile on her face.

'I know,' she said. 'We saw your husband and David manhandling it into the house yesterday afternoon. What did Sally say?'

'She's over the moon. She wanted to come straight round and tell you but I made her wait.

You've been so kind I almost hesitate to ask you for another favour.'

'You'd like me to have a look at it. Of course, you want to know if it's good enough. Shall I come now?'

Her sister fussed a little, bringing a grey cardigan and placing it round her shoulders and she smiled in thanks.

'Would you like to come too, Miss Pritchard?'

'I'd love to, I want to see Sally's face.'

Though the elder of the two sisters, Constance, had the most contact with Sally, the younger sister, Muriel, had become very fond of the child too and loved to watch her as she listened to the music.

Eva led the way, followed by the elder and then the younger sister. During all the years they had been neighbours, she had been into their house only twice and they had never been in hers.

'Do come in; it's in the front room.' She raised her voice a little, 'Sally, Miss Pritchard's here.'

Sally was in the front room, perched on the piano stool, eyes shining. She stroked her hand across the keys without striking a note.

'Isn't it lovely, Miss Pritchard, isn't it?'

'It looks lovely. Shall we see what it sounds like?'

Sally jumped up to let Miss Pritchard sit.

Eva and Muriel stood inside the doorway watching them and Arthur and David were in the kitchen, not wanting to overwhelm the old ladies.

Constance settled herself at the keyboard, looked at Sally and started to play the first piece she had ever played for her, "The Dream of Olwen". To Eva's untutored ears, it sounded wonderful. The music rose and filled the small front room. She hardly noticed that first

David, then Arthur, had appeared and were standing in the hall listening too.

As Miss Pritchard's hands came to rest, they burst into spontaneous applause.

She coloured slightly.

'It's a long time since I've had such an appreciative audience. Thank you.'

Arthur stepped forward. Usually so confident, he was reticent in the presence of someone he subconsciously thought of as a "real lady".

'Thank you, Miss Pritchard, that was wonderful.'

Sally was almost beside herself with the excitement of having Miss Pritchard playing *her* piano and having her mum and dad so enthusiastic about the music. Even David looked impressed.

Eva hesitated but she needed to know.

'How is it, as an instrument, I mean?'

'It's as good as you're going to get. The tone is beautiful. It's a joy to play.'

She looked at Sally, tilting her head slightly.

'You're a very lucky young lady, Sally. Are you ready to start lessons?'

Sally looked to her mum and then to her dad for confirmation. They smiled and nodded.

'Yes please, Miss Pritchard. When can we start?'

'I want you to be sure you know what this entails, Sally. As well as a lesson once a week, you'll need to practice every day for at least half an hour.'

Sally nodded.

'I will, I will. When can we start?'

'Why don't you come round on Wednesday as usual and instead of listening, you can start to do the playing.'

During the following weeks, Sally made enormous progress. The first lessons had taken place in the school holidays. At the piano for an hour at a time, she ran up and down the scales until she could play them quickly and accurately. She had learned two complete pieces, practising when her mum and dad were at work. She wanted to surprise them with a concert but not until she could play without faltering.

On the day of her dad's birthday, she had written out invitations to Mr and Mrs Steadman and Mr David Steadman, inviting them to a concert in the front room at seven o'clock. Three dining chairs were arranged in a row.

Her parents fell happily into the charade, as did David, and they stood in the hall at two minutes to seven and knocked on the door. Sally looked at them solemnly and waved them in. David thought she was getting a bit obsessive about this music lark and struggled to keep his face straight. Eva frowned and shook her head at him.

Sally seated herself at the piano with a flourish, announced the name of the piece, and began to play. Even David was impressed.

Turning on the piano stool, she announced her second piece. This was a bit trickier but she'd practiced hard. Though the tongue protruded slightly through the lips during the middle section, she reached the end without mishap.

The applause was thunderous and shouts of encore, encore resounded.

'And now, one final short piece, in honour of my dad,' Sally announced and launched vigorously into "Happy Birthday, to you".

The three of them crowded round the piano, Eva, David and Sally, singing at the tops of their voices while Arthur looked on, as pleased as punch.

Despite initial concern from Eva and Arthur, Sally had kept up with her piano lessons and practice. Eva might sometimes have to nudge her to help in the house but she never had to push her to play the piano.

***

Tom Phillips passed a pleasant enough summer. Despite an offer from his father-in-law to foot the bill for a hotel in the South, they spent two weeks in a chalet on the outskirts of Blackpool. The weather was fine and the boys were tanned and fit. He spent hours building sandcastles and playing cricket on the beach and was stunned to find Margaret could put a wicked spin on even a tennis ball when he was batting, causing him to flinch or lash out.

'You never cease to amaze me,' he whispered in her ear as they walked up the beach, his arm round her waist and each of them holding a child by the hand.

'A woman of hidden talents. Is there anything else you're not telling me?'

She chuckled.

'I may still have a trick or two up my sleeve. You'll have to wait and see.'

Tom sat in a worn armchair in the shabby chalet. Margaret was in the bathroom with the boys and he looked around at the tired furnishings.

What does it matter? Margaret and the boys are happy enough although a week of rain in this place would have been depressing.

'Deep in thought, Tom? You'd better rouse yourself; the boys are waiting for a story.'

He hauled himself up, rubbing the small of his back and went through to the bedroom where he could hear Michael and Peter giggling.

An hour later, with the children asleep, Tom and Margaret sat facing each other in mismatched armchairs. Both had a book and a drink, beer for Tom and a sherry for Margaret.

She spoke.

'Tom, I've been thinking.'

Looking up from his book, he thought how attractive she looked. Her open necked shirt exposed her tanned neck and her freckles were out in force.

'What have you been thinking, love?'

'Well, when Peter starts school in September, Michael will start half days at the nursery.'

'And?' he smiled.

'I'm going to have a lot of time on my hands and I've been wondering what to do with it.'

'Have you made a decision? A part time job?'

Few married women worked, except in the higher professions or the very poorest communities.

'I've loved being at home with the boys but now I'd like to use my brain again. I don't want to go back to nursing or a humdrum routine. I want a challenge?'

'What sort of challenge?'

'I've been considering working in a hospital, as almoner. Would you mind?'

'Mind, I'd be delighted. Have you checked it out?' he asked.

She looked a little shamefaced.

'I met Mary Matthews in town a couple of weeks ago. You remember, I went to school with her. She's working at Withington Hospital and loves it. She got me all fired up. I'll need a certificate and I'm not sure what that entails. I didn't want to go ahead until I'd talked it over with you.'

'It's a great idea. I'm all for it. Make some enquiries about the training and we'll talk about it again when you know a bit more.'

He smiled at her encouragingly. All the blandishments of fancy holidays and the like from her father could never woo her from the ordinary looking chap facing her. With a sigh of relief, she wondered why she'd been so anxious about broaching the subject.

***

While Tom was spending a pleasant couple of weeks with his family, practically living on the beach, Nick Metcalfe, his deputy head, was tramping around northern France.

After two weeks and brown as a gypsy, he felt better, physically, than he had since he left the army. He had been sobered by the graves from the First World War and in a military cemetery; he looked along the seemingly endless rows of white crosses. There was no one else around so he sat for a while, soaking up the peace until the stiff breeze across the open spaces roused him.

What a waste, all those men. And we had it all to do again a couple of decades later.

He gave silent thanks that he and his immediate comrades had been spared, even in the worst of the fighting.

He remembered his parents as he had last seen them, standing on the platform at Victoria Station. Dressed in their best, they had come to see him off to his posting. Dad had shaken his hand firmly and said gruffly,

'All the best, son, take care of yourself.'

Mum had been unable to speak. She'd put her arms around him, the khaki uniform rough against her face. Kissing him on the cheek, she'd given him a little push towards the open carriage door.

After throwing his kitbag in, he'd climbed aboard and managed to get a place at the window where he could wave as the train pulled out. Dad had been standing with his arm round Mum's shoulders and she'd been clutching a white hankie to her mouth, trying not to weep until he'd gone.

He leaned out of the window and waved until they were specks on the platform. Three weeks later, he received a telegram. His home had suffered a direct hit and everything was gone, even his parents. He'd thought them indestructible.

Still in a thoughtful mood, he made his way past the cenotaph bearing hundreds of names and out through the gates. It put his current problems into perspective.

The brisk walk and the heat from the sun warmed his chilled bones and he decided to find some food and a bed for the night. According to his map, there was a village within reasonable walking distance.

An hour later, the road showed increasing signs of habitation. The odd cottage and then up ahead, more buildings and finally, the sign for an inn.

After an absence of several years, his French had come back, slowly at first, but he was becoming increasingly fluent. The inn looked pleasant enough. It could have done with a lick of paint but there were bright geraniums in tubs and window boxes and a yellow rose rambling round the door.

The place seemed deserted but when he called out, a short, rotund woman came bustling from the back, wiping her hands on her white apron. Hair neatly back in a bun, red cheeks and twinkling eyes, she spoke.

'Oui Monsieur?' she asked.

There was a room available and she would be happy to feed him although he was warned it would be plain fare. Following the proprietress up the narrow staircase, he nodded at the sight of the room. Although small, with only a single bed and a chest of drawers, it was spotlessly clean and looked out over the garden. A price agreed for the room and food, he ordered a beer which he took out into the garden.

He sat quietly, watching the sun set. In the grand scheme of things, his break up with Heather and her subsequent pursuit of him seemed a great deal less important. Although he still felt guilty and wryly admitted to himself that, yes, he *had* run away, he tried to look on it in a different light. He hadn't run, he told himself, he'd retreated from a battle he couldn't win.

He had moved to a slightly bigger flat a little further away from the school and in the opposite direction from where Heather lived. It was less likely he would bump into her and she didn't know where he'd gone. The new place was stacked with boxes but he had thrown a few things into a rucksack and left. She would be batting off the chaps by now, able to take her pick.

He admitted he'd been flattered by her undemanding admiration. He had been alone and rootless for a long time and had missed the closeness of a relationship. She was no substitute for a family but had been easy to get along with. They had both had a lucky escape.

His thoughts were interrupted by voices coming towards him and a couple of farm labourers passed through the garden into the inn. He turned his head as other footsteps approached. The place was slowly filling.

'Monsieur, Monsieur.'

A pretty, dark haired girl gestured to him; his food was ready.

Twenty minutes later, he mopped up the remains of an excellent stew with chunks of crusty bread and sat back, pouring himself another glass of red wine; fairly rough but not unpalatable. His spirits lifted as he looked at the French faces surrounding him. There was a low buzz of conversation and the waitress, who had introduced herself as Marie, the landlady's niece, was smiling at him across the bar.

A round, red-faced Frenchman approached the table and gestured at the empty seat facing Nick. He nodded and the man pulled out the chair. Nick welcomed every opportunity to use the language and found himself listening to views about the difference between French and English farming, a topic he knew little about. The conversation inevitably turned to the war and its aftermath and the ways in which each country was recovering.

'How very pleasant to talk to an Englishman who speaks our language so well. You'll join me in a cognac,' he said and, without waiting for a response, raised his hand to signal Marie at the bar. She came over immediately with a bottle and two glasses. She winked at Nick as she placed the bottle on the table and glided back to the bar, hips swaying as she went.

'Quite a handful, that one,' muttered his newfound friend. 'Now where were we?'

An hour and a couple of large cognacs later, Nick's companion rose unsteadily to his feet.

'I'll bid you adieu, my friend. It was a pleasure talking to you.'

He walked a little unsteadily to the bar, settled the bill and, giving a mock salute, departed.

Nick realized how much cognac he'd put away and decided bed was the best place. Making a conscious effort to walk straight, he nodded to the people at the bar and to Marie and her aunt and carefully mounted the narrow staircase.

Throwing off his clothes, he stumbled into bed and was sound asleep as soon as his head hit the pillow. There would be no soul searching tonight.

He awoke in the dark, as the mattress dipped with the weight of another person. Still fuddled, he lay still, trying to focus. A warm body slipped under the sheet and lay against him and a silky thigh rubbed against his own. He started to pull away.

'Shhhhh, cherie, shhhhh!'

He recognized the voice and the unseen smile. A slightly work roughened hand stroked his chest and then his face. He cupped her shoulder and pulled her towards him.

'Are you sure?' he whispered.

'I'm here, aren't I?'

She was no novice and knew how to take her pleasure, guiding his hands and murmuring instructions. It was so easy in the darkness; just a willing body and a hot mouth.

'There, yes, there. That's good, that's so good,' she purred.

As her body spasmed, he climaxed too, a long juddering burst and at the final moment, Janet Marsden's face appeared behind his closed eyes.

He lay spent and still half-drunk as she swiftly slipped into her dressing gown and pulled the door closed behind her.

'Au revoir,' she murmured.

In the early morning light, he thought he'd dreamt the whole thing. There were sounds of activity in the kitchen so he got out of bed, feeling better than he deserved, just a slight thrumming behind the eyes. Washed and dressed, he packed up his rucksack then stood hesitantly at the head of the stairs, listening to the bustle below. He didn't know what to expect but took a deep breath and started down.

'Ah, good morning Monsieur, I trust you slept well.'

Thank heavens, just Madame, looking much the same as the day before, snow-white apron and all.

She pointed towards a table and he sat, placing his rucksack beside him for a quick getaway if necessary. A tray appeared with a huge bowl of milky coffee and a couple of croissants. It smelled wonderful and he demolished it in minutes. His coffee bowl was taken, refilled and returned with a bill sitting discreetly under the saucer. There was no sign of Marie and he didn't know whether to be relieved or disappointed.

He settled up, shook Madam's hand and picked up his rucksack. There was nothing to do but leave.

As he opened the door, she called after him.

'Monsieur, Marie asked me to tell you she enjoyed your company and hopes you pass this way again. Bon voyage.'

The early sun warm on his back, he set off. At a steady pace, he could reach his next port of call in time for lunch.

He realized Marie had taken what she wanted. There were no strings attached and the physical release had eradicated the gloom of the previous day. As he walked, he recalled the sudden flash of Janet's face at the moment of climax; something to ponder on - but not now. Surrendering to the joy of the countryside and the sense of wellbeing, he strode out along the highway.

Chapter 8

Already two weeks into the summer holidays and Hettie still hadn't broken the news to Maurice.

Harry had left school on a Friday and started work the following Monday. Five days later, he'd brought home a pay packet, proudly passing it to his mum over the kitchen table. She had taken it quietly, with a lump in her throat. It was such a short time since he'd been a babe in arms and although he still looked like a boy to her, he was earning his own living.

'Look, son, this is an important day for you.'

She pushed the pay packet unopened back over the table towards Harry.

'You need a few things and I want you to have this. Treat yourself.'

Tears filled Harry's eyes; he could barely speak but muttered 'Thanks, Mum.'

'Every week from now on, I'll give you a third of what's in there. You'll be getting more than the other lads and there's the Saturday money from your dad. If you've got any sense, you'll open a post office account and start putting a bit by each week. It'll soon mount up and having a few bob behind you can make all the difference.'

'I will, I'll do it on Monday in my dinner hour.'

'There's something else I've got to tell you.'

She launched into the story of Johnnie's eleven plus pass and the fact that Maurice still didn't know.

'I can't believe it. I knew he was a clever little beggar but I never expected this. What are you going to do about Dad?'

'I'll have to tell him soon, I'm just waiting for the right time.'

'Look, Mum, I know he's going to need all sorts of gear.'"

He pushed the pay packet back over the table.

'Take some of this; it'll give you a start.'

Hettie smiled and shook her head.

'No, I meant what I said. I want you to have it. Leave your father to me.'

'If you're sure.'

She nodded and he whipped the packet off the table and into his back pocket.

The following Friday, Harry delivered up his wages and his mum split the cash between them.

'Have you told Dad yet?'

'Not yet, but it will have to be soon.'

A couple of hours later, Maurice came home. He'd had a few drinks, enough to make him more talkative than usual. He settled into a chair and looked across at Hettie.

'I'll have another before I have a kip. Pass the bottle, Het.'

She pulled the bottle and a glass out of the kitchen cupboard and plonked it on the table.

'Get yourself a glass, girl, you'll have a snort with me?"

Hettie didn't show her surprise, but placed another glass next to the first and waited until he poured the drinks. She picked up the glass and looked at him, saying nothing.

'I got a surprise this afternoon,' he said.

'Oh, what was that?'

'I was having a pint with Jimmy Gill, you know, the foreman at the bottling plant.'

'And?' Hettie prompted.

'He said our Harry's a bright lad. He's really pleased with him.'

'Can't say it's news to me. He's never been book clever but he's good with his hands.'

'Funny you should say that. Jimmy says if he shapes up, he's going to put him in the workshop to learn lorry maintenance. One of the lads has had his call up papers and they need a replacement. Hettie flushed with pleasure. It was rare for Maurice to take any notice of the boys. She sipped at her whisky, waiting.

'He's shaped up with the Saturday betting too. He's not keen but he does what he's told and doesn't moan. I expect he's glad of the extra couple of bob.'

Hettie cleared her throat. This could be her chance. The time was right.

'He could go far and earn a decent wage. Our Flo was talking to Eva Steadman the other day and their David is doing really well. There's talk of him going to university.'

She was taking a chance by changing the subject and waited.

'Well, the Steadmans think they're a cut above the rest of us anyway,' he replied.

The sharp look from Arthur in the pub still rankled.

'The way he's going, our Harry could be earning good money before David Steadman even leaves school.'

This was the response she'd hoped for.

'You know, Maurice, he's younger than David Steadman but I'll bet you our Johnnie is just as clever.'

'What, that little devil. All he's good for is giving lip.'

She was pushing her luck but ploughed on.

'I'm not kidding. He's passed the exam and could go to Whitworth Street.'

'This is the first I've heard of it. Why didn't you tell me?'

'I never thought you'd let him go. The uniform and all the other stuff costs a fortune.'

Ever reluctant to part with cash except in the pursuit of his own pleasure, the words 'cost a fortune' were like a warning bell.

He frowned and Hettie sweated.

'I'm not sure I agree with all this education anyway. It'll give him big ideas.'

'Maurice, he's got big ideas already.'

Maurice had to smile.

'Things are changing,'' she continued. 'Sooner or later, they'll make off course betting legal and there'll be all sorts of new regulations. Paperwork has never been your strong point and Johnnie might well go into the business with you. Heaven knows, he's sharp enough.'

She waited silently. Had she blown her chance? She could practically see the wheels turning in Maurice's head.

He picked up his glass and leaned back in the chair. On the one hand, there was the cash but on the other, this could be one in the eye for cocky Arthur Steadman. He felt the same way about Arthur that Johnnie felt about David.

Show him my lad is as good as his, he thought.

'He can go. How much will it cost?'

Hettie was nothing if not an opportunist.

'Twenty quid should cover it.'

'Twenty quid?' he yelped.

'I know, I know, that's why I didn't ask you. He'd need piles of stuff. Blazer and trousers, a couple of shirts and a school tie and cap. Then there's a gym kit and shoes and a satchel…'

'Enough,' Maurice interrupted, fumbling in his back pocket for the roll of money he always carried. He counted off twenty one pound notes and flung them on the table.

'That should cover it.

He stood and stretched, hoisting the trousers that had slipped down over his gut.

'Right, I'm off for a kip.'

Having parted with the cash, he wouldn't give it another thought. He would never ask about Johnnie's progress or show any interest until she asked for more. The Steadman card could come in handy in the future too.

As Hettie heard the door close behind him, she slumped in her chair. She had pulled it off, not only pulled it off but excelled herself. The cash on the table would leave some over to add to her stash. This was a triumph.

She weighed up the bottle. He'd never miss another tot so she poured a shot in her glass before putting the scotch back in the cupboard.

Maurice wouldn't reappear for a couple of hours so she fanned the pounds notes flat on the table and anchored them with a sauce bottle.

The back door banged open and Johnnie wandered in. He hadn't been his usual cocky self for a while; the uncertainty was wearing him down. He stopped short, gawping at his mother lounging at the kitchen table with a glass in her hand.

'Mum?'

Hettie gestured broadly towards the cash on the table.

'That, my lad, is your ticket to Whitworth Street. I've squared it with your father.'

Johnnie's expression changed from doubt to joy. The worry was gone and a broad smile took its place.

'When can we go and get the stuff?' he asked hurriedly. 'There's that list and I have to have everything on it.'

Hettie sighed, deflated now.

'We'll go into town on Monday and see if we can get the lot.'

Johnnie was thrilled. He hadn't been sure she could do it. His mind raced ahead, the gang would need sorting out. There would be trouble when they found out but if he had to, he'd punch a few noses to keep them in line. No need to tell them yet, the rest of the summer holidays still lay before them.

His problems temporarily solved, he put them out of his mind and asked,

'Tea not ready yet?'

'About ten minutes,' said Hettie wearily.

Not a word of thanks. What did I expect? Some are givers, some are takers and Johnnie will always be one of the takers. He's just like his father. No doubt he'll go far.

***

Arthur's second interview was again, conveniently on his half day. Eva had laid out a clean white shirt and brushed his best suit. He'd come home and changed before going back into town. Turning up for work on your half day in your smartest clothes was a dead giveaway.

Eva had been on pins all day, finding it hard to concentrate. With a sigh of relief, she picked up her next job, a straightforward hem to shorten. She could have done it in her sleep so her thoughts wandered and she watched the hands of the workroom clock.

At five thirty, Arthur was waiting for her outside the staff entrance and the grin on his face said it all.

'I don't have to ask how it went. You got it didn't you?'

'Yes, I did. Come on, let's go for a drink.'

The children were to go to grandma's for tea. Eva had known whichever way the interview went, Arthur would expect her undivided attention.

Congratulations or commiserations would be required, and in fairly large doses.

The barman was opening the doors of the Shakespeare on Fountain Street and they were first into the lounge bar. Arthur put a port and lemon in front of Eva and placed his pint on a mat. He laid his coat and hat on a chair and sat down facing her.

'Come on then, what happened?' she asked eagerly.

'They couldn't have been nicer. Michael Grey was there and Mr Samuels, although there was no sign of the other director. We'd gone over a lot of the ground at the first interview except for the complete pay structure. I can tell you, it's very generous. The basic wage is more than I'm getting now and the commission is higher.'

'We'll be on Easy Street then?' Eva smiled, before sipping at her drink.

'Better off than we are now.'

Sitting back, she let him tell the story in his own way. He sometimes used three words where one would do but she was so relieved, she would listen to a sermon if she had to.

On he went. I said this, he said that and then I said, and so on – and so on. She paid careful attention. He would expect her to remember every word. Finally, he got to the point she wanted to hear.

She had hardly noticed her glass was empty until Arthur asked,

'Another?'

He was deliberately spinning out the story and she could have choked him but played along in the face of his sly smile.

Putting the fresh drinks on the table, he sat back and lit a cigarette, more delaying tactics.

A few more people had wandered in and were ordering at the bar while Frank Sinatra's dulcet tones murmured in the background.

Eva could play a waiting game too and she swirled her drink round in the glass.

Finally, he carried on.

'I start on the first of the month. Down to head office on the train to go over the journey plans with Michael Grey, look at the accounts we've already got and where there's room for new business.'

He hadn't even started and it was already "we".

Bursting with curiosity, she asked,

'Come on, Arthur. What about the car?'

"I'll be there two days. The rest of the week and the following week, I'll be doing the rounds with Michael Grey. I pick up the car on the second Friday, it's a Ford Popular.'

'What colour?'

'My God, woman, how would I know? I don't care what colour it is. Michael's car is already three years old and they're letting him have it as part of his retirement package. Mine will be brand new.'

Impressed, she said,

'That's very generous. Sounds like a good firm to work for.'

Eva laughed and he went on,

'There's only one fly in the ointment. I have to give my notice in tomorrow.'

'They won't begrudge you a chance to get on. You've worked hard for them.'

'I hope you're right. Still, it has to be done. Now then, get that down and we'll go and have a bite to eat."

'Another celebration? I'll be letting your trousers out if you carry on.'

He smiled, well pleased with the world.

Later, on the bus, holding hands like teenagers and still elated, Eva asked,

'What are you going to tell the kids?

'I'll tell them I'm changing my job; that I've got to be away a couple of weeks for training. I won't tell them about the car, just arrive at the front door, give them a surprise.'

'They'll be thrilled,' she said, smiling.

'We won't tell anybody until I've got it. It'd be tempting fate.'

Arthur worked his notice, making sure the records were up to date and compiling copious notes for the new man starting in a week. He hadn't realized how much information he held in his head. He made a new address book listing the suppliers' details with telephone numbers and names of contacts. The receipts for the previous year were checked and he made a separate list of regular customers. The shop window and the showcases were emptied in turn and the glass cleaned.

It was a matter of pride, and a matter of conscience, to leave the place in good order. Mr Simon had been good to him over the years and this was a way to show his appreciation.

At four o'clock on the last afternoon, Mr Simon called him into the office and handed over his final pay packet.

'Here you are, Arthur. You've done a great job. The shop has never looked better.'

'It's the least I could do. Now it's come to it, I'm sorry to be going.'

'I don't begrudge you the chance to get on. You've worked hard for us and deserve this opportunity. It was always likely you would move on at some stage. There doesn't seem to be anything else to do. Call it a day and get along home?'

He put out his hand and they shook warmly.

'You know I wish you every success in the future,' he said.

'Yes, I know.'

Arthur could hardly speak he was so choked up.

'Of course, we'll be seeing you again in the not too distant future. No doubt you'll be calling to show us the new range.'

Arthur cleared his throat.

'That's right, before the end of the month. I'll get going now, see you soon.'

He turned to leave the office, putting his wages in his pocket and as he opened the door, Mr Simon spoke again.

'Arthur,'

He turned.

'I'll make sure the first order's a good one,' he said and winked.

Arthur grinned and closed the door behind him. He turned on to Market Street. Ten minutes earlier he'd been quite emotional but now he was like a kid let out of school and with a spring in his step, made his way towards the bus stop.

***

Sally

It was funny that first week without Dad but it was nice in a way. Mum made quick and easy teas and we all sat down together. I found myself half-listening for his key in the door a couple of times and had to remind myself he wouldn't be home until Friday.

On Sunday afternoon, I'd stood on the front step with Mum's arm round my shoulders, David on the other side, and watched my dad walk down the street carrying a suitcase. He'd turned at the corner and waved and I'd had a real lump in my throat. Mum was a bit upset too and she blew her nose and wiped her eyes. She gave my shoulder a gentle squeeze.

'Come on Sal, cheer up. He'll be home on Friday. At least this time I'm not seeing him off to war,' she half murmured.

I'd only been about four when he came home from the army. He'd been on leave a couple of times so I knew who he was and he always brought us a present but he'd no sooner arrived than he was gone again.

I remembered when I realized he was here to stay. He didn't wear that scratchy uniform any more and liked me to sit on his knee while he read me stories. I kept expecting him to pack his bags and leave and for Mum to have a little weep. It didn't happen and gradually, I realized he wasn't going away again. There were four of us now instead of three and Mum was happier and smiled more.

It would only be a week away but I missed him. Mum did too.

He came home the first weekend and told us all about the place he was staying and some of the new people he was working with. I could hear Mum and Dad talking when I was in bed. I couldn't hear the words, just the hum of their voices, and soon dropped off.

Now it was the second Friday and he was coming home for good.

He was expected about five o'clock and we were all there waiting. Mum looked really excited, fidgeting around and checking the clock, her eyes bright and a wide smile on her face.

The sound of his key in the door made me jump and I ran down the hall to meet him and fling my arms around him. I couldn't hang on hard enough.

'Come on Sal, give us a chance to get through the door' but he was smiling.

'Go and get your Mum and David, I've got something to show you,' he said.

I put my head round the kitchen door,

'Come on, you two. Dad wants us.'

We hurried down the hall and on to the front step. I couldn't believe my eyes, a shiny new car, a black one, stood on the cobbles in front of the house. My mouth fell open and Dad joked

'Catching flies, Sal. Come on, climb in and I'll take you for a spin.'

I still couldn't speak and even David looked a bit shell shocked as he and I climbed in the back. Mum didn't look surprised, she must have known all about it, but she did look pleased.

She pulled the front door closed and climbed carefully into the front seat next to Dad. By this time, loads of kids had gathered. I could hear them muttering,

'Is it theirs?' and 'Look at it, it's brand new. Think we'll get a ride?'

It was seldom we saw a car in our streets, just the odd delivery van. I was so proud, sitting in the back and waving to the kids on the pavement. I'd never been in a car before.

Dad tooted the horn and pulled away. We went down Clowes Street to the end and then turned up Hyde Road towards Belle Vue. We cut off by the Corona and back towards home, finally pulling up again outside our own front door. Alice Spencer was looking through their front window and she gave me a little wave. I couldn't stop grinning and as I climbed out of the back, I caught sight of Mickey Smith, wiping his nose on his sleeve but with eyes like saucers. Wasn't I pleased too, when we drove past Johnnie Marshall's gang and I saw the look on his face?

A couple of the neighbours had appeared on their front steps. News travelled fast. Dad had caused a sensation.

As David got out of the car, he looked slowly at all the kids. He knew them all and looked round the crowd, fixing his gaze on one or two faces.

'Right, you lot, nobody lays a finger on it. Got it? Not one finger or you'll have me to deal with.'

He was older and a great deal bigger than the kids hanging around and most of them looked up to him.

'Be sure I'll find out and I'll find out who.'

Mutters all round, a few nods and a couple of them stepped back a bit.

'Right, David,' and 'OK' and from the back of the crowd, 'got it.'

Dad looked a little surprised but nodded and I could see mum trying not to smile.

When we were all settled in the kitchen and Mum was dishing up the tea, Dad said

'We'll have a proper run out on Sunday. Eva, what would you say to a picnic if the weather's decent?'

'I'd say that was a good idea, what do you think, Sal?'

I was so excited I was speechless. I could only nod and grin.

David took one look at my face and started to laugh. Then Mum and Dad joined in and though they were laughing at me, I didn't care. I couldn't help it, I started laughing too.

***

Poor Alice looked wistfully through the window at the kids gathered in the street gazing at the new car. If only she could go and have a look but if her dad found out there would be murder. He'd be cross with her but even crosser with her mum and she hated it when he spoke so harshly. She never answered back but her mum got upset and sometimes she heard her blowing her nose and snivelling a bit in the kitchen.

Then there would be a couple of days of hardly any talking at all. He would warm to her again quite quickly but punish her mum for longer, only speaking to her in a cold, distant voice when he spoke at all.

She hated upsets so she did what her dad said. His word was law. It didn't stop her wishing things were different.

A toy carpet sweeper and dolls' clothes didn't keep her occupied the way they used to. She spent so much time at the front window watching the others, she'd become an expert in their games. With two tennis balls, she practised against the back of the house. She reckoned she could have beat Sally Steadman, who was the best in the street.

It wasn't the same has having someone to play with but if she ever got a chance, she would be ready.

Though they never told Jack, they had incorporated a detour through the park when they went shopping. Brenda was concerned Alice wasn't getting enough fresh air or exercise. They set targets for her, to run to the bandstand and back or round one of the circular paths while mum kept count to see if she could break her own records. Sometimes, she caught sight of Johnnie Marshall watching her but he never said anything.

On rainy days, when the park was out of the question, they still played cards and listened to the radio. Alice was now drawing complicated pictures, sometimes out of her head and sometimes copied from magazines.

Her best refuge on a wet day was to stick her head in a book. Fortunately, her Dad didn't disapprove of reading and said it broadened the mind but he looked carefully at the books she brought home from the library.

Despite her mother's best efforts and her father's indulgence when he was at home, she was a lonely little girl. Her mother was lonely too.

Alice loved the library; the stately staircase and the brass handles on the big swinging door, the smell of books and the quietness as you walked up to the highly polished desk. The librarian, in a black skirt and cardigan with a white blouse underneath, looked stern when she looked over her glasses. Nevertheless, she always spoke kindly to Alice and sometimes had a bit of a twinkle in her eye when she was stamping the books. After a whispered consultation with Alice's mum, she had brought a book called "The Principles of Drawing" off a high shelf and put it on the counter.

'Take it over there, dear', she'd said and nodded towards a table and chairs.

Alice put the book on the table and pulled out a chair. Her feet didn't reach the floor but she didn't notice once the book was open. The language was difficult but she could get the sense of the sentences and the diagrams needed no explanation. She was engrossed, turning the pages slowly and trying to remember it all.

Brenda took her time making her selection and tears came to her eyes when she caught sight of Alice's head bent so seriously over the book. She was on the verge of tears more and more often recently. She needed to get a grip of herself; she'd be no use to Alice if she cracked up.

'Come on sweetheart, it's time to go,' she said. 'You can take that one out if you like.'

Alice's eyes widened in delight as she closed the book and carried it over to the counter. She couldn't believe her luck.

The librarian did smile at her this time.

'It's the same as the other books. You can keep it for two weeks but then you can renew it. Bring it in, I'll stamp a new date in it and you can keep it another fortnight.'

'Thank you,' she said softly with a shy smile and put the book carefully into her Mum's shopping bag. She could hardly wait to get home.

The following Tuesday, they went to the library again. Brenda got through at least two books a week and apart from the book on drawing, Alice had had nothing else to read.

To her delight, Sally was in the children's section and smiled broadly when she appeared. If they made a noise, the librarian would be on them like a ton of bricks so they stood close together whispering.

'If you've got what you want, let's go and wait on the steps. Ask your mum.'

Alice nodded and they found their mothers in quiet conversation. Given permission, they took their books to be stamped and went outside the swing doors. Halfway down the steps, they plonked themselves down, each with a book on their lap.

They talked about books and about school and going upstairs into Miss Marsden's class in September.

'How come you don't play out with the other kids?' asked Sally.

Alice reddened, not knowing what to say.

'It's my dad. He won't let me.'

She didn't tell Sally he thought she was too good for the likes of her and her friends.

Sally could see Alice was embarrassed. She didn't want to make it worse and changed the subject, telling her all about the new car.

In the library, Eva and Brenda were in the furthest corner away from the desk having a low pitched conversation.

'How are you anyway, Brenda? I haven't seen you for a while.'

The two women could not have been more different. Eva stood tall, hair well trimmed and cared for, smartly dressed and bright eyed. Brenda stooped a little and looked downtrodden, hair shoved behind her ears, mismatched cardigan and skirt and slightly red-rimmed eyes. At a few kind words, her eyes filled again. She cleared her throat.

Eva reached out and rubbed gently at her arm.

'Not so good, eh, Brenda?'

Eva had been the recipient of many secrets over the years. People knew instinctively she could be trusted and no one had ever heard idle gossip from her lips.

'Oh, Eva, it's all so grim. Me and Alice are like prisoners, we can hardly leave the house without permission and he wants to know exactly what we've been doing all day. It's bad enough for me but it's poor Alice I feel sorry for. She stands at the window and watches the other kids but he won't let her play out. Honestly, I'll be glad when the holidays are over.'

She fished a grubby hankie out of her pocket, blew her nose and gave her eyes a wipe.

Eva knew the value of listening and nodded and tutted a bit as Brenda carried on with her tale of woe.

'Look, Brenda. You can't go against him, I know that. Do you still go to your mother's on Saturdays?'

'Yes, every other Saturday morning when he's working. He hasn't stopped me, he's afraid my brothers will come looking for me if I don't go. I can't tell my mother, she'd tell my dad or the lads and then there would be hell to pay. But let me tell you, two weeks is an awful long time to wait for someone to talk to.'

Eva remembered when word spread that Jack Spencer was marrying Brenda. She had thought he had his sights set elsewhere but three months down the line, the reason began to show.

'Look, I come to the library every week. I can easily arrange to come on a Tuesday and bring Sal with me. The girls can sit outside on the steps and you and me can have a bit of a natter. We could go up to the reading room if there's nobody in there. Nobody needs to know.'

'You're a life-saver, Eva. I'd love that.'

'Sally would never pass up a chance to come here. Jack can't say anything if they meet by accident, this is a public place after all.'

Brenda nodded.

'I feel better for getting it off my chest. You won't say anything to Arthur, will you?'

'Course not. Trust me – and you can trust Sal too. I'll meet you here next week at the same time.'

The librarian wielded her stamp and they left the library, collecting the girls on the way out. They walked home together with the girls dawdling and chattering behind them and parted at Eva's front door.

Brenda let them into the house.

'That was nice, Mum. I like Sally.'

'Yes, she's a nice girl,' she said distractedly, searching for words.

'Look Alice, you don't have to tell your dad about spending time with Sally. I don't want you to tell him fibs but you don't have to tell him if he doesn't ask. We can go again next week and Mrs Steadman and Sally might be there again. Dad knows we go to the library and all he's interested in is what kind of books you've got. We can't help who we bump into, do you know what I mean?'

'Yes, Mum. I'll be careful.'

Alice was too grateful for half an hour's company to take any chances. She would be very careful indeed.

***

Brenda's encounter with Jack Spencer had left her leaning in the darkness of the back entry, sobbing and trying to get her clothes straight. She didn't know what to do, she felt dirty. Her head hurt from being pushed against the wall, her lower body throbbed and she could feel a trickling sensation down her inner thigh. She didn't know how long she stood there but finally managed to pull herself together and make for the safety of her own home.

She pushed open the front door and made her way along the darkened hallway where a light shone under the kitchen door. She hoped and prayed the lads and her dad would be in the pub and there would only be her mother to contend with. Her luck was in.

'What on earth's the matter, Brenda? You like you've seen a ghost. White as a sheet you are," said her mother from the armchair in front of the fire.

Brenda muttered.

'It's nothing, Mum, I just don't feel so good.'

'Are you sure? You look as though you've been crying.'

'I just feel rotten. Think I'll go straight up.'

Her mother looked at her closely; it looked like more than period pains. Brenda looked shocking.

'Go on up then love, I'll bring you a hot water bottle and a couple of aspirins.'

Brenda was already in bed when her father and brothers came in. She heard the front door open and clutched the hot water bottle to her aching body. The aspirin had helped with the pain but she was deeply ashamed and the tears leaked from her closed eyes. It was unthinkable her brothers should know what had happened.

The low murmur of voices from the kitchen usually made her feel safe but there was no comfort tonight.

'Brenda in?' her father asked.

'Yes, she's in bed. She looks shocking, says she doesn't feel well but I'm worried about her.'

'Don't fuss, woman, it's probably nothing serious.'

The lads showed some concern and Jim, the eldest, asked.

'Should I go up and see if she's OK'

Brenda's mum shook her head.

'No, leave it for now. She's fast asleep. I can tell you this, if she doesn't look better in the morning, I'll have her at the doctor's.'

It was amazing that she got through the next few days without anyone being the wiser. Her eyes filled with tears unexpectedly and she shrugged it off as a cold coming on if anyone noticed. She went through the motions; going to work in a daze, stumbling through the day and sitting in at night, looking at magazines and staring into space.

She learned to cope as many people learn, by refusing to think about it. She didn't notice when she missed her period, she'd always been a bit irregular. A few weeks later, she realized she'd missed not one but two. Her breasts were tender and she was increasingly queasy first thing in the morning. She didn't make the connection.

Her mother was now watching her like a hawk and when she heard Brenda retching in the toilet, she crossed herself quickly.

'Mother of God, no.'

Brenda appeared white faced and red eyed and all but fell into an armchair. Her mother knew her awful suspicions were justified.

Whatever will her father say? And the lads will go spare.

Brenda, still blithely unaware, finally spoke.

'I feel rotten, Mum. I can't go into work. I've been feeling a bit off for a couple of days but not as bad as this.'

Brenda's mum held back a sob and patted her on the shoulder.

'I'll put the kettle on, love. We need to have a talk.'

She brought Brenda a cup of weak tea and a couple of plain biscuits and watched as she struggled to get them down.

'Better?'

'Yes, much better, thanks Mum.'

'You know what's wrong with you, don't you?'

'No, but I'm not right. Do you think I ought to see the doctor?'

'The doctor will only tell you what I already know, Brenda. You're going to have a baby.'

'What? That can't be right. It can't be right, Mum can it?'

Brenda's mum looked at her again. She really was that green.

'I'm afraid it is. Look, you must have been with somebody. You know what I mean. The first thing your father will want to know is who the father is?'

Brenda, who had been holding back tears, now sobbed out.

'Don't tell Dad. Please don't tell Dad or the lads.'

Soothingly now,

'They'll have to know. They'll find out anyway. We don't know how far along you are but my guess is you'll soon start to show. Is it someone you've been seeing regular?'

Brenda was still sobbing and her mum passed her one of her dad's hankies. She blew hard and tried to pull herself together but she looked, and felt, a sodden mess.

'No, no. It only happened once and I couldn't help it. I never thought this would happen.'

She had always been open and honest without the guile to tell fibs to get herself out of trouble.

'Well, who is it?'

Slumped in the chair, wringing the hankie with both hands and nose red from wiping, she looked up.

'I can't tell you Mum. I can't'

Her voice was rising and the sobs started again, she was almost wailing now.

It was no use telling her not to get upset, there was going to be a lot more upset before this was sorted out.

God forgive me, she thought. If she gets upset enough, perhaps she'll lose the baby. That would solve the problem.

She put her arms round Brenda, who was now almost hysterical, rubbing her back in circular motions. It had always calmed her through childish upsets and her outburst subsided into sniffles and hiccups.

'Why don't you go back to bed? I'll call in work when I go to the shops and tell them you're not well. We'll talk about what's to be done when I get back.'

Brenda nodded and her mother could hear her slowly dragging herself up the stairs. She sounded like a sixty year old not the lively girl of nineteen they were used to.

Brenda's mum walked down to the shops, worrying at the problem. The old feller would have to be told, and the lads, and the sooner the better.

The name of the man would have to be winkled out of her and she vowed under her breath, that he'd be made to pay.

I'll give them something nice for tea, soften them up and I won't tell them until they've been fed. No one should hear this kind of news on an empty stomach. Brenda can keep out of the way until they've calmed down.

It was a disaster. The family would close ranks and sort something out. An unwed mother was a disgrace to her family. There were places where unmarried girls went in the late stages of pregnancy and stayed until after the birth. Such children were removed almost immediately for adoption, leaving many young mothers bereft of comfort and mourning the lost child for the rest of their lives.

I won't get in front of myself. Let's wait and see what happens. Maybe we can get her married before it's too late.

Plans laid, as far as plans could be laid in this dreadful situation, she carried on with her errands, told the boss at Brenda's work she'd be back in a couple of days and made her way home.

Brenda's dad pushed his plate away and watched as his wife put a mug of tea on the table in front of him. They had all finished and she brought tea for her sons as well.

'That was grand, lass. What's the occasion?'

She took a deep breath.

'I want you to keep your hair on. I've got something to tell you.'

They all looked up at the serious tone in her voice.

'What's up, lass? Out with it.'

'I'm as sure as I can be that our Brenda's in the family way.'

There was a stunned silence. Then Jim, the eldest, jumped up, knocking his chair over backwards.

'What? Who's the father? I'll kill him.'

'She won't tell me. She just keeps crying and saying she's sorry.'

All three men were visibly upset but it had hit Jim hardest. He idolized his little sister.

'Leave it to me, I'll get it out of her,' he said.

'Don't be too hard on her. She's upset enough.'

'Leave it to me,' he said and started for the stairs, leaving the rest of the family speechless at the kitchen table.

He opened Brenda's bedroom door and peeped in. She was sitting with her back to the headboard, knees drawn up and looking like a frightened rabbit. Her hair was all over the place and her nose and eyes were almost raw from crying. His anger disappeared and tenderness took its place.

He sat on the edge of the bed and put his arm round her, hugging her tightly.

'Come on, love. You know we've got stuff to talk about if we're going to sort this out. You'll have to tell us who's responsible sooner or later and sooner would be much better all round.

You don't have to say it in front of everyone. Tell me quietly and then we'll all decide what's to be done.'

Slowly, the whole sorry story came out with Jim doing his best to hold on to his temper. He didn't want to frighten her any more. She was already terrified.

'Now tell me love, are you saying he forced you?'

Despite her current hardship, there was still a spark of hero worship for Jack Spencer. She couldn't deny what had happened but tried to make it sound better.

"He was a bit upset and a bit drunk and I was giving him a bit of a cuddle and then it just happened.'

Jim wouldn't push her any harder but he could see the whole sordid picture playing in his head. He had murder in his heart.

'Does he know?'

'I didn't know myself until Mum told me. I'm so stupid. What am I going to do, Jim?'

Tears were leaking from under her eyelashes. She hadn't the energy to sob. She looked beaten.

'You look worn out. Try and rest while we decide what's best to be done. What would you say if he wanted to marry you when he finds out?'

A glimmer of hope showed in the red-rimmed eyes. In five minutes, she would be picturing married bliss with Jack Spencer, problems solved and everybody happy.

'Do you think he will?' she asked eagerly.

'I'll go round and have a word. Will that suit you?'

He kissed the top of her head and went back downstairs, grinding his teeth and muttering,

'I'll make bloody sure he wants to, one way or another.'

The four of them sat around the table talking it over. Brenda's mum, ever the pragmatist, stated the case.

'It would be best if they got married. What do we know about him?' she asked Jim.

'Not much, he works in some fancy office in town, always wears a suit and goes for a pint in the Queens most Friday nights.'

Brenda's dad spoke up for the first time.

'I could tear him limb from limb but it would do her,' he nodded towards the stairs, 'no good at all'.

Without a husband, Brenda and an illegitimate child would have a hard time, even with the support of her family.

'She could go to my sister in Wales until the child's born,' suggested Brenda's mum. 'Then we could put it up for adoption. She could come back and start again here as though nothing had happened.'

'Not bloody likely, that's my grandchild you're talking about.'

'And my niece or nephew,' added Jim.

'Does she want to marry him?' asked Mum. 'That's the first question. If she wants to and he's willing, it's the best solution all round.'

'Ay, she'll have him I'm sure and he'll be willing after I've had a word.'

He looked at his brother and then at his father.

'Come on, let's go and find him. Dad, you stay here with Mum and leave this to us.'

Not the first and surely not the last time strong-arm tactics would be used in similar situations. Jack Spencer had a nasty shock coming.

Jack was at the bar having a quiet pint. He'd felt bad about the way he'd treated Brenda but had been so drunk, the details were a bit fuzzy. He hadn't much of a conscience and had been able to shrug off the niggling but incomplete memories.

He was thinking about work and weighing up the possibilities for promotion when a voice from his right disturbed his train of thought.

'Hello there, Jack, how's it going?'

He turned his head to see Jim standing beside him, one elbow on the bar.

'All right then?' came from the other side and there was the other brother, he wasn't sure of his name.

'Fine, you OK?' he was trying to address them both at the same time, suddenly very nervous.

Ignoring the question, Jim leaned forward and said in a confidential tone.

'We need a word on a private matter. Either you come with us or we can clear this up in public. It's up to you.'

He hesitated, wondering if he could face them down. He took a good look at the expression on Jim's face.

One or two of the other customers looked interested in what was going on at the bar. Jack Spencer didn't usually drink with those two.

He quickly considered his options. If he didn't go with them, whatever was on their mind would be round the pub and then round the streets like wildfire and he'd get thumped anyway. If he did go with them, it was likely he'd get a good hiding but at least everybody wouldn't know the whole sorry story.

Downing the rest of his pint, he placed the empty pot on the bar and said,

'Ok, let's go.'

The three of them left the pub and Jim pulled him into the first back entry round the corner. After the narrow entrance, the passage widened out into a square that couldn't be seen from the street.

Jack was terrified and leaned against a wall for support, putting his hands in his pockets to hide the trembling.

'What's it all about, lads?' he half whispered, barely able to trust his voice.

'You don't speak, you listen, got that?'

Jack nodded.

Jim explained the situation in short, terse sentences.

'So there's going to be a wedding. Right Jack?'

Jack nodded.

'And it's going to be pretty quick. Right Jack?'

Jack nodded again.

'You get yourself round to our place tomorrow night at eight o'clock with a box of chocolates. You ask my Dad for his permission and then you pop the question. Right Jack?'

Jack's eyes were open wide, staring into Jim's angry face. He could only nod again. He was too scared to bluster, too scared to start throwing questions about how could they be so sure it was him.

'One more thing, Jack.'

Jim leaned towards him and put one hand either side of his head, his breath hot against Jack's face, and moved in close. It was as well he didn't know this was almost a mirror image of what had happened between Brenda and Jack just a few weeks earlier.

'We're not going to give you a good hiding. We don't want a damaged bridegroom, do we?'

He looked at his brother, who was happy to leave the talking to Jim, but who added,

'That's right, Jim. No damage - at the moment.'

'If our Brenda ever comes round and tells us you've hurt her in any way, any way at all, we'll kill you. You don't tell her what happened here tonight and we'll keep out of the marriage. We won't interfere unless we have to but we'll be watching.'

Without another word, the brothers turned and left Jack leaning against the wall, still quivering.

His first thought was to run. He feverishly examined the possibilities. Where could he go? He could run away to London, they wouldn't find him there.

No, he didn't know anybody there – and what would he live on?

He could get a job, they had insurance companies in London, didn't they?

How could he get a job without a reference? There'd be no decent reference if he left without working his notice.

There was only a few quid in the bank - it wouldn't last long.

The ultimatum loomed. If he didn't show up the following night they'd come looking for him. If he did show up, he'd be committed.

He could disappear, go and stay with his uncle on the other side of Manchester. No, that was no good either. Someone was sure to tell them where he worked and they would come to the office. That would be a disaster.

He decided to go home and think about it. Maybe inspiration would strike.

In desperation, he even fleetingly thought of the French Foreign Legion.

By the morning, he'd resigned himself to the inevitable. He hadn't the nerve for anything else.

Three weeks later, he was standing before a registrar, repeating his vows. Brenda stood beside him.

She didn't look half-bad. Unaware he was there against his will, she was glowing. The colour from her pink suit highlighted the blush on her cheeks and the little hat perched on the back of her head gave her a jaunty look. She put out her hand and, under the eyes of her grim faced brothers, he had no alternative but to take it.

Although he made the right responses, the words of the ceremony washed over him. He couldn't bring himself to look at Brenda although he could feel her adoring gaze. It was the other gaze that bothered him, the one burning the back of his neck. Both the brothers were scary but he was terrified of Jim, the elder of the two.

It was over. He was a married man. As they turned to face the audience, Brenda took his arm, hanging on possessively. He could see his mother and father in their best clothes, looking a little bewildered. Brenda's mother was sniffing and dabbing her eyes while her dad patted ineffectually at her hand.

Jim reached out and pulled Brenda towards him, enveloping her in a huge hug.

'Congratulations, love. I hope you'll be very happy.'

He looked Jack straight in the eye and Jack flinched.

Brenda was a bit weepy herself now and he gave her another squeeze.

'It'll be all right, love, you'll see.'
There would be no fancy reception and they piled into taxis outside the registry office to go to the city centre pub where a cold buffet had been booked.
Jack and Brenda were in the first taxi and Brenda's parents and brothers in the second.
'She wanted a white wedding and all the fuss but it can't be helped,' said Brenda's mum wiping away another tear. 'I hope she'll be OK.'
Jim looked at his mother.
'I'm sure she'll be fine. Folk will talk but they soon forget. There'll be someone else to gossip about soon enough. Anyway, let's look on the bright side. You've got a grandchild on the way and I'm going to be an uncle.'
Brenda's mother couldn't help but smile as she stuffed her hankie into her handbag.
'We'll all have to make the best of it.'

***

Johnnie had kept quiet about the change of school and hoped not to have to say anything until near the end of the holidays. One Sunday morning, he found his mates in the park and faced a furious Jimmy Gill. His lieutenant was spitting mad, face red and eyes flashing.
'What's going on? Why didn't you tell us?'
Johnnie's heart sank. Who could have spilled the beans?
'Tell you what?'
'Tell us you're off to Whitworth Street. It's a right carry-on when your dad tells you something about your best mate and you didn't even know. He was in the pub last night and said David Steadman's dad told him.'
'Bloody hell, how did *he* know?'
'It doesn't matter how he knew, he knew. Probably everybody knew except me and the gang.'
The rest of the lads were behind Jimmy Gill, all facing Johnnie and looking mutinous. This could be serious.

'Yeah, well, I was going to tell you today. What's it matter anyway?'
'*What's it matter?* You'll be up and off in September and we'll all still be here. Why do you want to go there anyway? You'll finish up a swot like that David Steadman.'
Johnnie decided to face him down.
'Well I'm going and that's the end of it. D'you want to make something of it?'
'Me and the lads have been talking it over and we're not sure we want you to be the boss of the gang any more.'
'Put yourself up for the job, have you? I thought we were mates.'
Johnnie had a choice, walk away now and be on his own for the rest of the holidays or fight. He looked speculatively at Jimmy. He was pretty sure he could win and lunged, grabbing him by the collar and dragging him down. Jimmy grabbed him round the knees and they were both down, struggling and punching.

The other lads formed a ring around the grappling pair, shouting encouragement to first one and then the other. Most of them didn't care who won, they just liked a scrap.

Johnnie knew he had to finish this fast.

He watched for an opportunity and punched Jimmy straight in the nose. Blood spurted, it was quite spectacular and bloodshed usually ended any fight amongst the lads.

Johnnie got to his feet and held out his hand to Jimmy who was holding his jumper up to his nose. There was blood all over him.

It was touch and go but he put out his other hand to take Johnnie's - a sign of surrender.

'Come on, Jimmy, I'll walk home with you, you'll need to get that cleaned up.'

He turned to the other lads and nodded.

'You lot wait here. We'll be back.'

He hadn't escaped unscathed; a grazed knee from hitting the gravel, bruised knuckles and his eye was closing. It had been a close thing but he'd drawn first blood and was back on top, for the time being at least.

Hettie wasn't too surprised when Johnnie turned up sporting a black eye. She cleaned up the graze on his knee, put arnica on his knuckles and made him lie down on the settee for ten minutes with a cold compress on his eye.

He lay there, wondering how Jimmy's dad knew.

Maurice had told the landlord in the pub about him passing the exam. Landlords love a bit of gossip and he passed it on to someone else who had mentioned it to Arthur Steadman when he was having a pint with Jimmy Gill's father.

Maurice too had had his nose put out of joint when he heard Arthur Steadman was now driving around in a brand new car.

All Johnnie knew was that the Steadmans were to blame for the fight. If they'd kept their flaming mouths shut, he could have coasted until September and faced the music then.

Too wary of David to have a go at Sally, he tried to think of something else. He had heard David had put out the word about damage to the car and action there would be tempting fate.

Short of sneaking out in the middle of the night, there was nothing he could do. Maybe he would touch lucky and come across the car parked somewhere quiet, away from home. He could bide his time.

His dad was just as narked. Maurice had praised his son, and even bragged a bit, not in Johnnie's hearing, of course, but in the pub. For once, Maurice had taken some notice of his boys, one doing well at work and the other one on his way to high school.

He deflated like a pricked balloon when his triumph was trumped by the news of Arthur Steadman's car, which had whipped round the pub like wildfire, overshadowing other topics of conversation for half an hour or so.

* * *

1954

First children receive Doctor Jonas Salk's polio vaccine.

Boeing tests the 707, the first jet-powered transport plane.

Roger Bannister runs the four minute mile

Rationing ends

Winston Churchill becomes the first, and only, British Prime Minister to reach his 80th birthday while still in office.

First Wimpey Bar opened

Published: 'Lord of the Flies' - William Golding
'Lord of the Rings' - J R Tolkien

Best film Oscar: 'On the Waterfront' - Marlon Brando, Rod Steiger and Eva Marie Saint

Hit Parade: 'Secret Love' - Doris Day

Born in 1954: Oprah Winfrey, American TV host
John Travolta, film star
Iain Banks, author

Chapter 9

Hettie's life had become a little easier over the last couple of years. Harry was bringing home his wages every Friday and she managed to tuck a fair bit away.

Maurice was approached periodically for more cash for stuff for Johnnie and although he muttered, he coughed up.

She'd brought the receipts home and laid them on the table so he could see how much she'd paid

'Costing me a bloody fortune,' was his frequent remark but he didn't go back on his word to pay for what Johnnie needed.

At the point when he stopped looking at the receipts, she'd started to push up the prices, a couple of bob here and a couple of bob there.

She now had a proper bank account but kept the records hidden behind a loose brick in an upstairs fireplace.

Deposits were made at a branch in the city centre when she went to buy clothes for Johnnie. The street was checked for familiar faces before she went into the bank. She didn't want anyone to know about the account.

It was gratifying to be treated with respect. They knew her now and invariably greeted her with,

'Good morning, Mrs Marshall' as she passed over her bankbook and cash.

Harry gave her no cause for concern and had done well at work but it was only a matter of time before he received his call up papers and that source of income would disappear.

Johnnie was a different matter. He was getting cockier and cockier. He still walked warily round his father but was now trying to ride roughshod over Hettie. He didn't ask, he told her what he needed. If he got too cheeky, she made him wait. He needed to know she still had some control and he wasn't yet brave enough to approach his father directly. Hettie still acted as go-between but she never got any thanks.

Things were easier in other ways too. The school holidays were no longer a trial. Harry was at work and Johnnie had made new friends at school. In practical terms, Harry paid for his own clothes, Maurice paid for Johnnie's and she didn't have two boys who wore out their shoes playing football every day.

Her sister, Flo, was in a better situation too. She had a couple of kids working and the others were growing up. One of her boys was now bigger than his father and the threat of violence decreased when the boy finally stood up to him. He still raided her purse occasionally but mainly confined himself to going to the pub on Friday and Saturday night.

'Course he's under me flamin' feet every other night,' she'd moaned to Hettie. 'But you can't have everything; sooner that than a black eye on a regular basis.'

Flo still nipped round to see Hettie on a Saturday night when Maurice was out. Occasionally, instead of a cup of tea, Hettie would fish her whisky supply out of the back of the cupboard and they'd each enjoy a tot. Though money was no longer so tight, Hettie never bought whisky and never increased her raids on Maurice's supplies.

Maurice left her largely alone. As long as his food was on the kitchen table on time, a clean shirt on a hangar, his shoes polished and his trousers pressed, he had little interest in her, the boys or anything else in his home. In public, he showed an occasional passing pride in his lads' achievements but naturally, it never crossed his mind to say well done to either of them. As far as they were concerned, they were almost invisible to their father.

There was never any idle chatter when Maurice was in the house. He liked things quiet when he got up in the morning, after a day's racing or when he was snoozing in the front room.

Conversation was mostly limited to such exchanges as,
'More tea, Het'
'Yes, Maurice.'
'Shirt ready?'
'Yes, Maurice.'

The wireless in the kitchen was switched on only when Maurice was out of the house.

In the evening, Hettie listened to radio plays and had developed a surprising love of classical music. The boys were often out and she had more time on her hands.

She had been a bright student herself but had been forced to leave school at fourteen. Her wages were crucial. Never questioning things might be different; she had accepted her lot.

When Johnnie had first changed schools, he had often shown her his books and told her about the stuff they were learning. She looked in wonder at the French textbook and wished she'd had a chance. Maurice had picked the book up off the kitchen table and responded typically,

'What are they teaching them all this for? What use will this stuff be when he's trying to make a living? Waste of time,' and he'd tossed the book contemptuously back on the table.

The English classics and plays Johnnie was studying fascinated her too. Although he had been glad enough to show them off in the early stages, he couldn't be bothered now. He didn't call her stupid to her face but it was often implied.

'What do you want to know all that stuff for anyway, it's bad enough I have to learn it,' he'd said, snatching a book back and stuffing it into his satchel.

Although he grumbled continuously, he sat at the kitchen table every evening and did his homework. Hettie sometimes had a look at what he'd been working on and it was all beyond her. The work was impeccably neat and well laid out, thanks to her. From the marks in his books, he appeared to be holding his own.

For Maurice, life went on as usual. He bought a new suit every year, even during the war years, and always had three good suits hanging in the wardrobe. Two were worn in rotation and one kept for weekends and special occasions. When a new suit was collected, the oldest of the three was relegated to be worn in the house and when he was taking bets in the yard.

He was the only man for miles around who had suits made to measure and his tailor, with downcast eyes, had tactfully mentioned his increasing girth and offered to let out any trousers which might be getting too tight.

Maurice frowned but couldn't deny the facts. It would never have occurred to him to adjust his eating or his drinking for the sake of his health but he didn't care for the proof around his waistline.

'What will it cost?' he asked.

'I'll do it at a special rate. After all, you're a good customer. Trousers don't hang right if they're a bit tight.'

He was having a fitting for his new suit and could see these new trousers, even marked up with French chalk, looked better than the ones he'd taken off.

'It will be cheaper than replacing your other suits.'

Maurice accepted the inevitable.

'All right, I'll send our Johnnie round with a couple of pairs. How long will it take?'

'Only a day or so, I'll do them straight away. I've got the measurements so I can get cracking,' he said, pulling on the tape measure round his neck.

'Put the alterations on the bill for the new suit and I'll pay the lot together. OK?'

'Fine, Mr Marshall.'

The day was warm, a little cloudy but random breaks in the clouds lit up the windows of the shops along Market Street. In comparison with the war years, the shops were well stocked and the street was busy with shoppers.

As always, he thought, the sun brings them out of the woodwork, like sunny weather on a race day.

Despite his cynicism, he enjoyed the warmth of the sun on his back and hoped the good weather would last a little longer.

As he reached Piccadilly, he fished his gold watch out of his waistcoat pocket and saw there was time to spare. He bought an ice cream from a van parked outside Woolworths and crossed the road to sit in the Gardens.

Idly checking out the women walking by, he graded their attractiveness. Young girls, teenagers and early twenties had no appeal. He liked women who looked like women. For him to find them attractive, they needed to be well dressed, good looking and shapely and look as though they knew it. In the half hour he sat there, very few came up to the mark and a picture of Eva Steadman popped into his head. Now there was a woman to be reckoned with. She looked good but no doubt, she'd be more trouble than she was worth.

Fifteen minutes later, he was pushing open the door to the saloon bar of The Church Inn in Ardwick Green. The pub smell, a mixture of beer, tobacco and floral disinfectant, enveloped him. He'd heard the bolts being drawn as he'd walked across the pavement and was the first customer of the evening. The bar was empty, apart from the barmaid.

'Hello, Maurice, how's it going?'

'Not bad, Edie, how are things with you?'

She smiled cheekily and winked.

They were old friends and for a while had had an arrangement which suited them both. When the landlord had offered to make an honest woman of her, she had jumped at the chance. She'd fulfilled her part of the bargain. She never strayed and more than pulled her weight in the pub.

Arthur cast an appreciative eye down the front of her low cut blouse and winked back.

'Well, what you havin',' she murmured.

'I'll have a scotch and soda, join me?'

'Are you crackers? If I started drinking this early the old feller'd skin me alive.'

'I guess so, but take for one later.'

He passed a pound note over the bar and knew she would take the price of a whisky from the change and drop it in her tips jar.

A couple more people came through the door and she moved along the bar to serve them, passing the time of day and laughing and joking. She was a good barmaid and knew how to make the customers welcome.

Maurice stood, swirling the whisky in his glass, idly watching the other punters.

The door opened again and Doris McGuire, his girlfriend, walked in. He'd been expecting her. Swaying gently across the room, she drew the eyes of the other men at the bar. The last three years had been kind to her and she looked good.

He had never expected their affair to last so long. Usually, his women came and went at regular intervals but she'd stuck. He wasn't sure why. She suited him, always even tempered and obliging, she did as she was told.

Unlike Hettie, he thought, who he'd had to knock into shape. This one knew which side her bread was buttered.

She smiled at him.

'Hiya, Maurice. Been here long?'

'I was a bit early, what do you want?'

'I'll have a port and lemon, ta'

What had started as an odd tussle on a Friday night had become something far more regular. She kept him supplied with sex and whisky. He no longer relied on bumping into her in the local. They now made firm arrangements and he called round a couple of times a week after closing.

He kept her supplied with cash and she showed her appreciation. She'd gone up in the world, from working in the local bread shop to one of the stores in Manchester. The bright red lipstick and brassy hair were gone, as were the overtight skirts and blouses. Even more attractive now the rough edges had been smoothed off, she had a lot to thank Maurice for.

He had bought her first good suit, well fitted but not tight, with a tailored blouse. She wasn't stupid. She was at the hairdresser the next day, toning down the blonde and, with a couple of extra quid he'd given her, into Lewis's for new makeup.

He wanted someone he could show off and often took her out to restaurants or clubs when he met his bookmaker friends. In turn, Doris was grateful. Everything he gave her, including cash, she regarded as a present, not as payment for her favours.

She was onto a good thing. Her wages from work more than covered her living expenses and she and her sister split the rent on the house they had lived in all their lives. Their father had been killed in a bombing raid and their mother had died shortly after so there was just the two of them.

Maurice wasn't too demanding in the bedroom department. He wanted easy sex and she was happy to oblige. She was better off than his wife, poor cow, who always looked so downtrodden. There was no need to feed him or look after him and he wasn't under her feet all day. A demanding husband and a houseful of snotty nosed kids wasn't what she was looking for.

She went over to a table and parked herself and Maurice picked up their drinks and joined her.

'Here you are, lass.'

'Thanks. Did you get your suit sorted?'

'It should be ready by next weekend.'

He neglected to tell her about the extra couple of inches in the trousers and was vain enough to think she wouldn't notice.

'You always look smart, Maurice, you really do.'

It was true. Hardly a good looking man, and growing more corpulent by the year, he had a certain presence. His bad leg had kept him out of the army and he'd put the war years to good use. Always immaculately dressed; trousers pressed, shoes polished and hat brushed, Doris didn't know or care Hettie was solely responsible for that.

He was open handed but not foolish and she was canny enough not to overstep the mark.

'You're looking nice tonight,' he said, dropping his hand to her knee and giving her a squeeze.

'I always try to look nice for you, Maurice.'

His hand rubbed along her thigh under the table. She smiled and placed her hand on top of his and looked at him from beneath her mascara.

'That's nice,' and she pressed his hand down a little more, making the strokes firmer.

He carried on talking and there were two different scenes going on at the same time, one above table height and one below it.

He went to the bar for more drinks and sat down again. Resuming the stroking, he slid his hand under her skirt, above the top of her stocking and on to the bare, silky flesh of her thigh. She felt the sweat on his palm and moved her thighs apart to show her approval.

'Ok, that's it. Let's get out of here before we get arrested,' he said hoarsely and rose, turning his back to the room to fasten his jacket over the budding erection.

They picked up a taxi and were in her front room in twenty minutes. The sister was out or in her bedroom. She had been warned to make herself scarce. After all, she too reaped the benefit of Doris's association with Maurice.

She put a glass of whisky into his hand, not the cheap Woolworths glasses she'd formerly used, but a decent tumbler.

Moving against him and stroking his shoulder, she leaned in and whispered,

'Tell me what you want.'

His libido was not what it had been even three years earlier. He now needed stimulation and titillation. First the clumsy foreplay in public, then she teased and coaxed him, stopping and starting to heighten his pleasure.

He pulled her towards him, rubbing himself against her.

'Let's go up, love,' she whispered, as though she could hardly wait.

It was like a well-rehearsed play and she knew what was expected of her. She would be active and he fairly passive, lying on his back while she moved above him. She wasn't cold or impervious, she enjoyed the sex and perhaps, more importantly, the fleeting feeling of power.

***

Alice now had some measure of freedom, nothing like Sally, of course, but better, much better than ever before. Her salvation had come from an unexpected quarter.

During the last year, she had looked forward to her Tuesdays in the library with Sally while her mum enjoyed a half hour's stolen conversation with Sally's mum. She had no idea what they talked about but they always looked very serious.

In the meantime, Jack had been struggling with his demons.

If she doesn't pass, she can stay where she is until she's fifteen. Then Brenda can take her to school and bring her home for another couple of years at least. But if she doesn't pass, God forbid, I'll never hold my head up.

Then again, even if she does pass, I don't have to let her go. But can I do that? She'll finish up in some dead end job. I don't want her in a shop or a factory; she's too good for that.

The idea his total control over Alice's movements might cease made Jack's blood run cold. Could he insist Brenda travel with her on the bus in the morning and meet her again outside school every afternoon?

His thoughts swung first in one direction then another and finally, he pushed the decision away. He still had time. He didn't consider any discussion with Brenda. She would do as she was told.

Brenda, a woman of little spirit, had always been in awe of Jack and done his bidding. Now she was worried. Alice suffered under her father's rules; she suffered herself. So little outside contact couldn't be healthy for a growing child. Brenda feared it would only get worse as she got older.

For the first time since their marriage, Brenda was about to take independent action.

In desperation, Brenda had confided in her mother, knowing she was setting something in motion. Her mother would tell her brothers and she didn't know what they'd do but they'd do something.

Jack was wary of them, these two huge working men, tall and muscular and very protective of 'our Brenda'. He gave them a wide berth, the memory of humiliation still strong. If he saw them in the pub, he nodded and turned away and they left him alone.

One Friday evening, he called for a drink on his way home and was sitting in a corner in the local with a pint and a copy of "The Evening News".

The only other customer in the room, was standing with his elbow on the bar, chatting with the barmaid.

He raised his head as the door opened and his heart sank when he saw who was coming in. Brenda's brother strolled over and pulled up a chair.

'Time for a chat, Jack. You ready for another?'

Jack nodded, ashen faced. Perhaps it won't be so bad this time, at least there's only one of them, he thought. They hadn't spoken since the wedding.

Jim came over with a pint in each hand and put them down on the table. They were an unlikely pair; Jack in his collar and tie, pale faced and anxious and Jim in his work clothes, broad shouldered and ruddy faced, an appraising look in his intelligent eyes.

'Thought I'd catch you while it's quiet. I'm a bit worried about our Brenda and especially about young Alice.'

'What's up,' Jack stammered, picking up the remains of his first pint and knocking it back.

'It's like this, Jack. When we had our last talk, about twelve years ago, wasn't it?'

Jack nodded again. He couldn't speak.

'When we had our last talk, I promised I wouldn't interfere unless you gave me good cause. Isn't that right?'

Jack managed a strangled yes.

'Our Brenda's never complained about you, never said a word to make me think things weren't OK. I knew you kept her and Alice on a fairly tight leash but saw it as your affair. How you manage your marriage is your business.

Now you're a reasonable man and when I've explained, I'm sure you'll see things my way.'

Perhaps things weren't as bad as Jack thought.

'I'll try.'

'I find out now, those two can barely leave the house without your say-so. You want to know where they are every minute of every day. Alice isn't allowed to play with the other kids and has to be brought to school and collected by Brenda.

Now Brenda's one thing, she made her choice when she married you, but Alice is another matter.'

'What do you mean?' Jack tried a bit of bluster.

'I think the world of her. She's bright and as good as gold, like Brenda was at the same age. It's like she's living in a prison. It's not normal, the way you keep 'em under control and it's not good for Alice, you must see that.'

'I'm only trying to protect her.'

'Protect her? You're stifling her. How's she ever going to manage in the world if she's locked in all the time? She needs to be a normal kid doing the things normal kids do. She's big enough to go to school on her own and big enough to play out with the rest of them. You can't wrap her up in cotton wool, Jack. You'll smother the life out of her.'

Jack was getting braver and said huffily,

'I'll decide what's best for my own family. You can't tell me what to do.'

'No, I can't - but I'll tell you what I *can* do.'

Jack thought he was on firm ground.

'What *can* you do?'

'I can pack up Brenda and Alice and move them lock, stock and barrel round to my mother's place. Now me and my brother are married, there's plenty of room.

Alice can easily get to her new school from there and my mother'll be there to look after her when she gets home. Perfect solution, eh Jack?'

The sweat trickled down the back of Jack's neck and he put his finger inside his collar to ease it off the damp skin. How could he face the shame if his wife left him? How could he face a day without the sight of his darling Alice?

Hands shaking, he picked up his pint and downed half of it.

'What do you want me to do?'

He couldn't look Jim in the eye and stared down at the rings the pints had left on the table.

'Ease off. Let Alice off the leash. It won't do her any harm and the same for Brenda. You'll still have your meals on the table when you get home, your washing done and your house clean, all in return for freedom for those two lasses. The alternative is that you'll see little of Alice, I'll make sure of that, and you'll be fending for yourself into the bargain.'

'What does Brenda say?'

'Brenda doesn't know anything about it. I wanted to give you a chance before I rocked the boat. What do you say, Jack?'

He was over a barrel. Wait 'til I get home, he thought. Brenda will pay for this.

'One more thing, any whiff of retribution for Brenda will have them out of the house before you can say 'knife'. It's up to you.'

Jack bowed his head in acknowledgement. He was beaten.

***

Sally

I was on the bus with Alice going home from school and that horrible Johnnie Marshall was three seats behind. We'd had two years without him at junior school and although I saw him on the street now and then, I didn't think about him at all when he wasn't there.

He was now a third year and like most of the older boys, he ignored the first years. We were beneath them. Even so, more often than not, he was on the same bus going home and always sat behind us and I felt his eyes boring into the back of my neck. He was creepier than ever.

In the last year in Mr Metcalfe's class, Alice and I sat side by side and became good friends. We'd met in the library in the holidays and her mum and my mum always had plenty to say to each other.

We were both clever, pretty much the same. When we had tests, either she was top or I was top and sometimes we were level but there were never more than a few marks in it. There was a boy who was part of the competition but he rarely beat both of us. He'd passed his eleven plus too and we sometimes saw him on the bus. He was a bit of a wimp.

A few of us had passed but the other girls had chosen Levenshulme as their school, so Alice and me were together even more.

The first day we went to the new school, I was glad she was there. We didn't know what to expect. The school was much bigger than we were used to. Instead of a class of around thirty five in each year, there were five classes of around thirty five. Multiplied by five different years and two sixth forms, this was an awful lot of girls.

Both our mums were at the bus stop to see us off, telling us to stick together and be careful on the bus coming home. Did we have hankies? Were we sure we had everything? They were making us more nervous not calming us down.

My brother, now in the sixth form at the boys' school in the adjoining building, was supposed to take us and bring us back but he was in bed with 'flu. I didn't want him to be my nursemaid but I would have been glad if he'd been there the first day.

If it hadn't made us feel like little children, we would probably have held hands as we got to the gate.

The first hour whizzed by. We were organised into forms and Alice and I looked at each other in relief when we found out we were both to be in 1A. A lady who introduced herself as our form mistress took us along to a classroom on the second floor. This was to be our form room and we would start every day there.

Although she looked a bit stern, with short, dark hair and a black gown thing over her dress, she said to us kindly,

'Well girls, I know this is all very confusing but you'll soon get used to us.'

I looked across at Alice. We'd managed to bag two desks together on the third row. Only two of the other girls knew each other and all the rest knew nobody else in the class. We would
be together for the next year at least and many of us for another four years after that.

A timetable was up on the blackboard to show where we had to be every hour of every day for the next twelve months.

'Copy this out neatly and then you'll know where you're supposed to be for all your lessons.'

'Trust me, you'll soon find your way around and if you get lost or have a problem, ask one of the mistresses or one of the older girls. They'll be happy to help.'

Suddenly, an electric bell rang right through the school and we heard an enormous clatter as girls left their form rooms and moved along the corridors and down the stairs. This was called break and not playtime.

'Now girls, go down to the school yard and when the bell rings, come back here.' She glanced at the blackboard. 'This will be your first French lesson.'

We went down to the playground, now called the schoolyard, and congregated in one corner, huddled together for safety. Only girls from the first three years were in the yard but some of them looked enormous, more like women than schoolgirls. There was a netball game going on at one end and it looked fairly rough to me.

I had been pleased when I got my uniform, even the tie. It made me feel more grown up. It was strange to see all these girls; all dressed the same, a moving sea of navy and white. I inched a bit closer to Alice.

We introduced ourselves to the girls nearest to us and got their names but there were so many new faces, I despaired of ever remembering them all. For once, Alice was braver than me.

'Don't worry, Sally, we'll be all right. At least we've got each other and we'll soon get to know the rest.'

By the time the final bell rang, we were loaded up with exercise books and textbooks for subjects we'd never studied before. Each book was to be taken home, given a new paper backing and not brought back to school until that subject was on the timetable again.

We walked along to the bus stop on London Road. A few of the girls and some of the boys were going the same way and by the time we got there, the queue was enormous. It wasn't as bad as it looked as several different buses stopped at the same stop and people got on each bus as it came along until there were only a few of us waiting for the 109.

At the front of the queue, Johnnie Marshall was laughing and joking with some other lads. He just nodded and turned away. Alice had spotted him too and gave me a nudge.

'Look who's there. I guess we'll be seeing a bit more of him now.'

She wasn't bothered. She didn't dislike him as much as I did.

***

For Nick Metcalfe, things were going well. He looked across the classroom at his new class. They looked much like the classes of the two previous years. Some of them were reasonably dressed, some of them scruffy and some of them very scruffy. You never can tell, he mused, I'll have to see what they're made of.

The familiar smell of the classroom enveloped him, particularly noticeable after a six weeks break and he breathed deeply. The place smelled of kids. They were shuffling around for places. In theory, they all knew where they were to sit; their desks were in the same position as the previous year but in different classrooms. A couple of the lads were playing the fool, swapping desks and jostling the girls. He watched for potential troublemakers and was prepared to split them up even if alphabetically they should be next to each other.

He glanced at the notes Janet Marsden had given him at the end of the previous year and identified those who had done well and perhaps more importantly, those who hadn't. He picked out a couple of them. Naturally, they were the ones causing the ruckus. Boys who did least well were the most disruptive.

Two of the girls had also done poorly and although they weren't sitting together, they were constant companions outside the classroom. The teaching staff watched the playground for bullying but these two were potential victims and stuck together.

'Right then, settle down. You all know me and believe me, I know you. Jenkins, I've got my eye on you.'

Better watch him, could be another Johnnie Marshall in the making. He'd soon lick him into shape.

He gave a couple of the other lads hard looks, letting them know he had them marked. The children were now all standing quietly by their desks.

'Sit down and we'll get started, first lesson arithmetic. You and you,' he pointed at children at either end of the front row, 'take these books and pass them to the rest of the class.'

There was a low groan from some of the children and he suppressed a smile. Some things never changed.

As deputy head, he always volunteered for playground duty on the first day of term. This was partially selfish; he wouldn't have to listen to protracted accounts of summer holidays and first day moans. He also wouldn't have to give an account of his own summer and that suited him too.

On his way across the hall, he exchanged a warm glance with Janet Marsden before making his way to the stairs and out into the playground. He was grateful the weather was fine. Wet days could be hard work and on the first day back, they needed to let off steam. Most of them had been running wild all summer.

His mind drifted as he watched individual children from his new class and wondered how many of them were exam material. He wanted better things for the children who were able to grasp their chance and a decent education too for those who would remain in the school until they were fifteen.

He was quietly pleased, and Tom Phillips was too, that their eleven plus passes had risen each year and the coming year should be even better. He found it hard to believe three academic years had gone by since he and Tom had joined the school and compared the atmosphere today with the lethargy they had faced when they arrived.

Glancing at his watch, he realized playtime had sped by in idle thought. He blew his whistle and the children lined up in classes to go back into school.

Tom was waiting for him at the top of the stairs.

'Time for a quick word after school, Nick?'

'Yes, I'll come to your office after my last class.'

He wondered briefly if there were a problem.

School finished at half past three and within minutes, the children had disappeared. Nick made his way along the corridor to Tom's office, passing the caretaker carrying a brush and shovel.

A brief rap at the door and he went in to find Tom sitting with his feet on the desk.

'Come on in and have a seat. I wanted to have a chat.'

'Sounds ominous, what about?'

'I wanted to put you in the picture. You know Margaret's father's just died?'

'Yes, please tell her how sorry I am. We only met a couple of times but he was a real character.'

'He's left her a lot of money. I'm not talking a few thousands, I mean a fortune. I may need to ask you to cover for me for an odd half day while we get stuff sorted out.'

'Of course, be happy to help. How is Margaret?'

'I was worried about her for a while. She took it very hard – and then this on top of it. I thought she was going to crack up but things have settled down and she's coping.

Anyway, how are things going with Janet?'

The quick change of subject disconcerted Nick and he looked surprised.

'I didn't know you knew, not that there's much to know.'

'I didn't know for sure but I've seen you looking at her and thought you might be keen.'

Nick was not happy about the turn of the conversation. The thought they might be the subject of idle conjecture unsettled him. Though he regarded Tom as a friend as much as his boss, he resented the intrusion into his private life. He frowned.

Declining to say anything further on the subject, he added,

'If there's nothing else, I'll get off.'

'No, nothing else, I'll see you in the morning.'

Tom realised from Nick's stiff response he'd been offended. He hadn't wanted to intrude but to warn him gently that if *he* knew, it would not be long before the whole school knew. There were no secrets in such a closed environment.

Nick strode out of the school gate, unsure why he was so angry. The September sunshine didn't distract him. He always walked when he was troubled and he was troubled now.

Tom had been his mentor for some years and Nick looked up to him. Today, Tom had overstepped the mark. Janet was none of his business out of school hours.

The relationship was still very tentative. She'd agreed to see him out of school only after a great deal of persuasion and they always met on neutral ground; occasional trips to the cinema or the theatre but often with other people along. Clearly reluctant to see him alone, she made excuses when he asked her out to dinner and he had never invited her to his flat.

The problem is, he thought, I don't know where I stand. Could she care for me or does she regard me as just a friend? I'm afraid if I push her, she'll run for the hills. The worst thing that could happen is for rumours to start running round the school. I can't let it go. I can't take the chance someone will say something to embarrass her or the kids will start sniggering. I'm afraid to speak and afraid not to.

It will have to wait one more day, he thought. I'll try to find a moment to talk to her tomorrow, perhaps early on. We're usually in school before anybody else. As far as she is concerned, we might not even have a relationship and she could laugh in my face.

On reflection, he realized he hadn't given Tom enough credit. He'd been trying to warn of the consequences of a school romance. It was all so nonsensical when there wasn't even a romance going on. He only wished there were.

The following morning, he was first in school and put the kettle on in the staff room, hoping Janet would appear before anyone else.

The click of the latch alerted him as she came through the door. Her face chalky white and her eyes puffy.

'What on earth's the matter?'

'My mother's ill. She was rushed into hospital yesterday, an emergency operation. My dad 'phoned last night.'

Her sentences were disjointed as if she were trying to make sense of what had happened.

'I have to go home. I have to go home straight away, today. I need to see Mr Phillips. Is he in yet?'

'Why don't you go along to his office and see? He's usually here by now,' he said, checking his watch. 'I'll find out the train times. Go on now.'

She dumped her handbag on a chair and he could hear her heels clicking along the corridor as he picked up the phone book to check the number for rail enquiries.

Ten minutes later, she was back.

'He said it was OK, I should go now. He said he'd cover my class but I should ring him as soon as I know something.'

'There's a train at twelve, will you have time to go home and pack?'

'Plenty of time, I'd better get going.'

She had steadied now there was something positive to do and turned to leave.

'Thanks, Nick,' she said over her shoulder as she disappeared through the staff room door.

At break the next afternoon, Nick put his head round the door of Tom's office.

'Any news from Janet?'

'She phoned about an hour ago. It's not good news, I'm afraid. Her mother is very ill and Janet and her father were at the hospital all night. It sounds as though its touch and go. She won't be back in a few days.'

Nick's face fell.

'That's bad news.'

'Yes it is and it leaves me with problems too. Much as I enjoy being back in the classroom, I can't stand in for Janet indefinitely. It's never easy to organize a temporary teacher and they can't send anyone until Monday. Let's hope it won't be for long.'

'Let's hope so.'

The days passed and then the weeks and there was no sign of Janet. The last he'd heard, there was no prospect of her returning for the foreseeable future. Her mother was now out of immediate danger but needed constant nursing.

He hadn't heard from her directly and couldn't write without approaching Tom for an address.

Perhaps she'd felt nothing for him after all and he had been deluding himself. He'd hoped against hope she'd get in touch but so far, the only message had been "regards to the staff", nothing specifically for him.

For the first time, he had a real sense of how devastated Heather had been when their relationship ended. He felt like a lost soul, the absence of Janet almost like toothache; always there, always nagging.

***

Three years into the job, Arthur was doing well. The management and customers liked him and his figures had increased steadily. The years of working nine to six in a closed shop environment, with the same routine day after day were gone. Now more or less his own boss, he planned his own journeys and calls.

Sometimes he had to stay away overnight to call on the customers who were furthest away but never stayed away two nights if one would do

At first, it had been a novelty to stay in hotels. He thought himself a man of the world and enjoyed sitting in a dining room to have his breakfast served. In the evening, he would sit in the bar and write up his orders for the day, glass of beer on the table, and then go and read the paper while eating his dinner.

On fine evenings, he would often go for a walk round unfamiliar cities, perhaps calling in somewhere for a pint, always able to strike up a conversation. He was a good-looking chap and the occasional lady looked after him regretfully when he walked away.

In a normal week, if his calls were further than twenty miles away, he was up and out on the road early, leaving his family asleep. He hardly noticed he was working longer hours than before but he finished early on Friday and now had the whole of Saturday free.

Always a keen football fan, for the first time in years, he was able to go to United's home matches with one of his brothers-in-law.

The travelling never palled but his heart lifted when he'd made his last call on a Friday and was on his way home. The routes were familiar and he welcomed the landmarks as he neared home.

I'll be home by five and United are at home tomorrow. What more could a man ask?

Eva didn't know, and had never known, exactly how much he earned. He had increased her housekeeping money and gave her extra at the end of the month to put in their savings.

During the war, Eva had handled the family cash and continued to do so. She paid the rent and the gas and electricity and settled up for things like coal and the family groceries.

The subject of her job had come up again, as she had known it would.

Both the kids were out and she and Arthur were sitting in their armchairs in front of the low fire. Eva was still dressed in her dark work clothes and Arthur had whipped off his tie and rolled up his sleeves. His order book was looking healthy and he was full of Eva's steak and kidney pie. He asked expansively,

'Why don't you chuck that job now? We don't need the money and you could stay at home, perhaps do a bit of sewing.'

This was the last thing Eva wanted. She loved the independence having her own wages gave her. There had been enough scrimping and saving over the war years.

Arthur felt it didn't reflect well on him that his wife went out to work. They were better dressed and ate better than most of their neighbours – and she had paid for Sally's piano. He didn't take *that* into account, she thought resentfully.

She responded sharply,

'Come on Arthur, it's only a few hours a week. Even Sally doesn't need me. She does her homework whether she's here or at my mother's.'

Arthur frowned; this conversation was not going the way he wanted.

'I'm thinking of you, Eva.'

She looked at him sceptically, folded her arms and squared her shoulders, not a good sign. Her voice was still chilly.

'Look at it this way, despite my few hours' work, all the jobs get done. There's a hot meal on the table every night, you've always got a clean shirt and the kids are doing well,'

Arthur, surprised at the hornets' nest he'd stirred up, nodded. She'd given him a choice. If he let the matter drop that would be the end of it. Eva would fall into line if he put his foot down but she wouldn't make things easy for him. Her expression suggested his usually compliant wife would be unhappy and resentful should he insist.

He was weighing up his loss of face against his prospective loss of comfort and wavering between the two.

Knowing he hated to think he wasn't in charge, a little soft soap to smooth the way might be in order. Her tone softened.

'If you think taking in sewing is better than working a few hours a week, you've got some funny ideas. I love that job … but if you insist.'

He looked at his wife's set face.

'Well, if you put it that way.'

Eva let out a sigh of relief; he'd capitulated.

Ever after, Arthur referred to "Eva's little job" with the implication he was indulging her but Eva didn't care.

***

Johnnie's move to the new school had not been easy. As always, he was too cocky for his own good and for the first time, his older brother wasn't around to protect him. He had to stand or fall by his own efforts. After one or two cuffs for giving lip to older boys, he had finally learned to keep a low profile.

Like Sally, he had found some of the changes strange. He had never been in an all-male environment before; no girls in the classrooms and no women teachers and some of the masters were hard cases. His mum was his only female contact and he was discounting her more and more.

There were girls on the other side of the school wall, he could hear them in the yard at break and there were girls on the bus going to and from school but for them, he didn't exist.

He felt isolated and sometimes invisible, one more navy blue blazer among the many, indistinguishable from the rest. From being the boss of his own gang, the younger brother of a tough guy and the best footballer in the school, he'd become a nobody.

In the absence of any other option, he buckled down to his schoolwork. During the first six months, he had even considered asking his mum if he could leave and go back to the other school with his mates.

He dismissed this idea after wandering into the park early one evening and found his erstwhile pals kicking a ball around. They'd studiously ignored him for a while and then Jimmy Gill, previously only a lieutenant in the gang but now obviously the leader, shouted magnanimously, if a little condescendingly,

'Fancy a kick around Johnnie?'

Johnnie weighed it up. There was no chance he could re-take control, he wasn't around enough and he hated to be on the outside looking in.

'Nah, thanks Jimmy, got to be somewhere,' he muttered and sauntered off, hands in pockets, desperately trying to suppress the tears prickling behind his eyelids.

He could hear the lads muttering behind him and one of them sniggered but he didn't turn round.

Upset at being shut out, he spotted that weasel, Mickey Smith, who had seen him coming and was legging it out of the park gate. He couldn't even be bothered to chase him. Walking steadily out of the park, he turned towards home. There was nowhere else to go.

Other lads who had left junior school to go to grammar school often had a hard time. Caps were stolen and tossed from hand to hand and school bags kicked around. At least his reputation saved him from that ignominy but it was little consolation.

By the end of the first term, he had found his niche at the bottom of the pile with the rougher element of his year. With no real mates in his own form, he'd drifted towards a few lads who congregated in one corner of the schoolyard.

By the time they were fourteen, these were the crafty smokers and the lads who continually used bad language. Johnnie had a sharp tongue and had learned the value of sarcasm. It wasn't always necessary to punch someone in the mouth to cut them down to size; ridicule worked just as well. Once again, he had a gang of sorts.

Working for his dad every Saturday gave him more cash in his pocket than any of the other lads. He had money for smokes and money for bus fares so he could roam during the school holidays.

A few of his pals had working mothers, leaving their homes free for the lads to meet during the holidays. These council estate houses were cheaply furnished but the kitchens had fitted cupboards and the bathrooms were modern. Above all, they were light and airy and a far cry from the Marshall's dingy, old-fashioned dungeon.

They smoked and cursed and, by the third year, were talking about girls. What they had done or would do to them given half a chance. Occasionally, they met in Manchester and sat in Piccadilly Gardens, watching the talent pass, with an occasional shoplifting foray into Woolworths for a laugh. One or two of the lads got their collar felt and were thrown out of the store but Johnnie was never caught. He got bored with it. What was the point of nicking stuff you had no use for? It wasn't worth the effort.

His life at junior school was now a distant memory. He had adapted to his change in circumstances. The only fly in the ointment was the hard look he got from David Steadman, now a sixth former and a prefect, when they passed in the corridor. Johnnie kept out of his way.

As he was going into his third year, Sally and Alice were entering their first. He could still have thumped Sally without any provocation but David was still in the background like a guardian angel.

The only bonus was that Alice Spencer had made it too. She and Sally were inseparable and travelled to and from school together.

Even though Johnnie was becoming interested in girls and keen to get a bit more experience, he was still fascinated by Alice.

He looked at girls his own age and at the older girls too. He checked out their legs and their breasts and imagined what they looked like unclothed. Like many boys of his age, he was in a semi-permanent state of arousal and although they didn't talk about it much, he knew all his mates, like him, were masturbating at frequent intervals.

Johnnie was a good-looking lad, still smooth skinned and slender although his shoulders were filling out. He always looked tidy, his clothes were always clean and he took some pride in his appearance, sure some of his father's air of authority lay in the way he dressed.

He was, of course, still growing and Hettie bought his clothes. Although Maurice had agreed to cover the cost of school uniforms, she had to cover the rest herself. Her budget was tight and she knew exactly how much stuff cost.

She was no fool but he knew when to soft-soap her to get his own way.

'Look, Mum, it's got to be a pain in the neck for you to go on the market. Let me save you the trouble. I'd like to pick my own stuff.'

Hettie knew he wasn't bothered about her, only interested in getting his own way. She considered.

I can't see the harm. At least I won't have to listen to him moaning about what I do buy. But I hate giving in to him.

Johnnie waited. He couldn't rush her; she was still a force to be reckoned with.

'Well, Mum? Can I?'

'I suppose so but don't get any big ideas. You'll only get what I would spend.'

'Thanks, Mum.'

Now he'd got his own way, he couldn't get out fast enough.

'See you later,' he shouted over his shoulder as he left the house.

Out of school hours, the lads wore shirts bought mainly from local markets and Johnnie had dressed much like the rest. Now he was choosing his own clothes. Hettie gave him cash for a shirt or a pair of trousers and he put a little of his own money towards what his mother gave him so he could buy better quality.

Hettie noticed but said nothing. After all, it was his money and the clothes weren't costing her any more.

There were still plenty of Teddy Boys knocking around town but Johnnie didn't hanker for that extreme style. He thought they looked a bit ridiculous.

When he turned up in the first shirt he'd bought for himself, pale blue with a dark blue trim across the pocket, it could have gone either way. It wasn't startlingly different from what the rest of the lads wore but it *was* different. He braced himself for snide remarks.

'New shirt, Johnnie? Where'd you get it?'

He'd bought it in a city centre store but didn't want the lads to know he was shopping where they wouldn't or couldn't buy stuff so he let the question go.

'Well?' he asked.

His pal narrowed his eyes and walked right round Johnnie, giving him the once over.

'Looks great, different but good.'

One of the girls chipped in,

'It looks lovely, dead smart.'

Somebody else murmured,

'Yeah, it looks good.'

Johnnie breathed a silent sigh of relief; he'd got away with it. His need to be better than the other lads constantly struggled against his need to fit in. None of the other lads cared about their schoolwork and he played down his achievements, shrugging them off.

'Got to be done or the old man will kill me.'

They all understood that kind of threat and weren't to know Maurice didn't care, one way or the other.

A few girls hung out with his set in someone's kitchen during the holidays. They were all mad about the latest rock'n'roll music and Bill Haley's "Rock around the Clock" had caused a sensation. With the furniture pushed back, they danced for hours, trying out new moves and practising for the time they would be old enough to go to dance halls.

Though some of the girls were regulars, some of them came and went, fascinated by what they perceived as the bad boys. A couple were fairly compliant and were happy to disappear with one or other of the lads into a hallway or upstairs into a bedroom where a fair amount of kissing and fumbling went on.

He came in for more than his fair share of favours. His blue eyes and dark hair were a lethal combination and his sardonic smile was the envy of his mates. He could be a charmer; not enough to persuade someone to go all the way, but enough to be able to undo a bra and massage a breast or gently slide his hand up someone's knickers.

The unwritten code was that the lads stopped when the girls said so and although he was sometimes teeth grindingly frustrated, he followed the code.

Alice was another matter. Lurid thoughts never entered his mind when he looked at her. She was so fragile, so perfect, so quiet and neat. He looked at her like an art dealer would look at a masterpiece, almost in awe and happy to feast his eyes. Nobody knew about his fixation. His mates would laugh him out of the schoolyard if they got an inkling. He just contemplated her quietly whenever he got the chance.

***

Tom had known Margaret's father was a wealthy man but the extent of the estate had been staggering. Margaret was now a very rich woman.

The day after the funeral, he had arrived home to find Margaret at the kitchen table, nursing a cup of tea and looking dazed. There were dishes in the sink, the usually tidy kitchen was in disarray and the children were running riot. Margaret's eyes were red from weeping, her hair a mess and even the collar of her blouse was crooked.

'Margaret, what on earth's the matter. Are you ill?'

She looked up at him, struggling to focus.

No, not ill, overwhelmed. It's Daddy's will.'

'What about it. Not cut you out of it, has he?'

His flippancy passed unnoticed. This was more serious than he had thought.

He pulled her to her feet and when he put his arms around her, he could feel her shaking. Murmuring words of comfort, he led her into the sitting room and gently pushed her into an armchair. He poured half a tumbler of whisky and placed it into her cold hands.

'Drink this. Take your time. I'll see to the boys.'

She grasped the glass and took a sip, then another.

Tom went into the hall and shouted up the stairs. The boys came running, yelling like Indians.

'Look lads, Mummy isn't well so I need you to be very quiet for a while, can you do that?'

They nodded sheepishly.

'Go upstairs and do a jigsaw or read a book. No more running around, hear me?'

They nodded again and quietly climbed the stairs.

Margaret hadn't moved but the whisky level in the glass had fallen and she had regained a little colour.

He went back into the kitchen, cleared the table, put jars back into cupboards and wiped the counters. Nothing irritated Margaret more than a messy kitchen. This was all so out of character.

Back in the sitting room, he pulled a pouffe up to Margaret's chair so they were sitting facing each other, knee to knee and took her hand.

'Can you tell me about it now?'

She took a deep breath and put down the glass.

'Mummy and I went to the solicitors this morning. He was very professional and read out the terms of Daddy's will. I wasn't surprised at first. He left the house in Bowdon to Mummy for her to live in or sell as she sees fit and an income from trust funds which will leave her very comfortably off.'

'That's what we expected, isn't it?'

'He's also left trust funds for the boys, which will mature when they're twenty one and will give them a decent start.'

Tom squeezed her hand to encourage her. He had never been comfortable around wealth, particularly not that of his father-in-law, which had sometimes been used as a weapon. In fact, he disapproved of inherited wealth on principle.

'Of course he left us this house outright. He paid cash for it when we got married.'

Tom had been saving for years to repay the cost of the house.

At that moment, Tom didn't think about the cash in the bank, which would now be at his disposal. The old man had bested him in the end. Crafty old devil, he thought, he finally got his way.

'Margaret, what exactly is it that has upset you so much?'

'He's left me thousands; thousands and thousands. I had no idea. The thought of so much money frightens me half to death. I have no idea what we'll do with it. I don't want it, it's too much responsibility.'

She clutched at Tom's hands, her eyes filling again.

'It's too much, it's just too much.'

'How much are we talking about here?'

Her voice wavered and she gripped harder.

'It's about five hundred thousand pounds.'

Dumbstruck, Tom was having trouble taking it in. For God's sake, he didn't want George's money. As far as he was concerned, this was now Margaret's money. He wanted no part of it. A couple of hundred, or a couple of thousand even, he could have stomached but this was too much. If the old man had still been around, he would have told him what to do with his money.

He looked at his wife and held his temper. She was struggling with the death of her father as well as this latest development. Her distress was clear from the grip of her hands.

He put his hand on her shoulder and spoke,

'It's crazy, anyone else would be turning cartwheels and here we are; you're crying and I'm angry. What a pair.'

Margaret managed a weak smile and he went on,

'The best thing we can do is put the whole thing to one side for the time being. There's no need to rush into anything. Let the idea settle for a couple of weeks until you get some kind of perspective. Try to carry on as normal, unless you want to rush out and buy a mink coat.'

With another weak smile, she said quietly,

'Not my style. I'm sorry I went to pieces. It was the shock and the thought this could change our lives completely.'

'We don't have to let that happen. Take your time and I'll help you all I can although heaven knows, I'm no financial expert. Let it all lie for a while.'

Tom had serious misgivings. He didn't want the money to become a wedge between them. Margaret had always supported his view he should be the provider and had continually refused offers of treats from her father. This was different; the money was now hers. He tried to gain some kind of perspective,

I'll have to trust her, he thought, she's never let me down yet.

He gave her shoulder a squeeze and spoke,

'Anyway, on a more prosaic theme, what are we going to give the boys for tea, something quick and easy? What about beans on toast? It won't hurt them for once.'

Margaret was now calmer, her faith in Tom had settled her. She was back to her usual practical self.

"Good idea, I'll go and get started and you can make sure they wash their hands. As for the rest, we'll take it easy and not rush into anything.'

1958

The Manchester United FC team plane flying back from a European Cup tie crashes on take-off after refuelling in Munich. 21 of the 44 people on board are killed. Seven of them were Manchester United players.

Bertrand Russell launches the Campaign for Nuclear Disarmament.

First parking meters installed in Britain.

The Preston Bypass, Britain's first motorway, is opened by Prime Minister, Harold Macmillan.

First boutique opened in Carnaby Street, London, by John Stephen.

Published: 'A Bear Called Paddington' – Michael Bond
'Saturday Night and Sunday Morning' – Alan Silitoe
'Dr No' – Ian Fleming

Best Film Oscar: 'Gigi' – Lesley Caron, Louis Jourdan and Maurice Chevalier

In the Hit Parade: 'Jailhouse Rock' – Elvis Presley

Born: Michael Jackson
Madonna
Jules Holland

Chapter 10

Hettie looked around the kitchen. Even to her jaundiced eyes, it looked shabbier than ever. The sunshine coming through the kitchen window and open door showed up the yellowed walls and the threadbare curtains.

Maurice was slowing down, now carrying a fair sized paunch and breathing more heavily after any exertion. Mentally, he was as sharp as ever and kept an eagle eye on his runners and on the books and takings but he had mellowed. She hadn't had a slap for several years although she knew this could change if she stepped out of line. Over the last few months, he didn't always go to the pub in the evening on race days

His presence in the house irked her. She had been used to having the place to herself in the evening. There would be no cosy chats and crafty drops of whisky with her sister while Maurice was in the house.

The murmur of voices in the back yard faded. They must be finishing for the day and a few minutes later, Maurice came through the back door with a pencil behind his ear and his tally book and metal money box under his arm.

Johnnie followed him in. At eighteen, he was now an active member of the firm.

'Not a bad day, eh, Dad?'

Never having admitted to having a good day, Maurice grunted,

'Not bad. Could have been better.'

Hettie deftly placed two plates on the table. The Saturday menu hadn't changed. Succulent steak nestled on the plate surrounded by golden chips and covered in fragrant onion gravy.

Johnnie breathed in the smell, smiling in anticipation.

Maurice picked up his knife and fork and got stuck in.

Hettie didn't ask Johnnie if he were going out, it was Saturday night. There'd be half an hour's activity while he got himself ready, disappearing upstairs to come down, close shaved and smartly dressed.

Maurice finished his tea, gesturing Hettie to fill his mug. He might have been mellowing but his manners hadn't improved.

Johnnie was moving about upstairs and Hettie raised her eyes to the ceiling.

'He doing all right, then?' she asked.

'He's bright all right. Still needs watching round the cash box but he'll do. He reckons the odds and pay-outs nearly as fast as I do – and that's saying something,' he said grudgingly.

Maurice was still the boss but who knew how long that would last, given Johnnie's conniving nature?

Taking a closer look at him, Hettie could see he was tired. The skin around his eyes looked puffy and his face was an unnatural pinkish colour.

'You going out Maurice?'

Only a couple of years earlier, she'd have been told to mind her own business but now he responded.

'Nah, can't be bothered. I'll go out tomorrow instead.'

She started to clear away the plates and mugs. If he didn't go and have his usual after tea kip, she wouldn't get her own tea in peace and a letter from Harry was burning a hole in her pocket. He stirred again in the chair and then spoke.

'I might get a television, put it in the front room for when I stay in. What do you think?'

It was rare enough he asked her opinion. She was slow to answer.

'Not a bad idea. D'you know someone?'

Maurice had contacts for practically everything which could possibly fall off a lorry.

'Course I do. I'd better get a settee while I'm at it, something comfortable. That old horsehair thing in there's seen better days; some of the springs are coming through.'

Hettie could hardly believe her ears. Maurice, talking about spending money? True, it was for his own comfort and entertainment but it was out of character.

Her heart sank, he must be planning to spend even more time at home but never one to miss a chance, she jumped in.

'If you're spending that kind of money, you might as well have the place decorated and get some new curtains. I could run 'em up.'

He scowled while he considered.

'Harry Marsden's handy with a paint brush and he owes me money. He can work some of it off. I'll tell him to come round and measure up.'

Hettie hesitated, should she push for the curtains now? The chance might not come again and there was nothing to lose by trying.

'And the curtains? They wouldn't cost much.'

He scowled again. Parting with cash was always painful but at least there'd be somewhere decent to sit. He fancied the idea of sitting in front of his own television with his feet up and a glass of whisky in his hand.

'How much?'

'Ten quid should do it.' Trying to distract him, she added 'I could go on the market on Tuesday, then get my old machine out, I could have 'em finished in a couple of days.'

Maurice had no idea what anything cost, apart from his suits and his drinks and the cost of food in a decent restaurant but he had to object on principle. He'd learned from experience, whatever he gave Hettie for specific purchases, there was never any change. It was too much trouble to chase her for a couple of bob and he let it go.

Hettie knew if she didn't get the cash now, it would be a long time coming and might never arrive. She waited. She'd been playing this game for years.

'All right then,' he grumbled and pulled a roll of notes out of his pocket. He counted ten pounds on to the table and then a few more notes.

'And there's your money for this week.'

Hettie had counted with him and knew she was a bit short. He had to show who was boss and who held the purse strings but she didn't care. She'd manage and Maurice had forgotten the parcel of sausages and pork chops passed into the kitchen this afternoon. Her cash would spin out until next Saturday. Naturally, there'd be a surplus from the curtains too.

He put his hands flat on the table and pushed himself to a standing position.

'Right, going for a kip.'

He need say no more, Hettie would wake him in an hour with a cup of tea. He'd skip the wash and brush up and sit in the front room for the rest of the evening with the paper, the radio and a bottle of whisky. She didn't need to check the cupboard, she knew to within a swallow how much was in the bottle and it would last the night.

Johnnie was still upstairs as she put the chip pan back on the stove. He'd be out in ten minutes and she could have her tea in peace, have another read of Harry's letter and then the paper and a cuppa before she woke Maurice.

She grinned as she stashed the cash in her apron pocket. She wasn't much of a machinist but she could manage curtains and ten quid would go a long way.

Her own tea finished and a cup of tea in front of her, Hettie settled contentedly into her chair and pulled the letter out of her apron pocket and unfolded it.

Dear Mum,

Glad to hear you are doing OK. I read your letter and it looks as though nothing much changes your end, Dad and Johnnie still slogging it out.

Things are pretty much the same here, the garage is going well and more people are buying cars than ever. All the more business for us.

Mr Jones has decided to go into the used car business, just in a small way. It was my idea, and he really went for it. It means I get out now and again to look at cars that are for sale. Even if they are a bit battered, we can soon put them right in the garage and sell them on at a decent profit. He's a fair bloke and said any profit over £100 will be mine, seeing as I do most of the work.

This means a lot to me and makes it worth my while to put in the odd Saturday and Sunday to go and look around and he lets me use the van. If she's got nothing better to do, his daughter sometimes comes with me. She's a very nice girl and very friendly.
I'm not making much extra at the moment but am sure that will change. He's no fool though, he said he'd review the situation in three months. (Just in case I'm making too much, I suppose.) But don't worry. I'm fine and still putting a few bob away every week.
Write back when you can, I like to hear the news from home.

Your loving son,

Harry

PS I'm enclosing ten bob for you, treat yourself.

Naturally, the ten shilling note had been stashed as soon as she'd opened the envelope.

The letter re-folded and back in her pocket, Hettie quickly checked Maurice's packet of cigarettes. There were plenty left and she lit up.

Harry was doing fine but she missed him. It only seemed five minutes since she'd had both the lads under her feet and now, with Johnnie out all day and most nights, there was only her and Maurice and he wasn't much company.

As usual, he'd shown little interest in Harry's letter; hadn't even asked to read it. Just asked,

'He doing OK? Still working at that garage?'

'Yeah, he's doing fine and likes the job.'

'Don't know why he didn't come home when he finished his National Service. He could have gone back to the old place. They'd give him a job like a shot.'

Hettie knew exactly why he hadn't come home. He was glad to be out from under Maurice's thumb and away from his father's illegal operation. He'd always been an outdoors kind of lad, out in all weathers, and now he was living practically in the country. Good luck to him, Hettie thought, I'm glad he's out of it.

Maurice was stirring in the front room and she got up to put the kettle on, best keep him sweet.

***

Alice and Sally had thrived at their new school. Better friends than ever, they were now inseparable.

They travelled to school together, each leaving home at twenty past eight and meeting on the pavement outside Sally's house. Now they were in the fifth year and the girlish gymslips of earlier years had disappeared in favour of skirts. They wore regulation uniform. Neither of them had pushed the boundaries like some of the other girls who were wearing pencil skirts and Cuban heeled shoes.

These girls were the equivalent of Johnnie's gang of bad boys and were often seen hanging around at the bus stop, giggling and flirting. Alice and Sally rolled their eyes when they saw them. All they could talk about was lads and lipstick, clothes and rock and roll.

Maybe it was their background or their influence on each other but at sixteen, neither of them had yet shown much interest in the opposite sex. They had their crushes on film stars, both near swooning over Paul Newman and Steve McQueen and the more exotic Harry Belafonte and Rossano Brazzi but there was no connection between these heroes and the boys banging about at the back of the top deck of the bus.

Sally still hero-worshipped her big brother and Alice was a close second. She'd had a crush on David since she had watched him stop Johnnie Marshall from tormenting those two old ladies. She'd had a grandstand view from behind the lace curtains in her mum's front room.

Brenda and Alice's house arrest had miraculously ended during the school holidays immediately before Alice started at the new school.

She didn't know why and she didn't ask. She welcomed the change with open arms.

During the first week at the new school, one of the rougher girls and her cronies had begun to pick on Alice. It had started slowly, sniggering conversations that stopped as she passed. Then a few names called in a voice calculated to reach her but not the teacher on duty.

Sally said, 'never mind, they'll soon get fed up. Keep away from them.'

Easier said than done. They stood behind her in the dinner queue, giving her the occasional shove. When it started, Sally made sure Alice always stood in front of her.

Thwarted, one lunchtime, the ringleader tripped Alice as she was carrying her plate to the table. Sally could only watch in horror as the crash of the breaking plate brought a hush to the dining hall and then an outbreak of whispers and craning necks. Every head at every table turned towards them.

Alice was crimson with embarrassment, looking in dismay at the mess on the floor.

'Quiet, you girls,' from Miss Powell, who was took no nonsense, and who was now bearing down on them across the dining room.

Before the teacher could get close enough to see what was happening, Sally slid her foot into the mess and threw the contents of her plate all over the girl who'd tripped Alice.

"Oh, Miss Powell, I'm so sorry. Alice tripped and dropped her dinner and I slipped on it and look what happened.'

The girl sat there, turned towards them, with mashed potato and gravy all over her face and blouse. She was redder than Alice and grinding her teeth with rage. The girls who were sitting close by, even her friends, were laughing.

Miss Powell was nobody's fool and had had her eye on this particular girl for a while. Alice and Sally were normal girls, a bit overawed by their new circumstances and unlikely to make a fuss without extreme provocation.

'Look at the state of you, girl. Go and clean yourself up. Take that blouse off and put on your gym shirt. Rinse that through before you put it in your bag.'

She turned to Alice and Sally.

'"And you two, you'd better go back to the end of the queue and hope there's something left by the time everyone else is served. Tell the supervisor what's happened and someone will come and clear up.'

She looked at them sternly but Alice was sure there was a twinkle in her eye. She had a good idea what had happened.

'Go on, off you go.'

Sally had the protection of her older brother but he'd never intervene in anything involving girls. Although Alice was unaware, she'd always been protected by Johnnie Marshall. The fact both boys were at the school next door was no help to them now.

They collected fresh plates of food and found two seats amongst the first year pupils, far removed from the empty seat vacated by the gravy stained bully.

Most of the first year girls were afraid of her and there were several whispers along the table,

'Good for you, Sally,' and

'She deserved it,' and

'That'll teach her a lesson.'

Alice and Sally looked anxiously at each other, they weren't so sure.

Sally was more streetwise than Alice would ever be.

'It'll go one of two ways. Everyone's been laughing at her. She'll either crawl into her shell and keep quiet or she'll be out to get us; both of us now, not just you.'

Alice's eyes filled with tears and her voice wobbled a bit.

'I'm sorry, I never meant for you to get in trouble too. What are we going to do?'

172

'Don't know. We'll have to wait and see. It was worth it. What did she look like with gravy running down her face?'

Sally started to giggle and looked at Alice, eyes still filled with tears, who started to giggle too, shoulders shaking with suppressed laughter. They didn't see Miss Powell coming up behind them.

'Unless you care to share the joke, girls, I suggest you get on with your meal. You're behind everybody else and the second sitting is waiting to come in.'

She moved away while they struggled for control.

They carried on eating, trying to keep their faces straight. They didn't want to fall foul of Miss Powell too.

At half past three, they set off for the bus stop. This could be tricky as the bigger girl travelled home on the same bus.

They were anxious and stood even closer together than usual. Johnnie Marshall sauntered up and took his place in the queue behind them, nodding at Alice as he passed. Sally breathed a sigh of relief as the bus came down the hill towards them and there was still no sign of her.

As they climbed the stairs, they heard a sudden racket behind them and the conductor raised his voice.

'You silly young madam, do you want to get yourself killed?'

There was a low mumbling and someone started to climb the stairs. It was her. They clutched their school bags convulsively. There was a good chance one or both of them would get thumped while the conductor was out of sight collecting fares on the lower deck.

She was breathing heavily.

'Thought you'd got away with it, did you?'

There was no right answer to this so they said nothing.

'I'm going to teach you a lesson. You first,' she nodded at Alice, 'and then you' pointing at Sally.

There was silence on the bus. There were two middle aged women in headscarves on the top deck, smoking their heads off, and the rest of the passengers were all from school. Nobody said a word though it was clear what was going on. They were at her mercy. She was only a first year but she was big for her age and stocky. She raised her arm to strike.

Johnnie came from nowhere, catching her arm and twisting it until she yelped with pain. Big as she was, he was two years older and even bigger.

'If there's any lesson teaching going on, I'll be doing it.'

He gave her arm another vicious twist and pushed her away. Staggering, she grasped at the rail but didn't fall. She looked petrified.

'I won't say this again. Leave her alone,' he gestured at Alice. 'If I hear you've even looked at her funny, you'll have me to reckon with. Have you got that?'

He had no qualms about manhandling someone younger than him, even a girl.

White faced, she nodded and stumbled down the bus to find a seat. He looked at the two girls cowering in their seats and spoke to Alice,

'You all right?'

She nodded.

'You heard what I said. Any trouble from her and you let me know.'

He looked down the bus at the white faced girl rubbing her shoulder.

'Thank you,' Alice croaked.

Sally was ignored. He still hated her guts and would have watched cheerfully while she got a thumping. Alice was another matter.

He nodded at Alice again and gave Sally a filthy look, reproaching her for getting Alice into trouble in the first place.

Johnnie moved into the seat behind them and Alice could feel his eyes on them. Her face was burning and she felt sick. She could have wept with gratitude.

She knew who Johnnie Marshall was but she didn't really know him and he didn't know her. They'd been in the same school and lived in the same streets but he'd never even spoken to her before. Why would he rush to their defence?

The girls looked at each other, glad to have escaped so lightly but still silent. Johnnie was right behind them and would have heard every word.

As the bus pulled into their stop, he rose and ran down the stairs, jumped off walked away without a backward glance.

When they got off, they looked up at the top deck. She was still there but her face was turned away as though she didn't even dare look down.

They stood on the corner, face to face, a bit dazed.

'What do you make of that?' Alice asked.

'I don't know. He's no knight in shining armour, there must be something in it for him.'

Sally instinctively distrusted everything about Johnnie Marshall.

'He did save us though didn't he?' said Alice nervously.

Sally hadn't missed a thing.

'He saved you and couldn't help saving me at the same time.'

'Come on, she'd have thumped both of us. I'm grateful to him. She won't come near us again, either of us. She looked terrified.'

That filthy look had cut Sally to the quick. She should be looking after Alice and had got her into trouble instead.

'Maybe it's about him,' she said. 'You know, us living round here and going to the same school. Perhaps he still thinks he's cock of the walk and we're part of his territory.'

Though she was relieved it was over, she was uneasy about Johnnie's intervention. He never did something for nothing.

That was all now in the distant past and they rarely saw Johnnie Marshall these days. He had left school two years earlier and they guessed he was working when they saw him in a dark suit. Sally wasn't interested and Alice didn't know anyone she could ask. Sal could have found out but if the subject came up, it was dismissed with a wave of her hand and a look of disgust.

They'd seen him going into the cinema one Friday holding hands with a dark haired, pretty girl in a pencil skirt and high heels. He looked better than ever, a good haircut, smart navy trousers and a deep blue sweater and he'd nodded at Alice as she passed but looked straight through Sally.

He does have some style, Alice thought but didn't say a word to Sally who'd sniffed and tugged at her jacket.
'Come on,' she hissed. 'I don't expect those two will see much of the film anyway.'

The girls now had the O-levels behind them and the summer holidays before them and later that evening, Alice said,
'I'll be glad when the results come in. How about you, Sal?'
'I wouldn't say this to anyone else but I'm pretty sure I've done all right. I probably ought to cross my fingers when I say that, it's tempting fate.'
'Don't worry Sal. You'll have done great, you always do and always will.'
Sally smiled and gave Alice a nudge.
'You're not behind the door yourself. There's nothing we can do and I can't see either of us having to do a re-sit.'
'We've got six weeks to do what we like. What do you fancy?'
'Plenty of sitting around, doing nothing, for the first week at least, after that, we'll see.'
Sally was unaware of the long reaching changes waiting in the wings.

***

Arthur Steadman had risen in the world. He now wore more expensive suits and drove a slightly bigger car.
Eva had her sights set high. In the eight years since Arthur had changed his job, she'd extracted a proportion of his earnings each month and put the money into a building society account. Each salary increase and commission cheque had also been similarly taxed and their savings had grown steadily.
Had it not been for Eva, Arthur would have spent money more freely. Although she'd had no objection to his improved wardrobe or a week's holiday at the seaside in the summer, she'd often said,
'There's no point throwing money away, now is there, Arthur?'

Arthur could only agree. She'd always handled the family finances to 'save Arthur the bother' and he was happy for her to do so.

Their standard of living had improved and there was a new three piece suite and bedroom furniture for Sal, who was growing up fast.

'She might as well move into David's room and we can fit it out for her. He comes home so rarely these days, he can manage with the box room.'

Arthur's promotion to Regional Sales Manager had meant another hefty increase in salary and Eva had plans.

Not wanting to take the shine off his pleasure, she waited before raising her next project. Let him enjoy his success, he'd worked hard and deserved his rise in the company.

A week or so later whilst they were sitting quietly after tea, each with a cup and saucer balanced on the arm of their chair, she said,

'Do you realise we now have more than enough for a deposit and with your wage increase, we can easily afford mortgage repayments?'

'Really? Are we so far ahead? It's a big step,' he sounded a bit uncertain.

Arthur sat back in his chair, deep in thought. The evening sun was shining through the window, the light catching the brass candlesticks on the mantelpiece and reflecting off the mirror. Eva could almost hear the wheels turning in his head. He was surveying his kingdom and wondering whether he wanted to move at all.

'We need to find a house first, don't we?'

Arthur had agreed in principle but now it looked as though it might happen, he was anxious. A mortgage was a big responsibility. Nobody in his or Eva's family had ever owned a house. In fact, he didn't know anybody, apart from his bosses, who did.

'If we're still set on Denton, I can start looking around.'

'As long as we're not too far from a bus stop, Sally will still need to get to into town every day.'

There was no mention of Eva getting to work, the subject was skated over as usual.

She fished a newspaper from under a cushion on the armchair, folded open at one of the back pages, and passed it over.

'Have a look,' she said, pointing to an advertisement.

Arthur, brow furrowed, read it out,

> *"A small estate of new houses near completion;*
> *Fully fitted kitchen, three bedrooms, garden, etc. etc."*

'Do you know where it is?' Eva asked.

It was crucial some of the decisions should appear to fall into Arthur's hands and Eva waited.

'I've got a good idea. It's not far from Debdale Park.'

'Any chance, you could go and have a quick look. If you like the look of it, maybe we could go together at the weekend. There's no need to rush into anything.'

Arthur nodded.

'I'll do that, may be able to drop by tomorrow. Are you sure we can afford it?'

Eva nodded and prompted,

'It can't hurt to have a look, can it?'

'I suppose not,' he said, still looking worried.

'Don't mention it to Sally for the time being. Nothing's settled and it might not even happen.'

'Right you are.'

Eva let it go and changed the subject, asking him about his new journey plan and what was happening at the office and, as ever, he was happy to hear the sound of his own voice.

***

On the back row of the cinema, Johnnie sat with his arm loosely around the shoulders of the girl with him, waiting for the lights to go down.

Alice and Sally were a couple of rows in front and he watched them, heads together, whispering. Alice looked as pretty as ever, her shiny hair falling softly round her face. The shy, reticent girl he'd known at school was gone and she now looked confident and self-assured although she was obviously still an innocent. She'd smiled at him as they passed and he couldn't help but compare her freshness with the mascara and lipstick of the girl sitting beside him. Sally Steadman was as cocky and surly as ever.

As the lights dimmed and the raucous cock crowed at the start of Pathe News, wreaths of cigarette smoke rose through the light from the projection box. The heavy stuff first; British paratroopers had landed in Jordan to come to the aid of King Hussein. He thanked his lucky stars he wasn't there. Never mind all that rubbish about seeing the world, he'd no interest in being shot at.

The rest of the news was of little interest. The Queen had given Prince Charles the official title of Prince of Wales, as if he cared.

He laughed at the sight of parking meters, like lollipops on London streets and people feeding them coins like some alien life form. What a brilliant idea, somebody must be making a fortune, he thought cynically.

The cartoon started up, Tom and Jerry, and the whole cinema was laughing, Johnnie too. He loved the idea the little guy could win if he worked smart. Working smart had always appealed.

While all this had been going on, Johnnie had been idly stroking the shoulder of the girl beside him. The credits started for the main feature and Johnny settled back in his seat. He didn't care what was showing, it was rarely the purpose of a trip to the cinema. If there was a good Western or a thriller, he'd occasionally go with some of his mates but out with a girl, it was a whole different matter.

Over the last couple of years, he'd had a string of girlfriends, none of them lasting more than a couple of months.

He'd been seeing Sandra, the girl beside him, for just a few weeks. They'd met at the Plaza on a Sunday night and he'd liked the look of her. She'd been wearing a red dress with a full skirt and petticoats underneath so the skirt swung out as she jived, showing her shapely legs. Leaning back against one of the pillars, he watched her dance. She was light on her feet and much in demand.

His method was always the same. He'd find a girl he liked the look of and fix her in his sights until she became aware he was watching her. It was usually only a matter of time until she was watching him too, waiting for him to ask her to dance. Then he'd wander off to weigh up the rest of the talent. The place was always crowded and young people came into town from all the suburbs.

There were always new faces although Johnnie was familiar to many of the dancers. He was a regular, well dressed and with an air of superiority many of the girls found attractive. Sandra was no exception.

The dance floor was crowded. There were no quicksteps and waltzes and no band, just a disc jockey playing the latest hits; jiving for most of the evening and a couple of smoochy records at the end. Bill Haley was seldom heard, now it was The Everley Brothers, Elvis and an odd Chuck Berry thrown in. The crowd was predominantly young with very few people beyond their early twenties. The older crowd tended to congregate at the Ritz, five minutes' walk away.

As he made his way between the small round tables, each with a couple of gilt chairs, towards where she was dancing, he could see her scanning the crowd and knew she was looking for him. She smiled when she caught sight of him and as the record ended, moved to stand with her friend, turning her face away so as not to appear anxious. He knew all the signs.

The music had started when he made his move. He heard her friend whisper,

'He's coming over. He's going to ask you.'

She turned when he tapped her gently on the shoulder and he asked her quietly,

'Want to dance?'

'Sure,' she said and moved on to the dance floor and into his arms.

The music was slow and people were dancing more traditionally, hands clasped, boys' hands on girls' waists and girls' hands on boys' shoulders. A few were shuffling round, some of them snogging and holding each other very close.

They chatted for a few minutes and when the record finished, neither of them made a move to leave the dance floor. Johnnie was relieved Connie Francis had finished wailing. Peggy Lee with 'Fever' was more to his taste.

Sandra was glad he didn't try to hold her too close and didn't try to kiss her but she was a bit disappointed too. There'd been envious looks from a couple of other girls as she looked over her shoulder. How could she have known there were at least two he'd taken out once and never asked to see again and another he'd slept with and left with the parting words, "see you around"?

The last record was announced and they continued to dance. Sandra was half hoping he would ask to take her home. That wasn't his style. He liked to keep the ladies waiting. Instead he asked,

'Do you want to go out one night next week? I'd like to see you again.'

There was an instant response.

'I'd like that. What did you have in mind?'

They'd made a date for the following Wednesday and he'd been seeing her a couple of times a week since then.

They lived a short bus ride apart and could easily meet in town or on each other's home ground. The progress from a quick kiss on the cheek to a full blown, hands-on necking session had been fairly swift. Sandra sometimes thought too swift but once she'd taken the step, she couldn't go back.

In the cinema, they now spent practically the whole film kissing and cuddling on the back row with Sandra trying to cope with Johnnie's wandering hands. She wondered how far she should let him go, he was very persuasive and had a crafty way of taking liberties but he always stopped when she asked him.

He had no way of knowing Sandra was beginning to think they were going steady but was wary of broaching the subject. He could be unpredictable but was good company and so good looking, she thought he could have any girl he asked.

Money was plentiful and how he afforded what he spent on entertainment on a junior clerk's wages was a mystery. His family were another mystery. They were never mentioned and he deftly deflected any questions about them.

Johnnie liked her too. Sharp and sparky, she wasn't afraid to speak up for herself but the idea of going steady had never crossed his mind. He'd dump her in a minute if she became difficult or if something better came along. Where girls were concerned, his standards were high. It went without saying they had to be good looking but they also had to dress well. Anyone who looked or spoke what he called 'common' wasn't given a second glance.

Such girls were often less inclined to be straight laced and even possibly allow the ultimate liberty but there was no room in Johnnie's life for anything he regarded as second rate.

At sixteen, he'd lost his virginity to a mate's older sister and was naturally delighted. The other lads were still talking about their imaginary and intended sexual exploits but he never said much, just smiled inwardly.

A good looking girl of eighteen and more womanly than girls of his own age, she already had a bit of a reputation, never mentioned in the presence of her brother, but there were a few whispers.

They met occasionally and she clearly had a soft spot for him. When he called round for his friend one Saturday afternoon, she'd invited him in.

'I don't know where he is, do you want to come in and wait?' she said, holding the front door open so he could follow her down the hall and into the back room. She waved him towards the settee.

'Have a pew. Fancy a cuppa?'

Johnnie nodded, a bit overwhelmed. Her dark hair fell to her shoulders and her low cut summer dress exposed the top of her full breasts. Smiling seductively, she handed him a cup and saucer which he balanced on his knee to steady it. She sat down beside him. So nervous he thought he might rattle the cup right off the saucer, he could only sit tight. Was she just being friendly? Inexperienced as he was, her eyes told him otherwise and his feelings were a mixture of fright and hope.

'Don't worry,' she said. 'I don't bite. Why don't you put that down before you drop it and give me a kiss?'

So he did. He'd had plenty of practice at kissing and she showed her approval. His thoughts whirling, he sank deeper into the embrace, wondering what she expected of him. Should he try it on a bit further? Tentatively slipping his arm between them, he grasped at her breast, squeezing gently. He was still on familiar ground and when she leaned away slightly, he managed to undo the top two buttons of her dress and slide his hand inside, not only inside the dress but hallelujah, inside the bra too. He thought he'd gone to heaven.

By this time, they were both breathing heavily and she drew back a little, pulling down the skirt which had risen over her bare knees during the tussle.

'I think that's enough, don't you?' she asked in a heavy whisper.

Not by a long chalk, he thought, but she was older, a woman even, and he felt like an inexperienced oaf.

'Tell you what we'll do,' she said. 'You get hold of something, you know what I mean?'

He took a deep breath and nodded. He was almost bursting out of his trousers.

'Then you come round here on Friday night about eight o'clock. Everyone'll be out and we can have some fun.'

Barely able to speak, he nodded again and managed a strangled, 'Right, I'll be here.'

'One more thing,' she said. 'If you breathe a word to anyone, if I hear one whisper about this, your name will be mud. I'll tell our kid you were round here trying it on and what's more, you'll never get within ten feet of me again.'

'I won't say a word, that's a promise,' he said fervently.

'Better be on your way then,' she said looking down at the bulge in his trousers. 'See you Friday.'

Before he knew it, he was back on the pavement, gazing at the shabby front door. In a state of almost unbearable arousal, he set off to walk the long way home.

At the barber's, he'd been red to the tips of his ears but managed to ask for a packet of three. The poker faced barber had slipped them into Johnnie's top pocket and put out his hand for the cash. He'll be sniggering as soon as I'm out the door but I bet he's only jealous. He won't be getting any, he thought. The bell jangled behind him as he left the shop, relieved he'd got what he'd come for.

The week dragged by until Friday finally arrived. Freshly bathed and with the few errant whiskers surreptitiously removed with his dad's razor, he stood on the doorstep, almost trembling with anticipation. He waited. Suppose she's changed her mind, he thought. The door opened quickly and she took his hand and dragged him inside. She looked younger without the usual war paint and the creamy colour of the silky looking robe gave her face a soft glow. The fabric clung to her and there was little but skin beneath it.

'Follow me,' she said, making for the narrow staircase at the end of hall. Hanging on to the banister, he climbed, watching the slow slide of the fabric over her thighs and hips, desperate but not daring to put his hands on her.

When they reached her bedroom, she closed the door behind them and put her arms round him. Breathing in the scent of her skin and hair, he nuzzled against her neck. The skin was soft and smooth and warm to the touch.

'Did you get something?' she whispered.

He fished the packet out of his pocket and showed her and she smiled.

'Ambitious, aren't we? Packet of three.'

The next two hours exceeded his wildest dreams. She coached him, showing him where and how to touch her, how to give her pleasure while receiving pleasure in return. He was a very quick learner.

Finally exhausted, they lay back in her bed, her head resting on his chest. Looking down at her, he could see her lips were slightly swollen, her hair tangled and her face flushed.

I did that, he thought proudly.

The room wasn't very big, but there were flowers on the wallpaper and a small lamp on the dressing table shed a gentle light. It smelled of talcum and make up and something indefinably feminine.

They were a bit cramped in the single bed but he'd only just noticed. The sheets were tangled and the candlewick bedspread was in a heap on the floor, so he pulled her a little closer, savouring the moment.

She kissed him swiftly on the mouth and got out of bed, wrapping the gown around her.

'Come on, better get a move on. Mum and Dad will be home from the pub soon. Don't want them to catch you, do you?'

His first thought rose to his lips.

'When can I see you again?' He really meant, 'When can we do it again?'

'We'll see. I don't know when I'll have the place to myself. Anyway, I call the shots. I say where and I say when and *you say nothing.* Clear?'

'Clear,' he said, like a chastened schoolboy.

Over the next six months, he saw her maybe half a dozen times. There was no future in it, he knew. They could never go out together. The two years age difference put them worlds apart. He never kidded himself he loved her but he was sexually besotted and waited impatiently from one meeting to the next, ever eager for more.

It was beyond him why she'd even looked at him in the first place when she could take her pick of lads her own age. Maybe it was the female equivalent of the male fantasy of seduction, of being in charge.

They were lying, limbs entangled, in her narrow bed when she broke the news.

'This'll be the last time.'

He'd been half expecting it. Her brother had mentioned she now had a steady boyfriend a couple of years older than her.

'I don't know what to say,' he muttered.

'Don't say anything. It's been great and you did me a world of good when I was down in the dumps. Look on the bright side. You know more about women now than many a lad years older than you.'

He couldn't help but grin and she grinned back. It was true.

'Go on now, get your clothes on and get off.'

She pulled on her dressing gown and watched while he dragged on his trousers. Putting her arms round him, she spoke softly in his ear,

'I'll miss you but I'll see you around.'

'Yeah, see you around,' and he ran down the stairs, suddenly anxious to be away, and closed the front door behind him.

Yes, he was lucky. He knew all sorts of things the other lads didn't but it didn't make it any easier. Sometimes, her muttered or gasped instructions of where and how to touch had irritated him but he learned.

Now more than a bit disgruntled the excitement and sexual fulfilment of these last months had come to an end, he suspected a quick fumble in the dark with some inexperienced girl would be an enormous let down. The suspense had been part of it; wondering when he'd be summoned. At sixteen, resignation and acceptance weren't part of his vocabulary and he felt like kicking something.

His experiences in that back bedroom stood him in good stead in years to come. It wasn't the pleasure he took or was able to give future partners, the feeling of being in control when they moaned in his arms turned him on.

***

Life for Alice had changed drastically. When the reins had started to slacken, she hadn't reasoned why, she'd welcomed the changes with open arms. She was now able to leave the house on her own, go and meet Sally or go to see her grandparents.

Initially, she'd been like a bird with its cage left open, teetering for a while on the threshold but she'd found the nerve to fly free.

Her dad was often touchy, frowning as he asked where she was off to and questioning her on her return. His vigilance was still constant but he'd taken a step back. She was a truthful child and he could rely on her to be where she said she was going to be.

The atmosphere in the house was constantly strained and Alice felt it keenly. Her mum and dad had never talked much but now Dad rarely spoke at all. He hardly ever smiled except when she came home full of some triumph at school or when she delivered up her end of year report. Over time, he'd started going to the pub almost every night and she'd heard him hauling himself up the stairs, cursing as he stumbled or knocked his elbow on the banister. The days of a story on Daddy's knee and a goodnight kiss were long gone.

Alice's freedom became Brenda's freedom too though Jack was grumpier than ever. There was no longer need to keep an eye on Alice and make a full report every evening. Never a great talker, Jack spoke mostly in monosyllables and he was out most evenings.

Alice's exams were over so there was no more constant revision and she and Sally were out together a couple of times a week.

With time on her hands, Brenda read avidly, visiting the library twice a week and becoming friendly with the librarian, who'd stop for a chat if she wasn't too busy. She might have spread her wings further afield if there'd been a little more cash in her purse. Although Jack wasn't ungenerous with the housekeeping money, he did demand decent food on the table and there was very little left at the end of the week.

Relief that Alice had some measure of freedom sustained her for a long time but gradually, she realised how empty her life had become.

Once she'd cleared up after breakfast and done a few chores, the day stretched before her. Some days, apart from a brief respite at tea time, she was alone all day and all evening. She took up knitting again and tried her hand at dressmaking but had to hoard her resources in order to buy the materials. Wool was put aside so she could buy a couple of balls a week.

In the bad old days of clothing coupons it had been difficult and although things were easier to get hold of now, it was still a struggle if money was tight.

On a trip to the wool shop, she'd seen a notice in the window:

Part time assistant required. Apply within.

After buying what she needed, she went home, put the kettle on and then sat at the kitchen table, a cup of tea in front of her.

She'd always envied Eva Steadman her independence and the thought of having her own money in her purse was intoxicating. Jack would go spare, she thought and then carefully figured it out. He didn't have to know, did he? None of the men he drank with were ever likely to go in the wool shop, nor were they likely to enter into conversations with their wives about knitting or sewing.

Of course, she might not get the job but how would she know if she didn't try.

To hell with it, she thought and before she could change her mind, she put her coat back on, banged the front door behind her and set off briskly down the street.

Sally

I'd seen Alice looking at Johnnie Marshall and given her a bit of a dig. Why she could be bothered was beyond me. He wasn't the scruffy kid he used to be and I had to admit grudgingly he looked better than he'd ever done. It changed nothing; he was still the sly, crafty character he'd always been.

He'd still been on the back row as we left the cinema. His girlfriend had her compact out and was putting lipstick back on her mouth. He didn't look at me and I didn't look at him but I saw his eyes following Alice as she walked towards the exit.

It made me uneasy and the pleasure of the film we'd just seen dissipated. I'd enjoyed the music. Mario Lanza sang beautifully and the idea of Italy made my head spin, even though for us it might have been Mars. Alice was humming the theme tune, "Arrevederci Roma", under her breath and it got on my nerves.

The lights came on as we wandered along the cobbled street, past the pubs and the sweet shop and turned the corner towards home.

I wanted to tell her to put a sock in it but didn't say anything. Alice knew something was wrong.

'What's the matter with you? You've got a face like a wet weekend. I thought you wanted to see that.'

'I did,' I said and tried to pull myself together. 'Rome or Paris – I'd love to see those places.'

'So would I, Sal. Think we'll ever make it?'

'It's fairy story stuff, as if we'll ever get anywhere,' I muttered.

At the corner of the street, Alice said,

'I'll leave you to it. Perhaps you'll be a bit more cheerful in the morning.'

She turned toward her own front door and her Dad was watching from the window as she crossed the road. He must have come home early tonight.

It wasn't late and Mum and Dad were in the kitchen drinking tea, There was something going on. I could feel it in the air. Dad was fiddling with his cigarette packet and Mum was turning her cup and saucer round and round.

'What's up?'

They were both smiling.

Sit down Sally, we've got some wonderful news,' said Mum, eyes shining.

I was still a bit grumpy and couldn't raise much enthusiasm but had to ask,

'What's that then?'

'We're moving. We're buying a house in Denton.'

I couldn't take it in and just gawped.

'You'll love it. It's brand new and there's a garden and a modern bathroom. You can have the middle room, which is loads bigger than your bedroom here. It's five minutes' walk to the bus stop and ten minutes to Debdale Park.'

Dad was grinning now too and chipped in,

What do you think about that, our Sal?'

I couldn't help myself, I let rip.

'What if I don't want to move? What if I'm happy here and don't want to go to godforsaken Denton?"

That stopped them in their tracks. The smiles disappeared and Mum sat silently. Dad spoke,

'We thought you'd be pleased. It's as much for you as it is for us. A nice, new house to live in, somewhere you can bring your friends from school and our own garden. It'll be lovely.'

Not so sure of himself now, he'd gone pale and Mum looked near tears.

'What about Alice? What about my piano lessons? What about the extra travel to school?'

My voice had risen and I was almost shouting. They looked shaken. I'd never raised my voice to either of my parents before.

Mum's eyes had filled with tears and I could see Dad was upset too. He took a cigarette out of the packet on the table and fumbled for his matches, playing for time.

'Don't be so hasty, Sal. Alice can come up and stay all weekend. You'd like that - and you can stop off next door for your piano lessons on the way home from school, it's on the same route. There'd be nothing stopping you going to the pictures with Alice, I'd come down and meet you afterwards and bring you home or you could stay the night with your Gran. She'd be happy to have you."

I was all but crying myself now, gulping to keep back the sobs. I'm ashamed to say I wailed out the misunderstood child's eternal mantra.

'*It's not fair.* It doesn't matter what I want, you'll do what you like anyway. I'm going to bed.'

I flounced, yes flounced, out of the room, banging the door behind me; another first. Running up the stairs, I could hear Dad's voice trying to sooth Mum and could imagine what he was saying.

'It's a bit of a shock. She'll come round, you'll see.'

My head was spinning.

Whose tin pot idea was this anyway? Mum had always thought herself a cut above the rest round here, putting on airs and graces. Dad was no better; first car in the street, one of the only dads to go to work in a suit; brushing his trilby before he left the house and rubbing a duster over his shiny shoes while the rest of them wore overalls, flat caps and boots. I dismissed the fact I'd always been proud of them and didn't even feel guilty about this sudden condemnation of their values.

I didn't want to live in Denton. It was miles away and what's more, it was miles away from Alice. As if her dad would ever let her come and stay overnight. Even if I could still go to Miss Pritchard's on my way home, the extra travel would cut into my time, time I needed for practising and homework. What did I care about a bigger bedroom and a garden? I was happy as I was. Why did they have to spoil things? I didn't want change. I wanted everything to stay the same.

They didn't care about me or they wouldn't do this to me. I sobbed into my pillow, feeling sorry for myself.

My room, my lovely bedroom, I thought, squinting at the curtains Mum and I had picked out, the posters on the walls and the china lady on the dressing table. I didn't want a new bedroom, I wanted this one.

Next morning was Saturday and they were both at home. I was a bit shame faced as I went down to the kitchen. Mum and Dad were sitting in the same chairs, as if they'd been there all night but of course they hadn't.

Dad nodded at me.

'All right, Sal?'

There was nothing I could do to change their minds. I hadn't accepted the move was inevitable and replied sulkily, my earlier shame replaced by resentment.

'I suppose so.'

Dad was trying to jolly me along but Mum looked a bit wary.

'What are you doing today? Seeing Alice later?'

I suppose so.'

Mum put my breakfast on the table and I ate without speaking. I couldn't pretend nothing was wrong and as I got up to put my bowl and cup and saucer in the sink, I mumbled,

'Going to practise,' and, pushing my chair under the table, I made my escape to the front room. In front of the piano, I flexed my fingers and started to play; all the angriest and most dramatic pieces I could think of.

I hammered at the piano for an hour or more, trying to get rid of the knot in my chest. Still unresigned to the move, at least I was calmer and finally stopped to take a break.

A tap on the door interrupted my thoughts and David poked his head round the door.

'Is it safe to come in? That piano's had a good hiding this morning. I don't want to be the next in line.'

I flew across the room and into his arms and he hugged me tight. I was sobbing again.

'Come on, Sal. Don't take on so, it's not the end of the world. I'd have thought you'd be pleased.'

David had always been my hero and I thought he'd be on my side. I hadn't known he was coming home from university for the weekend. If anybody could make it right, he could. I still held fast to my childhood belief David could fix anything. I was to be bitterly disappointed.

He held me at arm's length and looked straight in my eyes.

'Let's go for a walk, talk things over.'

I nodded and he shouted down the hall,

'We're off to the park. Won't be long.'

I heard Dad shout 'okay' and knew they'd be hoping David would talk me round. Fat chance.

We walked to the park in silence and on through to the band stand and sat on the edge, swinging our legs. A gang of lads was kicking a ball around but I didn't know any of them, they were much too young. Watching them fool around, I felt quite grown up but then David started talking.

'What's it all about, Sal?' David asked in a quiet voice, his grey eyes focussed on my face. His expression was serious but sympathetic.

I poured out my troubles, about how I didn't want to move and all the reasons I'd concocted. It sounded a bit childish even to me.

'I'm surprised at you. Don't you realise how long it must have taken them to get the deposit together. You've never gone short of anything but Mum has scrimped and saved for years. It's important to them to own their own house after always renting. They both work hard and want to go up in the world. I can't see anything wrong with that.'

I hung my head and looked at my shoes.

'I never thought you'd be so selfish. You're well on the way to spoiling it for Mum and Dad. They'd both be miserable if they thought they'd made you unhappy.'

I was snivelling again now and fished around in my pocket with no success. As usual, David had a great big white hankie, ironed and folded into a square.

'Here,' he said, passing it over and grinning, 'give us a blow.'

I took the hankie, blew my nose and wiped my eyes and tried to smile. He'd made all my objections sound so petty. I'd been so busy being outraged, I hadn't even thought about how they must be feeling.

'You might as well make your mind up; this is going to happen. You can accept the inevitable with good grace or you can make everybody miserable, including yourself.'

David had always talked to me as an equal and I'd always listened. He was right, there was nothing I could do so I might as well make the best of it.

Dad was out when we got home but Mum was pathetically grateful when I started asking questions about the move. I felt bad all over again but David gave me a broad wink behind Mum's back and I could see he was pleased.

The following morning after breakfast, we all piled in Dad's car and drove up Hyde Road to have a look at the new place. There were twelve new semi-detached houses in a short, newly paved cul-de-sac, four on each side and two at the end.

'That one's ours,' said Mum as Dad pulled up outside. The front garden was just churned up mud but the house did look nice and we all crowded round peering through the front window.

'Come on round the back,' Dad said. 'You can have a look at the kitchen.'

The back garden looked even worse than the front, even muddier and there was some kind of cement mixer parked near the house.

Under David's watchful eye, I was trying to show some enthusiasm but it was hard going. Dad had disappeared and re-appeared a few minutes later, waving a key in the air.

'The site foreman just pulled up to check some of the work and he said we can have a look if we're quick and don't touch anything.'

We trekked back to the front and waited while Dad ceremoniously opened the front door, flinging it wide. I was mortified when he suddenly picked Mum up and carried her over the threshold, thanking my lucky stars there was no-one around. David thought it was a hoot and gave me an almighty dig in the ribs.

The empty house smelled of paint and had an odd feel to it. Our voices echoed and our footsteps on the bare floorboards made a terrible clatter. David and I trailed after Mum and Dad, first into the sitting room where she pointed out the settee would fit under the window. Then we had to ooh and aah at the fitted kitchen, which I grudgingly had to admit was a vast improvement on our current kitchen.

'Wait 'til you see upstairs,' she said and we wandered up behind her. The rooms were bigger than ours and the bathroom, with its sparkling new white suite and tiles, was clearly Mums pride and joy.

'Once the carpets are down and the curtains are up, it'll look as different again,' she said, looking at me as if for approval.

I did my best. "It's lovely, and so big. When's the move?"

'A week on Friday, we've given our notice at the old place and the van's booked.'

It was all happening so fast. They'd wanted to give me a lovely surprise and I tried to give them credit. It was a surprise all right, more of a shock really, I scarcely believed it was happening.

If only theyd given me more time, told me earlier or consulted me before they committed themselves. Would that have been worse? Would they still have bought the house even if I'd said I didn't want to move? Perhaps it was as well I'd never know.

David brought me down to earth with a nudge.

'It'll be great, won't it Sally?' and I had no alternative but to say yes.

Dad rubbed his hands together, looking relieved.

'Come on then, you lot. We'll have the beef overdone if we don't get a move on.'

Even the thought of a Sunday roast, my favourite meal of the week, and "Family Favourites" on the radio, wasn't much consolation.

As we drove away, I looked back at the house. It was just a shell. I couldn't see it ever feeling like home.

***

Although Hettie had never missed a chance to skim a bit from what Maurice gave her and she'd always been careful, pickings were now slimmer than ever. The times he came in straight from his floozy and full of whisky were fewer and further between. He often sat in front of the television until the white dot appeared and then went straight up to bed.

The roll of notes was still left temptingly in his trouser pocket when he got into bed but it was too risky to help herself, even to a couple of quid. She couldn't take the chance he'd wake and catch her or that he'd notice the shortage.

Her savings hadn't diminished but they weren't growing much either. She wracked her brains for some other way and came up empty handed. The answer fell into her lap from an unexpected quarter.

She never went to Flo's. There were always a couple of her kids underfoot. Heaven knows, she wasn't living in the lap of luxury but thanked her lucky stars she'd only had two. How Flo managed to keep food on the table and the place half decent with five kids and a shiftless husband, she'd never know.

On Saturday morning, Hettie was in the butcher's buying steak for tea when Flo came in for brisket and sausages. Hettie waited outside, watching the cars and buses pass until Flo had been served and they walked down to the greengrocer's together.

'Maurice'll be out tonight,' Hettie said. 'Fancy coming round for an hour, I've got a drop saved.'

'Lovely, mine's sure to be out too. About half eight?'

Hettie nodded.

'See you then.'

Hettie glanced at the clock and put down the paper she'd been reading. She didn't bother with the television much. She preferred the radio and a newspaper or a book. Occasionally, she watched "The Black and White Minstrels" or "I love Lucy" but the rest left her cold. Though she said nothing, she thought most of it was rubbish. Maurice watched indiscriminately, everything from "Gunsmoke" to "77 Sunset Strip" and even "Come Dancing". Despite his bad leg, he hadn't been a bad dancer in his youth but what he saw in those high falutin' couples prancing around in what amounted to fancy dress was beyond her.

A tap at the back door signalled Flo's arrival and she came in, pushing her headscarf into her coat pocket and smoothing her hair.

She was looking older these days, older and careworn. Two years younger than Hettie, she looked ten years older.

'Sit yourself down,' said Hettie, pouring whisky into the two glasses she'd already put on the table.

'There, get that inside you.'

Flo picked up the glass and took a sip, smiling at the warmth sliding down her throat.

Full throttle came the usual moan about him and the kids and Hettie countered with moans about Maurice and Johnnie, who was treating her increasingly as though she were invisible.

With the formalities out of the way, they settled down to the local gossip; who was in the family way, which wife was sporting a black eye, whose kids were in trouble with the law.

'Did I tell you about Maggie Evans that lives next door but one?' Flo asked.

'No, what about her?'

'She's in that much trouble, doesn't know which way to turn.'

'What's she been up to?'

Getting a story out of Flo was like pulling teeth, Hettie thought.

'She put her husband's suit in pawn a couple of months ago and thought she was safe because he never wears it. Now they've got a funeral to go to middle of next week and she hasn't got the cash to redeem it. He'll kill her, he doesn't hold with borrowing money and the interest has been mounting up, you know how much they charge.'

It was as though someone had switched a light on in Hettie's head.

'Don't tell her who's asking but find out how much she owes. I might be able to help her.'

Flo looked at Hettie open mouthed.

'What, you? Why would you want to?'

'Never you mind Find out and get round here and let me know.'

What?' said Flo again, looking more confused than ever.

'Just do it. Stop asking questions and do it.'

She picked up her glass and downed what was left and Flo did the same. Why on earth would Hettie want to help Maggie Evans?

She shrugged into her old brown coat.

'Right then, I'd better get a move on. See what the kids have been up to.'

She looked at Hettie again, who was sitting waiting.

'I'll find out,' she said fishing the scarf out of her coat pocket and tying it over her head, 'and I'll let you know.'

The following morning just before ten, Flo tapped on the kitchen door. The coast was clear, Maurice was still in bed.

There were no preliminaries, Hettie jumped straight in.

'How much?'

'She owes a tenner, pretty much a week's wages and she's desperate.'

'Listen carefully, Flo. This is important. I can trust you, can't I?'

Flo nodded solemnly.

'You've not to say a word to anybody, not anybody. Cross your heart?'

Hettie fell back on the old childhood promise and Flo nodded again, wetting her finger and drawing a cross over where she thought her heart was situated.

'This is the deal. I'll give you the ten quid to give her. She's to pay it back at ten bob a week for twenty five weeks and she's to pay it to you. Never, ever, tell her where you got it?'

'I won't, Hett, honest.'

'You can tell her as well, if she misses even one payment, her old fella will find out about it. That ought to keep her prompt.'

'That's blackmail, isn't it?' Flo looked unsure.

"It's not blackmail, it's insurance. I've got my investment to protect,' Hettie smiled.

'If you do this right, Flo, and it all works out, there'll be a couple of bob in it for you.'

Hettie pulled two five pound notes out of her apron pocket and passed them over. Flo, who was enjoying the intrigue, tucked them neatly into her purse,

'Better get off then, I'll pop round later on when her old fella's gone for his Sunday pint.'

'Don't forget. If she doesn't agree to the terms, you're to bring the cash back.'

'She'll agree all right and be glad to get herself out of bother.'

'Not a word to anyone,' Hettie stressed.

Flo stood at the kitchen door with her finger on her lips, then slipped out.

There was no sign of life from upstairs and Hettie put the kettle on for a cuppa. She'd thought it over and could see nothing wrong with her strategy. It would be a slow return on her money but far in excess of what she'd make if the cash were in the bank. Twenty five percent wasn't to be sniffed and she felt a twinge of guilt at the exorbitant rate. Never mind, she wasn't running a charity and the woman would be grateful as hell. Silly cow, shouldn't have borrowed money she couldn't pay back in the first place.

Hettie had always planned ahead. Yes, she was taking a chance with this first ten pounds but if it worked out, there were plenty of women in the same boat, women who needed cash quickly. At the point of borrowing, they were unlikely to work out the interest rate and how much the loan would cost them, they couldn't see so far ahead. She'd have to be selective about who she lent money to and make sure there was some kind of leverage before she parted with anything.

She hoped she could trust Flo to keep her mouth shut.

Maurice had no idea what Hettie was up to. He had no idea she could even lay her hands on two five pound notes.

He was in the front room, balancing a cup of tea on his paunch. This place looks all right, he thought, glancing at the new television, which had pride of place. He settled himself further into the comfortable armchair. For the first time, he had some real comfort in his own home. In the end, he'd decided to go the whole hog and after the decorating and hanging the new curtains, he'd even sprung for a carpet.

Hettie had the extra job of lighting a fire when the evenings were cool but that's what she was there for, to look after him. He'd been surprised when new curtains appeared in the kitchen and even more surprised to find her up a ladder walloping the left-over paint on the kitchen walls. As she hadn't asked for more money, he didn't much care.

The business was running much as usual. Hettie got her housekeeping money, Johnnie got an extra couple of quid on Saturdays and odd bottles of Scotch regularly fell off a lorry and landed in his kitchen.

He knew his performance in the bedroom wasn't what it had been but brushed the thought aside. Doris wasn't complaining and wouldn't as long as he treated her right. The extra fiver here and there worked wonders.

He'd fleetingly considered moving in with her but dismissed the thought immediately. Apart from the bedroom and the restaurant, she didn't know what he liked. Hettie was an expert, food on the table on time, shirts ironed the way he liked, trousers pressed and jacket brushed and she didn't argue.

He reflected how things had changed since the end of the war. In those days, bets had been small and he'd needed to take lots of them. Money was now more plentiful and a lot of it came his way. The working man was still betting but now the bets were higher.

He turned his thoughts to his youngest son. Harry had disappeared off his radar.

Johnnie was smart, there was no doubt about it and although only eighteen, there was a good head on his shoulders. Maurice smiled wryly, remembering their first real dust up. Johnnie had reached the end of his fifth year and as far as Maurice was concerned, his education was complete and he could come and work in the business. Johnnie had had different ideas.

They were sitting face to face at the kitchen table and Hettie was clearing up. She could tell there was going to be trouble.

'Look, Dad, it's not that I don't want to work for you, but not yet. I've still got a lot to learn.'

'I'll teach you what you need to know,' Maurice had huffed.

'That's just it. I know nobody could run this like you do.'

Maurice was not immune to flattery.

'But there are going to be changes. Sooner or later betting will be legalised and we need to be ready. We'll need capital and there'll be all sorts of rules and regulations. You'll need proper accounts and someone who knows how to find the loopholes.'

Maurice was surprised Johnnie had given the situation so much thought but was reluctant to give him his head. He'd be boss in his own house if it killed him.

'So, what are you saying?'

'I want to train as an accountant, get properly qualified, specialise in business accountancy. It'll take five years.'

'Five years?' Maurice spluttered. 'Go as a clerk in some poxy office, earning peanuts for five years? You've got to be crazy. Besides, I need you here and you'll do as I say.'

Johnnie knew if he didn't get this right, it would be the end of his plans. He couldn't stand up against his dad. Maurice held the purse strings.

'It's not so bad, Dad. I'll be around at the weekend to help and I'll be learning all the time. When off-course gambling becomes legal, a lot of people will go under and I guarantee some of those blokes you drink with on a Sunday will be amongst them. They won't be able to move with the times, they won't know how. You can be a step ahead and be ready.'

Hettie, leaning against the sink, had watched the exchange, turning her head from one to the other as though she were watching a tennis match. Would Maurice capitulate or would Johnnie have to do as he was told?

Maurice remained silent for a minute or two and finally nodded.

'I'll think about it. I make no promises but I'll think about it.'

He could see the sense in what Johnnie was saying but he was heartily sick of all the speculation. There were constant rumbles about legalisation but nothing ever happened.

Johnnie knew he could push no further.

'Fair enough. You'll let me know when you've thought it over. I know I need to know the business inside out but I learn fast and I'll be here every weekend.'

'All right, all right, I said I'd think about it,' snapped Maurice.

Johnnie pushed himself away from the table and with an imploring look at his mother, went upstairs to get ready. Hettie was still leaning against the sink, a frown of concentration on her face.

Johnnie was anxious. He felt as he had when he passed his eleven plus. Mum had saved his bacon then. Could she, and would she, do it again?

He'd given it his best shot. It was in Maurice's hands now.

Downstairs in the kitchen, Hettie had cleared up and poured Maurice another cup of tea. She could see he was mulling things over.

'That lad will be the death of me,' he said. 'Talk about big ideas.'

Hettie smiled.

'You know where he gets that from. He's a chip off the old block.'

If she could do anything to push Maurice in the right direction, she would.

'It might be worth it. If and when it all goes legal, there'll be paperwork and regulations and checks. Do you want to tackle all of it when Johnnie could do it with his eyes closed?'

'Pearls of wisdom from you, that's all I need, he said dismissively. 'It might never happen and then Johnnie'll be working for peanuts and not much good to me except at weekends.'

Although still resisting the thought of the changes to come, he was reluctantly coming round to Johnnie's point of view. It couldn't hurt to take precautions and if nothing happened in the next couple of years, Johnnie could always leave the job and come and work for him.

Maurice leaned forward and put his elbows on the table. His face was red and he looked tired. He was obviously weighing up the pros and cons and Hettie thought he was weakening. She pushed her hair back behind her ears and pulled her apron straight, without looking directly at Maurice.

'And besides, if he does the five years accountancy, he'll get deferred from National Service. He won't have to go until he's twenty one and the call up will be finished by then.'

'True enough but I could probably get him out of it anyway.'

'What do you mean?' Hettie spoke quietly, 'Get him out of it.'

'There's ways and means if you've got enough cash and the right contacts.'

Maurice didn't notice Hettie had gone deathly pale. She clasped her hands and asked,

'Do you mean to say you could have got our Harry off but didn't bother?'

'Why should I? He was never going to be any use to me with his head full of motors and engines. He never wanted to work for me. I had enough trouble getting him to do the look out on a Saturday.'

Hettie turned back towards the kitchen sink and picked up the tea towel. She needed to hide her face before Maurice saw the raw anger there.

'Johnnie's a different kettle of fish,' he said. 'He'll need watching but he's a clever lad and what's more, he wants to work with me as much as I want him. Together, we can go far.'

Too furious to speak, Hettie picked her coat off the hook on the back of the kitchen door and struggled into it.

'I'm nipping to the corner shop,' she managed to mutter, picking up her purse off the kitchen table and bolting.

Maurice scarcely looked up. What's up with her, he thought?

Hettie's eyes filled with tears of fury and frustration. She'd always known Maurice was as hard as nails but this was the absolute limit.

The thought Harry needn't have gone in the forces was like a red rag to a bull. If Maurice had done his stuff, he'd still be here at home, more use to her than Maurice and Johnnie put together.

Still, she thought, he's better off where he is. He's made a new life for himself. Maurice is right, he'd never have gone into the business and there'd have been constant strife. But I miss him.

As for Johnnie, She'd done what she could. Typical Johnnie, she thought bitterly.

Anger bubbling to the surface again and unable to go home in case she blew up, she walked and walked, scarcely noticing where her feet were taking her. Maurice wouldn't miss her for an hour or so. He'd be in the front room by now, sleeping the sleep of the just.

Little did Maurice know he'd strengthened Hettie's resolve. He'd get his come-uppance but not yet. She could wait. All the rest; the slaps, the floozy, the constant demands, paled into insignificance compared to this.

Calmer now, she turned towards home. Maurice had landed a body blow without even knowing, but he'd pay.

***

Sally

While other kids were playing kissing games in the park, at fourteen, Alice and I were doing our homework and going for walks. When I was practising, Alice was usually busy with her sketch pad.

At sixteen, the others were starting work and pairing up. We could have come from a different species, especially the girls. Many of them wore overalls for work but at weekend, tight skirts, high heels, cheap jewellery and heavy make-up were the norm. To us, they looked like parodies of grown women.

Our clothes were simpler; flared skirts and jumpers and we still wore uniforms to school. They thought we were weird and we, in a patronising teenage way, looked down our noses at them.

While most of them were working eight hour days, we were still going to school and coming home with piles of homework. I practised daily and Alice often worked on art assignments. They had money to spend from their wages and all we had was pocket money but we still thought we were better than them.

We often took the bus into town at the weekend. A stroll down Market Street followed by a tour of the more expensive shops in St Ann's Square. We ventured into Kendal Milne, the most expensive department store in town. The smell of cosmetics and perfume as we came through the doors was the smell of luxury itself. We took the moving staircase from floor to floor looking at everything, clothes to shoes and even the furniture. The evening dresses in the ladies department took our breath away. The prices were breathtaking too. Although I was familiar with the other department stores, especially the one my mother worked in, this was a world apart.

Both customers and staff were more expensively dressed and though we couldn't afford to buy anything, we loved the quality and class of what was on show. Half-jokingly, we promised each other one day we'd be shopping there ourselves.

There were other treats too and we were happy to share each other's interests.

'The Halle's at the Free Trade Hall on Friday. Shall we go?' I'd ask and Alice was almost as keen as me.

We'd go down early and stand in a queue for the cheapest seats. The bustle of the entrance hall with people milling around looking for the doorways which would lead to their seats was heady in itself. We'd sit in the gods, so high the musicians looked like miniatures on the stage.

I loved the contrasts; complete silence from the audience during a performance while music filled the hall and then, after silence fell, the uproar of applause and sometimes whistles and cheers.

When one of these outings was planned, my dad would roll his eyes and look at Mum but put his hand in his pocket and slip me the price of a ticket.

Although I knew Alice's father didn't altogether approve of me, the concerts were highbrow pursuits suitable for his daughter and he too would pass over extra cash. Putting up with me in his daughter's company was the price he had to pay, especially as my dad insisted on driving into town to pick us up so we wouldn't have to brave the late night bus.

Alice kept an eye open for special events at the art galleries and when something she fancied turned up, we'd make an outing of it on a Saturday afternoon.

Walking through the doors and into the gallery, we left the noise of the streets behind and entered an oasis of calm. People spoke in quietly as they stood before one masterpiece or another.

Alice was surprisingly knowledgeable and we'd stand in front of a picture while she explained the finer points in a low whisper.

I loved all the traditional art, a picture that was a picture of something, but despite Alice's enthusiasm, I couldn't make head or tail of some of the modern stuff she loved so much.

Dressed in our best, we'd spin out the treat and walk back up Mosley Street and down Market Street and into the Kardomah for a coffee. We drank coffee occasionally at home but it was nothing like this. As I pushed open the door, I'd wait for the smell of the coffee being ground behind the counter to envelop me and it never disappointed. I'd stand still and breathe deep. Next to the smell of a roast dinner, this was the best smell in the world.

Older ladies and couples gathered on the ground floor but we headed down the stairs to the basement where the city's young and smart gathered on Saturday afternoons. We'd try for a table in a corner or against the wall and sit with our coffee, looking them over.

A couple of years older than us, these young people were fashionably dressed and, to our inexperienced eyes, were the height of sophistication. Of course we looked at the boys, some of them very smart, but we'd have been terrified if any of them had approached us.

To my disgust, I spotted Johnnie Marshall as part of a crowd one Saturday afternoon, laughing and joking with his friends. Alice saw him too and nudged me.

'Look who's there.'

'I've seen him,' I snapped.

'You've got to admit, he looks good. Is it the same girl?'

When I looked again, I grudgingly had to admit he did look smart and the girl looked good too.

'Yes, it's the same girl. She must be something special to have lasted this long.'

As though she'd felt our eyes on her, she looked across at us. She looked puzzled, as though she couldn't place us and, putting her hand on Johnnie's arm, she whispered in his ear.

I couldn't hear what he said but he'd obviously dismissed us as nobodies.

Nevertheless, I caught him looking at Alice a couple of times even while he had his arm round the girl next to him. As we left, Alice smiled at him and I could see his eyes following her.

***

When Johnnie was charming, he was charming beyond his years, opening doors and holding her chair but he could change in an instant and be cold and distant.

Naturally, it was his appearance that had attracted Sandra. His clear blue eyes and well-groomed hair already put him a cut above most of the lads she knew. His clothes were smart and well cared for and he carried himself with an air of confidence which made him appear more mature.

It didn't hurt either, that he always had cash in his pocket and took her to places she'd never been before.

At the weekend, he liked to go to one of the city centre hotels and mix with an older, more affluent crowd. Drinks were served from trays by smart waiters in the lounge bar and the atmosphere was far removed from the local pubs they used during the week.

Sometimes, they went on to a night club, situated down a flight of stairs, where they put their coats in the cloakroom before finding a table in the dimly lit cellar. Drinks were more expensive but Johnnie never flinched. They danced on the miniscule dance floor to the three piece band, listened to the singer, a local celebrity, and watched whichever cabaret act was appearing. The club was open late and it was often after one when he put her in a taxi and paid the fare up front. Her friends were green with envy at the sophisticated life she was leading and the handsome, worldly wise boyfriend.

They'd been seeing each other almost a year and got along pretty well, provided Sandra toed the line. It was implicit they go out together on Saturday night and again on Tuesday or Wednesday. Implicit too, was Sandra shouldn't go out with other young men or even go dancing with her girlfriends. She went to the cinema occasionally with her mum or her friend from school but anything else was frowned on. What Johnnie did on the other evenings, she had no idea.

By the time she realised how thoroughly in charge Johnnie had become it was too late, she was hooked; not only on the trappings he provided but on Johnnie himself and was anxious and eager for his approval.

If she looked good, he was generous with his compliments but if he looked disapprovingly at what she was wearing, the outfit was either pushed to the back of her wardrobe or unloaded on to a friend. Over a period of time, she was dressing solely to please Johnnie.

Their physical relationship was another area where Johnnie ruled. She'd been relatively inexperienced at eighteen when they met and had never progressed further than snogging. It had been easy to stay in control of her former boyfriends. She enjoyed the kissing and the cuddling but it never roused her and she was able to push them away if it got too hectic. Johnnie was a different matter.

A sexual animal, Johnnie knew exactly what he was doing. Kissing wasn't a means to an end, it was an end in itself and he was good at it. On the back row of the cinema, Sandra found her breathing deepening and new sensations creeping through her. For the first time, she wanted more and when he finally put his hand on her breast, she gasped in pleasure and felt Johnnie smile through the kiss.

He was tired of quick fumbles or an odd hour in someone's house when their parents were out. The thought of sex with the same girl over a period of time was appealing.

Many girls would have jumped at the chance but Sandra fitted the bill. She looked good, dressed well and had something to say for herself without being pushy. He didn't want to frighten her off and softened her up slowly, prepared to wait. An odd one nighter would tide him over and she'd never know.

One summer evening, they'd taken the bus out to Daisy Nook, a local beauty spot, and although the weather was fine, he had a light mac over his shoulder. They passed a couple of kids climbing trees and walked until they found a secluded spot away the footpath. He spread his coat on the gentle slope and gestured to her to sit down. Dropping down next to her, he put his arm around her shoulders.

She turned to look at him and he kissed her, slowly and skilfully, and gently lowered her to the ground. Her arms tightened around him as she kissed him back and he stroked her shoulder and slid his other arm beneath her, pulling her to him. He lowered his face to her neck and breathed on her, delivering swift kisses up her neck and around her ear. She was practically squirming with desire as she gripped him tighter. This was his moment and it was quite calculated.

He pulled away and sat up quickly, dropping his head in his hands. She lay for a minute, with the palm of her hand against his back and tried to breathe normally. She whispered,

'What is it? What's the matter?'

'I can't do this any longer, it's driving me crazy. This so far and no further and I go home tied up in knots. You can't tell me you don't feel it too.'

Her hand trembled against his back. She was sniffling and rummaging for a handkerchief.

Her voice, when it came, was shaky too.

'I know, Johnnie. I do feel it and I do want to. When you hold me and kiss me I want it to go on but I'm scared, I'm really scared.'

'What are you scared of? It's the most natural thing in the world.'

'I'm scared my mum and dad will find out. I'm scared somebody else will find out and look down their nose at me. You know what they say about girls who go all the way. Most of all, I'm scared of getting pregnant. It would break my dad's heart.'

He finally turned and put a hand on her shoulder. She couldn't look at him and kept her eyes down, looking at the hankie twisting in her hands.

He put his hand under her chin and lifted her head.

'Listen to me. We'll be careful, no-one will find out, not your mum and dad, not the lads, no-one. I won't tell anybody.'

She blinked, still tearful but now she couldn't take her eyes off his face.

He spoke again, slowly and deliberately.

'I won't get you pregnant. That's a promise. *I will not get you pregnant.*'

'Come here,' he said gently, pulling her into his arms. 'Don't worry, it will be all right, sssh now,' and he rocked her gently and soothingly.

She gripped him tightly. She'd acquiesced without even realising. No longer if, it was now a question of where and when.

Johnnie held her against him, gazing over her head and planning ahead.

1960

Mau Mau Uprising - state of emergency lifted in Kenya

First traffic wardens

Last man enters National Service as conscription ends

Manchester City Football Club sign 20 year old Denis Law for £55,000

First Episode of Coronation Street

Published:	'For Your Eyes Only' – Ian Fleming "Lady Chatterley's Lover" - D H Lawrence (sold 200,000 copies in one day)
Best Film Oscar:	'The Apartment' - Jack Lemon and Shirley MacLaine
In the Hit Parade:	'My Old Man's a Dustman' – Lonnie Donegan
Born in 1960:	Linford Christie, athlete Jeremy Clarkson, TV personality Kenneth Branagh, actor

Chapter 11

Life had changed for Brenda. Two years earlier, she'd screwed up her courage and gone back to the shop where she bought her wool. A regular customer for years, Brenda knew Mary Jones, the owner, quite well and been surprised at the warm reception.

"'Course you can have the job. You'd be ideal, nobody round here knows their way round a knitting pattern like you. When can you start?'

Brenda flushed with pleasure, it was the first compliment she'd had for years.

'"Come into the back and we'll put the kettle on and sort the details out.'

Bustling around the kitchen, warming the pot and making tea, she sat Brenda in one of the armchairs in front of the fire. As she settled down, Brenda looked around the crowded kitchen. A drop leaf table stood against the back wall, piled with boxes and cellophane wrapped packets of wool, obviously overspill from the shop. Mary sat down heavily in the other armchair and looked speculatively at Brenda, wondering aloud that Jack would let her take the job at all. He was not known for his liberal views.

Brenda flushed and then stammered,

'He doesn't know – and he doesn't need to know. I mean, who's going to tell him what's going on in a wool shop?'

Mary Jones gurgled with laughter, shaking so much she almost spilled her tea.

'Good for you. I'll keep it under my hat.'

Since then, she'd been in the shop on Tuesdays and Fridays from two o'clock until five. On Wednesdays, Mary often went to the wholesaler or into town to meet her sister and Brenda worked from ten until four.

The day to day running of the shop was easier than she'd imagined. She could add up quickly and give the right change almost without thinking. After a couple of weeks, she started to make a note of which items were running low so Mary could re-order without checking through the stock.

The job couldn't have suited Brenda better. There was plenty of time to keep the household running and she shopped on her way to and from work. Between customers, she sat in the shop and knitted. A few of her sample pieces had been placed in the window and Mary had paid her in cash for the extra work when the jumpers were sold.

The downtrodden drudge was disappearing. On Jack's instructions, Alice had always been beautifully dressed. Brenda had come a poor second.

The transformation had started one spring morning. She'd put the finishing touches to a dress made as a surprise for Alice's birthday. They were much the same size and, wanting to check the hem, she'd tried it on in front of the mirror on her wardrobe door. It looked fine, Alice would love it.

She stepped back and squinted at the mirror and, for the first time, saw the whole picture and not just the dress.

Is that me? I look different. It must be the colour.

A bit shaken, she took off the dress and noticed the contrast against the grey of her own clothes. A seed had been sown.

The following morning, she was leafing through the patterns in the shop, stopping at an intricate pattern knitted in cream.

'That's nice,' said Mary, coming up behind her, 'For Alice is it?'

'I might do it for myself. Not too young is it?'

'Get away with you. Not brown or grey again, surely?'

'I fancy a bit of a change.'

Mary ran her hand along the shelves, passing through the colours, pausing at a deep pink and then stopping at a lovely, clear cornflower blue.

'This would be perfect for you.'

Unsure about this radical change, Brenda took the wool off the shelf. Mary nodded her approval.

I can always give it to Alice if I don't like it, she thought, looking at the pattern and picking up her needles.

When she wore the jumper for the first time, Alice had beamed with pleasure.
'It looks lovely, Mum. You look like a different woman.'
Brenda glowed with pleasure.
Jack didn't notice.

***

Since Sally had moved away, Alice had been at a bit of a loose end. They saw each other at school and often in the holidays but it wasn't the same. Changes were coming thick and fast and in September, Alice would start at art school and Sally would be going to study music. They would see even less of each other.

By the time she was eighteen, Alice was sketching ideas for clothes and cutting her own patterns. She looked in expensive shops and tried on clothes she could never afford. Under cover of the changing rooms, she turned the garments inside out to see how they were put together.

She had a good eye and knew what suited her; pale colours and classic styles set off her straight blonde hair and fair complexion. Sally's mother, Eva, had always dressed well and as a child, Alice had been in awe of this smart, elegant woman. She wasn't exactly ashamed of her own dowdy mother but had sometimes guiltily wished she looked a bit more like Mrs Steadman.

These last two years had been a substitute for the years Brenda had missed. Married at nineteen and constantly kept in her place, she'd never had chance to blossom. The plain teenager had matured into a good looking woman and although Jack may have been vaguely aware she looked a bit different, he only saw Alice.

Any confidence she'd had as the younger sister of two doting brothers had been leached away by Jack's indifference and intolerance.

She now took pleasure in her improved appearance, walked taller and dressed with care, particularly on workdays. The customers liked her and asked her advice and Mary never bought new stock without consulting her

***

Sally

I finally bowed to the inevitable and made the best of the move. Though I had to admit, albeit grudgingly, the house was better than expected now it was furnished, it didn't feel like home. I didn't know the neighbours and didn't want to. The roads were unfamiliar and I never bumped into a single soul I knew. I was surrounded by strangers.

Mum and Dad had changed too. The cool, calm mother I'd always known was now constantly fussing; tweaking curtains and cushions and re-arranging furniture. Before the move, we'd gone to the market or into town and looked at shoes and dress fabric. Now Mum only wanted to look at lamp shades and ornaments and wander through the furniture department. The whole palaver was yawningly boring. When Mum asked me what I thought, I had to stifle the urge to mutter "who cares?"

As for Dad, he was a different man. It had always been a family joke he was so ham fisted Mum changed the fuses or tightened the screws on the kitchen cupboards. Anything more demanding had involved one of Mum's brothers coming round. He'd now developed a passion for gardening and had spent a fortune on spades and forks. If he were late home from work, it was because he'd stopped somewhere to look at plants.

The old, easy camaraderie of the household had disappeared. Instead of a game of cards or a chat about the day over a cup of tea, Dad was engrossed in gardening books or standing at the back door surveying his empire while Mum leafed endlessly through housekeeping magazines or fiddled with shade cards for paint or curtain samples.

The new, streamlined kitchen held no attraction for me. It was cold and clinical compared to the shabby comfort of the old place. I spent more and more time in my bedroom, the only room in the house I liked, packed with my stuff from the old house. My piano was in the front room, which was now called the lounge, and I played daily for an hour or more at a time.

Once, I heard Mum's voice from the kitchen,

'She's still playing all that fiery stuff. We never hear anything soothing these days.'

'Don't worry, love,' I heard Dad whisper, 'She'll come round.'

If I hear that sentence one more time, I'll scream, I thought.

The rest of the holidays stretched before me like a wilderness. It was easy enough to get down to see Alice but nothing was the same. We'd always been able to sit in our kitchen and natter but our kitchen was now a bus ride away in Denton.

I felt like a bird, fluttering from perch to perch between Alice, Miss Pritchard and my Gran but knowing my permanent roost was further away than any of them.

One Friday night not long after the move, we went to the cinema as usual. All the usual crowd were there, people we'd gone to school with and old neighbours but they just nodded or said hello, unaware how much my life had changed. Only Mickey Smith, came over to ask how I was doing. As far as I knew, I was the only person he ever approached. He spoke if people spoke to him but generally kept his head down. He sneaked a glance at Alice, almost adoringly, and when she smiled at him, he blushed to the roots of his ginger hair.

I could tell Alice couldn't make out why I was so grumpy.

'What's up Sal? You don't look too happy,' she said gently.

'I don't know. It's only been a couple of weeks but I can't settle. Everything's different, even Mum and Dad don't seem the same. I suppose I'll get used to it.'

'It'll be all right. You'll soon find your feet,' and she rubbed her hand along my arm to comfort me. 'I can't understand why you're not over the moon, I'd love to live up there.'

Walking back from the cinema, we passed one of the local pubs as the door swung open and Johnnie Marshall emerged with his girlfriend, laughing his head off. He stopped short.

'Hello Alice,' he said. 'All right?'

I was invisible, as usual.

Alice flushed and nodded. 'Fine, you?'

'Yeah, see you,' and he turned down the street pulling his girlfriend with him.

'Who's that? Who *is* that girl,' we heard her say and his response,

'Oh, someone I went to school with. Come on Sandra, the Crown will be calling last orders if we don't get a move on.'

If anything could have made a bad mood worse, it was the sight of Johnnie Marshall and Alice. She'd had a soft spot for him ever since he saved us from the bully on the bus.

'Never mind him,' she said. 'What time shall I meet you?'

I was going to stay the night at my Gran's and Alice was coming home with me the following morning to see the new house.

'I'll meet you at the bus stop at ten, all right?'

'Sure, I'll be there. I wish I could come and spend the night but my Dad would never allow it.'

'We don't always get what we want,' I quipped and laughed properly for the first time all night.

I turned the key and pushed open the front door.

'It's only me,' I called.

This was more like home than the place in Denton; the familiar striped curtains and cushions in the front room, the polished furniture and the scent of lavender polish.

I'd had a key to my Gran's house since I was ten when I wore it on a string round my neck. Now though, I had the key so Gran wouldn't have to get up to answer the door. One thing the move had brought home to me was Gran wasn't getting any younger. When I saw her every day, I hadn't noticed she was slowing down.

'Hello, love. Enjoy the film?' she asked, smiling.

'I've seen worse.'

'Well that's something. Put the kettle on. Let's have a cuppa before we go to bed.'

The cups and saucers were already on the table and it only took a minute for the water to come to the boil. I poured the tea and handed a cup to Gran and watched her settle it on her ample stomach as she sat in her old rocking chair. I'd sat on her knee and been rocked in that chair many times when I was little. She opened fire.

'Your Mum's worried about you. She was down here the other day, fretting about how unsettled you are.' She waited.

What could I say? Gran was as concerned about Mum as she was about me, she hated to see her eldest daughter unhappy.

'Oh, it's nothing Gran. Just so many changes all at once; leaving school, moving house and all the trailing up and down on the bus. I'm not really worried about starting a college in September but that'll be all new too. This time I'll be on my own, there'll be no Alice to prop me up.'

This *was* a genuine concern but as usual, Gran could see through the waffle.

'Your nose has been put out of joint. You've always been the centre of attention, specially since David left home, and now your Mum and Dad are concerned with other things. They didn't just move for their own sake, you know. They wanted to give you a better start, a nicer place to live.

I can't say I'm happy not to have them living round the corner but I'm glad they've got what they want. They've worked hard for that house and I'd never do anything to make them regret it. I'll have to make the best of it.'

The implication was, of course, I should make the best of it too. My face was hot with shame. Gran was right.

She held out her cup and saucer for me to take and as she heaved herself to her feet, I knew she'd say no more. The subject was closed.

'You go on up, Gran. I'll rinse these cups.'

She held out her cheek for a kiss and I gave her a quick hug. I loved her dearly and knew she loved me too. As she climbed the stairs, I was concerned to see how long it took her to get to the top.

Lying in bed later, I turned things over in my mind. That was the nearest to a telling off I'd ever had from Gran. Although I reluctantly admitted she had a point, it still seemed everybody was getting at me. First David, then Alice and now my staunchest ally was having a dig. The fact they were right made me feel guilty but there was also underlying resentment. Nobody likes to have their faults pointed out to them. Why couldn't they leave me alone?

***

Hettie's little side line had taken off and for two years she'd been making regular loans to the women of the neighbourhood. There was great speculation about who was financing the loans. Everybody knew Flo was the go-between and some suspected Maurice was behind it. He was the only one around with plenty of money. Nobody suspected shabby, downtrodden Hettie.

Flo was happy enough, she got her cut for very little effort and up to now, all loans and interest had been paid on time. She had never told anyone where the money came from, despite constant quizzing.

Caution was Hettie's watchword and she now had a hundred pounds out in loans. That was her absolute limit, with a maximum of twenty pounds to any one person. Once the limit was reached, Flo got the word no more cash would be forthcoming. Lending would only recommence when the oldest loan had been repaid in full.

The first time this had happened, Flo had arrived in Hettie's kitchen with a desperate plea from one of her neighbours.

Hettie showed her exasperation.

'I told you. No more loans. I'll let you know when you can start again.'

'But she's at her wits end. I said I'd see what I could do,' she said ingratiatingly.

Hettie gave Flo a straight look.
'No more loans! You can't do anything unless you want to lend her the money yourself.'
Flo blanched.
'I can't do that. Where would I get that kind of money?'
'Exactly, the answer's no.'
'You're as hard as nails, our Het. I never thought I'd see the day.'
"It seems to have slipped your mind I'm the one taking the risks. I decide the rules, I decide the limit and I decide who I lend to. This isn't a charity and I'm not a soft touch. Have you got that?'
Flustered now at Hettie's tone, Flo nodded.
'Yes, I've got it. I won't do it again,' she mumbled without looking Hettie in the eye, fiddling with the buttons on her cardigan.

Hettie had always been the dominant sister and Flo had followed where she led. The first time she'd tried to act on her own initiative it had blown up in her face. She would play safe from now on.

The first hundred pounds was kept in circulation and the interest was scooped off and paid into the bank, minus Flo's small cut. Her commission was only paid on the completed repayment of every loan.

It'll keep her keen, Hettie thought. She'll chase the payments if she gets nothing until it's paid up. She's always needed a firm hand.

With her bank balance growing steadily, Hettie felt much safer. Life had changed again. Johnnie was hardly around, coming home only to eat and change his clothes and he often didn't come home at all on Saturday nights. At twenty, she could hardly scold him and as Maurice either didn't care or didn't notice, she kept her peace.

Like father, like son, she thought, in more ways than one.

On the other hand, Maurice was under her feet more and more. Sunday evenings were still spent in town and she supposed his floozy went with him. He still went in the local on Saturday after the racing but during the week, he was at home on his new settee in front of his television more often than not.

When Johnnie stayed in, which wasn't often, he sat in the front room with his father and watched the television. He knew which side his bread was buttered.

Letters from Harry arrived on a regular basis and Hettie carried them around in her apron pocket, taking them out constantly and re-reading them.

She'd read the last one so many times she thought she might wear the ink right off the page. Thrilled with the news, she'd kept it to herself for a couple of weeks, knowing Maurice and Johnnie would have something sarcastic to say. She'd have to tell them eventually but she'd bide her time.

She confided in Flo and on Saturday night, when Maurice was in the pub and they'd tallied up the books, Hettie poured Flo a measure of scotch and said,

'Get that down you, this is a celebration,' and she raised her glass.

'Oh, what we celebrating then, won the pools, have you?'

'No, our Harry's getting married. Had a letter on Monday and the wedding's in October. She sounds like a lovely girl and Harry's doing well. He works in her dad's garage.'

'Fancy, what does Maurice say?' Flo leaned forward, eyes bright and eager.

'I haven't told him yet. I doubt he'll be interested. He only cares about Johnnie and that's only 'cause he's looking to him to be doing the donkey work at some time in the future.'

'What about the wedding, where's it to be?'

'Down there, in Sussex. She wants to get married in her local church where she was christened and I can't blame her. There's nothing up here for them, is there?'

She fished the envelope out of her pocket and pulled out a photo.

'Look there, doesn't Harry look well and isn't she a bonnie girl. Can you imagine a girl like that up here in these miserable streets? This is the cottage where they're going to live. It's even got roses round the door, like in the songs.'

'They make a lovely couple. Will you be able to go? You'll have to tell Maurice sooner rather than later. You can't just spring it on him.'

"I'm going and that's the end of it. I don't know what he'll say. I'll have to play it by ear, as usual. Course, this means our Harry won't ever come home," she said wistfully. "I can't say I blame him but I do miss him. He's the only one who made all this worthwhile,' she said, waving her arm around the kitchen.

In truth, she didn't just mean the house; she meant the life she lived in subservience to Maurice and now to Johnnie.

"I can't wait to hear what Maurice says.'

***

Jack was in decline. All traces of the self-confident, bossy head of department had gone. His appetite had dwindled and he now rarely called at the pub on his way home. He was losing weight and his face was pale and drawn.

Alice, now eighteen, would be leaving school at the end of term. He watched his daughter with saddened eyes. She would soon be stepping into the wide world. He was eaten up with anxiety. How would she cope with this new and very different life? Her relatively safe environment would be exchanged for one filled with predatory males.

Brenda, who'd always been self-effacing and rarely spoke unless spoken to, had started to nag.

'It's not right, Jack. You're not eating enough to keep a bird alive. Why don't you go to the doctor's?'

He'd brushed aside her concern. It was head in the sand time. If he didn't acknowledge the problem, it didn't exist.

In the evening, he sat in his armchair, scarcely moving. His eyes moved only when his daughter was in the room and he watched her constantly, rising with difficulty to stand at the window when she left the house and watch her walk away.

Like most homes in the street, there was a television in the corner of the front room. Brenda watched everything, invariably knitting some fancy garment or other. Jack stared at the screen but little caught his attention. He was oblivious to the content of the programmes, didn't laugh at the comedies or show any interest in the news. Often in bed by ten, he lay on his back, listening to the indistinct sounds from the television downstairs and watching the light from the street lamps play across the curtains.

Between his concern for Alice and the increasing stomach pain, he was unable to focus on anything else. He was drifting through life like a ghost.

Things finally came to a head one Friday afternoon. He left the office early.

'Not feeling too good,' he said to his clerk. 'I'm going home.'

'You don't look well. Perhaps you should see a doctor.'

He gave her a withering look but made no comment, just turned and left the office.

'Please yourself,' she muttered under her breath and carried on putting letters into envelopes. The slight concern she had felt at his obvious discomfort dismissed by his rudeness.

The walk to the bus stop was endless; he was almost shuffling now and sweat was breaking out under his shirt and on his forehead. He leaned heavily against a wall and then struggled to move when the bus turned the corner and pulled up.

The conductor, watching as he grasped the rail to drag himself onto the bus, reached out and pulled him on.

'You all right, mate? You look a bit dodgy.'

Jack couldn't respond but hauled himself into the nearest seat. He could think of nothing except his need to get home, to get off this bus and get to his bed. The journey was familiar and the bus was nearing his stop as he tried to stand. Vision blurred, his legs buckled and he was lying between the seats, staring up at the ceiling.

Fading in and out of consciousness, he could hear the panic in the conductor's voice, the repeated ringing of the bell to alert the driver and a voice saying,

"There's a phone box over there, somebody call an ambulance.'

Then there was only darkness and silence.

Brenda was behind the counter in the wool shop serving a customer when the ambulance, lights flashing and siren wailing, passed the window. Her customer went to the door and popped her head out.

'It's stopped up the street behind a bus. Someone must have been taken ill.'

Brenda followed her to the door and they stood watching the small crowd milling around the bus, the conductor and driver standing on the pavement, looking worried. It was hard to see what was happening until two ambulance men carrying a stretcher bearing a prone figure manoeuvred their way off the bus. The crowd surged closer, trying to see the man on the stretcher.

The driver stepped forward and his voice drifted down the street,

'Stand back there, give him some air. Let them do their job. Come on now, stand back.'

With the stretcher loaded, the ambulance men climbed back into the vehicle and drove off, light flashing.

Drama over, the crowd dispersed. The passengers got back on the bus with the conductor behind them and the driver climbed into his cab and drove away. Now there was nothing to see, the rest of the crowd went about their business.

Back in the shop, Brenda wrapped up the wool she'd sold and took the money.

'Poor soul, I wonder what was the matter with him.'

'Pity his poor family, they'll wonder what's happened to him,' the customer replied. 'Must get on, they'll be home for their tea in an hour. See you.'

The 'poor soul' in the ambulance had already been dismissed; a few minutes' excitement in an otherwise humdrum day.

Mary Jones lived on the premises and was currently in the kitchen behind the shop.

'I'm off now,' Brenda called. 'See you on Tuesday.'

Wiping her hands on a tea towel, Mary came to the door into the shop.

'See you then, take care.'

Brenda closed the shop door behind her and walked down the street towards home. There was plenty of time. Jack wouldn't be home for another hour and tea was all but ready. It didn't matter what she cooked these days, Jack only picked at it. Her brow wrinkled in concern, he was far from well.

She'd never known what had passed between her brother, Jim, and Jack but whatever had been said had brought about a change. Jack had eased off his constant demands to know exactly where she and Alice were almost every minute of every day. Alice was allowed to travel to school on her own and now, at eighteen, had a certain freedom of movement.

It still wasn't right but it was better. Jack still watched Alice almost obsessively and there was a strict curfew. She had to be in by half past ten, without fail. She always was. She'd do anything to keep the peace.

***

'Have another look, Alice.'

Alice moved to the window in the bay and looked down the street. It was half past six and there were a couple of kids riding bikes but still no sign of Jack.

'Botheration!' This was the nearest Brenda ever came to swearing.

'The tea will be ruined. I suppose he's stopped for a pint, though he hasn't done that for ages.'

He had looked so poorly when he left for work this morning she'd expected him to come straight home.

"He hardly eats anything anyway. Come on Alice, we'll eat and I'll keep your Dad's warm.'

She dished out the stew and cut a couple of rounds of bread.

'That smells good,' said Alice as she pulled out a chair and sat down. Jack had always insisted they eat in silence and the habit was ingrained so, as usual, they concentrated on the food until the plates were empty. Alice rose to clear up and put the dishes in hot water.

At seven o'clock, Brenda went out onto the front step and looked down the street again. Still no sign of Jack and she was worried. In the not too distant past, Jack had occasionally come home late with a couple of pints inside him. Since he'd been under the weather, he'd been home on time every night.

Her unease had spread to Alice and she joined her mum on the step.

'Tea's made. Come back inside, watching the street won't make him come any sooner.'

Brenda washed the dishes and Alice wiped. The familiar routine had distracted them for a while. Still not talking, they were both fretting and Brenda was gnawing at her fingernails. Their silence was interrupted by a loud knock on the front door. They looked at each other apprehensively until Brenda jumped up and ran to open the door, followed by Alice who peered over her mother's shoulder.

Brenda clutched at the neck of her jumper at the sight of a tall, young policeman on the step. Her heart sank; it had to be bad news.

'What is it? It's Jack isn't it? Has he been in an accident?'

The young man shuffled his feet and then spoke. He hated to be the bearer of bad news. The best policy was to get on with it.

'Jack Spencer, is that your husband?'

'Yes, that's my father,' Alice replied. Brenda seemed incapable of speech.

'I don't have any details but they found a letter in his pocket with this address on it. He's in the hospital. He collapsed on the bus and was taken in an ambulance.'

'Which hospital?'

'Manchester Royal Infirmary, you'll have to ask at reception when you get there.'

'Thank you for telling us. We'll go straight away. Come on, Mum, we need to go.'

The policeman turned to leave and Alice pulled Brenda inside and closed the door.

'I'll have to sit down for a minute. Let me collect myself, I knew something awful had happened, I knew it,' Brenda muttered, wiping her eyes.

'We'd better take him a few things. We don't know how long he'll be in there.'

Alice ran upstairs and threw pyjamas, a toothbrush and shaving gear into a bag. Picking her mum's jacket from the back of the door and collecting her handbag from the kitchen, she went back into the front room. Brenda was visibly trying to pull herself together, sniffing and blowing her nose.

'Ready?' she asked.

'Yes, come on. The sooner we get there the better.'

Banging the door behind them, they hurried down the street towards the bus stop and stood waiting, willing a bus to appear.

So intent was Alice, looking down the road for a bus, she hadn't noticed Johnny Marshall pull up on the other side of the road. He'd been the proud owner of a car for just a couple of days and had stopped for cigarettes.

He could see Brenda was upset. She was clutching a hankie and dabbing at her eyes and Alice was speaking, trying to soothe her.

Johnnie had never been known for his kind heart but this was Alice.

Wonder what's up, he thought. Only one way to find out.

Surprising himself, he crossed the road and spoke.

'What's the matter, Alice? What's happened?'

Brenda was unable to speak.

'Oh Johnnie, it's my dad. He's in the Infirmary, taken ill at work, we think. The police have just let us know and we're on our way there now. If only a bus would come.'

'Come on, I'll run you down. You could wait for ages at this time of night.'

He shepherded them across the road, opened the passenger door and tipped the seat forward so Brenda could climb in the back where she sat clutching her handbag. Alice climbed into the front, smiling weakly in gratitude

He could hear Brenda trying to control her sobs and glanced sideways at Alice as he drove.

She looks like the ice princess, he thought but he didn't speak until he pulled up outside the main entrance.

'Do you know how long you'll be?'

'We have to go to reception and ask. They'll tell us which ward. I've no idea how long we'll be,' Alice said.

Brenda struggled out of the back seat, dragging her handbag and the bag with Jack's bits and piece out of the car after her.

'Come on, Alice. Let's find out what's happening.'

Alice turned to Johnnie.

'We might be here all night but thanks for the lift. I can't tell you how much it means to have got here so quickly.'

Brenda was walking at a fast clip up the path towards the main entrance and turned to look for Alice, gesturing madly.

'I have to go, thanks again,' and she turned, following her mother into the hospital.

Johnnie watched them disappear and shook his head. It was unlike him to get involved in anybody else's problems and now he would be late to pick up Sandra. He got back into the car and drove off. Sandra would wait, she always did.

At the reception desk, Brenda was trying to make herself understood when Alice caught up. She stepped in.

'We're looking for Jack Spencer; he was admitted as an emergency sometime this afternoon. The policeman who came to see us didn't know any more than that.'

'Just a minute,' the clerk responded. 'I'll check,' and he started shuffling through his papers. Brenda was fidgeting and muttering 'come on, come on,' under her breath but he wasn't to be hurried. What was life and death to them was routine to him.

'Here we are, ward 7B on the first floor. Take the stairs at the end of this corridor, first floor, second ward on the right.'

Alice nodded her thanks and they walked quickly along the corridor and climbed the stairs. The doors to the ward were closed. Alice took a deep breath and as she pushed open the heavy door, a nurse approached with a frown on her face.

'Visiting's over. I'm afraid you'll have to come back tomorrow between two and three or seven and eight.'

Alice spoke up. She was not about to be fobbed off.

'We've been told by the police my father's here. He was taken ill this afternoon and brought here in an ambulance. The man at reception said he was in this ward.'

'Sorry, love. We've been run off our feet today. Go and sit in there,' gesturing towards an office, 'and I'll fetch Sister.'

They sat in the office on the edge of their seats, Brenda clutching her handbag, Alice with the other bag on her knee. The longer they waited, the worse Brenda painted the picture. She took up the mantra, 'come on, come on.' She seemed incapable of saying anything else.

Firm footsteps down the corridor preceded the arrival of the starched and stern sister. They looked at her beseechingly, waiting for her to speak.

'Mrs Spencer?' she said to Brenda, who nodded.

'Your husband is here. He collapsed on the bus on his way home from work and the driver called an ambulance.'

'How bad is it?' asked Alice while Brenda wrung her hankie round and round.

'I'm afraid he's very poorly. The doctor's given him something to make him sleep and he's comfortable for the time being.'

Alice asked.

'Can we see him?'

'Yes, you can have a look but don't expect any response, he's sedated.'

'Is it his stomach?'

'Yes, he's scheduled for an emergency operation first thing in the morning.'

Brenda flinched. She knew how Jack hated hospitals and doctors.

'The surgeon wants to have a proper look. We'll know more after that. I'll take you to him but don't stay long. Come again at visiting tomorrow evening, he'll be groggy from the op for most of the day but I expect he'll be glad to see you by then. Come this way'

Two rows of beds stretched down the long ward, one on each side and several patients turned their heads to look at these new arrivals. It was unusual to see relatives after visiting hours.

The curtains were drawn around the first bed on the right and the matron pulled them apart so Alice and Brenda could step inside.

Brenda gasped and involuntarily put her hand over her mouth. It didn't even look like Jack, so small, shrunken and grey of face. They stood at the foot of the bed, Brenda clutching at Alice. They couldn't reconcile their image of Jack with the poor soul lying in that bed. They stood without speaking for five minutes. He didn't move and the bustle in the ward beyond masked the sound of his shallow breathing

Alice took a deep breath and said.

'Come on Mum. We can't do anything here. Let's go home. We'll come back tomorrow, like the sister said. Come on now.'

Brenda was so dazed and shocked it was all Alice could do to get her home. She got on and off the bus, up the street and through her own front door like a zombie.

Alice got her upstairs and into bed and brought her a cup of tea and a couple of aspirins.

'Try not to worry too much. We'll know better what's happening tomorrow. Try to get some sleep.'

She bent and kissed her mother and went into her own room and climbed into bed. Unable to sleep either, she lay and listened to the sound of her mother's quiet weeping.

***

Johnnie drove off after watching Alice and her mother go into the hospital. He was surprised how good it felt to do someone a good turn. Must be getting soft, he thought, but the picture of Alice hurrying into the hospital lingered.

He glanced at his watch, not too late after all, and he put his foot down. Sandra would give him earache if he was much later.

A few days earlier, he had been walking along the narrow corridor between reception and the general office and overheard a snatch of conversation through an open door. The voices were unmistakeable.

'He's a sharp lad," he'd overheard the senior partner say to the chief clerk and known they were discussing him.

He crouched to retie his shoelace, desperate to hear what was going on. It wasn't much of a subterfuge but it was all he could think of as the conversation continued.

'He works hard and can be relied on to do a thorough job. He doesn't cut corners like some of the other lads. We could send him out on some of the more complicated audits. Let him spread his wings a bit.'

'It's up to you but he'll be off like a shot as soon as he qualifies and we'll have trained him up for some other firm,' the chief clerk responded.

'All the more reason to get our money's worth now. Even though he's good, I won't be sorry to see him go. That business with Mrs Hutchins could have turned nasty'

'As you say. I'll take him with me to the Smith & Jones audit and see how he copes.'

Hearing movement through the open door, Johnnie straightened and moved quickly down the corridor. He mulled over what he'd heard, flattered the senior partner valued his work but the other remarks rankled.

Why I should care? He's right about one thing. I'll be off as soon as I'm qualified. I'll have bigger fish to fry. As for Mrs Hutchins, he's right there too, that could have ended in disaster.

The Christmas party had been much the same as the party the previous year and the year before. The partners had provided drinks, beer for the lads and Babycham for the girls, with a bottle of whisky for the senior staff, all male of course.

Because Christmas Eve fell on a Saturday, work was to finish for the holiday on Friday evening. Unsurprisingly, dedication to work started to peter out by lunch time and by two o'clock, desks were being cleared in the general office while the younger lads brought crates of beer up in the lift and stashed them in a corner. Two of the girls were fussing around with glasses and bottle openers and packets of crisps although the lads would be drinking out of their tea mugs, specially washed for the occasion by the office junior.

Finally, they were all assembled except the partners and nobody would help themselves to a drink until they arrived. Johnnie cast his eye over the girls' attempts at Christmas decorations. A small, scruffy tree stood on one of the windowsills. It must have been dragged out of a storeroom for at least ten years in succession. There were a few cards taped to the wall at the back of the office and a few tatty streamers attached to the lights. This feeble attempt at decoration emphasised the drabness of the office instead of disguising it.

The staff don't look much better, he thought, inwardly sneering, they all look tatty too, except for Mrs Hutchins. She looks terrific, as usual. The name didn't suit her at all and he idly wondered what she'd been called before she married. Bet she'd been something like Mortimer or Davenport.

All the lads, Johnnie included, had fantasies revolving around her shapely figure. Always polite but cool, she kept them at a distance, discouraging familiarity. As the boss's secretary, she regarded herself as a cut above the rest. Whenever she came into the general office in her smart suit and high heels, she left a lingering fragrance and more than one of the lads heaved a sigh as she left.

They were all hanging around, shuffling their feet and hardly speaking, when the partners came in together.

'Come on then, let's get this party started,' said the senior partner, rubbing his hands together. 'Let's have those drinks poured.'

A sudden burst of activity saw them all with a drink in their hands and then, at a cough from the chief clerk, silence fell.

There was the usual guff from the boss about how hard they had all worked, how their work was appreciated and the firm was growing from strength to strength.

Ya, de ya, de ya, thought Johnnie, I've heard it all before.

Finally winding down, he raised his glass and made a toast.

'Merry Christmas, everybody, and all the best for the New Year.'

Thank God, thought Johnnie. Now the fun will start.

Slowly, as glasses and mugs were emptied and re-filled, the noise level rose. The senior partner nursed his whisky, making a point of having a word with everyone. He left early.

The party progressed, as office parties do. A couple disappeared and was discovered snogging in the stationery cupboard. Engrossed in the clinch, they didn't realise there was an audience until someone sniggered in the open doorway. Blushing to the roots of her hair, the girl made a break for the ladies while the lad, trying to look nonchalant, managed only a sheepish grin.

The junior, who was too young to drink, had been emptying his mug at an alarming rate. He was now throwing up in the gents, supervised with amusement by one of the older lads.

Judging by the blush on one of the typist's face, the two young men standing by the beer crates were telling smutty jokes.

Johnnie had no close friends amongst the staff. He sometimes went out with them after work on Fridays but he had little in common with any of them. He watched them make fools of themselves. There would be a few red faces when work resumed after the holidays and he wouldn't hesitate to take a sly dig here and there.

When three of the lads started singing drunken carols, he decided he'd had enough and, putting his coat over his arm, headed for the stairs. No one would miss him.

He thought Mrs Hutchins had already left but he bumped into her coming out of the ladies, where she had obviously been making minor repairs, and they waited for the lift. Someone had left the sliding gate open and the lift was stranded on the floor above so they used the stairs. Raucous laughter floated up from the floor below; another Christmas party in full swing.

Only half the staircase lights were on and when Mrs Hutchins paused on the half landing, leaning back against the tiled wall, he looked closely at her face in the dim light. She'd had her fair share of the Babycham. Totally out of the character she presented at work, she started to giggle. He'd barely even seen her smile before.

'What's so funny?' Johnnie asked. He wasn't drunk but wasn't sober either.

'Did you see their faces when we opened the door of the stationery cupboard? It was hilarious.'

She giggled again and then started to laugh and although Johnnie hadn't found it at all funny, the sound was so contagious, he started to laugh too until they were both almost howling.

As their laughter petered out, he put a hand on her shoulder and gently pulled her towards him. She didn't resist and in seconds, he had her coat unfastened, his hand on her breast and his mouth on hers and she was co-operating enthusiastically.

Although he had been seeing Sandra for close on two years and sleeping with her at every opportunity for the last twelve months, he wasn't averse to a bit on the side and he was getting all the right signals.

She finally pulled away and whispered,

'I'd better get going. I need to get home.'

With the veneer of a gentleman, he solemnly re-buttoned her coat and escorted her down the stairs and they parted, without a word, at the entrance to the building.

What a surprise, he thought, a surprise and a bonus. He smiled and put it down as just a drunken fumble after the Christmas party.

Returning to work after the break, he'd half expected her to look a bit embarrassed but not a bit of it. Her cool exterior was intact and she barely looked at him so he was surprised when she slipped a note into his pocket as she passed him in the corridor.

It was the start of an affair that was to last three months. Her husband was a sales rep and away from home at frequent intervals. It was great at first, she'd let him know when and he'd travel by bus to her rented flat in Whalley Range for a couple of hours of grand passion. Her enthusiasm never waned and she was an eager and willing participant in anything Johnnie wanted to try. Sex on a regular basis, no strings attached, and in the comfort of her flat and her double bed was more than he could have hoped for.

He thought she felt the same, in it for the excitement and the experience. That had been true at the beginning but foolishly, she was now letting feelings come into the equation. She gave him long, lingering glances in the office, making opportunities to talk to him and standing very close when she did. It was only a matter of time until someone noticed and eventually, the rumours started. One of the lads tackled him head on.

'You getting some there, Johnnie?'

'I wish,' he replied, trying to laugh it off though inwardly panicking.

If it got to the partners' ears, it could be a sacking offence for both of them.

He tried to cool the situation but it made her the more eager. At his wits' end, he floundered, hardly speaking to her at all, not turning up at the flat when she asked him and showing a photo of Sandra round the office.

She looked at him with tears in her eyes and mouthed, 'please, Johnnie,' but he turned away, his only thought his own skin.

The situation was resolved unexpectedly when he heard she had given a week's notice and would be finishing on Friday. Her husband had been transferred to Coventry. He would be off the hook by the weekend and needed to keep out of her way until then. A last minute scene could be disastrous.

Thankful he was to be out on audit until late Thursday, he started a collection for a leaving present and bought a card from a local shop to pass round the office. He was the first to sign, writing 'with all good wishes for the future, Johnnie' before putting it on the desk behind him. Everyone in the office would eventually sign and the card and present would be given to her on Friday afternoon.

On Thursday, under the watchful eye of his superior, he totalled the figures for the audit, coughing at regular intervals. He had bought cough sweets, left them in full view on the desk, and sucked on them frequently, wiping his face on his hankie.

'Not too good, are we?' asked his supervisor with a knowing look. The last painful and embarrassing days of the affair had not gone unnoticed by senior staff although nothing was said.

Johnnie hung his head like a naughty boy, unable to meet his eye. He hadn't missed a day's work since he started at the firm but they both knew he would 'phone in sick tomorrow.

He was afraid of an emotional scene and sniggers from the rest of the staff. Management frowned on liaisons within the firm. If Hutchins were to become vindictive, she could easily get him the sack. She was leaving anyway and had nothing to lose.

He looked down at the scarred desk on which he was working, tucked away in a dingy little office as auditors usually were. The pile of ledgers, the adding machine and his handwritten notes were out of focus. Perhaps he was ill after all. He could only hope she would go quietly.

As he approached the hulking office building on Monday morning, his heart was truly in his mouth. He hung up his coat and when he sat down at his desk, the figures he'd been working on for the last week were already waiting for him. He pulled the file towards him, half expecting a summons from one of the partners, when one of the other lads spoke.

'Old Hutchie's gone then. Pity, let's hope the boss gets someone who is as easy on the eye. She cried a bit when we gave her the present and didn't want to go for a drink after work. Good luck to her, getting away from this place.'

Johnnie, who had been holding his breath, exhaled. He'd got away with it.

Over the next few weeks, he received several letters from her. He recognised the handwriting and the Coventry postmark. His mother noticed him tearing them in half and dropping them in the rubbish but made no comment. Hutchie might as well never have existed.

He pulled up outside Sandra's home where she was waiting on the step.

The small semi looked neat and tidy. The paintwork was fresh, the windows shining and the small, square lawn was closely mown with flowers, like soldiers on parade, in orderly rows round the borders. A far cry from Johnnie's own home, he was impressed every time he saw it. Sandra didn't live far from him but they usually met in town. There had been the occasional visit when Sandra's parents went somewhere special and could be relied upon to be away for a few hours. Once they had stayed away overnight and Johnnie had been there until the early hours of the morning.

No doubt he'd be here more often now he was driving. Sandra would expect to be collected and at the moment, it suited him too.

She came running down the path, eager to have a look at the car and even more eager to ride in it. Running her hand along the roof and on to the bonnet, she bent to look in at Johnnie. The proud smile on his face spoke for itself.

'It's great,' she said breathlessly. 'I'm so pleased for you. Where are we going?'

'I thought we might have a run out, go for a walk in Haughton Green and have a drink in the Hatters, make a nice change.'

'Lovely, I'll get my bag and tell Mum I'm off.'

She ran in the house and was out again in a couple of minutes, shouting 'bye' over her shoulder.

The curtains twitched as she came down the path, Sandra's mum, no doubt. Her dad must be out or he would have been down the path, giving Johnnie the onceover, again, and giving his studied opinion on the car, whether it was welcome or not. He had reservations about Johnnie. Sandra's mum had not had an opinion of her own in twenty years.

He pulled away smoothly and Sandra sat back with a sigh of satisfaction. She could get used to this. It had crossed her mind once he was mobile, he might well spread his wings in other directions but she pushed the thought away. He was here now, wasn't he?

'You were a bit late, was the traffic bad?'

'No, I took one of the neighbours down to the infirmary, her husband collapsed at work and she was in a right state.'

He made no mention of Alice. He'd seen Sandra's instinctive reaction to her once before and didn't want to rock the boat. He wanted to enjoy the moment, basking in her admiration of his newfound mobility and the sense of wellbeing still lingering from his good turn.

Sandra was surprised. It wasn't like Johnnie to put himself out for anyone.

'That was nice of you, quite the Good Samaritan.'

'Me all over,' he said and changed the subject quickly.

'What about the colour? Gulfstream Blue they call it.'

Sandra laughed.

'It matches your eyes. When did you get it?'

'It arrived yesterday. My dad sorted it out for me.'

Sandra knew better than to ask about his dad or any of his family. He shut up like a clam if she mentioned them, his terse responses discouraging further enquiry. Sandra asked no more.

As usual, Maurice had a contact and had pulled a few strings to find a bargain. Johnnie had the best part of the purchase price, a cash transaction of course, but Maurice agreed to advance the rest.

'I'll pay you back, Dad,' Johnnie had said.

'Too true you'll pay me back. I'll stop it out of your wages at a fiver week.'

***

Another letter from Harry confirmed the wedding was to be the first weekend in October. As usual, Hettie carried it around in her apron pocket for several days. Guessing she might show the letter to his father, Harry had chosen his words carefully.

"....... I know it will be very unlikely Dad will be able to take a weekend off and I suppose the same applies to Johnnie, now he's helping out. But it would be great if Dad could spare you for a couple of days, so the Marshall family is represented. I've checked the trains and you could travel down on Friday afternoon and back on Sunday morning, so you would only be away two nights. Let me know if you can come so I can fix up somewhere for you to stay.
Please write soon.
Love
Harry"

After worrying at the problem for a while, she decided to talk it over with Johnnie and when he came home a little early one night, she broached the subject.

'Have a look at this,' she said, pushing the letter across the table. 'I'll put the kettle on.'

Johnnie pulled the letter out of the envelope and she watched his face as he read. When he reached the part about her going to the wedding, his face fell. She could have picked the thoughts out of his head,

A whole weekend on my own with Dad? Who's going to look after us?

'Well,' she said. 'What do you think?'

He flushed a little and looked up. For the first time he could remember, Hettie looked vulnerable and unsure. It was obvious she desperately wanted to go.

He thought of all the times she'd bailed him out and covered for him with his Dad; the times Harry had stuck up for him at school and how Harry's shadow had protected him.

I'm getting soft.

'You should go. How are you going to get round Dad? Let's talk tactics.'

As usual when she wanted anything, Hettie waited until Maurice was fed. She was nervous and fidgety and looked meaningfully at Johnnie, willing him to start the proceedings.

He just smiled. For once he was in control of Hettie and was savouring the moment. Finally, at the point where Hettie thought they'd missed their moment, he spoke.

'Have you shown Dad Harry's letter?'

'What letter?' muttered Maurice.

Hettie fished out the letter and handed it over. It took him only a minute to read it and he threw it down on the table.

'He must be crackers. How will I manage on my own for a whole weekend?'

Johnnie spoke up in his mildest tone.

'It wouldn't be so bad, Dad. Mum can leave everything straight. It's only two nights and if she puts something in the oven for Friday night, I could go to the chippie on Saturday. It'd make a nice change.'

Maurice grunted, unconvinced and Hettie groaned inwardly. She turned to pour the tea, not wanting Maurice to see her face.

'Look at it this way, it doesn't matter what those yokels down there think but how would it look if your eldest lad got married and everyone round here knew nobody was bothered enough to go? '

'Mmmm.'

'And another thing, Harry isn't asking *us* to go, he knows how important the Saturday racing is. Surely me and you can manage for a couple of nights.'

'Mmmm'

Hettie was keeping busy, trying not to look anxious. She hadn't said a word so far and Maurice looked at her searchingly.

'Do you want to go?' he asked.

If she was too eager, he was capable of stopping her, just to show who was boss.

'I wouldn't mind. It'd be a chance to see what kind of girl he's marrying and check out he's doing as well as he says.'

'Yeah,' chipped in Johnnie. 'You'll have two sons in business if what he says is right. He'll be running the garage down there before you know it.'

Maurice was weakening. He'd be bragging in the pub about how magnanimous he was to let Hettie go, about how well Harry was doing.

'And another thing,' Johnnie chipped in. 'you'll have the big bed to yourself all weekend.'

'A treat in itself' Maurice said and Hettie could tell he wasn't joking.

'Come on, Dad. You won't have to lift a finger. I'll dish up the meals and wash the pots. I'll even polish your shoes for Saturday night. It'll be me and you, two lads together. What do you say?'

'I suppose it's going to cost me.'

'Not so much, just the fare. I'll give Mum something so she can buy an outfit for the wedding. We can't have her turning up like the poor relation.'

This was the first Hettie had heard of this and she blinked. Johnnie really had thought this through.

Maurice bridled and took the roll out of his back pocket and peeled off a few notes.

'No you won't,' he said. 'If there's any new outfits to be bought, I'll be buying 'em. After all, she'll be representing the family, God help us.'

He liked the sound of that and looking at Hettie, peeled off another couple of notes.

'Better get your hair done as well and don't get it done on the cheap. I know you.'

'Right, Maurice' said Hettie meekly.

'Buy something decent, something smart. Go into town, have a look in Lewis's.'

'Right, Maurice.'

She picked up the cash and stuffed it into her pocket. Maurice had no idea she had money of her own but she'd dip into if she had to. She wanted to do Harry proud.

'Right then, I'm for the telly,' puffed Maurice as he pushed himself up from the table and left the kitchen.

Hettie all but fell into the chair he'd just vacated and she and Johnnie sat grinning at each other.

'You pulled it off,' she said. 'Well done.'

Johnnie was pleased with himself. He'd got his way with his father and now his mother was in his debt. She'd never be in the driving seat again. To hammer this home, he took out his wallet and passed over some folded pound notes.

'Get yourself some shoes as well and you'll need a matching handbag.'

It was difficult for Hettie to swallow her pride and accept cash from Johnnie. The balance of power had shifted and he had the upper hand now.

She studied him across the table. He had a cocky grin firmly in place. He'd never need her to intercede for him again. Yet another tie had been loosened and Maurice had done himself no favours. Those unthinking, unkind remarks had stung.

***

Sally

I turned the corner and stopped short. I couldn't believe my eyes. Alice was getting into a car and Johnnie Marshall was holding the door open for her. Rooted to the spot, I watched him walk around the car, get in the driver's seat and pull away.

I didn't see Alice's mum huddled in the back seat, didn't see Alice's face was white and worried, all I'd seen was Johnnie Marshall leaning into the car to talk to Alice.

Betrayed, I thought dramatically. Why would Alice do that? We had a standing date for Friday evenings. At half past seven, Alice would leave her house and I'd leave Gran's and we'd meet somewhere in between. We often went to the cinema or if the weather was fine, got on a bus into town or went for a walk. There was no rational explanation for what I'd just seen.

Feeling like a fool, tears pricked behind my eyes but I fought them down. I couldn't be seen crying in the street. What to do now? Where to go? The evening stretched in front of me with no plans and no destination. I had to do something, I couldn't just stand there. Without thinking, my feet in motion, I walked disconsolately down towards the park.

A couple of young girls came skipping towards me, each with a rope and obviously in competition. It seemed a century since I'd been so carefree.

My thoughts tumbled. How could Alice leave me there without a word? We were supposed to be best friends. She must know how much it hurt - and Johnnie Marshall of all people. That it was Johnnie Marshall was the worst let down of all. I played the scene over and over in my mind. Fluctuating between anger and sorrow, I tried to pull myself together.

I looked at my watch, surprised to see it was only ten past eight. I couldn't go home with my tail between my legs and listen to my parents wittering on. What about Gran's? I'd get the same reception there. I'd go to see Miss Pritchard. It was a bit late but I was always welcome there.

It had been a few days since I'd seen them but I knocked at the door and waited. The younger of the sisters often went to the bay window to see who was knocking before she came to the door and Sally saw the curtain twitch and heard footsteps coming down the lino covered hall.

'What a surprise, I didn't expect to see you tonight. Come on in.'

'I was passing and thought I'd drop in. Your sister didn't look too well when I was here last and I wondered how she was.'

'That's kind of you, Sally. We're in the front room.'

The older Miss Pritchard was sitting in her armchair, propped up on cushions with a book on the table beside her. Despite the warm weather, she had a light shawl over her knees and still looked frail. A smile lit up her face when I came in.

'How are you, feeling any better?'

'Can't complain, I'm on the mend but these things take time at my age. Put the kettle on, Muriel, I'm sure Sally would like a cup of tea.'

Muriel bustled off down the hall and her sister looked at me searchingly.

'Is there something wrong? You look a bit upset.'

I brushed it off, with a shrug.

'Nothing too serious, it'll sort itself out.'

'Things are changing for you now, Sally. You'll be starting your studies in earnest in a few weeks and that will bring more changes. It's sometimes hard to let go of the way things have always been but you have to look to the future and adapt to the changes as they come.'

I nodded. I knew Miss Pritchard was right but couldn't see how I would adapt to a change in my relationship with Alice who'd been a major part of my life for most of my life.

The tea arrived on a tray laid with a cloth, patterned china and sugar tongs and a small plate of biscuits.

As Constance poured and passed around the tea, the conversation turned to music and one piece after another came under discussion. I could now hold my own although my knowledge was slight in comparison to Miss Pritchard's. Muriel took no part in the conversation but listened and watched her sister, looking for signs of fatigue.

'Why don't you play something for us before you go, Sally? I'm sure Constance would love to hear you. So would I, of course. It will give us something pleasant to go to bed on.'

This was the gentlest of hints her sister was tiring.

I checked the time, heavens, it was already half past nine and I knew they went to bed early.

'One piece, then I'll be off. What would you like to hear?'

'Why don't you play the piece on the piano? I was tinkering around with it this afternoon and would like to hear what you make of it.'

Although I was familiar with the music, I'd never played it so I concentrated, took my time and was happy enough with my efforts for a first sight reading. Miss Pritchard was pleased too.

'Well done! We'll make a musician of you yet,' she smiled.

I closed the piano but left the music on the stand. No doubt Miss Pritchard would be playing it again the following day.

'I'll be off then. I'll see you next week.'

'Bless you, we'll look forward to that.'

For the first time, in what had always been a fairly formal relationship, I crossed the room and kissed Miss Pritchard on the cheek. She looked surprised but pleased and she touched my hand as I turned to go.

At the front door, I bent and kissed Muriel too.

'You've saved my life tonight, thank you. I'll see you next week.'

She looked puzzled but smiled anyway.

'Goodnight, Sally, take care.'

The evening hadn't been a total washout. It soothed me to be so highly thought of and so welcome in their lives. I wouldn't say anything to Mum and Dad or to my gran. I couldn't bear them to feel sorry for me. I'd wait and see what happened but I hardened my heart towards Alice.

Whatever her explanation or excuse, I'll never forgive her for what she did tonight, I thought.

Now we'd left school, I had no other friends within easy reach. Me and Alice had never needed anyone else.

She can say what she likes, I thought bitterly, I'll never forgive her.

Chapter 12

Jack slowly became aware of the voices floating towards him. He couldn't make out the words but he cautiously opened his eyes.
By God, I hurt all over. I didn't know there could be so much pain.
He lay still, frightened to move, trying to see where he was without moving his head.
I'm in hospital.
Vague memories of the bus ride home from work filtered in but he remembered nothing else.
What's wrong with me? I need something to make the pain go away. This is unbearable.
The curtain round his bed swished open and a nurse popped her head through. Seeing he was awake, she came all the way in.
'Good morning, Mr Spencer. I see you're back with us. How are you feeling?'
She picked up his arm, taking his pulse and looking at her watch.
He could barely speak.
'The pain's awful,' he whispered. 'Can you give me something?'
Carefully placing his arm back on the bed, she replied.
'The doctor's doing his rounds. He'll be here in a few minutes. Hang on.' He moaned quietly. Hang on? There was no other option and he gritted his teeth.
The nurse disappeared and other voices approached.
Another swish of the curtains and the doctor came through, accompanied by the matron.
'Hello there, how's it going?'
Jack grimaced and couldn't suppress another quiet groan. He put his hand to his stomach, the major source of pain, but it was too tender to touch.
'That bad, eh? We'll soon fix you up.'
He turned to Sister and gave her some instructions and she disappeared, returning quickly with a syringe in a kidney bowl.

'This should do the trick,' the doctor said, injecting the contents of the syringe into Jack's arm. 'Take deep breaths, it will ease.'

Watching the doctor filling in the chart at the foot of the bed, Jack felt the pain loosening, leaving a dull ache around his stomach.

'What's the matter with me?' he said, his voice a little stronger. 'Is it serious?'

'You were in a bit of state when you came in, collapsed on the bus, I understand. We did an emergency operation this morning to see if we could sort you out, that's why you're so sore.'

Jack was panicking now. An emergency operation sounded serious.

'Was it a success?'

'It's early days, we'll keep you on medication for the pain and keep a close eye on you. We also need to do more tests. Your wife was able to give us some of your medical history but I need to ask you a few questions.'

The whole sorry story came out. How it had started, how long he'd been struggling and how he'd put off going to the doctor, hoping the pain would disappear.

'You're not the first to ignore serious symptoms and I don't suppose you'll be the last,' he said and the words "until it's too late" hung in the air between them.

'Try to take it easy. You'll be given regular pain relief and I'll be round to see you again in the morning.'

The pain had continued to ease and Jack's eyes started to droop. He couldn't speak, couldn't ask any more questions and his worries were floating away. He slid away into the darkness.

***

Alice had wakened suddenly, knowing there was something dreadfully wrong but it was a few seconds before she pulled together the memories of the day before.

The house was silent although the clock showed almost nine o'clock. She crept out of bed and across the landing to peep through her parents' bedroom door. Brenda was lying on her back with her arm flung over her eyes. After crying half the night, she'd finally succumbed to exhaustion. Alice had slept badly, the sound of her mother's weeping making it difficult for her to sleep.

There was a lot to do today but first things first. Alice went downstairs to put the kettle on and returned a few minutes later. She shook Brenda gently by the shoulder.

'Mum, Mum, it's almost nine o'clock.'

Brenda moaned, reluctant to wake and face the day.

'Come and have some breakfast. Put this on,' she said, pulling a cardigan from the back of a chair."

Like a zombie, Brenda reluctantly climbed out of the warm bed, shrugged on the cardigan over her nightie and made her way downstairs.

The table was laid, cereal already in bowls and bread cut ready on the breadboard. Everything was strange, only two cups on the table instead of three, only two bowls instead of three. Even Brenda in her nightie instead of being fully dressed was strange.

Alice could swan around in a dressing gown for half the morning but Brenda was expected to be at the table, fully dressed, before Jack came downstairs. She pulled the cardigan closer around her.

'What are we going to do?' she asked. 'What are we going to do?'

She was obviously in no fit state to make any decisions and Alice took charge.

'Try and eat something. You need to keep up your strength.'

Although the cereal might have been wood shavings, she managed to get it down. Alice buttered a piece of hot toast and put it on her mother's plate.

'See if you can eat that too,' she said.

The toast went down more easily and Brenda sat nursing her tea, waiting to be told what to do. She couldn't have acted independently had her life depended on it.

'First, I have to go down and phone Dad's office. It was his Saturday to work so there's bound to be somebody in his department. They'll need to know he's in hospital. We don't need to be at the hospital until two o'clock so why don't you have a bath and wash your hair so you look nice for Dad."

Jack never noticed how Brenda looked as Alice well knew but it would keep her mother busy for a while.

Fishing around in her purse to check she had enough change for the phone box, Alice wrote the telephone number on a scrap of paper, put in her pocket and set off.

It had been late when she remembered she was supposed to meet Sally at the end of the road.

Poor Sally, left hanging around. She'll be wondering what happened.

After making the call, listening to the commiserations of Jack's second in command and promising to keep the firm up to date, she decided to pop round to see Sally's grandma. Maybe Sally was there.

'No, love. She left here to meet you just before half past seven and I haven't seen her since,' was the reply when she asked after Sally. 'You could call at Miss Pritchard's, she sometimes goes there.'

'Thanks, I'll try them too. You will tell Sally what happened when you see her, won't you? I wouldn't let her down on purpose.'

'Don't worry, I'll let her know.'

On her way home, she knocked on Miss Pritchard's door and asked if they'd seen her.

'She did call in last night about eight o'clock and left about quarter past nine. I wouldn't expect her to call again today.'

'If you do see her, will you tell her I'm sorry I didn't turn up. My dad's been taken into hospital and we're going to see him again this afternoon.'

'Of course, I'll let her know. So sorry to hear about your father. I hope he's improved when you get there today.'

'Thanks, Miss Pritchard.'

Alice could do no more. She couldn't leave her mum for the length of time it would take her to get to Sally's and back. Hopefully, Sally would hear the news and call round.

Sally

The day after I'd seen Alice getting into Johnnie Marshall's car, I'd stormed around the house, slamming doors and banging books on tables. It was only luck there were no serious casualties amongst the cups and saucers.

In the evening, sitting in front of the television, hardly registering the inanities on the screen, I fumed and replayed the scene over and over in my mind.

Mum and Dad looked nervously at each other, they'd have to be deaf and dumb not to realise something was wrong. Finally, Mum spoke.

'Not seen Alice today then?'

I couldn't bring myself to tell them how badly let down I felt.

'No, I expect we won't be seeing so much of each other now. After all, she's going to one college and I'm going to another. We'll both have to make new friends.'

Mum shot Dad a warning look. I knew I was more prickly than usual and one wrong word could send me off the deep end. I hoped Dad wouldn't try to joke me out of it.

'If you don't have plans for Monday, why don't we go into town? We could get you a few things; a couple of jumpers and a skirt for college. It'd be nice to have something new to wear on your first day.'

I looked at their concerned faces with a twinge of guilt. What was I punishing them for? Anyway, the thought of another day stuck in the house gave me the creeps.

'Thanks, Mum. You're right, something new for the first day would be great and it's only a couple of weeks now.'

'Good, we'll do that' and she stood and pushed the hair back from her face. 'Who's ready for a cup of tea?'

I was left gawping at the screen as Dad followed Mum into the kitchen. I could hear their lowered voices.

'It looks like they've had a tiff. It'll blow over,' whispered Dad.

'I'm not so sure. You know what Sal's like when she digs her heels in. I hope they can sort it out.'

'It's a storm in a teacup, you'll see. They'll be best of friends again by the weekend.'

'Let's hope you're right.' Eva sighed. 'Sometimes I wish she was seven again and we could sort out all her problems for her.'

In the other room, I was on the boil. How could he reduce my battered feelings to such trivial expressions as tiff and teacup? He had no idea. I had to get out of the house. I didn't want to fall out with mum and dad as well.

'I won't have tea after all, Mum. I'm going for a walk,' I called, grabbed my cardigan from the back of the settee and was out through the door, heading for Debdale Park.

I walked off some of the steam, striding past young mothers with prams, kiddies on trikes and courting couples, all enjoying the early evening sunshine, and gave myself a talking to,

Come on Sally, pull yourself together. Things were bound to change. She's made her choice and there's nothing you can do. You'll have to get on with it. Make new friends, start again."

Slightly soothed by the vigorous exercise, I headed for home but as I lay in bed, trying to read, the feeling of loss overwhelmed me and I gave myself up to self-pity, snivelling into a hankie so Mum wouldn't hear me.

Sunday passed in a fog. I lay in bed, listening to mum and dad moving around downstairs, until hunger finally drove me down for breakfast. Mum was in the kitchen and Dad was in the garden, digging again. I wished David were home for the weekend, I could have talked to him.

Not knowing what to do with myself, I went out and watched Dad plant a bush and listened distractedly to him wittering on about the blossom we'd have in the spring.

Back in the kitchen, Mum looked pointedly at my pyjamas so I went up and got dressed. She'd obviously decided I needed to keep busy, so she passed me a bag of carrots and a peeler so I half-heartedly prepared the vegetables for Sunday lunch.

Though I'd hardly noticed, it was a lovely day and they decided to go out for a run in the countryside. Mum all but insisted I went too and what else was I going to do. I tried my best to be cheerful, to push my worries away for an hour or so but I wasn't very good company.

The best part of the day was the time I spent playing the piano after tea. I lost myself in the pleasure of the music for an hour or so and went to bed early after soothing my worries in melody.

The following morning, dressed in our best for the trip into town, Mum and I walked into Lewis's in Piccadilly. It made no sense to shop anywhere else. As Mum worked in the store, she was entitled to a staff discount.

'Let's look at the skirts first,' she said, 'then we can pick out jumpers to match.'

As we walked through the store towards the lifts, I noticed how many people behind the counters nodded and smiled at Mum. She was obviously well known and well liked and, for the first time in a long time, I was proud to be out with her.

We wandered through the ladies department and came across Mrs Marshall, looking flustered and trying on coats.

'Hello there, Mrs Marshall, treating yourself?'

Mum didn't say 'about time' but she must have thought it when she looked at the old grey coat hanging over the end of a rail. I looked at her, the mother of the famous Johnnie Marshall. He might be smart as paint but she looked decidedly scruffy.

'Our Harry's getting married and I'm trying to find something for the wedding. It's in October so maybe a coat instead of a suit but I want something I can wear afterwards too. I've narrowed it down to these two.'

Mum knew her stuff and was happy to help.

'The coat's the main thing; you can buy everything else around that. Let's have a look, try them on for me.'

I stood by, arms folded, almost grinding my teeth. Why my mum should help *his* mum was beyond me.

Eva studied Hettie. They hadn't spoken for years beyond an odd greeting when passing in the street. She wasn't a bad looking woman, younger than she looked at first glance and with a bit of care and the right clothes, she could look good. Of course Maurice had led her a dance for years and she wondered whether Hettie knew about Doris McGuire, Maurice's bit on the side. Probably, she thought, secrets aren't kept for long in that neck of the woods.

'The dark blue,' she said suddenly. 'It's smart and serviceable and the colour's right for you.'

'Do you think so?'

'I'm sure. You can wear anything with that; pale blue, cream or even pink. I'd pick a hat first and then match it up with a nice blouse and you can never go wrong with navy shoes and bag.'

Mind made up, Hettie nodded. She'd had the push she needed and, thanking Mum, went off to look at hats.

'Why'd you do that, Mum?'

'What, help her out? Why not? There's a lot more going on in that house than you know. She doesn't have an easy life. Don't be so quick to judge, Sally," she said more sharply than I was used to. 'Not everything is black and white.'

I was taken aback. Mum wasn't usually so quick to criticize me. I wondered what she meant and then thought, who cares anyway? Nevertheless, a little chastened, I started looking through the rack of skirts on display, pulling an odd one out and holding it up for Mum's approval.

The department manager came over to talk to Mum and I listened in.

'You should be on commission, Eva. That was a perfect sale and she'll buy everything else she needs here.'

Mum flushed with pleasure.

'Perhaps you're right, perhaps I ought to ask for a transfer from upstairs,' she said, laughing. 'Come on Sally, let's get you sorted out.'

On the bus on the way home and loaded with shopping bags, I'd heaved a sigh. The distraction had worked for a couple of hours but now my troubles were back.

'What's up love?' Mum asked gently.

'Nothing, I'm all right.'

'Do you want to stop off at your gran's? We could call in for a cuppa.'

'Not really, I can't face lugging all this stuff off the bus and then on again in an hour. Let's go straight home.'

In reality, I was reluctant to face my gran's sharp eyes. I couldn't believe Alice hadn't been in touch; hadn't made any attempt to apologise or explain. Outrage and resentment bubbled up all over again. I turned my face to look through the window at the passing shops and houses.

I could feel Mum's eyes on me but didn't turn to look at her.

'OK, she wasn't expecting us and I'm going to see her tomorrow anyway.'

Mum sat back and eased her shoes gently off her feet. We'd be home in half an hour. How could I have known a simple answer was to be found at my grandmother's house? Instead, the wound was left festering.

The next day, a letter dropped on to the mat. I recognised Alice's handwriting and turned the envelope over and over. What could she possibly have to say to justify leaving me stranded on a street corner, while she swanned off with that hooligan? I almost put it straight in the bin but curiosity got the better of me and I slit it open with a kitchen knife.

Dear Sally,

I'm so sorry I let you down the other night but something awful has happened. My dad is in the Infirmary and is very poorly. He was taken ill on the bus on his way home from work and taken straight to the hospital. Mum and I are visiting every day but I'm worried.

I left word with your gran and with Miss Pritchard but don't know whether you got either message.

I wanted you to know I wouldn't have let you down unless it was something really serious. I'll try and let you know what's happening.

> *Lots of love*
> *Alice*

There was no mention of Johnnie Marshall and no mention of when I would see her again. I was sorry about her dad and could tell she was worried sick but still, there was an underlying feeling of having been dismissed. I didn't know what to do now. Should I answer her letter or should I go down and take a chance on catching her. In the end, I decided to ask Mum what she thought.

***

During her father's illness, Alice was thrown on her own resources. While Jack lay slowly fading away, she and Brenda spent most of their time at the hospital. They were allowed unlimited visiting. Brenda was barely functioning and had to be chivvied to eat, bathe and get herself dressed. Meals were snatched, easily prepared food which Brenda barely touched and packets of sandwiches taken to the hospital.

Alice sat by the bedside, holding her father's hand. He was barely recognizable as the father she had always known. No longer robust and self-assured but grey and shrunken, drifting in and out of a drug induced stupor, the white whiskers on his face emphasizing his helplessness.

They'd been told to keep talking to him. He may not appear to register their words but the sound of their voices could offer some comfort on a subliminal level. When he did surface for short periods, Alice spoke quietly, trying to soothe and, as time went on, expecting less and less response. The rest of the time, she was babbling, telling the motionless figure on the bed about what was happening in the news, what they'd had for tea, how long they'd waited for a bus, how many people were asking after him and the messages they'd had from his place of work. She was pushing the silence away.

Brenda gazed blankly into the distance, incapable of accepting the inevitable. She rarely spoke above a whisper and then it was only to ask for reassurance that he would get better, wouldn't her?

As is often the case, extreme circumstances became the norm as they fell into the routine of hospital visits. They brought home Jack's pyjamas every second day and Brenda managed to wash and iron them, the only task she seemed capable of. They trudged down to the bus stop, never knowing how long they would have to wait. Occasionally stopped by neighbours, Alice grew tired of responding to enquiries, tired of the endless repetition.

'He's very poorly but doing as well as can be expected.'

She knew they were being kind but wished they'd leave her alone.

Despite the grimness of Jack's illness, they got up in the morning and Alice did what was essential, called at the shops and prepared the food. Without Jack to impose his strict standards, the house was showing signs of neglect. Alice had never realised how much work there was in keeping a household running. Now, everyday necessities were pressing for attention. By the end of the week, washing had to be done or they'd have no clean clothes and the reserves in the food cupboard were running low.

Alice tried to push her mum into action.

'Let's make a proper list. What do we need? We can't go on eating these scratch meals, we both need proper food inside us.'

Brenda made a couple of suggestions but fell silent standing in front of the open cupboard, unable to concentrate. Although far from accepting the inevitable, she had, at least, stopped saying,

'He will get better, won't he?'

Alice didn't know whether to hug her or shake her. She felt as though she was carrying the weight of the world on her shoulders.

The end, when it came, was undramatic. As they went into the ward, the nurse, who had been watching out for them, took Brenda by the arm and said,

'Sister wants to have a word. Why don't you go into her office and take a seat? She won't be a minute.'

Alice sat perfectly still, expecting the worst. Brenda was back to wringing her hankie and muttering,

'Come on, come on.'

As Sister came through the door, Alice looked up and asked calmly,

'He's gone, hasn't he?'

'Half an hour ago.'

'Did he ask for us?'

'No, he fell into a deep sleep and then slipped away.'

Alice nodded, tears rising, and leaned to put her arm round Brenda.

'Can we see him?'

Brenda stiffened.

'I don't want to. I really don't want to. You go. I don't want to.'

Giving her mother a squeeze, Alice rose and followed the sister to the closed curtains. Most of the other patients watched, some with sympathy and some rampant with curiosity, eager for anything which might interrupt the tedium of the ward.

'Ready?' asked the nurse as she pulled the curtain to one side to allow Alice to enter.

She took a deep breath and stepped inside.

The person in the bed did look like her dad but yet it didn't. It didn't look like the daddy who'd sat her on his knee and sung to her but it was a relief to see it didn't look like the grey faced, pain wracked dad she'd been watching for the last few days. His face was smooth, the pain lines had disappeared and although he didn't look as though he were asleep, he did look at rest.

Tears spilling down her cheeks, she stepped out of the privacy of the curtains and made her way back towards her mother. There was an overwhelming sense of relief, relief not only that his pain had stopped but that her ordeal was over. She had no idea of the turmoil to come.

Alice was at her wits' end. Brenda was sunk so deep in apathy she was almost catatonic, hands idle, staring into space. If Alice hadn't chivvied her around, she'd still be in her nightie at tea time. The food Alice put in front of her was pushed around her plate, barely tasted, until Alice could have screamed.

The aftermath of death was more complex than Alice could have imagined and she struggled.

From never having to worry about anything more than making her pocket money last the week, Alice now had the finances of the household on her shoulders. Jack had, naturally, dealt with everything. A death certificate had to be collected from the hospital before anything could be done and then there was the funeral to arrange. Her mother's brother, Uncle Jim, came with her to the funeral parlour to sort it out. It was all harrowing; choosing a coffin and making all the other decisions, which church, which cemetery and so on without the worry of how much all this would cost.

Uncle Jim gave her good advice.

'Go for the cheapest, love. Your dad won't care and you and your mum will need any cash that's left.'

After they'd sorted out the details, the undertaker suggested there might be a policy with death benefits which would cover the costs. Alice knew some kind of insurance man called at the house every week but she'd never known or cared what kind of insurance it was. She promised to go home and check. If there were such a policy, the undertaker would wait for settlement until the policy paid out. It was normal practice.

The insurance man called on Friday evenings, as did the rent man, to collect their money while there was still some left in the weekly pay packets.

She'd found the policy in the old tin box in the sideboard and was relieved to hear a pay-out could be made within a couple of weeks. It wasn't clear exactly how much but she was assured it would be sufficient to pay for any normal funeral.

The rent was due again, they'd missed a week when they were visiting the hospital and now they owed two weeks. She'd had to stand on the step and explain to the rent collector she wouldn't have the money until they got access to her father's bank account.

A familiar figure, belted raincoat and trilby hat, he'd been collecting for years. He wasn't unkind but he had a job to do and was uncomfortable dealing with this distressed young woman.

'Look,' he said, 'I understand what's going on and it's not unusual for there to be a bit of a hiccup when the breadwinner dies but I only have so much leeway. Up to all this happening, you never missed a week but now there's two weeks' due.'

Alice nodded but stood her ground even though she felt like a scrounger.

'You know we'll pay, the money's there, I just have to get at it.'

'I know, love, but I have to deal with the landlord. All he sees is the takings, he's not interested in anybody's troubles.'

'Can you wait a couple more days? I should have the money by Monday or Tuesday.'

'Look, I'll wait until next Friday but then there'll be three weeks due. If you're struggling, I'll take two weeks then and to keep him quiet for a bit but he's not a patient man.'

'I don't know how to thank you. I'll sort it out somehow.'

'There'll also have to be a change in the tenancy agreement. I suppose we'll be putting your mother's name in the rent book.'

'I think so,' said Alice unsurely.

'I can bring the necessary papers with me next week. Right then, see you next Friday,' and he tipped his hat and went to knock next door.

Alice closed the front door behind her and leaned against it. A temporary reprieve and she'd bought them a little time. She didn't want to ask Uncle Jim for money. He had his own family and couldn't afford to keep two houses going.

She hoped there would be enough in the bank to cover everything. The gas and electricity bills had arrived this morning but she had a little time before they became pressing.

The world and his wife needed the death certificate and she'd had to get extra copies.

She'd gone down on the bus to Jack's place of work to start the ball rolling with the pension people. It was crucial she have some idea how much would be coming into the house and how soon payments would start. The personnel officer had been sympathetic but she'd need Brenda's signature so Alice had to take away a form and bring it back the following day. She was promised a letter within a couple of days setting out the details of pension payments.

'I'll deal with it as quickly as I can and your mother should start receiving payments within ten days. In the meantime, there are outstanding wages. If you care to wait, we can sort them out now, it won't take long.'

She left her office but returned quickly with a small brown paper envelope. Alice could feel the notes folded inside. At least they'd have some cash to buy necessities, she thought, slipping the envelope into her bag.

The bank manager had been reluctant to disclose information or give Alice access to the funds. After all she was only eighteen years old. He'd insisted the widow sign various forms and other proof of identity be provided. Alice had gone home with the forms and found Brenda still at the kitchen table where she had left her an hour earlier.

The old tin box provided the rest of the paperwork and, to be on the safe side, Alice took out her father's and her mother's birth certificates, their marriage licence and her own birth certificate. Brenda listlessly signed yet another form and Alice raced back to the bank. It was a relief to find there were several hundred pounds in

Jack's account. At least they could pay the rent but serious decisions would have to be made.

It was never ending; visits here and visits there and then repeat visits with Brenda's signature and copies of documents.
When she wasn't running around trying to get everything in order, she was trying to keep the household running, doing a bit of shopping and a little cleaning but was struggling to keep on top of it and not altogether succeeding.
Under normal circumstances, people would rally round to help but Jack had kept them so isolated, the neighbours were reluctant to intrude.
Sally was Alice's only real friend and Eva was the only person Brenda could remotely call a friend and they were miles away.

Sally

When Gran told me Alice's dad had died, I was thoroughly ashamed of myself. All my resentment and self-pity and my best friend was going through the worst time of her life.
I didn't know what to do but Gran said I should call round, express my condolences and see if I could do anything to help.
As I approached the house, I could see the curtains were all drawn as people did when a family member died. Knocking gently at first, and then louder, I waited on the step until finally Mrs Spencer answered the door.
'I don't know where she is,' she said vaguely. 'She's doing a lot of running around, she never seems to be here.'
Not knowing what else to say, I mumbled something about calling back later and she closed the door on me.
I couldn't get home fast enough, Mum would know what to do.
'Honestly, Mum, she looked like a ghost. Her hair was all over the place, she was white as a sheet and hardly knew I was there. Alice was

out and her mum didn't know where she was or what time she'd be back.'

'The poor lass, it sounds as though Brenda's gone to pieces. She's been under Jack's thumb so long, she won't know which way to turn. We'd better get down there. Your dad can run us straight after tea, Alice is bound to be in later. She can't be left struggling with her mum in that state.

The funeral must be in the next few days. Go and put some stuff together. Alice is about the same size as you. We'll take one of your black skirts and cardigans and a white shirt for her to wear at the funeral and the same for Brenda out of my wardrobe. That'll be one less thing for them to worry about.

I'll put some food together. Heaven only knows what they're eating. Go on, get cracking. Here's your dad now, tea will be on the table in ten minutes.'

Relieved to be doing something, I ran upstairs and got the clothes together. Surely they'd both have a pair of black shoes. It crossed my mind they'd look like a pair of shop assistants at the funeral but it couldn't be helped.

Dad huffed and chuffed when Mum told him he was going out again but Mum was having none of it.

'What am I supposed to do while you and Sal are being angels of mercy?' he muttered.

'You have two choices. You can come home and come back for us later or you can go for a pint and we'll meet you in the pub when were done.'

Dad's reluctance disappeared.

'I'll wait in the pub, then you won't have to wait around for me to collect you.'

Mum gave him a look. He was choosing the alternative he liked best but implying he was being unselfish and caring. She knew him well.

Less than an hour later, we were on our way and the journey had never seemed so long. It was a pleasant evening and there were plenty of kids running about, letting off steam and being a general nuisance.

'For crying out loud, Sal, sit still will you? I can hardly see out the back window with you wriggling around,'

I hadn't realised I *was* wriggling. I was so anxious and so guilty, I couldn't get to Alice's fast enough.

Mum was out of the car with her bags and knocking on the door the minute Dad pulled up while I struggled to balance skirts and jumpers on hangers over my arm and get out of the back seat.

Alice opened the door straight away and stood in the doorway. She was white faced and red eyed and unable to speak.

'Hello, Alice, can we come in?' asked Mum gently.

Alice stepped back and nodded and Mum turned to wave Dad off.

'See you later,' she called and turned to enter the house.

Mrs Spencer scarcely registered we were there. Her gaze flickered over us and then settled somewhere on the wall facing her.

Alice flung her arms around me and sobbed.

'Oh Sally, I'm so glad to see you. I've been at my wits' end.'

The room looked gloomy with the curtains drawn. There was a thin layer of dust on the polished furniture and the whole place smelled musty.

Mum took it all in at a glance and took charge.

'Alice, put the bag in the kitchen and put the kettle on. Leave the back door open, we need some air in here. Then go upstairs with Sally, I want to talk to your mum.'

She pulled the curtains aside slightly and opened the window so there'd be some movement of air.

'Sally, don't stand there gawping. Take those clothes upstairs and put them in a wardrobe.

Alice seemed glad to be told what to do and she clattered up the stairs behind me and followed me into her bedroom.

We sat on her bed and I put my arm round her shoulders and it all came pouring out; the policeman on the doorstep, the rush to the hospital and the lift in Johnnie Marshall's car. I hadn't even had to ask her about it.

'It's been so awful. My Dad was so poorly and then when he died, there was nobody with him. We arrived too late and since then, it's been even worse. Mum can't do anything and there was the funeral to organise and I don't know what to do about money and the rent and loads of other stuff.'

She broke down again and all I could do was hug her and murmur in her ear it would be all right, it would get sorted out. I hoped it would, although I didn't know how. I'd never dealt with anything like this either. All the while, I was feeling so guilty she'd gone through all this on her own.

Mum would sort it, she'd know what to do.

We could hear voices from downstairs; Mrs Spencer was speaking at last. After a knock at the front door, we heard a male voice join the conversation.

'That must be Uncle Jim,' Alice said. 'He said he'd call round tonight.'

A few minutes later, Mum called up the stairs.

'Come on down, you two. We need to talk to you.'

There was a pile of papers on the table and Mum and Uncle Jim had been going through them. They looked at Alice and Mum spoke.

'I can't believe you've managed all this on your own, Alice. Everything's been done that needs to be done for the time being. We have to get the funeral over and the rest will sort itself out.'

Mrs Spencer gave a little cry at the mention of the funeral but at least she was reacting and she looked at Alice as though she hadn't seen her for weeks.

'I know it's been hard on you, Alice, but you've done wonders. Now you need a break.'

Thank heavens for Mum, she'd got everyone organised.

Uncle Jim was to take Mrs Spencer round to Alice's gran's for the night and Alice would come home with us.

'Brenda, go with Jim now and I'll meet you here in the morning. Alice has done more than enough and she can stay with Sally tomorrow and come back for tea. This place needs a proper going over and the two of us can do it in a day.'

Mrs Spencer spoke; the first time I'd heard her speak since we arrived.

'Jack would go mad if he knew.'

'I know, but you have to face it Brenda, Jack won't know and he'd be even madder if he saw the place going to wrack and ruin,' she said gently.

Alice threw a nightie and a toothbrush in a bag for her mum and held her coat while she shrugged into it. She gave her a kiss on the cheek and said,

'I'll see you tomorrow, Mum.'

Brenda fought back the tears and gave her a hug.

'All right, love, see you tomorrow.'

Alice gathered together a few bits and pieces for herself and the three of us went down to the pub to meet Dad.

He took one look at Alice and gathered her into a warm embrace, his eyes too filling with tears. He gave her a final squeeze and said,

'Sit down there love, I'll get you a drink. Shandy OK?'

Mum was at the bar, talking to the landlord who was nodding and trying for a sympathetic expression while silently calculating the extra profit.

She came back to the table with Dad, carrying two shandies.

'Look Alice, I've sorted everything out for after the funeral. He'll keep the back room for us and lay on sandwiches and a few cakes. You and your mum can't cope with trying to do a buffet on top of everything else. Any idea how many we'll be?' implying of course she'd be there.

'Not many, Dad had no family to speak of, just a few distant cousins and I doubt they'll make the trip from the other side of Manchester.'

Counting on her fingers, she said sadly,

'There won't be more than about eight. Will that be all right? There's money in Dad's bank account but I need to know what it will cost.'

'Don't worry about that now. We'll sort it out, it's the least we can do for our friends.'

I guessed the cash would come out of Mum's savings and I blessed her for it.

While we'd been talking, I'd seen Johnnie Marshall come in with his dad and they were standing at the bar, each with a pint in front of them.

Mum shot a look at Dad and nodded almost imperceptibly towards them. They didn't like the Marshalls any more than I did.

Meantime, Johnnie had caught sight of Alice and was looking at her searchingly. She didn't notice him until she got up to go to the loo. As she passed, Johnnie touched her arm briefly and leaned forward to speak to her. The sight of Marshall's hand on Alice made my blood boil.

'What was all that about?' I asked her when she came back.

'He said he was sorry about my dad. He was very nice.'

I bit back a sarcastic response. Alice had enough on her plate without me making waves. Still feeling guilty I hadn't turned up sooner, I let it go but wondered what he was up to.

Not long after, we set off for home. Alice was still pale and weary and when Mum caught her yawning, she sent us both upstairs.

'Go and get some sleep, you two. You'll have another busy day tomorrow.'

This was the first night Alice had ever spent away from home and it must have felt strange with no Dad to tell her she couldn't.

When we were settling down for the night, she said

'I can't tell you how relieved I am. All the worry has rolled away, your mum's a marvel.'

I had to admit she was and shamefacedly thought I'd given her a hard time too.

Alice was on a fold up bed in my room, the bed Mum had bought two years ago for just this eventuality. We'd never thought it would be used under circumstances like these. I'd thought she was dropping off when she spoke again.

'Sal,' she said hesitantly.

'What, love?' I asked.

'Can I get in with you?'

'Course you can,' I said and flung back the covers. 'Come on.'

She snuggled in with her back to me and I put my arm around her. It was a bit of a squash in a single bed but I lay still, holding on to her and heard her breathing deepen. I guessed this was the best sleep she'd had for a while and gave her a gentle squeeze.

Poor Alice, she'd had a hard time but I'd be there to support her from now on. Despite the upheaval, I hadn't been so happy for days.

***

Maurice smiled wryly. He'd been well and truly manoeuvred into letting Hettie go to the wedding and, he realised, Johnnie had done the manoeuvring.

He'd reached the unpalatable conclusion he'd never make the changeover to legal trading without Johnnie's input. He played down Johnnie's scaremongering tactics and waved them away. Nevertheless, the general view amongst his peers was that it was coming and once the legislation was passed, nothing would be the same. A few diehards were determined to stay as they were and carry on back street betting but much as he hated to admit Johnnie was right, there was no future for them.

As long as I hold the purse strings he'll have to toe the line. I'll show him a few manoeuvres.

He could block Hettie's trip, show them who was in charge but he softened. Hettie wasn't much to look at these days and he hadn't troubled her in the bedroom department for years but she wasn't a bad old stick. She ran the house, put good food on the table, looked after his clothes and didn't give him any backchat. She could go, might do her good. A sudden memory of Hettie in the early days of their marriage flashed past and he wondered fleetingly how things had changed so dramatically. He dismissed the thought It was all a long time ago.

They probably wouldn't even miss her. It didn't cross his mind he would have a weekend of freedom. Every weekend was a weekend of freedom. He always did exactly what he wanted. Johnnie would do the necessary in the house and he had Doris on standby for anything else. It was a surprise, even to him, that she was still around.

Until now, his liaisons had lasted a few months and then either he tired of the woman or she drifted away. He'd been seeing Doris now for some considerable time and she suited him. After he'd knocked her into shape, she'd become the kind of woman it was a pleasure to be seen with. Although his sexual appetite had diminished, she didn't care and often found new ways to stimulate him.

In a restaurant, she'd slip off a shoe, lay a stocking clad foot in his lap and start to massage. Smiling slowly, she'd watch him react; eyes glittering, face reddening until she felt an undeniable pulse under the sole of her foot. Her timing was good. She made sure the main course was over and would give him a couple of gentle rubs while the dessert was on the table. Maurice always took a brandy to finish his meal and once it was on the table, she'd start again, rhythmically rubbing until he waved for the bill and muttered,

'Let's get out of here.'

Smiling sweetly, she'd sashay across the restaurant and wait until a taxi was summoned and then lean against him in the back seat, rubbing him gently.

On summer evenings, even when they were out with other people, she'd lean over and whisper in his ear.

'No knickers tonight, think about that.'

And he did. He watched her cross the bar to go to the ladies, soft fabric swishing across her trim backside and know there was nothing between the dress and the soft skin of her buttocks. They'd sit for a couple of hours, the men talking about what was happening in their world and the women talking about whatever women talk about. Doris would sit and chat, sometimes gently moving against the seat and he would talk as usual while the vision of what was under the skirt would roll around in the back of his mind. At any sign of distraction, she'd give him a cheeky wink or a sly smile.

Once in a taxi, he couldn't wait to get his hand up her skirt. He wanted her ready when they got back to her place and if she climaxed on the way home, so much the better. Who cared what the driver thought.

This was the nearest Maurice came to foreplay. Once they were inside the house, Doris was expected to do whatever was necessary to bring Maurice to orgasm and it sometimes took all her powers of invention.

***

For Doris's part, she'd considered her options carefully. Maurice was more trouble, sexually, than he'd ever been but less frequently. She even enjoyed thinking up new tricks. He was getting older and fatter and if she let nature take its course, Maurice would become increasingly disinterested and wouldn't need her at all.

In the early days, she'd been happy with the odd present of cash but for a while now, Maurice had slipped her a few notes every weekend and always the same amount, which was more than Hettie could count on. With her wages and Maurice's contribution, she was doing very nicely. Her clothes and shoes came from Kendal Milne and she went to the best hairdresser in town.

She enjoyed her job, enjoyed shopping and spent money like water. The sexual innovations were a way of keeping her income intact. She was fond of Maurice and enjoyed being out with him but if the money dried up, she'd move on without a backward glance. At thirty two, she was in her prime and knew it.

***

Hettie made the trip south for the Harry's wedding. Never having been further than Blackpool, let alone as far as Sussex, she was a little apprehensive though no-one would have guessed.

The station was busy; noisy and intimidating. Trains were pulling in and steaming out and people were on the move, some carrying suitcases and looking harassed. Others were standing around, waiting to meet visitors from relatively far flung places.

The platform number was firmly embedded in her mind as she threaded her way through the Friday afternoon throng. Checking with the guard this was the right train, she walked along the platform, case in hand, until she found a comparatively empty carriage with a corner seat free. The young man already occupying the other window seat smiled as she climbed aboard and stood to put her bag on the overhead rack.

As the train pulled out of the station, she sat back and breathed a sigh of relief, watching the outskirts of Manchester disappear. The sound of the train beat a rhythm in her head, "I'm on my way, I'm on my way, I'm on my way." Streets and houses flashed past, replaced gradually by gardens and semis and leafy roads and finally, open countryside. The city of her birth was far behind her. The book on her lap remained unopened as she watched fields and woods pass the window.

She thought briefly of Maurice and Johnnie and then dismissed them. It was only two nights after all. No doubt she'd pay the price when she got back. Maurice would be more demanding than usual but she could cope. She'd had years of practice.

An unfamiliar sense of freedom settled over her. During the last couple of years, she'd spent a great deal of time alone but always with the spectre of Maurice hanging over her shoulder. His regimen never altered and her life was regulated around it. Now the weekend stretched before her and she relished the thought.

During the time Harry was in the army, he'd come home on leave occasionally. Once his father was out of the house, they'd sit in the kitchen while he regaled her with tales of routine in the camp and the goings on of his mates. Speaking about the countryside, the fields and woods, his face had lit up and Hettie came to terms with him never settling in Manchester again.

He was filling out, becoming a man both in physique and attitude and Hettie was impressed with his new found maturity. It was a pity he and Johnnie now had so little in common. Harry's experiences had broadened his mind while Johnnie's life was still confined to the narrow streets of his childhood and city centre Manchester.

Neither Maurice nor Johnnie cared whether Harry ever came home. Seen by Maurice as of no use in the business, he was rarely given a thought. Johnnie no longer needed his protection and was glad to have a bedroom to himself. Only Hettie missed him and although he wrote regularly, there was a huge gap in her life where once there'd been affection and laughter.

It was two years since she'd seen her eldest son and as the train neared her destination, mixed emotions raced through her; anticipation and apprehension in equal measure. Anticipation of the reunion to come and apprehension he might have changed; apprehension too about his wife-to-be. Had Harry made the right choice? Would she like Rosie and, perhaps more importantly, would Rosie like her? And finally, sneakily, was she good enough for Harry? Her hands trembled as she pulled her suitcase from the rack and she felt slightly sick.

As she stepped out of the train, Harry was on the platform, looking anxiously along the carriages. The moment he saw her, he gave a delighted yell and came running to wrap her in a warm embrace. She dropped her bag and hugged him back, tears filling her eyes. When the embrace finally loosened, his face was wet too.

Looking over Harry's shoulder, she could see a pretty, dark haired girl, dressed in yellow, at the entrance to the station, wiping her eyes and blowing her nose in sympathy. Hettie was already almost convinced.

Harry picked up her suitcase.

'Come on, Mum, come and meet Rosie. She's been on pins, waiting for you.'

As she walked along the platform, Hettie thought she'd been transported into a different world. The station was tiny, a far cry from the noise filled cavern she'd left behind, and it was freshly swept and tidy. There were even late geraniums in the boxes on the windowsills and a smartly uniformed stationmaster smiled and held out his hand for her ticket.

'Mum, this is Rosie.'

Rose stood shyly at the end of the platform but she put out her hands in a gesture of welcome and Hettie was quick to grasp them, both of them beaming while Harry looked on with a wide grin.

'I know you two are going to get along,' he said, watching their smiling faces. 'Come on Mum. Let's get you settled,' and he whisked them both to the car he had standing in the station yard.

'Wait a minute, Harry, I want to have a look,' said Hettie and stopped. Even the air smelled clean and the sky was the bluest she'd ever seen; the autumn sun shone down on the white painted cottages and neatly tended gardens. In the distance, she could see patchwork fields and hedges and beyond, clumps of trees and rolling hills.

It's like a picture postcard, she thought, but this is the real thing.

In the back of the car, Hettie didn't speak. She looked out of the window in wonder, wonder at the village and the lanes and the fields. She didn't notice Rosie put her hand on Harry's thigh and smile or Harry give her a little squeeze and whisper,

'I told you she'd love it.'

Hettie's body relaxed, the tension easing from her shoulders and her hands loosening in her lap as she gazed around her. A gentle smile broke out at the sight of the pair in the front seat. Harry looked so happy and although her acquaintance with Rosie had been no more than the exchange of a few words, she trusted her judgement. Rosie had passed muster.

'That's where we're going to live, Mum,' said Harry as he slowed to pass a small cottage on the High Street. There were late roses round the freshly painted door and bright flowered curtains at the shining windows.

'I'll bring you down this evening so you can have a proper look. There's Rosie's dad's garage'. That's where I work. And look, there's the church where we're getting married tomorrow."

Hettie looked and looked. She was overwhelmed by the prettiness of the village and people they passed raised a hand. Everyone knew everyone. Not much different from home except here, people were smiling. The sunlit road, with its smartly painted cottages and gardens, couldn't have looked more different than the narrow grey streets she'd left behind.

'Here we are. You'll be staying with Rosie's Auntie Sheila. She's looking forward to having you and we thought you'd be more comfortable than at the local pub.'

The car slowed and then stopped outside the village shop and Harry jumped out, pulling Hettie's bag out of the back seat.

At the door, a small, dark haired woman was waiting, a wide smile across her homely features.

'Come on in. I've got the kettle on,' and she put out her hand and drew Hettie gently through the shop and into the kitchen at the back.

'Harry, take your Mum's bag upstairs. I've put her in the back bedroom and then take Rosie home. I know you've both got things to do, so go and get on with it.'

Although she was smiling, she meant what she said and was obviously used to being in charge.

'Let your mum catch her breath and put her feet up for half an hour. Harry, you be back here for your tea at six o'clock and Rose, I'll see you in church tomorrow.'

'Right, Sarge,' said Harry. 'I thought I'd left the orders behind when I was demobbed but it seems I was wrong.'

Rosie leaned over and kissed Hettie's cheek.

'I'll see you tomorrow. I've so looked forward to it and Harry has told me such a lot about you. Maybe you'll be able to come again for longer so we can get to know each other properly.'

Hettie doubted it. She and Harry exchanged glances. He knew what things were like at home.

273

Unwilling to make promises she couldn't keep, Hettie smiled and laid her hand on Rosie's warm, brown arm.

'See you in church,' she said. 'Go on you two, shoo. Go and do what you've got to do.'

'Sit down there, love and make yourself at home,' said Sheila, gesturing towards a comfortable armchair and deftly pouring boiling water into the round bellied china teapot.

'There we are,' and she handed Hettie a cup and saucer and nudged a footstool forward so she could put her feet up.

'I'll show you where you'll be sleeping once you've finished and you can unpack your things. The shop's open for another hour or so but it won't be busy.'

Hettie smiled her thanks. She was taken with this little dynamo who bossed people twice her size around and ran her own business.

Unable to sit while someone else was working, Hettie set the table and cut the bread while Sheila put a meal together. A beautiful ham appeared from the pantry, pink and moist and smelling like heaven. A plate of local cheese and home-made chutney also appeared with a bowl of tomatoes and crisp lettuce and a couple of hard boiled eggs.

'That should do us and I've got a nice Victoria sponge for afterwards.'

Do us, thought Hettie, it's a banquet.

The bell above the shop door jangled.

'That you Harry?' Sheila called and when he responded, she added, 'turn the sign and bolt the door, will you?'

The food was of a quality Hettie had never seen or tasted, even before the war, and she ate with pure pleasure. This was all local produce and even tasted of the countryside and fresh air.

After a huge chunk of cake and a second cup of tea, Hettie started to clear the table.

'Hettie, leave it,' murmured Sheila. 'You and Harry go for a walk. He's dying to show you the cottage and this is your only chance to have some time together. Heaven knows when you'll get another quiet hour. Go on now.'

'Right, Sarge,' said Harry. It was obviously a standing joke between them and Hettie could see the kindly smile lurking below Sheila's stern exterior.

'Come on, Mum. Let me show you around.'

Walking through the village with her hand in Harry's arm, Hettie was bowled over yet again. The little Norman church sat within a quiet, orderly graveyard, the graves lovingly tended, with flowers on many of them. She was constantly making comparisons and thought of the bleakness of the huge cemeteries in Gorton and Phillips Park.

'We can have a quick look, if you like, it won't be locked,' and Harry pushed open the door and they walked into the quiet space. Late sunlight was pouring through the stained glass windows, lighting the pews with blues and reds. A snow white cloth glowed on the altar in the subdued light and two brass candlesticks were polished to a high shine.

Despite her feelings over the last few years, Hettie thought if there were a God, he'd surely be in a place like this. Peace and silence enveloped her and she stood for a moment, soaking it in.

'You'll be down there on the right, Mum, on the first row.'

Hettie was shaken to realise she'd probably be the only one on Harry's side of the church. Poor lad, the other side would be full of Rosie's family.

Harry must have read her mind and patted her hand.

'Don't worry, you won't be on your own. There'll be a decent turnout on my side; lads I was in the army with and some of their wives and my landlord and landlady. It'll be fine. Let's sit down for a minute.

They sat in the stillness, silent for a while and Harry held Hettie's hand.

'This'll be the only chance we'll have to talk so I want to tell you how much it means to me that you're here though I don't know how you pulled it off. Quite honestly, I'm glad Dad isn't. Can you imagine what he'd be like? He'd likely say something dodgy and as for

Johnnie; he's turning into such a man about town, he'd be calling us all country bumpkins.'

Hettie smiled wryly. She couldn't deny any of it but felt she had to defend Johnnie.

'If it hadn't been for Johnnie, I'd never have made it. He talked your dad round without him even realising.'

'He always had a knack of getting his own way but I'm grateful to him. Will you tell him, Mum?'

Hettie nodded and Harry went on,

'You're different from those two. You're the only one I could ever rely on, the only one who ever cared what happened to me. Though they're my family, I don't like 'em much.'

'Don't say any more, son. This isn't the time for recriminations. You've a lovely girl waiting for you and a whole new life ahead of you. Let the past go and look forward to the future.'

'You're right, as usual. Let's go and have a look at the cottage.'

Closing the door gently behind them, they set off down the road. The years they'd spent apart disappeared and they were on the old, easy footing.

The wedding went like a dream; the bride was beautiful in a white lace dress and wore fresh flowers in her hair. The groom was handsome, but nervous, in a navy suit and white shirt.

The church had been dressed with flowers and fresh greenery and was full of expectant faces. Hettie sat in the front row, next to Harry's best man, an old friend from the army.

As they made their vows, there was a lump in Hettie's throat and she had to take a deep breath, wiping her eyes and trying not to sob out loud. Rosie's mum caught her eye and they exchanged watery smiles as they turned to watch Harry put the ring on Rosie's finger.

As they walked back down the aisle, the stirring Wedding March had never sounded so triumphant and there was a smile on every face.

Later, at the reception in the well-proportioned room over the local pub, Hettie and Rosie's mum sat together, nursing glasses of sherry. The tables were almost groaning under the weight of country food. Polished silverware and dishes shone in the sunlight pouring through the windows. Wedding guests were milling around, laughing and joking and looking for their places at the table. Rosie's mum, a chubby matron with an open face and twinkling eyes, interrupted her reverie.

'It's such a pity Harry's father and brother couldn't have made the trip. I'm sure we would have made them very welcome.'

Hettie spluttered a little and wondered what Harry had told them. She should have checked with him. Now she had to tread carefully, not wanting to contradict whatever he'd said.

'It couldn't be helped,' she said and deftly turned the conversation. 'I'm glad I could come, I couldn't have had a kinder reception.' Another deft turn, 'they look so happy together.'

'Yes, it's lovely, isn't it? Harry fits in here so well, you'd think he was village born and bred. Everyone likes him so it's no wonder we've taken to you too. After all, you're the one who brought him up.'

Hettie considered briefly what that sentiment said about her and Johnnie. Clearly, he was his father's son and Harry his mother's.

'Well, I hope you find your husband in better health when you get home. It was good of your other son to stay at home to look after him.'

A clue at last and although it wasn't a hundred percent true, it wasn't exactly a lie either. She couldn't have seen Maurice, with his increasing girth, puffing and panting his way on to the train. He'd never have stopped moaning.

Rosie's mum leaned over confidentially.

'I understand Harry and his father don't get along. He never talks about him.'

'Let's say they don't see eye to eye. It happens sometimes.'

Harry had been clever. By not talking about Maurice, he'd not had to give any information about him. If the subject came up, he'd deflected the conversation, and eventually, people stopped asking. Because they all liked Harry, they assumed the fault lay with his father.

He's ashamed of him, Hettie thought, and so am I. I'd hate to admit Harry's father is a back street bookie, not much better than a spiv.

The kindness and openness of the people around her highlighted the cheerlessness of her life in Manchester. The freshness and sheer beauty of the countryside threw into stark relief the drabness of her usual surroundings. She'd lived there so long, she no longer noticed but for the first time in years, she was really breathing, really seeing.

Although she'd been nervous, she needn't have worried. Her clothes were just right, thanks to Eva Steadman, and she'd fitted in beautifully. They were all prepared to like her, for herself as well as for Harry's sake. She wasn't tainted here by Maurice, his reputation or underhand dealings. It was bliss.

Life could be like this, she thought. She was more determined than ever to leave the meanness and pettiness of her home and marriage behind her but she needed more time.

Harry interrupted her.

'Penny for 'em.'

Not wanting to load him with her darker thoughts on his wedding day, she shrugged,

'Just thinking how grand this all is. You're a lucky lad with your Rosie but I know you make your own luck. You could have come home and gone back to the same old grind but you didn't. You had the courage to make a new life for yourself. I'm so proud of you.'

Despite her good resolve, her eyes filled with tears.

'None of that today, Mum. It's the happiest day of my life. Come on, they're playing a quickstep, like you taught me in our old kitchen. Let's show them how we do it in Manchester,' and when he held out his hand, she rose to her feet and they took to the floor.

The evening passed too quickly as she ate her fill and took perhaps one sherry too many. She danced with Harry again, Rosie's dad and one of her uncles and couldn't remember ever having had such a good time.

As the party started to wind down, Harry came over to whisper in her ear.

'Sheila's ready to go. It's only a five minute walk down to her place. Will you be all right?'

''Course I will. Me and Sheila will be fine. Don't worry. You get off now.'

Rosie and Harry were to spend the night in the cottage that would be their home.

'I'll be round to take you to the station about twelve,' he said, bending and kissing her cheek. Rosie kissed her too and, hand in hand, they strolled through the room, smiling and calling good night to the people who were still lingering.

***

Hard decisions had to be made and Brenda was in no state to make them. Between them, Alice and Uncle Jim decided everything.

Alice's move to art school was in doubt. Jack's pension and Brenda's earnings wouldn't amount to enough to support them.

'I'll get a job, go and work in a store. I'm fairly sure Lewis's would take me on full time or I could apply somewhere else, Kendal's even.'

Although Jim had never had any time for Jack, he knew how he'd felt about Alice, and for once, took Jack's part.

'Your dad would turn in his grave if he heard you. His main aim in life was to see you do well. It's a sin to even think of giving up your place at college and going into that kind of work.'

Alice had been through so much, she was now a little braver, a little more assured and able to speak up when just weeks ago, she would have done as she was told.

'That's all very well, but how are we going to live? Even with my Saturday job and holiday earnings, we still won't be able to manage and Mum's not herself. Heaven knows when she'll be back at work.'

'There is another way,' said Jim, 'but I'm not sure if you'll like it.'

Alice's brow furrowed. She looked tired and pale and had lost a little weight but her hair was washed and shiny and her clothes were neatly pressed.

'Try me,' she said, ready to grasp at any solution.

Jim took a deep breath.

'You could give up the house and move in with your gran and granddad. They've got the room now we're all married. You'd have your own room and your mum could have her old room and there'd be someone to keep an eye on her 'til she's back on her feet. She'd have company all day and not be sitting here brooding on her own.

I've talked it over with them and they'd love you to go there. There'd be no rent to pay, perhaps a bit towards gas and electricity and with your dad's pension, you'd be able to manage easily."

The look of relief on Alice's face lightened Jim's heart. He'd been expecting opposition. She'd looked so worn and weary and suddenly, there was a beaming smile and a little colour back in her cheeks. She flung her arms round his neck.

'Uncle Jim, that's perfect, thank you.'

Flustered at the outbreak of emotion, Jim gave her a quick hug and, running his fingers through his now greying hair, said,

'Don't thank me. It's your gran and granddad you need to thank.'

'I know, I know, but I bet it was your idea. I don't know what I'd have done without you, Uncle Jim. I never would have coped.'

Alice's eyes had filled. She hadn't realised how heavy the burden she'd been carrying and the thought of passing it to someone else released a flood of relief. She blew her nose and in a shaky voice asked,

'What about Mum, have you talked to her?'

They were in the kitchen, facing each other across the table. The place was neat enough but far from the high standards Jack had imposed. Brenda was in the front room in front of the television but staring into space.

'I thought I'd talk to you first. The way your mum is at the moment, she'll do whatever we think best. She couldn't make a decision if her life depended on it.'

The landlord was given notice and the new tenants were waiting to move in. Apart from Alice's bedroom furniture and a few bits Brenda might want to keep, the contents of the house were sold lock, stock and barrel.

Alice was in the only home she'd ever known, while two flat capped, hulking great chaps carted their stuff out to the van parked outside. She'd insisted she'd be all right, it was only furniture after all but as she saw the contents of their home carried through the front door, a wave of grief hit her. Upstairs was cleared first; her parents' wardrobe, bed and chests of drawers. There were a couple of tea chests in the kitchen filled with pots and pans and the rest of the contents of the kitchen cupboards and they went next. Then the kitchen table and chairs were carried out and the settee where Brenda had spent so many hours, watching television and knitting.

'That's the lot, love. Is that going too?' The removal man gestured towards the chair she was sitting in, her dad's chair.

She stood hastily and managed a strangled,

'Yes, this is going too,' and watched as he hefted it and manoeuvred it through the front door.

You all right, love?' he asked. Without waiting for a reply, he muttered, 'We'll be off now' and left the house, leaving the door ajar behind him.

Alice stood in the bay window and looked around the room. It looked huge now but derelict. There were outlines on the walls where the mirror and a couple of pictures had hung and the carpet looked worn in places that had seen heavy traffic but, she realised, this wasn't her home any longer.

The removal of her father's chair was her undoing and she broke into bitter sobs. There was nowhere to sit except on the stairs and she perched there, all but howling. It hadn't hit her, even at the funeral. She'd been so wrapped up in things to be done, running around with paperwork and trying to keep the house straight, the harsh reality hadn't hit home. Her Daddy was gone, she'd never see him again and the last trace of him had disappeared. There was nothing left except a couple of photos in frames round at her gran's.

She didn't know how long she sat there, sobbing her heart out until she noticed it was getting dark. Gran would be worried. Blowing her nose vigorously, she pushed herself to her feet. Better get on with it, there was no turning back now and with one final look around the gloomy, empty room, she left.

Life at Gran's was easy; back to the old routine of food on the table when she got home, clean clothes in the wardrobe and no responsibility for anyone but herself. Her sick worry about her mother started to lift as Brenda responded to the warmth of her childhood home. She looked on as Brenda was gently, but firmly, chivvied into pulling her weight with the housework. Gran came home with a bag of apples and cajoled her into baking a pie and slowly, but with increasing confidence, Brenda came back to life.

By the end of the second week she was ready to go back to work, and everyone breathed a sigh of relief. Life didn't return to normal, there was no normal anymore but Alice was able to start at college as planned.

Unlike Sally, Alice didn't have a new wardrobe to signal her status as a student but managed with the clothes she had and even so, she was better dressed than most of the other students. Her tailored skirts and trousers combined with pretty sweaters, contrasted sharply with the rag tag bunch of other girls, dressed in jeans and tee shirts. She had no alternative but to grin and bear it. There was no spare cash and she couldn't be bothered anyway.

Her innate shyness and the upheaval of the past weeks made it difficult for her to engage with college life outside the classroom. Throwing herself into the work, mainly as a distraction, she'd acquired a reputation for being stand-offish and a bit miserable. When she overheard one of the lads refer to her as 'the ice queen' she'd blushed to the roots of her smooth blonde hair and had to hold back the tears.

She often sat alone during breaks. Occasionally, if she were already seated, someone joined her but she found casual conversation difficult and didn't have the confidence to join people who were already in groups. They couldn't know she was still grieving and she didn't know any of them well enough to confide in.

Her very real concerns about her mother had eased but there was a hollow feeling in her chest when she thought of her dad. Nobody else appeared to miss him and nobody talked about him. She'd felt the undercurrents from her gran and granddad and from Uncle Jim. Even Mum seemed to be pushing away the memory of him now she was getting back on her feet.

On a day to day basis, Sally was sorely missed. There was nobody to talk things over with, nobody to boost her confidence and more than anything, nobody to make her laugh. Their friendship was as strong as ever but the chances to meet were few and far between.

Sally had already made new friends and was engrossed in her college work and her new social life. Alice was frequently invited but on the few occasions she joined Sally's group, she felt out of place, the odd one out.

Most of her evenings and weekends were spent either in her room, working on assignments or in front of the television with her mum and grandma and granddad.

To her surprise, her mother had developed a taste for the cinema. Brenda was interested only in musicals, love stories and happy endings. She loved 'Pillow Talk' and 'The Bells Are Ringing' but anything more challenging was beyond her. Practically any soppy, sentimental scene could reduce her to tears.

It's come to this, she thought wryly. The highlight of my social life is a trip to the cinema with my mother.

Because there was no-one to go with, she went alone to see "Exodus" and wasn't surprised to see Mickey Smith in the cheap seats and gave him a wave. He went to the cinema every Friday night, regardless of what was showing.

Mickey, still a young man of very few words, was hanging about outside the cinema when she came out. He'd smartened himself up and shaved on a regular basis. His shirt was clean, his shoes were polished and his hair, which had darkened from ginger to auburn, was neatly cut and combed. Now he was working, he could buy new clothes for the first time in his life.

Alice paused and spoke to him.

'Are you waiting for someone, Mickey? Got a date?' she asked, smiling.

Mickey reddened but managed to put a couple of sentences together. He wasn't slow witted and he didn't stammer; he was just painfully shy.

'I saw you were on your own and ... er...thought I'd wait and walk home with you. You shouldn't be out on your own so late.' He struggled on, 'You never know who's ...er... knocking around.'

Alice dismissed any thought he might try something on. This was Mickey. She'd known him since they were kids.

'I'm sure I'm safe enough but if you're walking my way, I wouldn't mind the company.'

It was a fine night and the street lights were all lit, throwing a soft glow over the harsh outlines of the houses.

Their exchange couldn't have been called a conversation, it was more question and answer. Mickey didn't volunteer information but he did answer her gentle probes and she was surprised to hear that as well as his usual casual labouring, on Saturdays he worked as a runner for Johnnie Marshall's dad.

'What's Johnnie like now?' Alice asked, 'I thought you weren't too keen on him.'

She remembered Mickey in tears after being thumped by a ten year old Johnnie.

'I'm still not keen. He's still bossy, y'know, but he keeps his fists to himself these days. I've been working with his dad for ages now.'

'And the job, what's it like?'

'It's all right, a bit of running around, collecting bets and paying out winnings.'

'Doesn't sound too complicated.'

'No, it's not but Mr Marshall trusts me with the cash.' He smiled shyly. 'It's great when somebody wins, I like paying out although the boss isn't too keen. I hear some good jokes too.'

Alice laughed. 'I won't ask what kind.'

She could imagine him in the pub, on the edge of a circle of men, laughing at jokes but never quite part of the crowd.

They were at her front door and could see the lights in the front room. She turned and said,

'I would have been fine but thanks for bringing me home.'

Mickey shuffled his feet a bit. As always, he had trouble looking her in the eye and mumbled, 'S'all right. See you.'

He stood and watched her put the key in the door. He would have walked to the ends of the earth with her, never mind to the corner of her street.

1962

Margot Fonteyn and Rudolf Nureyev first dance together in a Royal Ballet performance of Giselle.

The Beatles play their first session at Abbey Road Studios.

Jamaica becomes independent.

Severe smog in London causes numerous deaths.

22 December – "Big Freeze" in Britain: no frost-free nights until 5 March 1963.

Safeway opens its first supermarket at a store in Bedford.

Published:	'A Clockwork Orange'- Anthony Burgess
	'The Ipcress File' – Len Deighton
Best Film Oscar:	'West Side Story' – Rita Moreno, Russ Tamblyn and George Chakiris
In the Hit Parade:	'The Young Ones' - Cliff Richard
Born in 1962:	Eddie Izzard
	Evil Knievel
	Steve Redgrave

Chapter 13

Ready to set up in business at last, Johnnie kept his eyes open and ear to the ground. His first application to take over a shop had been refused. The landlord was some kind of holy-roller who refused point blank to have the premises used as a betting shop. Buying property was out of the question. The capital required to set up premises, pay staff and running costs was just within their reach, thanks to Maurice's astute handling of their cash over the years and Johnnie's financial acumen during the time he'd been involved in the business.

In the end, it was Maurice who found the shop. The landlord in the local had leaned over the bar and asked confidentially,

'Still looking for a shop, Maurice?'

'Ay, have you heard something?'

One of the lads mentioned his auntie wants to sell up and move to St Annes. You know the one; the old fashioned looking ladies' shop, on the block next to St Marks?'

'Ay, I'll look into it. Thanks for the nod. I'll have another pint and take one for yourself,' passing a pound note over the bar.

'Ta, Maurice, I'll take for a whisky if that's all right. I'll leave it in the bottle until after closing.'

This was cheap information. He'd put Johnnie on to it first thing in the morning.

Grateful for the tip, Johnnie went round to see the shop and the proprietor early the next day. The bell over the door jangled as he entered and looked around. The place smelled of lavender and mothballs and was woefully old fashioned. A bank of drawers behind the counter held most of the stock, each drawer labelled appropriately; men's handkerchiefs, ladies' handkerchiefs, stockings and so on. A half-bust displayed an interlock vest a modern girl would only laugh at and the two hats on stands, the kind worn by grannies at weddings, belonged in the ark. Nevertheless, the polished counter and the gleaming windows indicated a level of care beyond the usual.

The elderly lady who emerged from the back echoed the same care; snowy white long sleeved blouse with a cameo at the neck and silver hair neatly up in a bun.

'Can I help you, young man?' clearly surprised to see someone of his age and sex on the premises.

He spoke politely and carefully.

'Good morning, Mrs Matthews, is now a convenient time to have a chat?'

'What about?' she asked suspiciously. What on earth could he want? She'd read enough crime novels to wonder if he were casing the joint.

'I heard a whisper you're thinking of selling up and wonder whether you'd be open to an offer.'

She sized him up, still suspicious.

'Aren't you a little young to be going into business?'

Used to holding his own and having his opinion listened to, Johnnie felt like a naughty schoolboy and a flush rose to his cheeks. If he hadn't wanted the shop so badly, he'd have walked out.

'My father will be backing the venture,' he said.

'Well perhaps your father ought to come round and see me himself,' she said briskly, 'I can't discuss this during business hours.'

A shrewd judge of character, Johnnie realised bombast wouldn't work here and turned on the charm.

'I realise I might look like a young whipper-snapper to you but I can assure you I'm acting with my father's full approval and authority. May I call this evening and we could have a preliminary discussion, go over your terms and so on? Of course I'll have to discuss details with my father but we could cover the groundwork.'

She looked him over again, taking in his air of confidence and his smart appearance. Perhaps there was more to him than she had initially thought. She sniffed.

'I suppose it can't hurt. Come round at eight, on the dot mind.'

Johnnie smiled.

'I'll be here.'

She followed him to the door and watched him cross the pavement and get into a smart car. Maybe she'd been a bit hasty, she could smell money.

Johnnie was quietly optimistic. The old lady was watching him from behind the shop door. He'd be able to handle her. As predicted by the partners, he'd finished his time with the firm and passed his exams with flying colours. Now fully qualified, he was branching out on his own. The business wouldn't entirely support him, at least at first, and he had other irons in the fire. He did the year-end figures for a couple of small businesses to give him a steady income. Some of the owners were cronies of his father and others had come by word of mouth recommendation but there was nothing he couldn't drop once the shop demanded his full attention.

Now on his way into Manchester to call on one of his new clients, he spotted Alice at the bus stop. Every time he saw her, she looked more attractive than the time before. She stood out head and shoulders above the other girls waiting for the bus, hair softly blowing around her face, her trim figure accentuated by a straight skirt and matching jacket. She looked calm and collected, not fidgeting and nattering like the rest.

Pulling up just beyond the bus stop, he flashed his lights, knowing she'd recognise the car and was happy to see her walk quickly towards him. He leaned over and pushed opened the passenger door.

'I'm going as far as Piccadilly, any use to you?'

'Thanks. Johnnie, that's great.'

'You're looking very smart, going somewhere special?'

With a blush rising in her cheeks, she responded,

'I'm going for an interview. I finished college last week and now I need a job. There's an opening at an advertising agency off Market Street and I'm hoping they'll take me on.'

'They'd be crazy if they didn't,' he said jokingly, admiring the colour in her fresh complexion.

As she looked embarrassed, he changed subject and they chatted about recent film releases. He didn't want to frighten her off.

He dropped her in one of the side streets and she was happy to go the rest of the way on foot. Before closing the passenger door, she leaned in and said,

'Thanks for the ride, Johnnie.'

He smiled and nodded and said,

'Happy to be of service, see you around.'

He watched her walk away. She really was something, still so fresh and innocent and he looked after her speculatively. No, not yet, he thought. I'll give it twelve more months and then I'll make my move.

At eight o'clock, Johnnie knocked on the side door and was whisked into a neat sitting room, with a vase of fresh flowers on a doily in the centre of the table. Johnnie sat down in the carved chair indicated by a waving hand.

'I've decided to consider your proposal,' she said. 'This is what I want for the stock and the good will,' and passed a folded slip of paper over the table.

Johnnie picked it up and looked at the figure. It was, of course, far in excess of the sum he'd had in mind. Either she was shrewder than he thought or completely naive. He looked at her speculatively and, seeing the steel in her gaze, made his mind up.

'Of course, there must be room for negotiation,' he said.

'Some room – but not much, I can't afford to take a heavy loss.'

They'd seriously misjudged each other. He'd thought she'd be a pushover. Lay on the charm and the soft soap and she'd be easily persuaded. She'd thought he was young and inexperienced and would take her proposals at face value. They couldn't have been more wrong.

Each now had the other's measure and negotiation started in earnest, he bidding down and she bidding up, to and fro until they reached a figure acceptable to both.

Johnnie was paying slightly more than he'd budgeted for and Mrs Matthews was getting slightly less than she'd hoped but the deal was done. They shook hands solemnly across the table.

'You'll join me in a glass of sherry to seal the deal?' she said, moving towards the sideboard where a bottle and glasses stood ready.

'I must tell you there is one proviso to the money changing hands,' he said a little nervously. His goal was in sight but there was still one potentially fatal hurdle.

She turned and stared and wondered if the deal was on the verge of collapse.

'What's that?'

'We're going to open a betting shop and the deal is provisional on the landlord approving the change of use. If we don't get his agreement, the shop's no use to us.'

She smiled, placed a glass in front of him and patted his hand.

'Don't worry, young man. The landlord's my cousin, on my mother's side, and I'm sure he'll see things my way,' she said and added, cryptically, 'I know where the bodies are buried. I'll speak to him first thing in the morning. Why don't you drop in tomorrow evening and we can firm up the details.'

Relief washed over him; he'd pulled it off. He didn't realise she was as relieved as he was but when she raised her glass in a mock toast, he did the same. With difficulty, Johnnie managed to down the dark, sticky sweet sherry and took his leave with a final handshake. Grinning uncontrollably, he drove slowly through the narrow streets. He was on his way.

Two weeks later, he stood on the pavement outside the shop, waving to Mrs Matthews who was in a taxi on her way to the station. The cheque had been paid in, cleared and the funds were now in her account. The furniture van had pulled away fifteen minutes earlier and he held the keys tightly in his right hand.

Pushing open the door, he surveyed his kingdom. Mine, all mine, he thought. There was work to be done but his plans were already in place. Johnnie knew the value of Maurice's contacts, built up over years. As usual, he knew a man who knew a man and the stock had been sold to a market trader who was coming to clear the shop that afternoon. A second hand dealer would follow to take away the drawers and cupboards. The proceeds of these two transactions would cover the cost of a new counter and enough paint to make the place presentable.

The 1961 Betting and Gaming Act had required licensed betting offices to discourage loitering. The punters were expected to enter, place a bet and leave. The House of Commons was intent on making betting shops as sad as possible so as not to deprave the young. They often ended up like undertakers' premises.

Installation of the counter would start the following morning and was scheduled to be completed within the day. The paint would arrive late afternoon and if all went well, the painting would be completed over the weekend.

Mickey Smith had been roped in to help. He was still wary of Johnnie, who treated him with off handed contempt. Although unlikely to show initiative, Johnnie knew he would work hard and do exactly as he was told.

Sandra had unwillingly been put on hold. Johnnie was determined to finish the job and he and Mickey worked Saturday and Sunday until late. By ten o'clock on Sunday night, the job was finished and they stood back and looked around.

The shop wasn't exactly inviting but it was clean and business like and conformed to the regulations.

'We've done a good job. Here's your cash," and Johnnie handed over a couple of folded notes. It was the nearest Mickey would ever get to a thank you but the extra money would come in handy.

'Anytime, Johnnie, let me know if there's anything else.'

'Will do, g'night.'

He was dismissed but left the shop happy enough, slipping the notes into his trouser pocket.

Before he locked up, Johnnie looked around at his new empire. The old man would approve, if grudgingly, when he came to inspect the place in the morning. Though outwardly as assured as ever, he sometimes struggled to subdue his doubts. He had to make this work, his whole future depended on it. Maurice would be implacable in the face of failure. There'd be no second chances.

***

Sally

Denton was finally home. I'd got used to the house and the bus journeys and acknowledged that yes, my room was bigger and better furnished and yes, the dining room where I could close the door and play the piano whenever I wanted was far nicer than the old place.

At Whitworth Street I'd mixed for the first time with girls from other backgrounds. I'd encountered Jewish girls who, although they looked different, were basically the same giddy schoolgirls and a few girls from affluent homes, whose blazers were tailor made and whose mothers collected them from the school gate in smart cars.

College was another complete change. We were treated like adults. There were boys in the class again and people from other towns and some from rural areas. Many of my contemporaries were in digs, going home only at weekends or for the holidays. Although I sometimes envied them their freedom, I was comfortable and spoiled at home.

One of the girls put it in a nutshell.

'You are lucky, you go home to a cooked meal every night, your clothes are washed and ironed and you've got a chance to practise whenever you want. Some nights when I'm looking at other people's dirty dishes and eating beans on toast again, I'd kill for one of my mum's roast dinners.'

'Why don't you come to tea on Sunday? My mum will always set an extra place.'

I became popular by default and friends often fished for invitations to meals over the week end.

Mum and Dad were delighted.

'Your friends are always welcome here, specially the hungry ones,' Mum laughed. 'The more the merrier.'

Her roast dinners and hotpot became famous. She treated everyone the same, regardless of background, and though Dad was initially overawed by some of my exotic friends, he soon got into his stride, laughing and joking and putting people at their ease.

Alice sometimes came on Sunday too and Mum and Dad welcomed her with open arms, almost like another daughter. She was prettier than ever and still dressed to suit her colouring and figure, uninterested in the more flamboyant styles of some of my fellow students. One or two of the lads gave her yearning looks but never plucked up the courage to ask her out. She didn't notice and treated everyone the same.

Our bond of friendship was still strong but different studies at different colleges made the opportunities to get together increasingly hard to come by.

Johnnie Marshall had disappeared from my life and I didn't give him a thought from one month's end to the next. Alice never mentioned she saw him occasionally, why would she? She knew what I thought about him. It wasn't worth mentioning he occasionally picked her up and gave her a lift into town.

My social life now revolved around music. We piled into concerts at college and scrimped and saved for tickets for the Halle. The pubs near the college were often filled with students, arguing and flirting in equal measure, and making half a pint of shandy last as long as possible.

Occasionally, one of the lads would ask me out and sometimes I went but rarely saw any of them more than once. I couldn't be bothered with the kissing and fumbling and couldn't see what the fuss was about. I liked the lads well enough and enjoyed their company and the banter but wasn't interested in anything more.

With the holidays ahead, I was glad to be busy. Although I'd done well in the end of year exams, I needed to play the piano for a couple of hours every day. Music was still the most important thing in my life and practising was no hardship.

There had been a shock in store when I started at college. From being the best musician any of my family or friends had ever heard, I'd moved into a different class. I was one of many and there were some really talented people around me. It wasn't too difficult to keep up with the theory but the only way I could keep pace musically was to practise and then practise some more.

Even though I was keen to do well, I couldn't practise all day, every day. I needed something to fill my time.

When I'd first started at college, Mum had fixed me up with a Saturday job at Lewis's and I'd now been there for two years. Brilliantly, she'd fixed up Alice too and though we were in the same store every Saturday, I didn't see much of her. We'd never worked in the same department and even our breaks rarely coincided.

Early on, we were sometimes moved from department to department and I didn't mind the change of scenery although I wasn't too keen to work in the food hall. The silly cap which covered my hair and the white overall weren't exactly stylish. Fortunately, it was only once in a blue moon and only in the early days when I lived in trepidation someone I knew, worst of all, someone from college, would come through and spot me.

After the first six months, I was in the dress department more often than not. The manager was a friend of mum's and had a soft spot for me; said I was worth my weight in gold. Obviously, mum's love of clothing had rubbed off on me. Although some of the women with more money than sense made me sometimes bite my tongue, I'd learned to smile and be pleasant no matter what the irritation. The pay packet at the end of the day was compensation enough. It meant I was relatively independent and didn't need to ask mum and dad for money.

Alice had gravitated to the makeup department on the ground floor. Her fair, clear skin, shining hair and skilfully applied but minimal make-up made her an asset on any of the counters.

We'd both been taken on full time for the run up to Christmas for the last two years, putting welcome extra cash in our pockets.

A job to tide me over the holidays fell into my lap one Saturday shortly before the holidays started. Talk about being in the right place at the right time.

I'd been serving a very pleasant woman who was looking for an outfit for a wedding. She had a pretty little girl about five years old, with soft blond curls and big blue eyes, who'd plonked herself on one of the chairs intended for long suffering husbands.

'My husband's supposed to meet me at half eleven,' and she glanced at her watch. 'He can't bear to hang around while I try stuff on but doesn't mind having the final say. Oh, here he is now,' she said looking towards the escalator.

Coming towards us was a familiar figure. I couldn't help grinning, it was Mr Phillips, the headmaster from my junior school. I'd never seen him off the school premises and he looked strange in these alien surroundings. I didn't think he'd recognise me but he smiled as he walked towards me.

'Hello, Sally, how are you?'

His wife looked at him and then at me.

'I see you two are acquainted.'

'We're old friends from West Gorton,' he said, examining me closely. 'You're looking well.'

'I'm fine,' I said. 'How are you?'

'I'm fine too. As you must have gathered, this is my wife and the rascal over there is our youngest, Rachel.'

The little girl slid off the chair and came over to take her daddy's hand.

Mrs Phillips showed him her selection. She'd narrowed it down to two smart suits.

'This one or this one?' she asked.

'That one,' he said. 'You always look good in blue.'

I could hardly believe it. Mr Phillips, who I'd regarded as the next thing to God, was behaving like any other husband.

'This one it is then,' and she went off to the cash desk, leaving her husband and daughter to wait, both examining me carefully.

I suspected Mr Phillips was disappointed to see me working in a store, he'd expected better, so I put him out of his misery.

'Don't worry, this is my Saturday job. I'm at the music college, about to start the summer break.'

A broad beam lit up his face.

'I knew it,' he said.

As his wife came back, carrier in hand, I could see the supervisor looking our way.

'I'm sorry, we're not encouraged to stand about chatting and the department head is looking this way.'

'What time's your break?' he asked. 'I'd like to catch up properly.'

He turned to his wife, 'Sally was one of my early successes. You don't mind do you, darling?'

She smiled as I looked at my watch.

'About ten minutes.'

'Good, we were going to have a bite of lunch. Why don't you join us in the cafe?'

I was pleased and flattered.

'I'll meet you there. It's still early so you should get a table easily.'

I was tickled pink to see Mr Phillips tucking into fish and chips. Back at school he'd been such a figure of authority, I couldn't have imagined him sitting down to eat anything, let alone something as plebeian as fish and chips.

He was pleased when I told him about Alice at art school and mildly amused when I told him about Johnnie Marshall and the betting shop.

'I knew that boy would go far,' he said. 'I can't say I'm surprised at the direction.'

He'd moved on too. He was now head of a school in Didsbury. Mr Metcalfe, his former deputy and the teacher who had pushed us for the eleven plus, was head at our old school.

Although Mrs Phillips hadn't known any of us, she showed a keen interest and turned to follow the conversation as each of us spoke.

The little girl, Rachel, polished off her lunch in short order and after her mother had wiped her fingers, she sat quietly, looking through a book she'd picked out of her mother's shopping bag.

'She reminds me of myself at the same age. I constantly had my head in a book,' I said.

'Yes, she's easy to amuse. Her brothers are quite grown up and a bit too old for her to play with.'

I'd had no idea Mr Phillips even had children. I almost had to pinch myself to believe I was sitting there with my erstwhile idol, chatting away as though we were old friends. He'd had no problem in making the transition to talking to me as an adult.

Mrs Phillips didn't say much and flushed when her husband started to talk about the marvellous work she was doing with handicapped children.

'It's not without its problems though. My main worry at the moment is finding someone to take care of Rachel during the holidays. It's become a bit difficult now she's started school. I don't suppose you're looking for a holiday job?' she asked, only half joking.

And that was that. I was in and my money worries, at least, were over.

Chapter 14

Hettie looked around the kitchen. Everything was tidy; dishes washed and put away, floor swept and surfaces wiped down. She'd left a dish full of hotpot on the stove and a note with instructions to heat it slowly on a low light.

The washing was done, the shirts ironed and the beds changed. The house had been cleaned from top to bottom and even the front step had been scrubbed. It had taken two whole days to achieve this state of perfection and she wondered wryly how long it would be before the place was a shambles.

She wasn't sure why she'd bothered, they'd be fending for themselves after tonight.

The envelope propped up in front of the clock on the mantelpiece was addressed to Maurice. Another note addressed to Johnnie had been placed on his pillow.

She had no qualms about leaving Maurice to his own devices but had sneaking feeling of guilt when she thought about Johnnie. This was no time to be getting cold feet, she'd been planning this for years.

He'll be all right, Johnnie will always be all right. It won't do either of them any harm to look after themselves. When the housework starts piling up, perhaps they'll realise what I've been doing for them all these years. Right, that's it. Better get on with it.

Her suitcase was already at the in the hall, so she slipped into her coat, the coat she'd bought for Harry's wedding two years earlier, and made her way down the hall. Picking up her case, she stepped through the front door, slamming it behind her. It sounded so final.

Flo was at the bus stop when she reached the main road.

'I thought someone should come and see you off,' she said, pulling her headscarf tighter, making her face look pinched and worried.

'Are you sure you know what you're doing? I'll be worried sick.'

This was typical of Flo, ever the ditherer.

'Flo, I'll be fine. Everything's set up. I'll drop you a line at the weekend and let you know how things are going.'

She turned and looked down the road, 'Look, here's the bus. Give us a kiss'

After one quick embrace, she was hoisting her suitcase on to the platform.

Flo was still dithering.

'Do you want me to come to the station with you?'

'No, stay here. You've got the kids to see to.'

Flo nodded and mouthed okay.

A final firm word from Hettie.

'Keep the business going. Keep to the terms and above all, Flo, keep your mouth shut.'

The bus was pulling away; Hettie on the platform and Flo at the bus stop.

'I will, Het, I promise,' and the threatened tears had started to spill down over her cheeks.

Softening, Hettie spoke over the noise of the engine.

'Take care of yourself, I'll miss you.'

Talk about tugging at the heartstrings, Hettie thought, another minute and she'd have had me bawling too. The sooner I'm on that flamin' train the better.

Hettie heaved her suitcase onto the rack, took off her coat and sat down. There were people milling around on the platform and gradually, the carriage filled.

That's it, I've burned my boats. I wonder what Maurice will say when he gets home. I'd like to be a fly on the wall.

As the train pulled out of the station, she sat back and breathed in, watching Manchester disappear.

The journey was familiar now. She was on her way, leaving the narrow streets of Gorton further and further behind.

Watching the miles fly by, Hettie gazed through the window and was lulled into a state of reflection. How had it come to this?

She'd first met Maurice in 1934 when he was a young man about town, already making more money than any of his contemporaries and not averse to spending it. She'd been nineteen years old and working in a city centre tobacconists. Maurice had dropped in by chance and the pretty young brunette behind the counter had caught his eye.

She'd thought him handsome and interesting looking, a little on the stocky side but smartly dressed, a trilby perched jauntily on his head. He'd been very polite and that always made an impression.

Like Johnnie in later years, he could have had any girl he set his cap at but there was something about this one. She'd served him quickly and efficiently and when she'd asked,

'Is there anything else, sir?' he'd caught a flash of her blue eyes. The combination of glossy dark hair, creamy skin and those laughing blue eyes had bowled him over. She was totally unaware.

He'd lifted his hat as he left the shop and she'd smiled back and then didn't give him another thought. She wasn't surprised when he called in again a few days later, why would she be? Maybe he was working nearby and would become a regular customer.

He started calling in a couple of times a week and waited until she was free to serve him. Always with a pleasant remark or a joke on his lips, she began to look forward to his visits.

Her boss, who missed nothing, warned her,

'I'd watch out for that one, all sweet talk but there's granite underneath.'

Hettie dismissed his remarks. What did he know? He must be forty at least and looked as though he'd never been young. Anyway, she could look after herself.

One Friday evening, he'd called in just before closing and as she passed over his change, he leaned forward and whispered,

'What time do you get off?'

'We'll be closing in fifteen minutes,' she whispered back.

He nodded, pocketed his change, and left the shop.

Would he wait for her? Her pulse raced and she felt decidedly fidgety; a bit anxious but excited too. She had little experience with the opposite sex. There was the odd old codger who came in the shop who tried it on but her boss, who kept an eye out for her, usually noticed and anyone who'd stepped even marginally out of line was served by him on subsequent visits.

At last, she thought, as she flipped the suspended notice on the shop door to 'closed' and went to get her coat and hat. She tucked her hair up neatly, put on her hat and carefully positioned the hatpin. After fastening her coat and brushing off the shoulders, she picked up her handbag and made for the door.

'Good night, Mr Jenkins, see you in the morning.'

'Good night, Hettie,' he said, adding in a gentle voice, 'Watch yourself, girl.'

He'd seen the exchange but could do nothing further to protect her.

As she stepped on to the pavement, she could see him waiting on the corner. She could have turned and walked the other way but why should she? That was the way she went home every night and she took a deep breath and walked towards him.

Smiling, he tipped his hat and put out his hand.

'Maurice Marshall, at your service, ma'am.'

She took the outstretched hand and shook it firmly.

'Hester Johnson, pleased to meet you.'

'Well now, Hester, which way are we going?'

He'd taken charge and she liked it. As they walked together through the busy streets, he was full of questions. Where did she live, who did she live with, and cheekily, how old was she? He walked with a slight limp but it didn't slow him down.

Hettie walked to and from work on a regular basis, taking the bus only when the weather was abysmal. Her wages had to be handed to her father on Friday evening and he grudgingly gave her a small portion back for bus fares and spending money. Hettie had learned at a very early age to make a little go a very long way.

When she asked in turn,

'What about you? What do you do for a living?'

He'd answered evasively, 'This and that, a bit of wheeling and dealing, you know.'

Hettie didn't know and wasn't sure she liked the sound of it. It didn't sound like a steady job but he was well dressed and he must have money, he bought expensive cigarettes.

As they reached the closely packed streets of Moss Side, the veneer of city life fell away and the narrow, grey streets were filled with scruffy kids tearing around and shouting.

'I live down there,' and Hettie gestured toward a cluster of houses at the end of a cul-de-sac. 'You'd better not come any further, my dad will have a fit if he sees you.'

Maurice tried to take her hand but she pulled away.

'Don't,' she said. 'Someone might see.'

She wasn't scared, just keen to avoid trouble. There was no point bringing it down on your own head.

She could tell Maurice liked her by the way he smiled at her, eyes twinkling as he listened intently to everything she said.

'I'll be off then. See you soon.'

He tipped his hat and Hettie stood at the end of the road and watched him disappear.

And so began their courtship.

Hettie pulled herself out of her reverie. She supposed it wasn't so strange she should be looking back to those happier times, now she'd abandoned Maurice completely. It was hard to reconcile that short happy time with the years of drudgery and abuse that followed. She'd seen how things had begun to slide and been powerless to stop the downward spiral.

She looked around the carriage, one couple were hand in hand, heads together, speaking in low tones. Two men each had a newspaper held up in front of their faces and the woman at the end was trying to placate a disruptive toddler. Her gaze returned to the window as they slid into a busy station. The courting couple got off and a few more people got in and bustled around, putting up suitcases and taking off coats and generally settling in for the journey.

A woman who'd just got into the carriage sat down facing her and smiled.

'Lovely day, isn't it?' She was obviously ready for a chat to pass the time.

Hettie smiled and responded, 'Yes it is, isn't it?'

The accepted thing would be to ask her fellow traveller if she were going far then an exchange of information would take place about destinations, who they were each visiting, their families and on and on.

Hettie couldn't be bothered. She'd been so deeply in the past she couldn't shake it off and resumed her vigil at the window, watching the countryside flash by.

Despite herself, her thoughts drifted back.

Maurice had pursued her with all the charm he could muster. They'd graduated to trips to the cinema and walks in the park. He took her dancing, holding her tight and whispering in her ear.

He was captivated by her pretty face, her trim figure and by her sharp wit and sense of humour. Though he never confided details of his business and she still wasn't sure what he did for a living, he often talked things over in a roundabout way, sounding her out and listening carefully to her opinions. She, in turn, was flattered to be taken seriously after years of being alternately threatened and ignored by her father.

After a few weeks, they took every opportunity to exchange kisses and embraces; in the park and on the back row of the cinema and even on the dance floor when the lights were low.

Maurice tried hard to push things further but she was having none of it and moved his hands away when they wandered too far. It was hard sometimes. She was as eager as he was but she knew the price paid by unwed mothers and had no intention of going that route. If she turned up pregnant, at best her father would throw her out and at worst, administer the beating of her life and then throw her out. Fear proved to be a reliable contraceptive.

Finally, unable to get her any other way, Maurice proposed. They'd been walking in the park and stopped to rest on a bench overlooking the flower beds. He'd produced a jeweller's box and held it out on the flat of his hand. Although he didn't go down on one knee, for once he looked vulnerable and unsure.

'This is for you,' he'd said.

Hettie had supposed it was some kind of trinket; a brooch or a locket perhaps and lifted the box but when she opened it and saw the contents, she gasped.

An engagement ring lay nestled in velvet. She'd never seen a diamond up this close. It was tiny and far from perfect but she was overwhelmed.

'Let me put it on,' Maurice whispered.

Unable to resist, the ring slipped on to her third finger and she held out her hand to admire it. It was a perfect fit and looked lovely on her slender finger.

She could hardly see the sparkle through her tears.

'What is it, Hettie? I thought you'd be pleased.'

'I am pleased. It's lovely but I daren't wear it. My dad will have a fit. You know I can't marry without his consent until I'm twenty one, and that's nearly eighteen months away. He'll never agree, he'd lose my wage, that's his drinking money."

Maurice put his arm round her and pulled her in close so her head was resting on his shoulder. He wasn't used to being thwarted and didn't intend for it to happen now.

'Don't worry about your dad, we'll get round him. I'm asking you now, properly, will you marry me?'

'Yes, Maurice, yes I will.'

If he'd thought a diamond ring on her finger would give him licence to take a few more liberties, he was sadly mistaken. She still wouldn't allow more than kisses and cuddles and it drove him crazy. An engagement ring was lovely but only a wedding ring would make her safe and she knew it.

As Maurice had learned from an early age, money would open most doors. The usual procedure would be for Maurice to meet Hettie's father and ask for her hand in marriage. That obviously wouldn't work.

Instead, he waylaid the old man in his usual haunt, the pub on the corner of their street.

He approached him, looked him over and saw a big man going to seed. What had once been muscle was now flab and the eyes, though sharp enough, were slightly bloodshot and matched the veins on his nose. He was near the end of his third pint.

Maurice, who'd been standing next to him at the bar, leaned forward and asked,

'Can I buy you another?'

'Ay, why not?'

Although he viewed Maurice with suspicion, he'd never turn down a free pint.

'I've got a proposal for you, put a bit of cash your way. Interested?'

'Ay, always interested in cash. What's it all about?'

Maurice pointed to a table in the corner.

'Why don't we take our pints and talk about it in private.'

A deal was struck. In return for a cash payment immediately and another the day they married, the old man would give his consent. He'd lose Hettie's earnings but quickly decided a bird in the hand was worth two in the bush. It would be good to have cash in his pocket. When it ran out, he'd find his beer money somewhere else.

In effect, Maurice had bought Hettie, a fact he was to throw in her face at frequent intervals in years to come.

Maurice was like a man possessed and Hettie was swept along, having little say in what was happening. She didn't have time to reconsider, Maurice was constantly organising. Underlying the romance and the excitement was the thought she'd be mistress in her own home and away from her overbearing, drunken father.

A house had been found in West Gorton, far away from Hettie's childhood home. The furniture had been bought through Maurice's contacts, most of it second hand, and Hettie hadn't been consulted.

She'd had to be at the house when it was delivered but she'd gazed on happily while the van was unloaded and the furniture placed around the house. A kitchen table and four chairs went into the back room and two armchairs from a three piece suite. The settee went into the front room, for the time being, Maurice said. A double bed, wardrobe and chest of drawers went upstairs into the front bedroom. The same furniture was still in place twenty years later.

She'd never been able to save anything and was reliant on Maurice for everything. Unlike most girls of her generation, she'd had no bottom drawer where she'd collected towels and sheets and knick-knacks for the home she might one day occupy. Her mother had an old sewing machine and she was able to run up curtains from fabric bought on the market, the only choice of furnishing she'd been allowed.

For once, her browbeaten mother had come to her rescue with a few shillings from her secret hoard, enough so Hettie could make a dress for her big day. She was so relieved, she broke down in tears. She didn't want to let Maurice down.

The wedding went without a hitch. It was over before she knew it and they were on their way to the local workingmen's club for a cold buffet and drinks. Maurice and her father were in a huddle at the bar and she was sure money had changed hands but was so happy, she didn't care. Her father had contributed nothing to the cost of his daughter's wedding but had stood back and let Maurice foot the bill.

She didn't know Maurice had instructed one of his cronies to get the old man as pissed as possible, as quickly as possible, so they could pour him into a taxi and get rid of him before he had a chance to put a damper on the proceedings.

The food cleared away, the club's resident pianist struck up a waltz and Maurice held out his hand to her.

'May I have this dance, Mrs Marshall?' and Hettie walked into his arms while the wedding guests clapped and whistled.

He whirled her round the floor, despite his bad leg, whispering in her ear about what they were going to do once this shindig was over and

Hettie could feel a blush rising. She was as eager as he was and now there was ring on her finger, she was ready to throw caution to the wind.

The eighteen months after her wedding were the happiest of Hettie's life.

Maurice couldn't get enough of her. He was far from inexperienced while she'd known little about what went on between married people. He'd found sex with someone he cared about was a far cry from the brief episodes of the past. He loved to watch her take her clothes off and would have her lie on the bed naked, so he could look at her. She was so beautiful, he occasionally had to blink away a tear and he'd lie next to her, stroking her and murmuring in her ear that she was perfect. Such adoration sometimes made her uneasy but she shrugged it off. With Maurice's help, she quickly overcame her shyness and became a willing and eager participant in their love making.

In the evenings, they sat in their kitchen and listened to the radio or talked and Maurice taught her to play cards. She learned quickly and had to be careful not to win too often. On Friday evenings he went out with his friends and on Saturdays he took her out, insistent she look her best, wanting to show her off.

She dismissed the downsides of marriage as unimportant. Maurice had insisted she give up work immediately and the days were sometimes long and empty. Without even the pittance her father had allowed her for bus fares, she was reliant on Maurice for every last penny. The habit of shaving a little off the housekeeping to put by had started then.

Maurice would have a face like thunder if his tea wasn't on the table on the dot of six or if his shirts weren't perfectly ironed and he sometimes came home the worse for wear on Friday nights. She thought all men were like that and at least he loved her.

They'd been lying in bed one Sunday morning, warm and cuddled together and Maurice had started to caress her but she'd winced slightly when he started to stroke her breasts. In a flash, he'd thrown the covers back and she was undergoing even closer scrutiny than usual.

'What is it Het, what's the matter?' he'd asked.

'Nothing, don't stop, you know I love that. It s a bit tender.'

He looked at her, following the track of his fingers across her skin.

'You sure?'

'Course I'm sure,' and she put her arms around him and pulled him to her.

It took another month and a second missed period before she suspected she might be pregnant. She had no idea how Maurice would take the news and was a little apprehensive.

Back in the present, she was unaware a brief smile had touched her lips until the woman facing her smiled back. She gave herself a mental shake.

It's no use going over the past now. What's done is done. I should be looking to the future.

Distraction, that was the thing, and she made the effort to strike up a conversation.

'Going far?'

***

Maurice and Johnnie came home to an empty house. The place was clean and tidy and the aroma of hotpot in the air but no Hettie. Maurice checked the front room then stood at the foot of the stairs, shouting,

'Het, are you up there? What're you playing at? Get down here, now.'

Johnnie had spotted the envelope on the mantelpiece and recognising the handwriting, passed it to his father.

'You'd better read this, Dad.'

Maurice blustered,

'I've no time for this tomfoolery, where the bloody hell is she?'

He ripped open the envelope, scanned the contents briefly, and flung the letter over to Johnnie. Shocked to silence for the briefest moment, they looked at each other blank faced, unable to take it in. Then Maurice exploded, red faced with rage and almost incoherent.

'How dare she? She'd better get back here double quick if she knows what's good for her. Leave me? Her, leave me? I won't have it, I'll swing for her, see if I don't,' he ranted.

Johnnie, white faced, was barely listening. The implications of Hettie's departure had hit him straight away. Who was going to look after them, do the cooking, provide clean shirts, and keep the place tidy? He'd found the instructions for heating the hotpot particularly telling. Tonight's meal taken care of but what about tomorrow and the day after? A future with the two of them rattling round, getting on each other's nerves stretched unappetizingly before him. Maurice wouldn't lift a finger and the whole shebang would fall to him. It had been bad enough when Hettie had been missing for two days for Harry's wedding. This was the thanks he got for helping her then. She'd truly left them in the lurch.

At last, Maurice was running out of steam and Johnnie pulled out a chair and gently pushed Maurice into it. Fetching the whisky bottle and two glasses, he poured two measures and sat down facing his father.

'What are we going to do, Dad?' he asked calmly.

Maurice took a hefty swig from the glass and a deep breath.

'She'll have to come home, that's the end of it,' he blustered.

'And if she says no, how are you going to make her? Are you going to go down there and drag her back?'

Maurice took another hefty swig from his glass and reached for the bottle, for once, lost for words.

Johnnie leaned across the table.

'There's more than one thing going on here. How will it look if it gets about that Mum's hopped it?'

'Absconded, more like it,' muttered Maurice. 'She's made a fool of me.'

'That's what we want to avoid. We'll put it about she's been under the weather, has gone to stay with Harry for a couple of weeks. No amount of shouting and carrying on will bring her back, she'll dig her heels in. We need to appeal to her better nature.

I'll write to her and say we can't manage without her. We need her, *you* need her. I'll tell her there'll be no recriminations, she can come home and pick up where she left off. Promise her anything, promise to stop taking her for granted, promise her more cash in her purse, she might see reason.'

'I refuse to grovel,' Maurice said sharply.

'Dad, you won't be doing the grovelling, I will. The main thing is to get her back. Apart from the loss of face, which is bad enough, how are we going to manage? I'm no cook and I doubt you've ever peeled a spud in your life and we need to eat. I don't fancy fish and chips as a steady diet and what about the cleaning and the washing?'

'Bugger the washing,' responded Maurice, who could look no further than his initial outrage.

'You won't say that when you haven't got a clean shirt,' Johnnie responded sharply. 'We need a plan.'

Maurice swirled the whisky round in his glass and raised it to his lips.

'How's this? You write to her and, much as it sticks in my craw, tell her she can stay down there two weeks and have a break. In the meantime, I'll have a word with Jimmy Gill. I know his sister's looking to earn a bit on the side. I'll get her to call round tomorrow night and you can have a word with her.'

The 'coping with the crisis' was already being pushed Johnnie's way and he bowed to the inevitable. He'd rather take charge himself than suffer Maurice's heavy handed efforts to sort them out.

'It'll cost, Dad, maybe not a fortune as she's so stuck for cash but it'll cost.'

'Hopefully not for more than a couple of weeks.'

Johnnie stood, took another look at the instructions for heating the hotpot, and put it on a low light.

Half an hour later, with some kind of a plan in place, they settled in to eat. Neither one of them gave a thought as to why Hettie had 'absconded'. There was no regret and no remorse, only outrage.

The letter Hettie had left for Johnnie lay unnoticed until he went to bed. Grasping the envelope in both hands, ready to tear it in half without reading it, he paused. It may hold something he could use as ammunition. After opening the envelope and reading the letter, he ripped it up in disgust.

By Saturday evening, they were organised, after a fashion. Johnnie's letter to Hettie was in the post and Jimmy Gill's sister agreed to come in on Friday, clean the house and collect the washing. Thank heavens, they both had clean shirts to last until then. She'd call in week days to leave them a dish to heat up or something simple, ready to cook.

Maurice had balked at the three quid Johnnie had agreed on but subsided when he realised the alternative was for them to do it all themselves.

It had been fish and chips after all on Saturday and on Sunday, Johnnie tackled a roast. How hard can it be? Mum does it every week, he'd thought. Needless to say, there wasn't a cookery book in the house and he'd had to play it by ear.

By the time they sat down in a slightly smoky kitchen to charred potatoes, a blackened piece of beef which bled profusely when they cut into it and watery gravy, Johnnie realised there was more to this cooking lark than he'd thought.

Both disgruntled, they pushed the food around their plates. No thought was given to what Hettie had done over the years; only resentment she wasn't here to do it now.

It was two weeks before her reply fell on the mat and a letter from Harry arrived at the same time. Johnnie had written to him too, hoping he'd see their point of view and put pressure on Hettie to come home and do her duty.

It was clear from Hettie's letter she had no intention of returning, not in the couple of weeks Johnnie had suggested, and not ever. Harry's letter confirmed it. He said he couldn't influence her in any way and her mind was firmly made up.

Johnnie shrugged on his coat and went off to the shop, leaving the letters on the kitchen table for Maurice to read when he finally surfaced. He'd be grumpier than ever. Even putting the kettle on was a chore for Maurice and now he had to make his own breakfast. The kitchen would be a disaster area by lunch time. Despite the efforts of Jimmy Gill's sister, who'd have to be kept on indefinitely, the place was scruffier than ever. Maurice was indifferent to the mess but it wore Johnnie down.

1963

Charles de Gaulle vetoes UK's entry into EEC

Dr Beeching calls for huge cuts to the UK's rail network

Dr Profumo, Secretary of State for War, resigns over affair with Christine Keeler

Great Train Robbery takes place in Buckinghamshire

Published:	'The Spy Who Came in From the Cold' – John Le Carre 'Ice Station Zebra' – Alistair MacLean
Best Film Oscar:	'Lawrence of Arabia' – Peter O'Toole
Popular Record:	'With Love From Me To You' – The Beatles
Born in 1963:	Natasha Richardson, actress George Michael, singer John Bercow, Conservative politician

Chapter 15

Alice was bored; bored with her boring job, bored with her boring boyfriend and bored with her boring life.

At the time of her father's death three years earlier, there had been more drama than she could handle. She would have given anything for life to go back to as it had been when she hadn't a care in the world, no decisions to make and everything to look forward to.

During the upheaval, she'd wished for a quiet life and now she had one, she was bored witless and fed up with her humdrum existence.

It was predominantly her gran who looked after her, running the household, doing the cooking and shopping. Brenda helped out with the cleaning and the washing. Alice's stint of running a household after her father died had been forgotten and she was, once again, treated like a princess.

Her boring boyfriend hadn't always been quite so boring.

Eighteen months earlier and a year into Alice's two year course, Sally had been the instigator of the relationship, albeit inadvertently. Alice knew Sally was concerned about her. She was still looking after Mr Phillips' youngest child during the holidays and Alice was still working in the make-up department at Lewis's but towards the end of the summer holidays after their first full year at college, they'd both had a free Friday afternoon.

Alice hadn't wanted to take up Sally's time. She didn't want to look needy, even with her best friend, but Sal had brushed her objections aside.

'Come on, Alice. It's only twelve months but it seems like years. The Halle's playing Sibelius and Grieg and I can get cheap tickets. Let's go into town and have a wander round the art gallery then get a bite to eat and go straight to the Free Trade Hall. Come on, it'll do us both good. It's too long since we treated ourselves and I miss you.'

Alice had been gratified to realise Sally meant what she said. Despite her new friends and new interests, the old bonds were still strong and she was clearly anxious for them to spend time together.

They were in one of the first floor galleries, looking at the Pre-Raphaelites. Whatever special exhibition was on, they always made a detour to this gallery to have another look at their favourites.

Alice was standing, lost in thought, in front of a Ford Maddox-Brown when Sally suddenly gave her a gentle shove.

'There's a lad over there can't take his eyes off you.'

Alice blinked and looked over Sally's shoulder, spotting a studious young man in horn rimmed glasses, dressed in jeans and a tweed jacket.

'I know him,' she said. 'He's at the college. His name's Alec something or other. He's in the same class as me for graphic design. He's not bad either.'

She giggled suddenly, 'I mean he's not bad at graphic design. I don't know about the rest.'

'He looks all right to me. Give him a bit of encouragement, smile at him for crying out loud.'

'Should I?'

'Sure, go on.'

Alice turned, caught the young man's eye and gave him a smile and a little wave.

Needing no further encouragement, he came over and joined them and was introduced to Sally, who smiled sweetly, winked behind his back and then looked at her watch.

'They'll be throwing us out any minute, it's almost closing time. We're going for a drink. Want to join us?'

Alice blushed, same old Sally, never been known to show restraint. She'd thought Sally was interested herself and then realised she was match-making on her behalf.

'I'd love to,' he said. 'Shall we make a move?'

At six o'clock, it was still a little early for the Friday night crowd. They found seats in the lounge and Alec went to the bar.

Although initially he'd been a little shy, he warmed under Sally's banter and they were soon laughing like old friends.

When Sally checked the time again, it was time to leave.

'Come on Alice, we've got fifteen minutes before the concert starts. We'd better get a move on.'

They were about to leave as the door swung open and Johnnie Marshall and his girlfriend came through into the lounge. He nodded at Alice, looked straight through Sally, and appeared not to notice the young man with them. His girlfriend gave Alice the once-over, taking in her clothes and her shiny hair then turned her back on them to take a seat in the corner.

Alec left with them and Alice knew he stood and watched them walk away, arm in arm.

'You've made a conquest there,' said Alice.

'You're crackers,' Sally smiled. 'He couldn't take his eyes off you. He didn't ask you for a date 'cos I was there and anyway, you'll see him next week at college. Mark my words, he'll move in then.'

'We'll see,' said Alice and wondered if Sal was right. She'd always been more streetwise than her.

'Did you see the look Marshall's girlfriend gave you? Honestly, if looks could kill.' Sally grinned and went on, 'I never had him down as the faithful type but he's been going out with her for ages. She must have *something* he wants.'

The sight of Johnnie Marshall could often sour Sally's mood and Alice changed the subject quickly.

'I'm looking forward to the concert. Thanks for getting the tickets.'

'No problem,' responded Sally. 'I'm looking forward to it myself.'

Sally had proved right and sure enough, when college started a week later, Alec had saved her a place at lunchtime on the first day and had asked her out.

Her first year had been difficult. She'd felt isolated and shut out and had even, for a brief time, considered throwing the towel in. Gradually, the pain of her father's death had lifted and now, more than ever, she wanted to do him proud. She loved the work and had done extremely well in the end of year exams.

For the first time, she was part of a group, thanks to Alec's intervention. People found her more approachable and wondered why they'd thought her stand-offish. Hardly anybody noticed the jeans bought from her holiday earnings. She still looked like a fashion plate, in the jeans or out of them.

She and Alec gradually became a couple. Although they often went out as part of the group, they spent time together too. She'd even asked him home to tea and her grandma had pronounced him 'a lovely boy.'

They shared occasional kisses and cuddles; on the back row of the cinema and sometimes in the park. Although Alice enjoyed their embraces, it didn't make her heart beat faster and want to throw caution to the wind. Alec, on the other hand, got a little hot and bothered occasionally.

It had worked well enough. She'd enjoyed being half of a couple and they had their courses and friends in common. Once they'd left college and worked on opposite sides of the city, Alec wasn't quite so interesting. Constantly moaning about people at work and the jobs he was expected to do, he was rapidly wearing out his welcome. She didn't want to hurt his feelings but the time to wave him goodbye was rapidly approaching. Their friends from college had largely disappeared, most of them returning to their homes in other cities and Alec, undiluted by other company, was becoming seriously hard going.

Her job was a disappointment too. She'd smiled and nodded at her interview. Said she'd be glad to start at the bottom, learning as she went along. The reality wasn't what she'd expected. In a predominantly male office and the youngest employee, she wasn't much more than a dogsbody; making tea, running errands and answering the 'phone.

The only other female was the boss's secretary, a bespectacled married woman in her thirties and they had little in common. The boss was kind and encouraging but the rest of the men treated her with condescension, often prefacing or ending their requests with 'there's a good girl' or making suggestive remarks. The office was always busy, either a deadline to meet or a new client to impress, and it could be exciting but she was given only the simplest of tasks. Although she watched and learned from the projects being prepared, nobody asked her opinion or whether she had any ideas.

At her lowest, she wished she hadn't jumped at the first job she'd been offered and then shrugged and supposed it wouldn't have been different anywhere else. I'll stick it for twelve months, she thought, and if it gets no better, I'll look around. At least I'll have some work experience by then.

Sally, who still had a year to go at college, was practically her only friend and although they met as often as possible, Alice spent much of her time on her own. There were no art projects to fill her evenings and though she spent some time making new clothes, there was a limit to how much would fit in her wardrobe. Her sketch pads were piling up too; quickly drawn pictures of her mum and her gran, bunches of flowers and bowls of fruit. There was one of her father she was particularly proud of. The photo in the frame in her bedroom had been the model and the pen and ink likeness was startling.

These were all stop gaps to fill her time. At twenty years old, and with two years of college behind her, she wanted a little excitement.

***

Johnnie's rise had been slow but steady. After a sticky six months, business had boomed. Maurice had wanted nothing to do with the shop apart from showing his face now then and throwing his weight about. Johnnie suffered in silence. Although he had control of the shop takings, Johnnie wanted to expand and Maurice still held the capital. No amount of fishing helped. There was money there but Johnnie didn't know how much and Maurice wasn't about to tell him.

Many of the old school punters were still suspicious of the betting shops, unwilling to accept change and they kept Maurice in business. Although the volume of bets wasn't what it had been, there was still a decent living to be made. The runners still turned up on race days, circulating the pubs and picking up betting slips, the lookouts still got their few bob for watching for the law. Maurice was able to cope single handed, operating from the back of the house, and Johnnie was in the shop all day.

It pleased them both to know whatever cash was around was being harvested by one or other.

The housekeeping situation had worsened. Jimmy Gill's sister kept the place as straight as she could but she wasn't there every day as Hettie had been. Their shirts were washed and ironed and put back in the wardrobes, the beds were changed and the kitchen floor mopped now and again but there was an overall look of neglect about the place. Maurice was pathologically untidy. He never rinsed a cup but always took a clean one out of the cupboard. He left his papers lying around, his coat over the back of a chair and his dirty shirts in a heap on the landing. The constant mess drove Johnnie crazy.

When Johnnie thought about Hettie, which was seldom enough, it was always with resentment. She should be here doing this stuff, not him.

One Saturday afternoon when the shop was crowded, the door burst open and Mickey Smith came rushing in, pushing through the punters watching their horses on the television tuned to the races and those queuing to place their next bets.

Fighting for breath, he gasped,

'Johnnie, you'd better come quick. There's something wrong with your dad.'

'What's wrong with him?' muttered Johnnie distractedly, still taking cash and placing bets.

320

'He's ill, had some kind of turn. He's sitting in his chair and can't move. It looks serious. You'd better come, I don't know what to do.'

It must be serious, thought Johnnie. I've never heard him say so much at one go. I'd better go and have a look.

Whispering to the cashier he'd wouldn't be long, he reluctantly left the shop, hoping chaos wouldn't follow if he weren't there to keep an eye on things.

The house was only round the corner and Mickey was all but running. Johnnie struggled to keep up. Surely it couldn't be so bad.

Like his father, Johnnie now used the front door and as he put his key in the lock, Mickey ran round the back. From the hallway, he could hear a strangled guttural noise coming from the kitchen.

Maurice was lying on the floor, his face distorted and pulled down at one side, obviously trying to talk but the sounds made no sense.

Johnnie didn't know what to do. Should he lift him up, should he leave him where he was? He shouted to Mickey who was coming through the back gate and together, they heaved Maurice's not inconsiderable weight into an armchair.

Johnnie grabbed the 'phone, dialled nine nine nine, and shouted they needed an ambulance, now. The calm voice asking questions at the end of the line did nothing to soothe him but he was finally assured an ambulance would be there shortly.

Maurice was struggling to speak and Johnnie could only keep repeating help was on its way. The place was a shambles and Johnnie couldn't bear for outsiders to see the mess so he moved dishes into the sink, stacked the papers in a neat pile and hung Maurice's jacket on a hook behind the door. Though Maurice couldn't speak, he was looking frantically at the table and when the penny dropped, Johnnie locked the cash box, put the key in his trouser pocket and shoved the box into a cupboard. He turned to Mickey, hanging around at the kitchen door.

'You stay here. Tell anyone who comes they'll have to go to the shop to place their bets.'

This wasn't a request but an order and Mickey nodded.

'I'll stay 'til you get back.'

He wouldn't have dared do otherwise.

There was a loud knock at the front door and Maurice was quickly loaded on to a stretcher and into the ambulance. Curtains were twitching in the houses facing and half a dozen kids had collected to see the drama. Talk about jungle drums, thought Johnnie; weddings, funerals and ambulances and a crowd will form in minutes. He climbed into the ambulance and sat next to his father. He didn't touch him, didn't even hold his hand. All he could manage was a muttered,

'You'll be all right, Dad. You're in safe hands.'

It was three hours before Johnnie got home. Maurice had had a serious stroke and the doctor had been unable or unwilling to say more.

'We can never tell with these things, the rate of recovery varies from patient to patient. We'll keep a close eye on him tonight and know more tomorrow. He'll be going up to the ward in a few minutes, do you want to go with him?'

Johnnie didn't hesitate but replied,

'There's nothing I can do, is there? I'd better get off, there's stuff to deal with at home.'

The doctor nodded, thinking perhaps of mothers or wives and children. Johnnie was thinking of outstanding bets and how he was going manage the following morning. As he walked along the grey hospital corridor, he realised his car was still outside the shop. Bugger it, he thought, I'll get a taxi. I can't be standing around at bus stops.

Mickey was still sitting on the back step and he jumped up when Johnnie appeared.

'There's a couple of blokes coming round at eight to collect their winnings. How's your dad?'

'Don't know yet. Know more tomorrow. Did you send the new bets round to the shop?'

'Yeah, I told 'em what you said.'

'Right, better call in the shop at lunchtime. There'll be some running around to do.'

'Right, Johnnie. I'll be off.'

Not a thought that Mickey had been there to help with his dad, not a thought he'd been hanging around in the cold for hours, no word of thanks. Johnnie's only thought was to check the cash box was intact.

There'd been no contact with Hettie or Harry since her refusal to come home but it might be worthwhile trying to smooth the way there.
Telephone directories gave him the number and Harry answered the telephone. Clearly not overjoyed to hear from Johnnie, Harry suspected the news wouldn't be good.
'Harry, Dad's had a stroke and is in hospital.'
'Sorry to hear that. How bad is it?'
'They can't tell yet, they'll know better by the weekend. He looks shocking and he's going to need looking after when he comes out. Mum may have to come home to take care of him. Will you have a word?'
The chill in Harry's voice was evident.
'I'll tell her he's ill but I can't tell her what to do. She'll make her own mind up but I don't hold out much hope. Ring me or ring her when things are clearer.'
He hung up without another word.
I must be slipping, thought Johnnie. Should have used a bit more soft soap, should have asked how he was, how Mum was, how things were going. I'll do it next time. I can always put it down to worry about Dad.
Discouraged by Harry's response, he could only hope Hettie's conscience would prompt her to do the right thing, to come home and do her duty. There was no way he could make her if she chose not to.

The next day was frantic. Johnnie had the takings from the previous day to check, he didn't trust anyone else to do it, and his dad's stuff to sort out. There were a couple of pay-outs to Maurice's punters but Mickey had to be sent round to the pubs and factories to pass the word bets would have to be placed in the shop for the foreseeable future.

It was six o'clock before he left the shop and he was relieved to find there was a hot meal waiting in the oven. The cleaner had been in and the place was straight and as he washed his plate and mug, he had the fleeting thought it would stay that way, at least until Maurice came home.

He set off for the hospital. Maybe there'd be some news and he could make plans. When he arrived on the ward, he asked to see the sister and was shown into her office. She looked him up and down, noting there was no real look of concern and no flowers, grapes or the like, and kept him standing.

'Your father's condition is much the same,' she said. 'We may see an improvement in the next day or so but he's unlikely to make a full recovery.'

'Any idea how long he'll be in?' Johnnie asked.

'It's hard to say but we'll keep an eye on him and make an evaluation towards the weekend.'

Fat lot of good that is, thought Johnnie. I need to get organised. This isn't a case where no news is good news, I've got a feeling things can only get worse.

'You can go along and see him. He's in the bed on the right, nearest the door.'

He'd been dismissed and didn't like it but he made his way into the stuffy, overheated ward and found his father lying in bed, propped up on pillows. His face was still drawn down on one side but he was asleep and snoring loudly. Grey whiskers were showing across his jowls and the dreadful hospital pyjamas made him look like a pauper. Johnnie couldn't have brought pyjamas from home, Maurice had never worn them in his life. He supposed he could send Mickey out to buy a pair tomorrow and bring them in.

Standing at the foot of the bed, the smell of the ward making him queasy, his mind raced with possibilities. Would Maurice recover at all? If he did, who'd look after him? If only he had some concrete idea of what would happen, he could start to look ahead. This marking time was killing him.

There was nothing to be gained by hanging around. Maurice didn't even know he was there. When one of the nurses passed, he whispered to her,

'I don't want to wake him up. Will you tell him I came and I'll try and get in again tomorrow?'

Less experienced than the matron, she was sorry for him and touched his arm gently. He was a good looking chap after all.

'Yes, don't worry. I'll tell him you were here.'

'Thanks,' he muttered and walked off briskly. He couldn't get out fast enough.

Looking briefly at his watch, Johnnie fished in his pocket for his car keys. He was supposed to be picking Sandra up in less than fifteen minutes. The upheaval of his father's illness had wiped her from his mind and when he remembered their arrangements, he couldn't be bothered. To hell with her, he thought, I'll give her a ring when I get home.

It had crossed his mind a couple of times recently perhaps it was time to cut her loose. She hadn't become demanding, she knew the consequences. Nevertheless, she looked wistful when one of their crowd arrived sporting an engagement ring or when they were invited to a wedding and had been almost tearful when her friend from school had a baby.

They'd been seeing each other for five or six years. He'd never been what anyone would call faithful and had had a string of one night stands and a couple of affairs with married women.

He'd tired of sex in the back of his car or waiting for Sandra's parents to be out or away. Although they went to a hotel occasionally, it was expensive and Sandra found it embarrassing when he signed the register as Mr and Mrs, keeping her hand in her pocket so no-one could see there was no ring.

The problem had been solved when he set up shop. Within two weeks, he'd installed a bed settee and a couple of other bits of furniture in the upstairs front room and he and Sandra used the place on a regular basis. She was still attractive to him and could still make him laugh. Above all, she made no demands. They were sexually matched. After all, he'd taught her well.

He shrugged. There was too much on his plate at present to make any other changes. A decision about Sandra could wait, he'd give her a ring when he got home and tell her he'd see her at the weekend.

***

Sally

With my second year behind me and my last still to come, I'd come to a cross roads. It was time to face the bitter truth. Although I was a more than competent musician and my marks for theory were excellent, the real fire or spark wasn't there. There was one student in my year who 'had it' and I wasn't the one. The discipline and knowledge were there but not that elusive something which brought an extra dimension to the music.

None of the other students seemed to be suffering the same soul searching. Was nobody but me concerned about the future? I had no patience with them. Some of them were missing lessons and spending too much time in the pub but at the moment, I didn't have the heart to socialise.

It was the first time in my life I'd suffered disappointment in any sphere. I'd always excelled at everything I put my hand to. No amount of hard work, no amount of practicing and no amount of watching and listening would give me the special something I lacked.

Better face it, there wasn't going to be a career as a concert pianist. It had only ever been a pipe dream. The best I could hope for was to be taken on as a trainee in an orchestra, filling in when someone was ill or playing the flute, my second instrument, when no-one else was available. There would be no working my way up to be a soloist, I wasn't good enough.

The pain of this admission was hard to bear, like a hard knot behind my ribs and the thought of disappointing all the people who'd believed in me was excruciating. I felt like a fraud and a failure and as guilty as hell.

All this mental thrashing around was driving me mad. I couldn't see my way forward. Should I finish the course or should I leave now? If I didn't do this, what else would I do? What could I do? My head felt it would burst with the pressure.

Alice would probably have understood but it was hard to admit, even to her, I was struggling. Though she was disappointed with her current job, I was sure she would eventually make her way artistically. The work she'd turned out, and was still turning out in her spare time, showed her talent.

Disillusioned as we both were, I felt like grabbing her, throwing a few things in a suitcase and making a run for it, the two of us against the world. It was unrealistic, of course, a complete fantasy.

During the summer holidays, I was again looking after Mr Phillip's youngest daughter and it was he who came to my rescue. A shrewd judge of character, he'd stopped me one afternoon as I was leaving the house. Mrs Phillips had arrived home and was in the kitchen with the little one, preparing the evening meal.

'I've been hard at it with paper work all afternoon, I'll walk down to the bus stop with you and stretch my legs,' and called to his wife he wouldn't be long.

'If you're not in a hurry, Sally, we could walk through the park.'

I nodded and murmured,

'That would be nice.'

Most of the kids had gone home and there was only one old man walking an aged dog. The large area in the park was nearly bald but the bowling green was smooth and tended, the surrounding flower beds filled with brightly coloured 'corporation planting.'

'Let's sit for a minute or two,' he said and I plonked myself down on a bench and waited until he settled next to me.

He looked much the same as he had while he was our headmaster. The hair, perhaps, was greyer and there were a few more wrinkles but his sharp grey eyes still missed very little.

He looked at me kindly and finally asked,

'What is it Sally? What's dragging you down?'

I suspected Mum and Dad and even Alice thought it was 'one of Sally's moods' and I'd snap out of it. They'd been handling me with kid gloves for the last couple of weeks, almost walking on eggs around me, and I felt guilty about that. They hadn't realised something was seriously wrong.

If he hadn't been so kind, I could have kept it together. I'd wanted to deal with it myself, find my own solutions but the sympathy in his eyes was my undoing. Before I could take a breath, I was snivelling and sobbing and the whole sorry story came pouring out. He waited until I'd finished then passed me a clean hankie from his jacket pocket.

'Well, Sally, this is a hard knock but you should be proud of the way you're facing it.'

'I'm not facing it all, I'm such a mess.'

'Not true. You've admitted to yourself you're not going to achieve your life's ambition. It's the first step, and the hardest. Time to regroup, look at other possibilities. You *will* overcome this, I've known you since you were a child and I know what you're made of.'

The confidence in his voice and in his eyes strengthened me and I blew my nose and wiped my running eyes and tried to pull myself together.

'It's not going to be easy,' he said, 'Music is such a large part of your life but it will always be there.'

'It's been the most important thing for such long time, the thought of putting something else first is killing me. That, and letting everybody down.'

'You're not letting anybody down, not even yourself. There's no shame if you've done your best. These are your ambitions, not your mum and dad's. They won't care what you do as long as you're happy. Admit that, at least.'

He was right. It was my own disappointment I had to deal with but I was pushing some of the blame on them.

We sat in the park for ages, talking things over and his grasp of my problems and his complete understanding grounded me. For the first time in weeks, my spirits lifted and I was better able to face the world.

'Are you ready to go home?' he asked. 'Mrs Phillips will be wondering where I've got to.'

I nodded and rose, pushing the soggy hankie into my coat pocket.

'Sally, I know you're bitterly disappointed but don't make any rash decisions. You need to give yourself time to look at all your options. Let things settle and we'll talk again early next week.'

Before he turned to leave, he put his hand on my shoulder and gave me a reassuring squeeze. My eyes filled again and all I could manage was a strangled 'thank you'.

'It'll all come right, Sally. You'll find your way.'

Watching him walk away, I fumbled for the hankie again but I felt better, better than I had for ages.

When I got home, I dashed straight to the bathroom and threw cold water on my face but as I sat down to tea, Mum was looking at me closely. She could tell I'd been crying but didn't ask and I was glad I didn't have to explain.

More cheerful, I laughed and joked a bit with Dad and their relief I was more or less back to normal was clear. It was hard to accept I wasn't letting them down but I knew they loved me and would back me whatever I decided.

My problems were far from over, difficult decisions still had to be made but I no longer felt the world was against me. Maybe Mr Phillips was right. The hardest part was facing the truth. I didn't know where to go from here but there would be answers, I only had to find them.

It was a relief to know I wasn't entirely alone. Somebody else knew the awful truth.

Chapter 16

Hettie was torn. Harry insisted she owed Maurice nothing. It was crazy to put aside everything she'd worked for.

With the money it had taken her so many long years to save, she'd bought the shop where she'd stayed at the time of Harry's wedding. Auntie Sheila, Rosie's aunt, had been past retirement age then and had been only too happy to sell up and move to a tiny cottage on the High Street. They'd become firm friends and because she'd been such a staunch ally, Hettie had gained acceptance in the village. It could have been much more difficult. After all, she was a 'foreigner' and a married woman who'd left her husband but between them, Sheila and Harry and Harry's wife Rosie had smoothed the way. Little had been said, just a few seeds sown, but people believed she'd escaped from a bitter and brutal marriage; not so far from the truth.

It was after hours and the shop was closed when she heard a tapping at the shop door and found Sheila on the step with a bottle of sherry in the wicker shopping basket over her arm.

'I thought you might like some company,' she said.

'Come on in, I'm glad you came. I could do with someone to talk to. Harry won't listen to anything I say. He keeps saying 'don't do it, Mum.'

They sat upstairs in the comfortable sitting room. Sheila had taken most of the furniture with her and Hettie had refurnished bit by bit, buying good second hand stuff from shops in local villages or at country house sales. The polished wood shone in the evening sunlight, two comfortable armchairs faced the fireplace where there was a low fire to ward off the slight evening chill. The scent of the sweet peas in the centre of the table filled the room.

'I blame myself in a way,' Hettie said, nursing a generous sherry in a graceful crystal glass, in itself a reminder of the cheap stuff she'd used at home.

'I should have gone for a divorce straight away. God knows I had grounds enough. Infidelity wouldn't have been hard to prove, I can tell you. But I wanted to be away, couldn't face the solicitors and maybe having to face Maurice in court.'

Sheila wisely made only appropriate noises and let her get it all off her chest.

'Although I owe him nothing, I'm still his wife. Is it my duty to go back and look after him? I don't even know how bad he is. Johnnie said he'd 'phone when there was news but we've heard nothing since the weekend.'

Sheila took a sip of her sherry.

'Harry's right. You've made a life for yourself here where you're appreciated. Think about moving back north, back to that house and leaving Harry and Rosie and the children behind. How often would you see them then? You'd be tied down looking after a man you detest.'

She paused, collecting her thoughts.

'Don't let young Johnnie rattle you. My advice is to wait and see how things stand before you make a decision. For all you know, he could make a complete recovery and then you'll have gone back for nothing.'

Seeing the sense of this, Hettie said,

'You're right. I'll wait and see how the land lies before I do anything. Come on, let's top your glass up.'

After Sheila had left and the evening was drawing in, Hettie sat in the dusk in the light from the fire.

Memories of her years with Maurice rose to the surface, not the happy ones of the early days but of when things had started to go wrong.

At the announcement of her pregnancy, she couldn't have said Maurice was overjoyed but initially, he revelled in the sight of her body, the fuller breasts and the slight mound of her stomach. She was blooming, her hair shone and her skin glowed but in the seventh month, sex became too painful.

He avoided looking at her without her clothes. Her formerly graceful body was heavy and unwieldy and her slim ankles slightly swollen. His distaste showed and made her weepy and he became even crosser.

'The sooner it's all over, the better,' he muttered.

When Hettie finally gave birth to a bouncing baby boy they were both relieved. Maurice bought drinks all round in the pub, telling everyone the child was to be called Harry, after his own father.

Hettie now had something to fill her days but Maurice was short tempered and resented the time she spent fussing over the child. When Harry was six weeks old and sleeping through the night, Hettie told Maurice the doctor had said it would be all right for them to 'resume marital relations'. She'd missed the physical contact. He hadn't touched her for weeks, not so much as a pat on the shoulder or a kiss on the cheek. She'd thought things would go back to normal.

They didn't. Maurice was slightly repelled by the lingering milky smell. She was still carrying a little extra weight and he'd been horrified to see stretch marks on her breasts and stomach. Her perfection was marred and his adoration of her had slipped through his fingers. Their formerly rich and satisfying sex life dwindled into more infrequent and fairly perfunctory performances which brought little pleasure to either of them.

When she'd discovered her second pregnancy eighteen months later, she dreaded telling Maurice but finally plucked up courage.

'What again?' he'd said shortly, as if it were all her fault, 'another flamin' mouth to feed.'

The second pregnancy wasn't as easy as the first. Hettie had suffered from morning sickness for almost three months and with Harry toddling, she'd had her hands full and looked washed out most of the time. It was unthinkable Maurice would help in any way. He paid little attention to his son except to express disgust when Hettie put the baby to her breast.

On the birth of his second son, Maurice again bought drinks all round but his heart wasn't in it. He looked morosely at the baby stuff cluttering up the house and was put out when Hettie was even more wrapped up in the kids.

Not until Johnnie was born did Hettie realise what an easy baby Harry had been. The new baby was much more demanding. He suffered from colic at two months and there was no comforting him. She walked the floor, patting his back and crooning for hours at a stretch. His constant crying drove Maurice out of the house.

'Is there no bloody peace in my own home, woman?' he'd shout, then shrug on his coat and head for the pub. Hettie was glad to see him go.

The early promise was gone. He no longer took her with him when he went out, even at the weekend. As a result, he no longer cared too much what she looked like. The stuff she had was getting shabbier and shabbier and she'd no time either to mess with her hair and it was kept tied back out of the way.

Before the children were born, when he came home from seeing his friends on a Friday night, she'd wait up for him and they'd sit in front of the fire and drink whisky while he filled her in on the latest gossip and passed on the current jokes.

Now he was out most nights and often came home the worse for wear. She was invariably in bed, worn out after a day with the kids and the housework. Although she feigned sleep when she heard him climb the stairs, she stiffened as he fumbled with his clothes and swore under his breath. Sometimes he made love to her roughly, breathing beer fumes into her face.

She'd thought it couldn't get any worse until the first time he gave her a crack. He'd been full of ale and she'd asked a question too many. He'd looked a little shamefaced in the morning but as time went on, his scruples disappeared and he handed out slaps on a regular basis if she 'got out of line'. She bit her tongue and kept her head down. At least he wasn't knocking the kids about. He'd have been horrified if anyone had called him a wife beater. He didn't beat her, he just gave her a backhander now and then to teach her who was boss.

There was even worse to come. When he climbed into bed reeking of perfume and of another woman, she felt physically sick. Lying rigid until his deepening snores allowed her to get out of bed, she retched herself empty.

There was no way out, no escape. She had nowhere to go. A return to her parents' home with two young children was unthinkable and the thought of leaving them with their father never crossed her mind. There was no way she could find work and still look after the kids. It was a bitter truth but it needed facing, she was trapped.

Things changed, in Maurice's eyes for the better. She made increased efforts to keep the kids out from under his feet. They were growing, and old enough to play out and old enough too, to be frightened of Maurice when he raised his voice.

The 'answering back' became a thing of the past and she did what was expected of her. Apart from putting food on the table and keeping the place straight, her other important job was to look after Maurice's clothes, keeping his shoes shined and his suits brushed and at least two clean shirts in the wardrobe.

It was all done without complaint but underneath she seethed. The determination to leave took root but she wouldn't leave without enough cash to give her a stake in the future. Her small raids on Maurice's cash increased. She had a goal but was wise enough to be cautious. Learning to wheedle and flatter when necessary made her wince but she learned.

At least, she'd thought bitterly, with a bit of luck he won't be bothering me with his drunken fumbling. It was the only relief in the whole sorry situation.

The first plan had been to leave when both the children were of school age. When the time came, there wasn't enough in the pot to set them up in a place of their own and at best, she'd only be able to get part time work.

Hettie stirred. The fire was out. Her glass was empty and she was sitting alone in her darkened, chilly sitting room with the faint light of a half-moon shining through the window. Her mind was made up.

After all those years of penury and humiliation she'd escaped and, she thought, I am not going back, not at any price.

Decision made, she took herself off to bed and slept soundly for the first time in a week.

***

After his initial visit to the hospital, Johnnie visited twice more. He'd sat for a few minutes on a steel framed, plastic seated chair and looked at his father. Maurice was unable to communicate. Only strangled noises came from his mouth and his frustration was clear. The more anxious he became, the more mangled the sounds. The eyes were pleading, pleading with Johnnie to understand but he couldn't make out individual words.

Johnnie couldn't stand it, not out of concern but because it was so pointless and because of his genuine antipathy to being in the enclosed space of the overheated and busy ward.

A visit was the only way to get any kind of progress report and he was desperate to know what was going on. Would Maurice recover? The sister, who'd taken an obvious dislike to him, wouldn't give him information over the telephone. On each visit, he'd hoped to catch the duty doctor, so far without success.

It hadn't gone unnoticed he came infrequently and always empty handed. Two pairs of pyjamas and some fruit had been brought in by a shy young man who sat by Maurice's bed for a while, his hand resting gently on Maurice's arm. He said very little but listened intently to Maurice's strangled attempts to communicate and seemed to understand. Maurice looked pathetically grateful for the human contact.

The sister gave Johnnie short shrift. 'As well as can be expected', was the only information forthcoming.

Fat lot of use that is, thought Johnnie. He was trying to run the business and handle the extra punters from Maurice's side, some of whom were difficult and suspicious. He'd need some kind of plan for

Maurice's care when he was discharged although it didn't look as though it would be any time soon. Perhaps he had a couple of weeks' leeway. The longer they kept him in the better.

Leaving the hospital with a sigh of relief, he made his way back to the car, thoughts racing. There was still no clue as to where Maurice kept his money. Johnnie's hands were tied. He'd had a perfunctory look around the house and at some of his father's papers but could find no sign. If Maurice made any kind of recovery and discovered Johnnie had been rummaging around, he'd never get his hands on the cash. Maurice would be outraged and that particular door would slam in his face, permanently.

For the second Saturday in a row, he put Sandra on hold, telling her he'd be in touch in a couple of days. She'd been understanding and asked if there was anything she could do but he choked her off and hung up quickly.

As he drove towards home, he regretted being so hasty. The evening stretched before him. He didn't want to go in his local. Everybody would be sniffing round, asking how his dad was with phony concern in their voices. It didn't cross his mind some of them might be concerned.

On impulse, he drew up outside The Church on Ardwick Green, it was unlikely anyone he knew would be drinking there.

The pub was filled with the rumble of conversation, not as crowded as it would be in an hour or so although many of the tables were occupied and there were several men standing at the bar. Most of the customers were dressed in Saturday night finery, obviously looking to have a good time.

As he ordered his first drink, he caught sight of a familiar face reflected in the mirror behind the bar. She leaned closer to the chap she was sitting with and whispered in his ear.

He watched Doris McGuire, his father's lover for years, stand and walk towards the ladies. Dressed in a smart dove grey suit, hair well cut and make up skilfully applied, she caught his eye briefly then looked away.

Still watching in the mirror, he saw her come out and then she was walking towards him. She's got a nerve. I thought she'd pretend she hadn't seen me, he thought.

He looked her over coolly from head to toe. She must be well into her thirties, he thought, but she looks good. I wouldn't throw her out of bed myself. No wonder the old fella hung on to her.

'You didn't waste any time,' he said, nodding towards the chap at the table.

'Oh, he's just a friend, in Manchester on business.'

Like many liars, she gave too much information, embellished the story a bit. 'He's a distant cousin although we don't see much of his side of the family.'

Knowing her effect on men only too well, she knew she'd made an impression on Johnnie and her clear brown eyes challenged him as she noticed his eyes drop to the swell of breast at the neck of her silky lilac blouse.

'Anyway, how's your Dad? I heard he was in the hospital.'

'Yeah, I was going to call round and see if you wanted to go and see him, let you know he's in ward three. He's not getting many visitors.'

It had crossed his mind he may be able to rope her in when the old man came out, give him a hand with looking after him. He was disabused immediately.

'Well, it did cross my mind to go down to the hospital but I've been busy. I've been doing overtime all week.'

Overtime my eye, he thought.

'Anyway,' she continued, 'I can't stand hospitals, feel sick as soon as I walk through the doors. But still, give him my love when you see him. Tell him I was asking about him.'

She turned and he caught a waft of her heavy, musky perfume. Walking back to the table, she leaned forward and spoke, giving her companion a full eyeful down her cleavage. As they made their way to the door, Johnnie got a good at him; smooth looking chap with a slight tan, dressed in navy with a flash of gold in the watch and the heavy signet ring on his right hand. Doris gave Johnnie a little wave and nodded. Had she no shame?

Yes, she'd asked about Maurice but hadn't waited for an answer. After all those years of taking the old man's cash, she'd obviously ditched him as soon as the going got rough. Poor old sod just didn't know it yet.

'Bloody women,' he muttered under his breath.

The peace of mind he'd been seeking in a quiet drink eluded him. He was angry and anxious all over again. He finished his pint, leaving the sound of conversation and laughter behind him. The thought of the empty house gave him the creeps but he couldn't face another pub so he gritted his teeth and started the engine.

The traffic was light and as he turned into Hyde Road, a girl at the bus stop caught his eye. Dressed in a belted pale coloured raincoat, bag slung over her shoulder and hands in pockets, he could see her foot tapping with impatience. She'd obviously been waiting a while, there was a queue behind her.

Pulling up beyond the stop, he gave the horn a tap and saw her turn to look. He'd been fairly sure it was Alice Spencer and he'd been right. She left the queue and walked back towards him.

He leaned over and opened the passenger door as she drew level,

'Need a ride home, Alice?'

Alice climbed gratefully into the car. The temperature had dropped and there was a chill in the air. She pushed her windblown hair back from her face and turned towards him. In contrast to the woman he'd so recently encountered, her perfume was light and floral. It suited her.

'Hello, Johnnie, it was nice of you to stop.'

'No problem,' he said. 'I'm going your way anyway.'

His usual debonair manner was absent and he looked strained and worried.

'How's it going?' she asked, remembering his father was in the hospital.

'Not bad,' he replied. 'Busy, as usual.'

Poor lad, she thought, thinking back to when her own father had been ill. People had asked how he was every five minutes and she'd had to give the same answers over and over again. He obviously didn't want to talk about it.

'What are you doing standing at the bus stop at this time of night, been to the Apollo?'

'Yes, marvellous film, 'To Kill a Mocking Bird,' have you seen it?'

'No, not been to the flicks much recently. Did you go on your own?'

'No, I was with a lad from college. I've been seeing him for a while but he can be awkward. I was fed up with him anyway and he turned up tonight already spoiling for a row so when we came out of the cinema, I told him to take himself and his bad temper home. I guess that's the end of that. I won't see him again.'

The flicker of irritation in her voice was unmistakable.

Surprised she'd been so candid, Johnnie's expression lightened. It was the only good news he'd had in days. The sight of Alice, her quiet beauty and the sympathy shining in her eyes soothed his soul. He made the usual response,

'I wouldn't worry, there are plenty more fish in the sea.'

'I suppose you're right,' Alice sighed.

He slowed as he reached the corner of the street where she lived with her gran and granddad.

'All right here?'

'Yes, it's fine. Thanks for coming to my rescue. You seem to be making a habit of it.'

She got out of the car and leaned forward before she closed the door.

'Thanks again, goodnight.'

'Goodnight, Alice,' he murmured, put the car back into gear and drove away.

The 'phone was ringing as he put his key in the front door. Glancing at his watch, he checked the time. Who would be ringing at ten on a Saturday night? He reached for the .phone.

'Yes?' he asked abruptly.

'Mr Marshall, Mr John Marshall?'

'Yes, who's that?'

'It's the hospital, your father has become very poorly. You should come straight away.'

Less than thirty minutes later, he was making his way along the almost deserted hospital corridor. There were few people around, only a couple of nurses, deep in conversation. The quiet was unsettling and the lights were dim, making him even more uneasy, wondering what to expect. He hurried along to the ward and pushed open the big swing doors, making his way to the sister's office.

The dragon usually on duty was missing and a rosy cheeked, plump lady in immaculate uniform sat in her chair. This must be the night sister, he thought.

'Mr Marshall?' she asked.

'Yes, I had a telephone call.'

'That was me. I'm afraid your father's had another massive stroke and we don't expect him to last the night.'

Johnnie was lost for words. He didn't know what to say or what to do, wrong footed for once. His self-assurance had deserted him.

'Let's go along and see him, shall we?'

She led the way down the short corridor. The ward was in semi-darkness, with one pale light over the nurse's station in the middle. Someone was muttering in their sleep, disturbing the silence. Maurice had been moved to the end of the ward and the regulation hospital curtains were drawn around the bed. Pulling the curtain aside, she waved him in, trapping him in the enclosed space.

He stood silently at the foot of the bed and looked at his father. Maurice looked dreadful, his breathing was loud and harsh and his face was ashen, the fingers of his left hand twitching with each breath.

Johnnie wasn't exactly unmoved but he didn't know what to do. He couldn't bring himself to sit on the chair by the side of the bed and couldn't have touched Maurice, not even his hand, if his life had depended on it. His eyes closed, Maurice was unaware Johnnie was there.

He stood and watched, idly thinking at least those dreadful hospital pyjamas had been replaced. He'd been shaved recently but the faint smell of unwashed flesh rising from the bed made him slightly sick.

Maurice's breathing became more and more laboured and with one final gasp, he was silent. Johnnie had been holding his breath and now released it gratefully. He stood for a few minutes, contemplating his father's face. Well, it's all over, Dad, he thought and went to fetch the sister.

There was nothing to be done and within a few minutes, he was on his way home.

Although it was turned twelve, he picked up the 'phone and called his brother. It didn't cross his mind to be a little considerate, to wait until morning. If he was up, Harry could be up too.

The 'phone rang for a long time before he heard Harry's flustered voice.

'Thought I'd let you know. Dad died an hour ago. Will you let Mum know? I'll ring again as soon as the funeral's been arranged.'

That was it. He hung up and went upstairs to his bed. The strain of the day had taken its toll and he was asleep in minutes.

Rarely in bed before the early hours on a Saturday night, he usually slept until lunchtime. This morning, he was awake at eight. He lay for a few minutes, assembling his thoughts. The house was silent, no heavy snoring from the front bedroom and at this hour, there was no one around in the street outside.

There was a lot to do, the most important, a thorough search of the house. As he reached the kitchen, he was relieved to find bacon and eggs and a loaf and made himself a decent breakfast, start the day right. No-one else knew the old man was gone and he'd be undisturbed.

The front bedroom was the obvious place to start and he systematically turned out all the drawers, a bag stashed on top of the wardrobe, looked under the mattress, checked the pockets in Maurice's suits, finding cash in all sorts of unlikely places, a total of several hundred pounds.

He'd found a couple of refuse sacks in the back of the kitchen cupboard and chucked in all the stuff of no further use; underwear and hankies, a couple of cardigans, old working trousers, belts, collar studs, shoes which showed signs of wear. Anything that might bring a few bob was left where it was; the rest he carried downstairs and dropped in the dustbin.

At lunchtime, he knocked off for half an hour. There must be more. There must be a bank book somewhere and maybe other papers worth something.

The funeral had to be organised too and even though it was Sunday, he 'phoned the local undertaker.

Fortunately, the senior partner picked up the 'phone and he was the man who could give Johnnie answers.

'Yes,' Johnnie had said. 'I know there are details to be arranged and I'll come in first thing in the morning to pay a deposit and sort out what we want but I need a date. We have family who have to come from down south and they'll need as much notice as possible.'

He didn't care whether they came or not. It was a way to apply some pressure.

At the mention of a deposit, the undertaker became remarkably co-operative.

'I've checked the diaries,' he said, in solemn undertaker's tones, 'and provided you can get here tomorrow with a death certificate and you don't have any special requests, it can be organised for Thursday, interment at four o'clock in Gorton Cemetery.'

Johnnie had no time for the niceties, there was still the rest of the house to go through.

'Fine,' he responded. 'I'll collect the death certificate from the hospital and bring it straight down. Should we say ten o'clock?'

He hung up and dialled Harry's number. His wife, whatever her name was, answered the 'phone. He couldn't be bothered with her and asked to speak to Harry.

'Funeral's on Thursday afternoon, four o'clock. Let me know if you and Mum are coming up.'

Harry could hear the coldness in Johnnie's voice. It hasn't touched him at all, he thought, typical Johnnie.

'I'll talk to Mum,' he said, 'and let you know.'

'Right, do that,' said Johnnie, hanging up and eager to get on.

***

Hettie heard a tapping on the shop door. She thought it was one of her customers, run out of something crucial. It wouldn't be the first time someone had knocked after closing but it was unusual for a Sunday.

Harry's silhouette showed through the glass. He was probably bringing news of Maurice. Her heart sank. She'd made her decision but would she be able to carry it through.

'Come in, son,' she said as she opened the door. 'You'd better come upstairs and tell me what's going on.'

In his late twenties and father of two, Harry looked well. He'd filled out a little but bore himself with confidence. The cowed lad who'd been largely ignored by Maurice was long gone. He was his own man now.

He followed her up the narrow staircase and into the sitting room. She motioned him towards a chair.

'You'd better sit down too. I've got some news.'

'Come on then, let's have it.'

Harry looked anxious, wondering how she'd react.

'For crying out loud, Harry, spit it out.'

He took a deep breath.

'Dad died last night. Johnnie 'phoned but I couldn't see any sense in coming over and waking you up.'

Hettie sat very still, gripping the arms of her chair. Her first reaction was relief. She wouldn't have to put her conscience to the test. Her second was she was finally free, free of Maurice, though she'd never be truly free of the memories of those dreadful years.

'Are you all right, Mum?'

'Yes, I'm all right. I can't believe it's over. I always feared he'd find a way to make me go back. If anything, I'm relieved. Does that sound awful?'

''Course not. I know what he put you through. Johnnie never saw the half of it. He was too wrapped up in himself.

The funeral's on Thursday. Do you want to go?'

'I think I'd better. After all, we were still married and there'll be stuff to sort out. What about you? Do you want to go?'

'I'll talk it over with Rosie and call round later.'

The implication was if she went, he'd go with her.

'Staying for a cuppa?' Hettie asked.

No, I'll get off. I promised to take the kids for a run this afternoon. Who knows how long this weather will last?'

'I'll see you later, then,' said Hettie and followed him down the stairs so she could lock up behind him.

Leaning back against the shop door, she was reassured. She wouldn't have to make the journey alone. Harry would go with her. The sunshine reflected off one of the glass cases dazzled her for a moment and, looking away, she focussed on the shop. The counters were wiped clean, all the shelves were neatly stacked and the floor had been mopped after closing. Although she'd made a few changes, the place essentially looked as it had the first time she saw it, a warm, inviting village shop. A sense of achievement filled her. I did it in spite of you, Maurice Marshall, she thought. You can never get at me again.

Chapter 17

Johnnie put the 'phone down. Arms crossed and foot tapping he was thinking. The cash he'd already found was stacked in Maurice's cash box, together with the takings for his last day of business and the contents of his wallet. There was already a tidy sum.

He knew there was more. He had to find it. There was another couple of hundred in an envelope in a drawer in the sideboard in the front room but nothing else, even after he'd almost dismantled the settee. Doubtful if anything except the cash box would be stashed in the kitchen, he nevertheless checked every cupboard, emptying each in turn and looked in all the boxes and canisters. 'God Almighty,' he muttered, 'some of this stuff has been here since before Mum left.' As the packets were checked, he dropped most of them into a rubbish bag. When he'd finished, only a packet of sugar and one of tea, a jar of coffee, a bottle of tomato sauce, a couple of tins of beans and Maurice's half empty bottle of whisky were left.

He took the cushions off the battered old armchairs and found another envelope stuffed with notes and added them to the growing pile.

The cupboard under the stairs was a jumble of all sorts of junk. It would take hours to go through this lot. There must be a bank account and paperwork of some sort somewhere and he'd looked everywhere else.

Wait a minute, he thought, I can't see the old man rummaging through this lot on a regular basis. It has to be easy to reach from the door.

His eyes settled on the tins of paint, arranged in rows on a high shelf running round the cupboard and he reached behind the two nearest the door.

'Eureka,' he said as the black plastic folder came into view. He knew bank statements when he saw them. He flicked the folder open to the statement on the top, the most recent, and whistled. No withdrawals were listed, only deposits and the final figure showed a total in credit of over nine thousand pounds; an absolute fortune. This was it, the jackpot. He only had to make sure he kept hold of it.

Pouring himself a shot of his dad's whisky and raising his glass, he said, 'Cheers, Dad.' and took the first sip. As he looked round the shabby kitchen, it was hard to believe they'd lived in what could only be seen as semi-squalor when all this cash was sitting in the bank.

With grubby hands and dust in his hair, he looked at the yawning cupboard and was tempted to close it and leave the rest alone but pushed himself. Having started, he was driven to get rid of the rest of the junk, make a clean sweep.

He had to clear the floor space so he could get to the shelves at the back and pulled out the boxes, checking each carefully before it went out in the yard. Spare blankets, old pans, paint brushes, all the miscellaneous rubbish accumulated over years. One box had all his stuff in it, from his first practice exercise books to the later grammar school books and all his photos and reports. It went out with the rest of the rubbish.

When only a box of dusters and polish, the vacuum cleaner and a brush and shovel was left, he could finally get to the shelves at the back. More old paint tins, where they'd come from he couldn't imagine, the house hadn't been painted for years but he soldiered on. As he removed the last of them, he found a dusty old tin, about eight inches by twelve, with a picture of horses embossed on the lid.

This looked more promising and he took it to the table and sat down to examine the contents. The lid was warped and he forced it off to find a stack of papers, some of them yellowed with age.

Leafing through them, he found birth certificates for all of them, even his mum, a letter from the Army Medical Board advising Maurice wasn't fit for active duty, Maurice and Hettie's marriage lines and a few ancient, sepia photographs. Having no idea who these people were, the photos were chucked into the rubbish bag. Right at the bottom of the pile, there were two large manila envelopes.

Intrigued, he slid the papers out of the first and found a letter dated ten years earlier from a firm of solicitors in Manchester confirming they were holding the deeds of the house for safekeeping. The old devil, Johnnie thought. I wonder if Mum knows. He'd had no idea Maurice had bought the property, had never noticed the rent man didn't call as he did at the other houses in the street.

The second envelope contained an even bigger shock. On the top of the documents, another letter from the same solicitor confirmed the purchase of the shop premises. He stared at the letterhead for a minute, hardly able to believe his eyes and hurriedly rifled through the rest of the papers. There was no mistake. The carefully folded, stiff buff papers were, indeed, the deeds to the shop.

He sat for a minute, quite still, hands flat on the table either side of the documents, mind racing, and shook his head in silent admiration.

Checking the date on the letter, he realized Maurice had bought the shop exactly a month after they'd moved in. Had the landlord wanted to sell or had pressure been brought to bear? The old lady had said she 'knew where the bodies were buried'. Perhaps Maurice had known too. Johnnie could only speculate, he'd never find out now.

It hardly mattered, the deeds were here, sitting on the kitchen table and, more importantly, Hettie couldn't possibly know anything about this. Now he had even more to lose.

Crucially, there was no Will. If it were anywhere, it would have been in this box with the rest of the stuff. Pity, if it hadn't been in his favour, he would have 'lost' it. He'd have to check with the solicitor. The Will might be there. If Maurice had died intestate, it was fairly sure everything would go to Hettie. She was his next of kin after all.

With the house thoroughly searched, he settled to count his 'takings'. Altogether, there was a total of three thousand and thirty two pounds and some change in the bottom of the cash box.

Nobody knows about this but me, he thought, so it's mine. Mum will have expected there to be some cash around but nothing like this. I'll tell her it was a couple of hundred, she'll never know the difference.

Looking at the stack of notes, he suddenly realised he was starving. He'd barely stopped all day and his stomach was rumbling. The evening stretched before him. He didn't fancy the pork chop in the pantry and didn't fancy sitting alone in empty house, even with the television for company. The silence was getting him down.

Picking up the 'phone, he dialled Sandra's number. Her father answered, disapproval clear in his voice. He took his time going to fetch her but eventually; she came to the 'phone, a little breathless.

'Sorry, Johnnie, I was in the garden. How are you? How's your dad?'

'He died last night,' he answered baldly, no sense in wrapping it up.

'I'm so sorry, is there anything I can do.'

'Yeah, you can keep me company. We'll go out for a meal. I'll pick you up at six thirty.'

Not even considering she might have other plans, he assumed she'd fall in with him and, of course, he was right.

He said nothing else, both her parents would be listening in and she'd get a talking to for dropping everything to go out with him. Her problem, he thought, and theirs.

His shirt was streaked with the years of dust from the back of the under stairs cupboard, his hands were filthy and there was grit in his hair. He hadn't been this dirty in years.

Half an hour later, his usual sartorial elegance restored, he put the cash box and the envelope of papers into a carrier bag, picked up his car keys and left the house. There was time to call in the shop and put the stuff in the safe. No point in leaving large amounts of cash lying around the house.

Sandra was at the window when he pulled up and was quickly on her way down the path. He avoided encounters with her parents. Indifferent to their disapproval, he couldn't be bothered going through phony courtesies and preferred to wait in the car. Invitations to Sunday tea had been made a couple of times but he'd always made excuses. No way he was going to sit in their dining room in front of a salad tea; two lettuce leaves, half a tomato, a slice of ham and a pile of bread and butter to fill up on, while her father cross examined him. His intentions weren't honourable and they never had been.

As she got into the car, Sandra glanced at his face. It was blank. There was no emotion there at all so, as she'd learned to do, she let him set the pace.

In the restaurant, in response to a tentative enquiry about his dad, he'd said,

'Look, I don't want to talk about it. Tell me what's been happening, what's going on, what you've been doing for the last couple of weekends.'

Assuming, incorrectly, he was upset, she chatted on, filling the silences. He, on the other hand, was trying to stop his mind jumping around, looking at future possible scenarios. He'd have to keep his wits about him.

The Chinese food disappeared at an alarming rate, he was starving. Sandra was only picking so he finished hers too. Raising his hand for the bill, he downed the rest of his beer.

'Let's go back to the flat for an hour,' he said. 'It's still early.'

It wasn't a question and she nodded eagerly. They hadn't been together for a couple of weeks and she'd missed him and, if she were honest, she'd missed the sex too.

He was different tonight. Usually, he was the master of a slow build up; the whisky, the soft music and the slow kisses and caresses. Gradually watching her arousal, he'd begin to undress her, one button at a time, pausing to kiss her neck or the side of her mouth, slowly squeezing her breasts through her blouse until she was breathing heavily and pushing against him. He didn't make love to a formula but constantly pushed the boundaries, trying out new tricks, things he'd learned with other women. She was a willing partner in all his innovations. This time was different.

They were hardly through the door when he started to undress her, kissing her hard and pushing her down on to the settee. She kissed him back and her underwear disappeared while she unzipped his trousers. This was a different kind of arousal, quick and sharp and exciting and she gasped as he pushed into her. His eyes were closed. There wasn't a thought in his head, only physical sensations. His body was here but the rest of him was somewhere else.

He shuddered and cried out. It was over and she was spread eagled on the settee, half dressed. Her blouse was on the floor and her skirt was pushed up around her waist. She felt more vulnerable than if she'd been naked. Hardly looking at her, he rose and went quickly into the bathroom.

It was so unexpected, she didn't know what to do. Was that it? Hurriedly shrugging into her blouse and pulling down her skirt, she thrust her underwear hastily into her handbag.

Johnnie leaned over the sink, his arms taking his weight, and looked into the mirror. Shaking his head at his reflection, he noticed his hair was a little mussed but he looked the same. There was some strain around the eyes but no other change. The loss of control had rattled him. He'd shown weakness and Sandra had seen it. She wouldn't see it again, he thought, as he threw cold water over his face. This Dad stuff must be getting to me after all.

Back in the sitting room, he was glad to see she was dressed and held out her coat.

'I'll run you home,' he said.

They'd been in the flat for less than twenty minutes and they were outside her house in another twenty. Johnnie hadn't spoken, just put his foot down. He couldn't wait to get rid of her.

'I'll ring you,' he said as she got out of the car, 'goodnight.'

'Goodnight Johnnie,' she whispered. Something had changed but she didn't know what. His father's death was bound to affect him even if he didn't show it. She couldn't help him, he wouldn't allow it. She could only sit and wait for his next call.

***

As Tom Phillips opened the kitchen door, a whiff of garlic came to meet him; spaghetti Bolognese, a family favourite. His boys, now sixteen and seventeen were starving, as usual, and waiting impatiently for their father to appear.

The evening meal finished, the boys scattered to play cricket with their friends and the little one, a picture in blue gingham, was in the garden pushing her doll's pram and scolding her pretend children, clearly visible from the kitchen window.

Margaret poured them another cup of tea.

'Everything all right?' she asked. 'Sally seems a bit distracted.'

'She's having a few problems but she'll sort herself out.'

Tom wouldn't betray Sally's confidence, even to his wife.

'I've had a letter from Janet, Janet Marsden. She's re-trained to work with handicapped children and is looking around for work. One of the staff is due for maternity leave and we could use another pair of hands. What do you think?'

'Ideal, it was a pity she ever left West Gorton. Those kids weren't easy but she had them eating out of her hand. I'd give her a reference any day.'

Margaret smiled.

'A reference from you is worth three from anybody else. I'll drop her a line, invite her over.'

'I wonder how Nick will take it. He was pretty keen and he's never been serious about anyone else as far as I know.'

'We'll have to wait and see – she hasn't accepted the job yet. She might not want to come back to Manchester. I'll get a letter off first thing. Time enough to worry about Nick when we know if she's coming.'

Tom nodded. He'd never interfere in the running of Oak House. That was Margaret's baby and Nick would have to take his chances. Perhaps any feelings he'd had for Janet had died long ago.

Three months later, Margaret wondered how she'd ever managed without her. She'd fallen into place at Oak House like the final piece into a jigsaw.

With Margaret's help, Janet found a ground floor flat in a converted Victorian villa ten minutes' walk from Oak House. For the first few weeks, she'd arrived home from each shift exhausted. Training was one thing, keeping control of a classroom of urchins in West Gorton another, but the full on experience of dealing with handicapped children for several hours at a stretch had proved more demanding than she'd expected.

She loved it, loved the challenge and now she had hit her stride, she loved her freedom. A life of her own was all she wanted, to please herself and not be at the beck and call of anyone. For the first time in years, she could eat what she wanted when she wanted, go for a walk with no questions asked and lie in bed until lunch time on her free days if she felt like it.

It was nine years since she had lived in Manchester and delighted in re-discovering the city, its galleries and theatres, shops and cinemas. She wasn't lonely, her work was demanding but worthwhile and although a thought of Nick Metcalfe occasionally slipped into her mind, it was dismissed. He must be married and settled by now. She never quite got round to asking Margaret.

Tom and Nick were still good friends; not as close as they had been when they worked together, but they met for a drink occasionally in the city centre pub where they'd had their early discussions about the move to West Gorton, often reminiscing about the early days.

'It's hard to believe that move was nearly fourteen years ago,' said Nick. 'I don't know where the time has gone.'

'When you think how windy we were; not quite sure what we were getting into. We really did make a difference there, got the results and put a lot of children on the road to further education. Thanks to you, Nick, things have only got better.'

'Enough of that, Tom, it's my job. Anything else happening?'

'I've been wondering whether to tell you, having had my head bitten off on this subject once before.'

'What subject?'

'Janet Marsden's back in Manchester.'

Tom watched Nick's reaction; a sudden loss of colour and his grip tightening round the handle of his pint pot.

'How strange. Is she here with her husband?' He was fishing not so subtly for information.

'She's not married and never has been, as far as I know. She's retrained and working with Margaret at Oak House.'

'How is she?'

'I haven't seen her yet but Margaret is full of praise. She's working wonders with some of the more difficult children.'

They fell silent, neither knowing what to say.

Nick's head was full of questions he couldn't ask and Tom looked at him sympathetically and decided on rescue.

'Going to the match on Saturday? What do you think of the new winger?' he asked and although Nick's response was a little disjointed, they managed to get back to their old familiar footing.

Margaret's birthday fell at the end of September and she and Tom had asked a few friends round to join them on Sunday afternoon.

Tom was becoming impatient with pussy footing around the Nick and Janet situation.

'Look,' he'd said to Margaret. You ask Janet but tell her that Nick's likely to be here and I'll ask Nick and tell him about Janet. If either of them doesn't want to see the other, they have the option of politely declining. Then everyone will know where they stand.'

'You're right, a perfect solution. I'll think no more about it,' she said, knowing she would.

After a grey start, the day was bright and clear, the sun now at the back of the house shining into the kitchen and dining room, lighting up the rooms and bringing out the scent of the white roses in the centre of the table.

The boys were on their best behaviour, opening the door to guests and taking coats, and their sister, flitting from room to room, was flushed with excitement and getting under people's feet.

Janet had arrived early to give Margaret a hand and they were in the kitchen putting finishing touches to the buffet. The doorbell rang again and as the voices wafted down the hall, Janet stopped dead in her tracks. It was unmistakeably Nick, she knew that voice even after so many years.

'Oh, God,' she muttered, 'I don't think I'm ready for this.'

Margaret put her hand on Janet's shoulder.

'Steady now, stay there, I won't be a minute.'

With her back braced against one of the kitchen units, Janet waited, hands clenched, wishing she were somewhere else. Could she sneak out of the back door?

The door from the hall opened slowly and Janet raised her eyes to look Nick full in the face. He looked as nervous as she felt.

'Margaret thought it might be easier if we met in private,' he said. The hair was a little greyer and he was carrying a little more weight but was still an undeniably handsome man.

'How have you been?'

Her voice not much louder than a whisper, 'Fine,' she said, 'and you?'

'I can't do this, not like strangers. Is that yours?' He pointed to a patterned cardigan over the back of a kitchen chair.

She nodded.

He picked it up, draped it round her shoulders and opened the back door into the garden.

'Come on, let's talk.'

They found a bench in a flower covered arbour, where it was quiet except for the buzz of a few late bees.

Janet was trembling and Nick took her hand, icy cold despite the September sun.

'Why didn't you write?' he asked.

'I intended to but when I got home, things were crazy; Mum in intensive care, not expected to recover, and Dad going to pieces and at the hospital all day and most of the night. When, beyond our expectations, she was allowed home, she needed constant care. Dad had the business to run so I stayed. It seemed pointless to get in touch. I had no idea whether I'd ever be able to come back. Far better to let you get on with your life.'

Nick didn't interrupt. He held her hand and waited with sympathetic eyes.

'She never complained. On good days, I pushed the wheelchair round the park or up to the shops. I thought we'd go on indefinitely but then she faded slowly away, leaving me and Dad heartbroken."

The tears were running down her cheeks but she took a shuddering breath and continued.

'She'd often say I should go back to teaching, even get a job locally. I'd say I'd think about it but I couldn't leave her.'

Nick pulled a handkerchief from his pocket and pressed it into her hands. She lifted her eyes to his gratefully.

'Go on,' he said quietly.'

'I muddled through the days, keeping house and shopping but barely existing. It sounds strange, but one spring morning, I was walking through the park and registered, really registered, the life around me. The early cherry blossom, the daffodils waving in the breeze, a small child on a red trike and I could hear Mum's voice in my head. Down to earth and straight talking, she was telling me to buck my ideas up, do something, get on with it.'

Nick watched her. There were traces of the girl in the hair and the eyes but she was a woman now. Her face had slimmed and showed maturity and determination. The attraction was as strong as ever.

'With only two years' teaching experience, I decided to retrain. The course got me out of the house but I dreaded going home to Mum's empty bedroom and Dad, who was miserable and grumpy.'

A burst of music and laughter broke the silence as the kitchen door opened briefly then closed. They'd forgotten the party at the other end of the garden.

Janet took a deep breath.

'When Margaret offered me a job, I jumped at it. Dad was upset but I had to leave. He'd never learn to cope as long as I was there.'

Nick put his arm around her shoulders.

'I'm glad you did,' he said. 'I thought about you often.'

'I thought about you too but it seemed hopeless. I wondered whether you were married, what you were up to and half hoped and half dreaded we'd meet.'

'It was a long time ago but perhaps we could start to get to know each other again.'

For the first time, she smiled, her eyes sparkling though tears still glistened on her lashes.

'I think I'd like that.'

They sat quietly for a few minutes.

'Do you want to go back inside?' he asked.

'I couldn't face it. I can imagine what I look like after all that weeping.'

'You look fine to me,' he smiled. 'Did you have a coat?'

'No, only my handbag in the kitchen.'

'Well go and fetch it and let's get out of here. Margaret won't mind.'

***

It had rained for most of the journey, the windscreen wipers swishing away the filth thrown up by other vehicles. They'd set off in the early hours, knowing it would be hard going to get to the cemetery by four. Harry was determined to get there and back in two days. Neither he nor Hettie wanted to spend an hour longer than necessary in their old home town.

The streets around the cemetery were filled with parked cars but at last, Harry found a space and pulled in.

'We'll have to walk from here. You OK, Mum?'

Hettie nodded, fastened her coat and reached into the back of the car for her handbag.

'Let's get on with it, shall we?'

The hearse pulled up as they approached the chapel, huddled together under a large black umbrella. The crowd sheltering in the porch parted to let the pall bearers through. Johnnie was fleetingly visible as he followed the coffin. The rest of the crowd followed, solemn faced, nobody speaking.

The organist burst forth with something vaguely religious and solemn while the mourners shuffled forward and took their seats, leaving Johnnie in splendid isolation on the front row.

Hettie and Harry followed the stragglers and found two seats at the back. Hettie wished she were invisible. Nobody had noticed her yet but perhaps heads would turn as the mourners left after the service. Someone might recognise her.

The chapel was chilly and an odour of decaying flowers and wet clothing seeped through the cheerless building. The coffin, covered in white flowers, lay centre front, clearly visible from every seat.

A jaundiced clergyman checked his papers before launching into the funeral service in a flat, well-practiced voice,

'I am the resurrection and the life,' he intoned, galloping through the opening phrases.

Hettie tuned him out, her attention wandering until the mourners were waved to their feet and the music, faltering at first, struck up. The first verse of 'Abide with Me' rang out strongly but few people knew the second verse and the volume weakened while they struggled to read the words.

Harry held the hymn book open but Hettie couldn't sing and, it appeared, neither could Harry. They stared silently at the words on the page while the rest of them warbled on.

Hettie was close to walking out and bugger the stares when the white gowned cleric at the front caught her attention, extolling the virtues of the deceased; an upstanding member of the community, beloved father, well respected, blah, blah, blah.

Upstanding, beloved? He can't have met him, selfish cantankerous old devil that he was. I bet this old sod has done half a dozen funerals today and didn't know any of the people he was burying; bloody hypocrite.

Pious tosh - she wasn't here to see Maurice laid to rest with phony sentiment. She wanted to be sure he was gone and get what was due to her.

Concentrating on the back view of the assembled company, Hettie tried to identify the dark clad mourners but her eye was constantly drawn to Johnnie. His shoulders were broader, filling the beautifully tailored dark suit, his hair was well cut and he stood straight and still, eyes presumably fixed on the coffin at the front of the chapel. She wondered what was going through his mind. Was there any regret at all?

She lost track of the service but when the organist started to murder another classical piece she vaguely recognised as 'Air on a G String', the congregation rose. The vicar, followed by the coffin and then Johnnie, walked down the centre aisle and the rest of the mourners gradually followed.

Johnnie caught Hettie's eye as he passed and nodded but there was no smile, no other acknowledgement as he took his place at the doorway to greet the congregation as they left the chapel. There'd been a 'good turn-out'. There must have been forty people in the chapel, predominantly men, and Hettie watched them pass, recognising only a couple of them from the early days of her marriage when Maurice had been proud to have her on his arm. Nobody gave her a second look, this good looking, smartly dressed woman who looked ten years younger than on the day she'd closed the front door behind her for the last time. She was glad of the anonymity.

They were the last to leave, their hands grasped in turn by the clammy handed clergyman. He had no idea Hettie was the widow.

For the other three, it was an awkward meeting. Harry put out his hand to Johnnie and it was firmly shaken.

'Johnnie,' he said.

'Harry,' was the only response.

Hettie leaned forward to kiss Johnnie on the cheek and although he didn't pull away, she felt him flinch. Cut to the quick, for the first time Hettie's eyes filled with unshed tears. Despite everything, he was her youngest child, the child she'd nursed, protected and loved. Harry moved closer and took her arm and she took a deep breath to steady herself.

Johnnie's voice was cool and unemotional.

'There'll be food laid on at the Kings Head after the internment. Are you coming?'

Harry looked at Hettie, who shook her head.

'I don't think so. We'll see him buried and then we'll be on our way.'

There was a look of panic in his eyes; not regret and not grief but panic. He needed something from her.

'Don't rush off when it's all over. I need a quick word,' he said.

Harry nodded. 'We'll wait.'

The rain had eased and a weak sun was trying to break through the clouds. Johnnie followed the coffin to the graveside, trailed by the other mourners, the mud from the path splashing their shoes and trouser bottoms. Harry and Hettie waited, the last to follow, and stood apart while the vicar intoned a final prayer and the coffin was lowered into the open grave. They were too far away to hear clearly but caught the familiar words, 'earth to earth, ashes to ashes, dust to dust'. The rest of it disappeared in a mumble.

Hettie felt nothing; not triumph or regret, and as the coffin disappeared, she breathed a deep sigh, not realising she'd been holding her breath.

It was over. The crowd started to disperse, making their way along the puddled gravel path towards the main gate and their cars. One or two of them looked enquiringly at Hettie and Harry. She thought she saw a flicker of recognition but they didn't stop. No doubt they'd be in the pub in short order, gossiping and raising a toast to good old Maurice, at Maurice's own expense of course.

Without a second glance at the yawning hole where they'd just placed his father, Johnnie turned to speak to them.

'I need half an hour of your time, there's stuff to sort out,' he said. 'Where are you staying?'

He'd given no thought as to where they would spend the night. Although his thoughtlessness didn't prick his conscience, he realised he may have made a tactical error.

'We're at The Church on Ardwick Green tonight. I'll be away first thing in the morning but Mum will stay for a couple of days to sort stuff out,' said Harry.

Hettie stood silently. Johnnie frowned. Surely, he hadn't thought she'd toddle off and not check on Maurice's money. There was cash there and she intended to get her share.

'I'll call in when all this is over,' he said, 'around seven?'

Nodding her agreement, she watched him leave the cemetery and climb into a flash car. Harry put his arm around his mother's shoulders and gave her a hug.

'Come on, Mum. Let's go and get something to eat. I'm starving.'

Johnnie pulled up outside the park, looking across to the pub where his mum and Harry were staying. How and why they'd fetched up there, he had no idea and, fleetingly, thought he should have been a bit more helpful but it was too late now.

The last few days had been hectic, dashing around and getting things organised and the funeral and the 'do' at the pub had taken it out of him. The landlord had been told to keep serving drinks and put them on a tab but to make sure there was no gin in Johnnie's gin and tonic. He needed his wits about him. An hour had been spent with his father's cronies, reminiscing about what a great character he'd been and Johnnie winced at being referred to as 'a chip off the old block'. His work on the accounts of the only two who'd made the transition to legal betting bolstered his income and he couldn't afford to alienate them yet. It was a profitable side-line he intended to keep going until he was in a position to expand. The others, still operating in the back streets, would slowly become extinct.

The weather had cleared and the temperature had risen compared to the chilly half hour at the cemetery and he took off his jacket and folded it on to the passenger seat and loosened his tie. Wouldn't do to look too formal and he squared his shoulders and crossed the road. A great deal depended on Hettie.

There were only a couple of men at the bar and Harry and Hettie were at a table with drinks in front of them. He crossed the room and bent to kiss his mother's cheek. He'd had thoughts about his earlier response and reconsidered. Sweetness and light were what was needed.

'I'll get you a drink,' said Harry, 'What are you having?' and he went to the bar to order.

Hettie and Johnnie looked at each other, measuring up. Now he could get a proper look at her, he was surprised how well she looked. The strained face, straggly hair and shabby clothes were gone and he was looking at a confident, mature woman, dressed in a navy skirt and light grey twinset, pearls in her ears and round her neck. She was looking straight back at him.

'Right, Johnnie, what's it all about? What do you want?'

Waiting until Harry came back to the table, he launched into explanations, pussy-footing around about the extent of the estate and what had to be done.

'The top and bottom of it is, there *is* money to come. As there was no Will, it comes to you as next of kin because you and Dad never divorced but it will take some sorting out.'

Hettie waited, not helping him out and asking no questions. He went on.

'It's not clear what will be left after the funeral is paid for and any debts settled but it might be easier if I were to do it from this end. You'd have to sign a form, giving me authority to deal with the estate. Otherwise, you'd need to organise a solicitor and that could cost a fortune.'

Looking sceptical, Hettie turned to Harry.

'It's up to you, Mum. You're the one the money comes to. You have to decide.'

Johnnie was sweating. If she went to a solicitor, he could still 'disappear' the cash. The bank account and the ownership of the house and shop would have to be disclosed. Would she share the proceeds with her sons? Even if she did, he'd get a third of it at best.

Watching him squirm, Hettie sat back and picked up her glass.

'Let me think about it. I'll nip upstairs for a minute, won't be long.'

The two young men facing each other across the table, neither knowing what to say. There was no longer any common ground.

Johnnie saw a well built, mature family man in a decent suit. Face and hands tanned to a nut brown, he looked confident and at ease. Whatever Hettie decided would be all right with him and he wasn't making this easy for Johnnie. Gone were the days when he could rely on Harry for support. There was no point asking about his family, it would sound too phony even for him. He could only sit; looking at Harry, looking at the other customers, looking into his glass on the table, waiting for Hettie.

Harry saw a good looking, smart young man about town, albeit with a city pallor. There was no trace of the scruffy kid he'd bailed out during their childhood, saving him from a good hiding when he'd got the wrong side of one of the older boys. Not so cocky at the moment, he looked ill at ease, waiting for Hettie and her decision. Harry had no interest in any of it. Hettie would make up her mind and then they'd put Manchester, Maurice and Johnnie behind them and go home.

'How come you fetched up here, in this place?' Johnnie finally asked; anything to fill the silence.

'I was in the army with the landlord's son and we used to drink here when we were on leave. He said I could stop over anytime so I took him up on it. I couldn't see Mum back in that house, not for a minute.'

'I suppose not,' said Johnnie. 'It's the same, except a bit scruffier. To tell you the truth, I had so much on my plate, I never thought to offer.' This was the nearest Johnnie would get to any sort of apology. He was distracted by the thought of Hettie upstairs, doing her thinking, not even sure he'd get an answer when she came down.

Hettie sat on the edge of the bed, miles away, lost in the past. The two people she'd loved most in the world were downstairs, like strangers. The escape to her bedroom had been an attempt to quell the emotions that were very near the surface. It never paid to show weakness when Johnnie was around.

His response to her kiss at the cemetery had been like a smack in the face and she'd struggled not to show it. Despite all reason, she'd hoped for some softening of his attitude. There'd been no forgiveness in his face, no understanding for her reasons for leaving, only blame she'd left at all. All the years of love and care meant nothing compared to the fact she'd left him to fend for himself. All the years she'd put up with Maurice for the sake of the lads might not have happened. From childhood, Johnnie had been his own number one priority. The minute someone was of no further use to him, they were gone from his consciousness as though they'd never existed. As he wanted something from her, she was temporarily re-instated.

There'd be no reconciliation, no warmth from Johnnie, whatever she did for him. Nothing would eradicate his bitterness towards her. Judgement had been made. The offer to help with the probate had nothing to do with her or with Harry. It had only to do with what he could get away with.

Devious as a boy, nothing had changed. The cheating at cards, the pilfering from her purse, the toadying to his father were all indications he wasn't to be trusted and she was ashamed for him, wondering why he'd turned out this way. Could she have done anything different, was she to blame?

None of the soul searching made any difference. Johnnie was what he was and she could see no hope of change. He'd cheat her if he could but she wouldn't give him the chance.

Rising from the bed, she walked over to the mirror, pulled a comb through her hair and touched up her lipstick, trying to ignore the knot of sadness lodged in her chest. Better get this over with.

Johnnie looked surreptitiously at his watch; she'd been gone for nearly half an hour.

'Got to be somewhere else?' asked Harry, looking amused.

'I wonder what's she's doing all this time?'

'She'll be down when she's ready,' said Harry, leaning back and picking up his pint. 'Here she is.'

Johnnie turned and saw Hettie making her way from the side door, across the bar to the table. She took a seat and said,

'Who's going to buy their mother a drink?'

Johnnie jumped up, 'same again?' he asked and Hettie nodded.

'Harry?' he asked, 'another pint?' and Harry nodded too.

There were more people in the pub and the buzz of conversation had risen. Balancing a port and lemon and a pint of bitter, he came back and sat down, looking nervous.

All his charm was no use with these two. They were the only people, apart perhaps from Sally Steadman, who recognised him for what he was. Looking at his mother's bleak expression, he feared things were going to go badly.

'What are you going to do, Mum? Have you decided?'

Johnnie was glad Harry had asked and leaned forward over the table to hear.

Hettie looked at Johnnie, sadness in her eyes.

'Here's what we're going to do. I don't know how much money there is but I'm guessing there's a great deal more than you're letting on, Johnnie.'

He didn't even look shamefaced, he should have known not to underestimate Hettie. She'd bested him too many times in the past.

'The good news is, I don't want all of it. Harry?'

'I wouldn't touch it with a barge pole. As far as I'm concerned, Johnnie's welcome to it.'

Johnnie was in shock, he couldn't believe his luck. He'd thought he'd have to account to Hettie for every last pound.

'However,' she went on.

Here it comes, thought Johnnie.

'I want five thousand pounds. The way I look at it, that's two hundred pounds a year for twenty five years. Little enough for the slaps, the scrimping and saving and the other stunts your father pulled,' she said bitterly.

Watching Johnnie's face, she knew he was working out the totals.

'And,' she went on, still keeping an eye on Johnnie.

'I want a thousand pounds each for Harry's kids.'

Kids, thought Johnnie, I didn't know there was more than one. His mind raced. An objection or a plea of poverty that the estate wouldn't stand it would bring dire consequences. She'd want a proper accounting. There'd no hiding the bank account or the property deeds.

Knowing she'd rumble him if he acquiesced immediately, he opened his mouth to speak but she interrupted.

'Otherwise, I'll have to stay over and go and see the solicitors myself. I know who they are and who he banked with. I can find out exactly what assets there are. If there'd been a Will in your favour, we wouldn't be having this conversation. You'd have taken the lot.'

Her threat of taking over frightened him. He'd get nothing past her and if she knew how much there was, she might take it all.

'Mum,' Harry interrupted. 'Me and Rose don't want any of it. The old man barely acknowledged I was alive. For all he cared, I could have been one of the runners, somebody off the street. I don't want his rotten money.'

'Well, I do. I want it for those kids. You don't have to touch it and they don't have to know about it. I'll invest the lot and they can have their share when they're twenty one. We might have to split it into more than two by then anyway. Come on, Harry, I don't want us to fall out about this.'

Harry sighed. 'Right, Mum. Do what you think is right.' Clearly this meant a lot to her and for her sake, he swallowed his scruples.

'For once, let's do something good with that tight fisted old bugger's money. It'd kill him if he knew,' and both she and Harry smiled at her inadvertently comical turn of phrase.

As Johnny watched their easy laughter, a twinge of envy touched him. Once he'd passed puberty, he'd never been close to anyone. Never mind, he thought, it looks as though things are going my way.

Their gaze returned to Johnnie, Hettie suspecting he would try to knock her down.

'Well, Mum....' he said. This was all pure gamble; he couldn't afford to make a mistake.

'Don't 'well Mum' me. This is the deal and you can take it or take the consequences,' her voice had hardened.

'You send me a cheque for a thousand pounds within the week and send the form for the probate. Once the cheque has cleared and the money is in my bank, I'll sign the form and send it back.

When you've got your hands on the money in the bank account, you'll be able to send me a cheque for the rest of it, and whatever's necessary for me to sign to pass the rest of the estate to you. Again, when the cheque has cleared, I'll send the forms back. I'll go to a local solicitor to get the signature certified.'

She'd done her homework and would leave nothing to chance but it was hard to accept, even now, that she needed safeguards against her own son.

He opened his mouth to speak.

'Don't bother telling me you can't get your hands on that kind of money. I know you can, I didn't live in with your father for all those years without knowing what was going on.'

There would be no arguing and no negotiation. Johnnie nodded his assent. He looked reluctant, hiding his jubilation. He'd got off lightly.

'Good,' she said. 'Now we know where we stand. Do you want another drink?' and looking at her watch, 'Auntie Flo will be here in fifteen minutes, are you going to stay and say hello?'

Knowing he would never willingly spend even two minutes with Flo, it was the perfect way to bring the meeting to an end. She needed it to be over.

'I can't, there's still a million things to do. I'd better get off.'

Pushing his glass away, he rose to leave and leaned over the table to kiss Hettie on the cheek. After all, he still had a great deal to lose.

'See you, Mum, see you Harry,' and he was gone.

Hettie sat unmoving, her hand over the place he'd kissed. She'd probably never see him again. Harry watched her face, concern in his eyes.

Through all the abuse and the humiliation of their childhood, Harry had never seen his mother cry and she wasn't going to weep in public. She managed a strangled, 'back in five minutes,' and made for the stairs.

The sobs broke out as she reached the safety of her room. She stood with her back against the door, chest heaving, tears streaming, her body racked with the pain of the loss of her child. She knew all there was to know about Johnnie and his methods but it didn't lessen the pain. Her mind sped back over the years, how had it come to this? He was gone from her life as certainly as if he'd died. She wasn't to know, but the feeling of loss would haunt her in the weeks and months ahead. Though the intensity would fade, even years later a random thought of Johnnie would bring unwanted tears to her eyes at the most unexpected moments.

She concentrated on bringing herself under control. Harry was sitting downstairs waiting for her and Flo would appear any moment. She had to get a grip.

Wringing out a face cloth under the cold tap in the washbasin in the corner of the room, she placed it over her face, cooling her throbbing eyes. .

There was a gentle tap at the door and Harry's concerned face appeared.

'You all right, Mum?'

'No I'm not, but I will be in a couple of minutes. I don't know what came over me.'

There was no need for explanations, Harry put his arms round her and held her close, rubbing his palm over her back, trying to comfort her.

'Come on, son, don't give me sympathy or I'll be off again.'

With a final squeeze, he stepped back.

'Flo's downstairs, are you all right to come down?'

Hettie groaned, 'You go on, tell her I'll be down in a minute.'

She looked in the mirror and found she didn't look too bad. The outward damage was nothing like as serious as the hard knot in her chest. She bathed her eyes again, combed her hair and touched up her make up for the second time in less than an hour.

All this emotion was wearing her out but she went downstairs to the bar, to have her sister fling her arms around her. Flo didn't mention her red eyes so Hettie guessed the damage didn't show.

The two of them sat at the table and exchanged news while Harry, out of his depth with the female conversation, stood at the bar talking to the landlord.

The years had been kind to Flo. She looked well, had put on a bit of weight and was dressed in a decent skirt and jumper. Even the headscarf has disappeared, heaven be praised, thought Hettie.

The tight economic circumstances of the post war years, when Hettie had made a small fortune lending money to hard up housewives, had eased. The majority of people were better off and the business Hettie had passed to Flo had declined.

''Course, there's still the odd silly beggar who bites off more than they can chew and comes running for a loan but there's not much doing. Nobody has any idea the cash comes from me, they still think I'm the middle man and answerable to somebody else. I never forgot what you said to me, our Hettie. I've never lent over the limit.'

'Well at least you're still making an odd bob or two. How's your Charlie doing, married isn't he.'

Flo was only too glad to talk about her family and what was happening in the neighbourhood and Hettie skilfully steered her away from references to Maurice, apart from agreeing it was good riddance to bad rubbish.

The sisters spent a pleasant couple of hours in each other's company, who knew when they'd see each other again and at ten o'clock, Flo said she'd better be going.

'Harry will walk you to the bus stop,' said Hettie, waving him over.

'It was lovely to see you, our Het. Keep in touch won't you?'

Flo was fishing in her handbag for a hankie. With so much port and lemon inside her, Hettie suspected she might get maudlin. There'd been enough tears for one night.

''Course I will, get along now. Time you were on your way,' and Hettie walked with her to the door of the pub and watched her walk along the park railings, her arm in Harry's. She looked a bit wobbly but it was a short bus journey and then not far to her front door. She'd be all right.

Twenty minutes later, Hettie lay in bed going over the events of the day. Glad it was all over, they'd be on their way first thing and tomorrow night, she'd sleep in her own bed. The small country village had become home.

Chapter 18

Sally

Me and Alice had been to the cinema. We'd missed 'Alfie' when it was on in town and had taken the chance to catch up locally. It hadn't matched up to the light hearted reviews we'd read and although we'd laughed, it wasn't the comedy we'd expected; a bit dark in places and no real happy ending.

We had plenty of time and decided to call in for a drink and sat over halves of shandy in Mum and Dad's local. They knew us there and we wouldn't have a problem with strange lads trying to chat us up.

Once we settled in the 'best room' and given the film a thorough dissection and giggling, agreed fellas were all the same, we got down to a real natter.

Despite everything we'd said, Alice was bemoaning her 'boyfriendless' state. Her relationship with the lad from college had come to an end and she was footloose again.

'The trouble is,' she said, 'I never go anywhere to meet people; not only lads but new people, interesting people. It was different when I was at college, there was always somebody doing something or going somewhere. Most of the crowd have gone and there's nobody at work even worth talking to.

The most interesting person I've spoken to in the last couple of weeks is Johnnie Marshall. He gave me a lift from Ardwick Green the night I broke up with you know who. I know you don't like him but he is good looking and there's something about him.'

'There's something about him, all right,' I said. 'Alice, he's bad news. Trust me, he'll only do you damage. Give him a wide berth.'

'Come on Sally,' she laughed. 'You've always had it in for him. He's not so bad. Did you know his dad had died?'

'I wouldn't wish that on anyone,' I said, 'but he'll be all right. Johnnie will make sure he'll always be all right. Anyway, enough about him.'

I hoped she'd heed my words. Although I wouldn't call myself experienced, I'd had a couple of sexual encounters; nothing too serious and nothing I'd wanted to go any further. Alice, on the other hand, was green as grass and Johnnie would make mincemeat out of her.

Although I was still unsettled at college and still had a year to go, the social life was still buzzing, plenty going on all over Manchester.

'Look,' I said, 'if you fancy something different, why don't you come with me to the Crown next Tuesday. The band is terrific; they play some really cool jazz. I never thought I'd develop a taste for it but I love it. There's a mixed crowd and it's not heaving with students either. Fancy it?'

'Why not? At least it's something different and I'll be out of the house.'

'Great, I'll meet you outside work and we can go and have a bite to eat and get there early so we get decent seats.'

Looking at my watch, I realised I'd better make a move if I wanted to get home before eleven.

'I'll come to the bus stop with you,' said Alice and we picked up our bags and jackets and made our way out on to the street.

The bus stop faced the Marshall's betting shop and Johnnie was pulling up outside.

'Speak of the devil,' I said, sarcastically.

To my surprise, Alice touched my arm and said,

'I won't be a minute,' and she crossed the road to speak to him.

You could have knocked me down with a feather. I couldn't hear what they were saying and she was back across the road in minutes.

'What was that about?' I asked.

'I wanted to say I was sorry about his dad. He was nice to me when my dad died and I thought I should return the favour.'

Although I suspected more than condolences had been expressed, what could I say? I turned to see the bus trundling up the road.

Alice was standing at the bus stop, waiting for it to leave and I couldn't help a final warning.

'Alice, do be careful. He's not the lad for you.'

She smiled and waved and called out,
'You worry too much, See you Tuesday' and the bus pulled away.

***

After he left Hettie and Harry in the pub, Johnnie had driven a couple of hundred yards and pulled up, his hands shaking with relief.

It could have been much worse, he thought. I didn't expect to get it all but she's a tough old bird. It was tied it up pretty tight too and there was grudging admiration for Hettie's tactics.

I won't worry about what can't be helped. It leaves me with three thousand in the bank, the cash plus the house and the shop. The takings from the shop will be mine too; not a bad evening's work.

The form for the probate application had been in his pocket all day. It had been a vain hope Hettie would sign there and then. If he paid a thousand from Maurice's cash box into his bank in the morning, he could have a cheque on its way to her. The rest he'd hang on to. He'd learned from his father a supply of undocumented and unrecorded cash could come in handy. With a bit of luck, he'd have access to the bank account within a couple of weeks. Hettie wouldn't go back on her word but she might make him sweat a bit.

Calmer now, he turned the key in the ignition and set off for home. There was little traffic on the road and in fifteen minutes, he pulled up outside the house. Looking at the shabby exterior, he couldn't face it. After the day, and evening, he'd had, the house with all its memories was too much.

Deciding to sleep over the shop tonight, he made another quick decision. The upstairs rooms were big enough to live in. With a few alterations, the place wouldn't be too bad. If Mickey Smith got cracking with the decorating and he bought some furniture, he could be set up and comfortable within a week.

He'd get the house cleared, have a coat of paint slapped over all the rooms and put it on the market straight away. With careful management, he'd never have to sleep there again.

Once inside the flat, he hung up his jacket, took off his shoes and poured a large whisky. If ever he deserved a drink it was now and for an hour, one drink followed another. Not normally much of a drinker, he'd half hoped for oblivion. Unbidden and unwanted memories of Hettie kept creeping in, almost like a slide show.

Himself at the age of about four, hiding behind her skirts and Harry cowering in a corner while she took a backhander to the face. Hettie looking over his work at the kitchen table when he was getting ready for the eleven plus, her crafty manoeuvring so Maurice bought his kit for grammar school, her nudging and pushing to get Maurice's approval for his accountancy training. He pushed the thoughts away. She'd left them to fend for themselves hadn't she?

Eventually sliding off into sleep, he smiled. Alice's 'phone number at work was fixed in his mind; a perfect end to a rotten day. He'd leave it a few days before giving her a call, he wanted her eager.

When he opened his eyes the following morning, for a moment, he didn't know where he was. The light was brighter, coming from a different direction, and there was a dull pounding at the back of his head. He dragged himself to a sitting position, holding a hand over his eyes, realising a trip to the bathroom was a matter of urgency.

That accomplished and a mug of tea in his hand, still dressed in his shirt, underpants and socks from the night before, he looked around.

The place looked seedy. His jacket hung crookedly on a hanger suspended from the picture rail, a pile of newspapers lay on the floor next to the crumpled blanket he'd slept beneath while a kettle, a packet of tea bags and a spare mug sat on one of Hettie's old tin trays on top of the cupboard next to an open bottle of milk.

The curtains were old fashioned and a dull, dark red and there were signs of wear on the carpet beneath his feet. Clean patches showed on the faded flowered wallpaper where pictures had been removed and a light shade with a tattered fringe hung forlornly in the centre of the ceiling. The 'love nest' which looked half way decent by the light of a couple of table lamps looked squalid in the broad light of day.

He groaned, this was more than he could handle. His watch showed eight o'clock; a couple of hours before the shop would be open. Wearing the trousers he'd found slung over the back of the couch, he made his way down to the local 'greasy spoon.' As the waft of frying bacon hit his nostrils, he realized he was starving. The funeral and the negotiations with Hettie had filled his head the previous day and he'd eaten very little. No wonder he was hung over. With a full English breakfast, two extra rounds of toast and another mug of tea inside him, he could finally face the world.

Needing a change of clothes, he'd no choice than to go back to the house where he found the cleaner half-heartedly pushing the vacuum cleaner round the front room carpet.

'I left your dinner in the oven last night, what do you want me to do with it?' She spoke out of the side of her mouth, managing to keep her cigarette in place and squinting to avoid the rising smoke.

'Leave it there, I'll have it tonight,' he said, knowing he'd have to speak to her at length very soon.

'Things will be changing in the next couple of weeks. Come in the shop about five o'clock on Friday and I'll settle up with you and tell you what's going on.'

Looking worried, she nodded, switched the cleaner off at the wall and pulled a duster out of her apron pocket. She probably thinks I'm going to stop her altogether, he thought. Let her worry, I can't be bothered.

Washed, shaved and dressed in fresh clothes, he walked back round to the shop. Opening the door from the street, he turned on the light. There was no natural light and the staircase looked gloomy and scruffy. The worn lino on the stairs could be a death trap and there were scuffs along the woodchip on the walls where furniture had been carried up and down.

He turned into the front room, it looked no better even with breakfast inside him and he stood in the doorway weighing it up. The room was almost twice the size of any of the rooms in the old place and for the first time, he noticed the mouldings on the ceiling and the size of the window. The other room was also of generous dimensions and gradually, a picture formed in his head of how the place *could* look.

The impulsive decision of the previous evening, to throw a coat of paint on the walls and buy some second hand furniture receded. There was money enough. It could be done properly. He wanted a decent place to live.

With no experience in the building trade and no idea what a renovation would cost, he needed advice. Who would know? Who could he ask? His father's network of contacts was no use to him here.

Down in the office, rummaging through the pile of business cards collected over a couple of years, he fished out the one he'd been looking for and checked the 'phone number. The card read, Mark Cunliffe RICS, Chartered Surveyor. Checking his watch, he picked up the 'phone and dialled. It was nine fifteen, perhaps he'd catch him in the office.

Although they were only slight acquaintants, Mark remembered Johnnie. To Johnnie's delight, he'd answered,

'You're in luck, I've got a cancelled appointment. I could come round about twelve and check the place over, see what needs to be done. Better give me the address.'

They'd walked through the flat together, Mark saying little but missing nothing and half an hour later, sitting in the local over a pie and a pint, they each took the measure of the other.

The pub didn't look much; Formica topped tables and leatherette covered chairs but the landlord knew his stuff. The beer was well looked after, with a dense, frothy head and the pies had been delivered that morning. A crisp pastry crust surrounded the clear jelly and succulent pork filling and the two plump pickled onions on the side promised a welcome sharpness.

Each of them had made a 'phone call before their meeting. A check on the reputation of someone you were dealing with could never hurt. As it happens, they'd both rung the same mutual acquaintance. The recipient of the calls sat at his desk, chortling in delight.

Well, there's a marriage made in heaven. Those two deserve each other,' he'd said to himself.

'The building's structurally sound, so you've no worries there. As to the renovations, there are two ways of doing this,' Mark had said. 'We can go in and out and the place will look OK. The second way is to make a proper job of it. I'm talking a complete rewire and putting the flat on a separate circuit, installing central heating and moving stuff around a bit.'

Johnnie knew this was going to cost and asked, 'moving stuff around, like what?'

'The only kitchen facilities are down in the shop. We'll take out the existing bathroom and move it upstairs to the attic room and put a kitchen in where the bathroom was. The bathroom suite is as old as the hills anyway. My grannie's is in better condition.'

The words 'central heating' struck a chord. There'd been too many winters shivering in bed, windows iced on the inside by morning and dressing under the blankets when the only source of heat in the house had been the coal fire in the kitchen. The thought swung the decision. He'd do it.

The punters and the staff downstairs could manage with the storage heaters already there. It wouldn't do to make them too comfortable.

'What will it cost?'

'Again, you've got two choices. I can make recommendations and draw up the specs and you can find your own workmen. Alternatively, for a fixed price, I can supervise the whole job and pull in people who've worked for me before. It could be finished in a couple of weeks. They might even be able to start at the weekend, if you'll pay overtime rates.

When you're ready to move on, you'll have a property to rent out. Even in this area,' he said disparagingly, 'it will bring you in a steady income.'

'OK, suppose you do the whole job. What would it cost?'

Johnnie blanched at the figure, rapidly weighing his options. God knows how long it would take to round up plumbers, electricians and plasterers and how would he know if the jobs were being done properly? He'd told Mark there could be more work in the offing. It would be in his own interests to do the job well and keep in budget.

'When can you start?'

Johnnie had decided and Mark nodded.

'I'll make a couple of calls and get back to you.'

They shook hands on the deal and Mark got into his car and drove away while Johnnie stood on the pavement and watched, excitement rising.

His initial resolve to move straight into the flat would have to be shelved. He'd put up with the house a while longer.

He rubbed his hand over his eyes to relieve the lingering headache and shrugged. Bugger the money, he thought. For the first time in my life, I'll have somewhere decent to live.

***

As Alice watched the bus pull away, Sally's concerned face had been framed in the window.

Johnnie disappeared through the door into the flat above the betting shop and she was glad she'd gone over to speak to him. Remembering how devastated she'd been when her own father died, she'd thought he must be fairly low.

There'd been a little quiver of excitement too. He had her 'phone number. Would he ring and if he did, would she go out with him? Silly question, of course she would. She wanted excitement and there had always been an aura of risk hanging around Johnnie.

By Tuesday evening when she and Sally met outside the Crown, he still hadn't 'phoned and although it was easy to shrug and tell herself she didn't care, a niggling disappointment lingered.

In the upstairs room over the pub, they found a table not too far from the front. The music hadn't started, apart from the pianist limbering up and odd notes from the trumpet player; a little discordant to Alice's ear.

The place was filling up and Sally smiled or nodded at a few people, Alice didn't know a soul. Most of the crowd were in their mid-twenties and some even older. To Alice's naive eye, they looked sophisticated and worldly wise.

Sally looked excited, eyes shining and clearly looking forward to the music.

'I hope you'll like this stuff, Alice. It's different to what we've been used to but I love it.'

Alice could only smile. How could she know until she heard it?

In a lightening change of subject, Sally asked,

'Seen any more of Marshall?'

Alice was glad she could answer,

'No, not since we saw him last week. Why?'

'I don't trust him, never have. He's always been so sly.'

Saved by the bell, Alice thought, as a long haired, smooth looking guy nursing a saxophone came to the microphone to introduce the first number and Sally's attention switched to the small stage at the end of the room. The bass player was draped over his instrument and the pianist leaned casually on the side of the piano, cigarette in an ashtray adding to the increasingly smoke filled atmosphere.

Silence fell as the leader put the mouthpiece to his lips. The first strains of 'Night and Day' rose hauntingly to fill the room. The sound so sweet and so clear brought goose bumps to Alice's arms. The trumpeter stepped in, weaving another melody round the first, then the bass added a thrumming, driving beat and picked up the rhythm. The pianist plunged in, raising the tempo even more and creating a harmonious whole.

The audience was silent, as reverential as any at the Halle. Not a word would be spoken while the music was playing. They were here to listen, not to natter.

Sally was entranced, mouth slightly open, gaze fixed on the tiny stage. The music advanced, ever more adventurous and ever more complex, but only occasionally did a wisp of the original tune break through.

Although Alice could hear how clever it was, that's all she could hear. Unlike Sally, it didn't hit her where it mattered and her mind wandered.

Suppose Johnnie did ring and ask her out, would she tell Sally? They'd never had secrets from each other. She trusted Sally implicitly, she was more street-wise than she was herself. But what was so very wrong with Johnnie? Surely Sally wasn't still nursing a grudge from junior school?

I give up, she thought, if he doesn't ring I won't have to make a decision but she half wished he would and half wished he wouldn't.

Applause erupted as the last note was drawn out and dragged Alice back to reality. Conversations started, drinks were ordered and people moved around while the band muttered together.

Sally's whispered, 'What do you think?' left Alice not knowing what to say.

'I'm not sure. Maybe when I hear a bit more I'll get the hang of it.'

Sally's disappointment was clear. She'd hoped Alice would 'get it' immediately; be as enthused as she was but Alice could be nothing but truthful. She hoped it would grow on her the more she listened. After all, that was only one piece and they had the whole evening ahead of them.

A young man standing in the doorway caught Sally's eye and she waved him over. As he threaded his way through the crowded tables, holding an instrument case in front of him, Sally said,

'This is Brad, from college. He plays the sax.'

The music was starting again so he sat down quickly, smiling and put the case carefully under the table.

Why the sax player bothered to name each piece they were about to play was beyond Alice. They played a few bars and then the musicians went wandering off, playing whatever they liked and occasionally wandering back to the initial tune. Brief applause broke when one of the musicians played a few bars of a solo but Alice waited until other people clapped before she joined in. To applaud in the wrong place was a fate worse than death.

After three quarters of an hour or so, to Alice's surprise, the leader nodded at Sally and raised one finger.

'Ladies and gentlemen, before we break for fifteen minutes or so, I'd like you to give a warm welcome to Sally Steadman and Brad Jones. They're new to the Crown and I'm sure we'll be seeing more of them.'

Alice's jaw dropped as the band left the stage and Sally and Brad, who'd retrieved his saxophone from under the table, walked up to take their places.

Sally didn't even look nervous as she played the opening chords of 'Just One of those Things'. Brad joined in after a few bars and Alice could tell he was good; not as good as the band leader and not as good as Sally, who was alight. Alice had watched her play many times but it had been a long time since she'd seen such joy on Sally's face.

They left the stage to loud applause. Sally was grinning from ear to ear and Brad blushed to the roots of his coal black hair while he packed his instrument away.

One of the band sent a round of drinks over and the two of them went immediately into an inquest about which bits had gone well and which hadn't. Alice sat and listened, out of her depth but full of admiration.

Riding on Sally's enthusiasm, Alice tried to follow the music, tried to understand why Sal was so captivated but failed. The music wasn't unpleasant, far from it, but it was too unstructured for Alice's taste. So many harmonious bits didn't, for Alice, make a harmonious whole. Perhaps it was an acquired taste and she'd learn to like it in time.

At ten fifteen it was all over and the band was packing up. Brad didn't linger, muttering something about the last bus and left Alice and Sally gathering their stuff together.

Surprise after surprise tonight; the band leader came over to speak to them and said to Sally,

'You were good, very good. There's room for improvement with your young friend but I could find you a gig, if you're interested.'

Sally looked so delighted, Alice thought she'd jump up and kiss him there and then.

'I'm interested,' and she hastily rummaged in her bag and scribbled her telephone number on the back of an envelope.

He looked amused.

'Who's your charming friend?' he asked, giving Alice a serious once over.

'This is Alice,' she replied.

'Well, Alice, please do come again, I'll look out for you.'

They hurried through the dark streets, making for the bus stop and hardly spoke until they were on the bus.

'I had no idea you were so keen,' Alice said. 'You were marvellous, do you think he'll ring you?'

'Maybe - but it'll be to stand in for someone who's on holiday but it's a start. I can't tell you how chuffed I am, there are so few women on the jazz scene. Will you come again?'

'I'll come again like a shot if you're playing. Perhaps it'll grow on me. Some of it seemed a bit haphazard.'

'That's the joy of it. The classical stuff will always be my first love but can you imagine what would happen in a concert if you played even one note not written on the page. The audience would be up in arms.'

It was true. Most of the classical crowd were dreadful snobs and very, very strait laced.

'With jazz, you have the basic structure, like a framework, but then you have the freedom to do whatever you like with the music. You can experiment, tinker around and find out for yourself what works. Know what I mean?'

Alice could see the attraction for Sally, who was more enthusiastic and lively than she'd seen her for weeks.

Changing the subject, she asked,

'What about that Brad chap, anything going on there?'

Sally laughed.

'Not likely, he's been going out with a cellist since their first year and they think it's 'lurv'. Her mind slid back to music. 'He's a good player but he could be terrific, he's got the spark. He'll muck it up and get married and have a houseful of kids.'

Finding Sally's cynicism a little disturbing, Alice asked,

'Well what about the band leader? Jules, isn't it?

'Him? He's as hard as nails. Had more girls than hot dinners but he's a fantastic musician.'

'He was very nice to you though, I thought he seemed keen.'

'Not on me, you crackpot, it was you he was looking at. Better watch yourself there, he's got a reputation for being a bit of a wolf.'

It was as well they were approaching Alice's stop. Sally had touched a nerve and as Alice stood up, she said, sharply,

'My God, Sally! What are you, Mother Superior and the guardian of my virtue? Good night!'

She hated to leave Sally on a note of discord but this was the limit. As bad as my dad, she thought, as she walked the final stretch home.

On Thursday afternoon, the boss's secretary snootily called out to Alice.

'There's a call for you, take it there,' she said, pointing to a 'phone on one of the work tables.

'Hello, Alice. It's John Marshall. I won't keep you a minute, I could hear the frost in that voice.'

'Hello, Johnnie. What can I do for you?'

The 'phone felt clammy in her hand and her stomach was fluttering.

'I want to ask you a favour. I'd rather ask you in person though. Can I meet you from work tomorrow night, perhaps go for a coffee or a drink?'

It wasn't a date then, thought Alice, both disappointed and relieved.

'Sure, I finish at five on a Friday.'

'I'll meet you outside your building at five o'clock. See you then.'

'Bye,' was the best she could muster. What could she possibly do for him and how did he know where she worked?

Chapter 19

There had been showers on and off all day but the sky had cleared though pavements and cars were still shiny with rain.

Johnnie checked his watch and when he looked up, Alice was coming down the steps of the office building, mac over her arm and bag over her shoulder. As always, she looked terrific; smooth and clean, out of place among the soot blackened buildings.

'Hello, Alice. All right?' he asked.

'Fine, thanks. You?'

It was all a bit stilted and Alice was looking at him questioningly, wondering what it was all about.

'Let's go for a coffee, shall we? Kardomah OK?'

They walked through to Albert Square, not the branch on Market Street where they might meet someone they knew.

Facing each other across a small table, a cup and saucer in front of each of them, they looked at each other.

Alice smiled and asked, 'What's this favour Johnnie? I can't think of anything I could do for you.'

'It's like this, I'm doing up the flat over the shop and I need help with picking out stuff; carpets and curtains, furniture and even paint colours. I don't know where to start. I don't know anyone else who might have any idea and you've got that kind of a background, what with art school and everything.'

Surprised, she almost choked on her coffee.

'Me? I've never bought furniture in my life.'

'But you must know about colours. This'll be my own place and I don't want to make a mess of it. Tell you the truth, it's frightening me half to death. Why don't we have a bite to eat and talk about it?'

She was intrigued, he could almost see the wheels whirring. Most people like to be asked for advice and Alice was flattered.

Then the questions started. How big were the rooms, did they get any sunlight, how many windows? She was hooked.

He'd never been this close to her for any length of time, looking at her full on. Sitting side by side in the car when he'd given her a lift was a different matter. There was no disappointment; skin flawless and smelling of fresh flowers, she was truly lovely – and clever too.

'Look, there's no-one around the shop at this time of night. Why don't you come and have a look? It wouldn't take long. Maybe you can give me a few ideas and it's on your way home anyway.'

The anxious look in her eyes gave her away and he smiled.

'Don't you trust me?' and placing his hand on his heart, he said, 'I promise you'll be safe or are you worried Sally wouldn't approve?'

That pricked. She didn't need Sally's approval.

'All right,' she said. 'Let's go and have a look.'

As he pulled smoothly to a stop, Alice looked around. She was nervous again and was worried about being be seen going into the shop with him. All the old clichés rose to the surface; she was a 'good girl' and he was 'a bit of a lad'.

Walking round the car, he checked the street and opened the passenger door.

'The coast is clear, not a soul around,' he said a little sarcastically and put out his hand to help her.

Alice flushed. Doubt whether she should be there at all was apparent on her face.

The entrance was murky but there was a light at the top of the stairs.

'That's funny,' said Johnnie. 'I thought I'd switched everything off.'

He climbed the narrow staircase and even in the dim light, it crossed her mind he *did* have a neat backside. She bit her lip to stifle a giggle and followed as he opened a door at the top.

'Oh, it's you,' she heard him say, 'I thought you'd be long gone.'

Mickey Smith was up a ladder, paint brush in hand, looking down at the two of them. Alice saw the shock on his face; he went white and swayed, leaning heavily against the wall.

Johnnie didn't notice and went on,

'Getting some overtime in? Have you got those paint charts handy? Alice is going to give me a lift with the colours.'

The room was littered with cans of undercoat, a pasting table and rolls of wallpaper stashed in a corner. Mickey gestured toward the settee, covered in a dust sheet, and Johnnie found the charts sitting on top.

'Come and have a look at the rest of the place,' he said to Alice. She looked back over her shoulder at Mickey as he came slowly down the ladder, looking as though he'd aged ten years in the space of minutes.

There was evidence of work in progress in every room. Tool boxes and bits of plumbing equipment were lying around, overalls slung in a corner and radiators leaning against walls but this didn't detract from the generous proportions of the two main rooms. In minutes, she was engrossed, checking the placing of the windows, the plaster detail and asking questions. Mickey already forgotten, she was decorating the place in her head, realising the potential and wanting desperately to have a hand in it.

***

Sally

I opened my eyes and saw a ceiling, an unfamiliar ceiling, a ceiling partially in shadow and a dim light. The sound of muffled weeping crept towards me and carefully, I tried to turn my head. My God, that hurt; I couldn't move.

I could manage only a muffled croak; lips, mouth and throat so dry I could barely swallow let alone speak and I closed my eyes again. A scuffle and movement and I heard my mum's voice,

'She moved, she made a sound. Arthur, she's waking up.'

I tried again and saw my mother's face floating above me. Tears were rolling down her cheeks and she gripped my hand so tight it hurt. Dad appeared and he was crying too. I croaked again, trying to focus, and she said sharply,

'Go and get a nurse, tell them she's awake.'

I was in hospital and I was hurt. How bad? Mum and Dad were in a right state.

I managed to turn my head but couldn't do much more. The fingers of my right hand moved but not the left. I was in plaster to the elbow. I tried the legs and the right one was OK but not the left, more plaster and it was strung up, hanging from a pulley.

A young doctor came bustling through the door, white coat flapping, followed by a stern faced nurse. He bent over me and spoke.

'Hello, young lady. I see you're back with us. How are we feeling?'

So dry I could barely speak, I blinked and managed a feeble, 'water', and the nurse stepped forward and held a spouted beaker to my lips. The slow trickle was bliss and although Mum was still weeping, she was smiling too, lips quivering.

The doctor busied himself; stethoscope on my chest, fingers on my pulse, waving a finger in front of my eyes.

He turned to Mum and Dad. He didn't speak to me, I was just a body in a bed.

'This all looks good. We'll keep a close eye on her but she needs rest. Go home, get some sleep and come back tomorrow.'

The relief in Mum's eyes was clear and as I tried to speak, she leaned forward putting her ear to my mouth, the comforting smell of her drifting towards me.

'It hurts, Mum,' was all I could manage. I felt about six years old and the tears were leaking out and running down my face. I hadn't the strength to sob.

She turned her head and all but snapped at the doctor,

'She's in pain, can't you give her something?'

'Of course, we'll give her something' and he nodded at the nurse, who hurriedly left the room.

Mum was going nowhere and when the nurse came back with a syringe in a metal tray, she blew out a sigh of relief.

'She'll rest now. Try not to worry. You'll see a big difference by tomorrow.'

I was floating away as first Mum, and then Dad, leaned over to kiss my cheek with a murmured,

'See you in the morning, sweetheart.'

As their footsteps receded, I tried to remember what had happened. How long had I been here and how bad were my fingers? Unable to concentrate, I drifted off.

For the next day or so, I slipped in and out of sleep, coasting from one injection to the next. Sometimes Mum was there and sometimes Dad but even when I summoned the energy to ask, no-one gave me any answers. 'It's early days' was the only response.

***

Mickey had packed up and gone home, looking paler than ever, and she and Johnnie had parked themselves on the settee with the paint charts spread out over the threadbare carpet.

The walls were to be covered in anaglypta and painted over. Alice suggested the woodwork, covings and plasterwork should all be white.

'White will set off whatever other colours you choose,' she said earnestly. 'Any idea what you want on the walls?'

'I'm out of my depth here,' said Johnnie. 'You pick the colours and I'll buy the paint. I trust your judgement.'

For once, Johnnie looked unsure and vulnerable. She'd half suspected a ploy to get her up to the flat but now she wasn't so sure. He really did want her help. Together, they picked out a pale, warm yellow for the bedroom at the back and a subtle cream for the sitting room.

'You'll have enough contrast against the white and the rooms will look bigger. You can hang a couple of pictures to break up the big spaces and bring a splash of colour.'

This was a revelation to Johnnie; pictures on the wall. The only picture currently hanging in his home was a calendar with a view of a garden and tear off leaves for the months at the bottom. Naturally, he'd seen pictures hanging in other people's homes but had never given them a second glance.

'God, something else to choose,' he muttered under his breath and Alice smiled.

'Don't worry, we can pick something together,' she said and was gratified to see the relief in his eyes. She was well and truly hooked; flattered by his obvious admiration, unable to resist a plea for help and excited to be involved in the project.

As she lay in bed later, she wondered what she'd got herself involved in. She furnished the rooms in her head several times over; what colour carpets, modern or traditional furniture, plain or patterned curtains? Johnnie was to pick her up from work on Wednesday to go and have a look round a furniture store run by one of his friends. Maybe then she'd have a better idea what he liked.

Her conscience pricked a little. Whatever *would* Sally say? Their last exchange on the bus still rankled and she decided to let her stew for a bit longer.

***

The following morning, Johnnie sat at the kitchen table nursing a mug of tea. Heartily sick of the dingy kitchen and the house in general, he'd been spending as little time there as possible. It was tidier than when his dad was around; no crumpled newspapers or empty mugs lying around but still it was dismal; battered furniture, faded curtains and walls in need of a coat of paint. The place was relatively clean but he wanted to be out of there. Like a kid waiting for Christmas, he was counting the days, ticking them off in his head. Ten days should do it, two weeks maximum and he'd be gone.

He'd been bowled over by Alice yet again; the fresh, wholesome look of her. She knew her stuff too and she'd brought the flat to life for him. In his mind's eye, he could see the colours already on the walls although the furniture was a worry. He didn't know what he wanted, didn't even know what he liked.

His plea for help had been a way to get closer to Alice but he *did* need help. The original sweeping idea of 'doing up the place' had turned out to be more complicated than he'd imagined. It was easy enough to agree to central heating, a new bathroom and a couple of window frames but they were the basics. The fine detail was another thing and he wanted to get it right. He wanted a place decorated in good taste and Alice could provide it.

She was meeting him again on Wednesday and then he'd need help with other choices; curtains, pictures, whatever. They'd be together in non-threatening situations, always in public and, for the time being, there'd be no move towards anything more familiar. His first target was for her to feel safe with him. The second was to distance her from Sally Steadman.

He put the mug in the sink, filled it with water and gave the table a quick wipe. His shoes were rubbed with a duster and the collar and shoulders of his jacket brushed before he slipped into it. A quick glance in the tarnished mirror on the kitchen wall and a run of the fingers through his hair assured him he was looking his best. Pride in his appearance was one character trait that came directly from Maurice.

The day lay ahead. It would be a busy one but he'd find the time to nip up to the flat and check progress. He was whistling as he left the house, leaving the car and deciding to walk in the early morning sunshine. Things were looking up. The business was thriving, he'd be moving into his own place in no time and he had Alice to look forward to. For the moment, all was right with the world.

His good mood hadn't gone unnoticed in the shop and everyone breathed a sigh of relief. He could be a nightmare if things weren't going his way.

The work upstairs was going well, he'd gone up a couple of times during the day and the progress was incredible. The radiators were on the walls, the boiler was in working order and Mickey had finished the paintwork and paperhanging in the front room.

Sandra was expecting him at seven. Her mum and dad were away for the weekend and she'd invited him for a meal, wanting to show off her housewifely skills no doubt. Unimpressed, he was becoming increasingly bored but didn't want to break it off while he still had a use for her. The flat was out of action for the time being so it suited him to go to her place. Her bed, though only a single, was more comfortable than the old settee anyway. It wouldn't be the first time he'd had to get out of bed to go home to bed. He doubted she'd ever see the new, improved set up but for now, she had her uses.

Shaking off the idle thought, he decided to call in for a quick half on the way home and stood at the bar, passing the time of day with the landlord.

'Hear about the Steadman girl?'

'No what about her? Has her halo finally appeared?' he asked sarcastically.

The landlord smirked.

'Hardly, Johnny. She's in the infirmary, got run over by a car, been unconscious for days and they can't say how bad it is.'

Johnnie struggled to assume a suitably serious expression.

'I bet her mum and dad are worried sick.'

''Course they are, they've been at the hospital non-stop, waiting for her to come round.'

'Must be off then,' said Johnnie, emptying his glass and placing it firmly on the bar.

As the door of the pub closed behind him, he had to restrain himself from laughing out loud.

'There is a God after all. My cup truly runneth over,' he muttered under his breath.

1966

BBC first broadcast in colour (four hours a week)

England beat Germany 4-2 to win the World Cup

Moors murderers found guilty

First credit card launched by Barclays

Anti-Vietnam protest at the American Embassy in London

Beatles top the British singles chart for the tenth time with 'Paperback Writer'

Published: 'When Eight Bells Toll' - Alistair MacLean

Best Film Oscar: 'A Man for All Seasons' - Paul Scofield and Robert Shaw

Popular Record: 'You Can't Hurry Love' - The Supremes

Born in 1966: David Cameron,
Mike Tyson,
Helena Bonham Carter

Chapter 20

Sally

Three years had passed since Alice came to visit me in the hospital with the bombshell that she and Johnnie were married, I'd thought there couldn't be any worse news. I couldn't have been more wrong. Push comes to shove, I'd thought, she can always get out of it if he shows his true colours.

It had been afternoon visiting and few patients had someone who could come in the middle of the day. Nevertheless, there was no-one wandering around the ward. Matron, a bit of a tarter, insisted everyone should be in bed, tops of lockers cleared and counterpanes tucked in tight, as regulated as an army barracks.

As the big wooden doors at the end of the ward swung open, heads turned. A trickle of visitors wandered down the ward and the patients who had none busied themselves with a book or pretended to sleep.

Alice stood out from the drab coated older crowd who made up most of the visitors and even the nurses reacted to her smiling face.

I hadn't seen her for a week or so and she was a welcome sight, hair falling over the collar of her red jacket, flared skirt swinging and carrying a bunch of pink carnations. She pulled up a chair, laid the flowers across the locker and bent to kiss my cheek

My leg injury still hadn't healed. I'd been back in surgery the previous week and was recovering, yet again, from the aftermath of an operation. Fed up with the injured fingers, the problematic leg and the itching stitches, I was doubly glad to see her. Through all the questioning about my progress and the chit chat about the happenings at work, I could tell there was something. Perhaps her eyes were too bright, her speech too fast; it was unlike her to babble. I couldn't put my finger on it and finally asked her,

'Alice, what's wrong? What aren't you telling me?'

I feared something dreadful had happened but hadn't envisaged something as dreadful as what came next.

She took a deep breath, gripped my uninjured hand and spoke.

'I married Johnnie last week in Scotland, over the anvil at Gretna Green.'

I couldn't manage more than a strangled, 'What?'

The story came pouring out; the drive north, only a few days and he'd been a perfect gentleman, single rooms all the way.

'It was a spur of the moment decision,' she said. 'He asked me and I thought, why not? He's got no family to speak of and my mum's pretty tied up in her own life. It was all so romantic, I couldn't resist.'

My unease must have shown and she squeezed my hand.

'I know you don't like him, Sally, but you don't know him like I do. Try and be happy for me. I love him.'

I could manage only a stilted wish that they'd be very happy. It was done – but 'spur of the moment' my eye. I'd bet my good arm he'd had it planned to the smallest detail.

I couldn't pretend. Couldn't be so phony as to ask the usual questions. What had she worn? Where were they going to live? Was she going to carry on working? I was shocked to silent horror. It was a relief when the bell rang for the end of visiting and she got up to leave, leaning over to kiss my cheek as usual.

I watched her go, shiny black shoes tapping down the ward, handbag swinging. I held the sob in my throat until she'd turned and waved, then lay down and turned my face to the pillow. The scent of the carnations which had delighted me an hour earlier was now sickening. I'd lost her. With the spectre of Johnnie Marshall standing between us, nothing would ever be the same again.

How could it? She was a married woman with responsibilities. My sense of loss overwhelmed me. Alice had abandoned me and I was desolate.

She did come to see me but less frequently. A coolness came between us as she felt my disapproval and inability to engage with her new life. Once we'd exhausted the topic of my recovery, how everyone was keeping and what was happening on the ward, we had little to say to each other. She didn't speak about Johnnie and I didn't ask and my heart ached, longing for our old, easy familiarity. I had to face facts; that was probably a thing of the past.

***

Johnnie's euphoria when Alice had whispered in his ear he was going to be a father had lasted until David was born.

When Alice said she thought it was time to go to the hospital, the normally cool Johnnie had panicked, running around and getting her into the car. She'd had to remind him to go back for her case, which had been sitting in the hall for days.

At the hospital, he watched her being wheeled away, a lump rising in his throat at the sight of her brave smile. Summarily dismissed to the waiting room, in time honoured fashion he'd paced the floor trying to ignore the other father-to-be who tried to strike up a conversation.

'This is our third but I still get nervous,' he said, lighting another cigarette.

Johnnie looked straight through him. Why would he possibly be interested? Any further attempt at conversation had been squashed with one look.

They waited and waited with the door open, expectantly looking up every time there was movement through a delivery room door.

An hour later, a nurse approached. 'Mr Hughes?' she asked.

Johnnie's companion jumped to his feet.

'That's me, he said. 'What's the news?'

She smiled and spoke, 'A bouncing baby girl, mother and baby doing well.'

'I'd hoped for a boy this time, but as long as they're both all right, I'm happy.'

'You can come along and see them as soon as we take them down to the ward.'

Grinning at Johnnie, he gave him the thumbs up and made his way down the corridor.

Only too pleased to be relieved of the unwanted company, Johnnie continued to pace, continually checking his watch, Alice had been in there for hours. One of the nurses brought him a cup of tepid tea but he couldn't get it past the lump in his throat.

Stopping to lean in the doorway, he looked down the corridor, wishing it were all over.

There was a sudden flurry of activity and a nurse appeared, almost running down the corridor to the doctor's office. The white coated medic emerged immediately and hurried up to the delivery room. Johnnie's heart thumped in his chest, this could only mean there was something wrong. He stopped a passing nurse and asked her to find out what was going on but was rebuffed and told to wait. Someone would be along to see him soon.

Another nail biting half hour and finally the doctor appeared.

'Mr Marshall?' he asked.

Johnnie nodded.

'Come along to my office, I need a word.'

In the doctor's pokey office, Johnnie sat on a straight backed chair, waiting and breathing in the smell of stale cigarettes from the overflowing ashtray.

Trying to listen carefully to the smooth tones he had difficulty grasping what was going on. He tried again for some control and it finally sunk in.

'I'm sorry to bring you such bad news but there's something you should know.'

The child had a condition called mongolism, was sub-normal and wouldn't live much beyond puberty, if so long. It depended on the degree and it was too early to tell exactly how handicapped he'd be.

It would be better for everyone, the child included, if he were put into care as quickly as possible. He'd never live a normal life and would need constant attention. Much better for the mother if he were removed as soon as it could be arranged.

Johnnie was furious. Why? Why him? Why them? Whose fault was it?

'It must come from my wife's family. There's no history of any mental problems in mine.'

He was looking for someone to blame and if there were no-one else, Alice would do. Irrationally, his first thought was she'd let him down. It was her failure, not his.

'Not true. It's a genetic disorder which occurs randomly. No-one is to blame, it couldn't have been foreseen and you could go on to have a dozen normal children.'

Johnnie shook his head. No he couldn't. He'd never father another child, he'd make sure of it. He couldn't take a chance and the thought he'd fathered a monster made him shudder in disgust.

Despite his professed love for Alice, all his thoughts were centred on himself. How *he* would deal with it. What would he tell people?

Unbidden, an image sprang to mind. A mongol child had lived in their street when he was young. The slitted eyes, slack mouth and shambling walk had been cause for hilarity amongst the other kids. They called him 'the loony', a great gallumping kid, hanging on his mother's arm, grinning vacantly and mumbling. Johnnie shuddered again.

He sat in silence, sifting through the information while the doctor looked at him compassionately. He spoke coldly, his mind made up.

'Can you organise a place where he'll be looked after?'

'Yes, it can be sorted out fairly quickly. The sooner he's separated from the mother, the better. The longer she has him, the more attached she'll become.'

'I can't face her. Will you tell her?'

The doctor, who'd been brisk and business like but not unsympathetic, suddenly became cooler.

'She'll need a lot of support. This will be very hard on her. It would be better coming from you.'

'No, I can't do it. I can't stand to be anywhere near her or that, that thing.'

The doctor raised his eyebrows.

'Very well. I'll tell her when I make my rounds. I'll put the rest in motion. A social worker will be in touch to make the arrangements.'

The voice was heavy with disdain.

'Your wife has been given a sedative and should sleep for a while. The baby is in the nursery on the third floor if you want to go and see him.'

Johnnie hesitated. 'Right,' he muttered, almost too overcome to speak. Could he bear to go and see the child? Maybe it would be better if he knew the worst so he made his way slowly up to the nursery where a nurse smiled at him enquiringly through the glass.

'Marshall,' he mouthed and watched her face fall and the smile slip. She walked between a row of cots and picked up a bundle wrapped in white and approached the window. Johnnie had to force himself to look. He saw it immediately, the folds around the eyes and the slack mouth and turned away in disgust, his eyes filling with tears. No way, there was no way that thing would come into his home. No pity for the child and no pity for Alice who would have to bear this too, just a deep, overriding disgust and rising fury.

He drove home like a lunatic, cutting corners and overtaking dangerously and finally, screeched to a stop amongst flying gravel.

Storming into the house and flinging his jacket aside, he reached for the decanter and poured himself a large shot. The rising aroma of the expensive single malt failed to sooth and he downed it swiftly and poured another.

It was stifling so he pulled off his tie, opened the top button on his shirt and pushed the French windows open. He was raging, face red and breathing heavily, his ugly expression making him almost unrecognisable.

He couldn't manoeuvre himself out of this one. He was powerless and floundering, furious and despairing and close to losing control. His glass was empty again so he poured another drink and paced; first in the house and then outside up and down the garden.

How could Alice do this to him? She'd let him down and, irrationally, the thought hardened. There was no sympathy in him, only resentment and outrage. How *could* she do this to him?

Another drink followed the first three, the decanter was empty and the smell of the alcohol made him feel sick – he downed it anyway. His reflection in the large mirror over the fireplace sickened him further and he lifted the crystal tumbler and hurled it. The glass and the mirror shattered and shards littered the carpet.

Forced by nature to make the stairs, he started for the bathroom. The open door of what was to be the nursery caught his eye, the gentle colours, soft toys and the sunlight sifting through the draped net curtains. A sudden flashback to the blank little face in the nursery made him gag and he barely made it to the bathroom, heaving and retching until his stomach was empty.

Despite his pounding head, he called the shop the following morning, leaving a message for Mickey to come round as soon as possible.

A 'phone call arranged a meeting with the social worker. He was to meet her at the hospital at eleven to sign the necessary forms. There were things to be done and he'd have them done fast.

His clothes from the previous day were in a heap on the floor and he kicked them into a corner. He'd slept in his shirt and it was stripped off and thrown on the floor with the rest of his clothes. Bathed and shaved, he looked better but still felt like hell.

As the doorbell rang, he started down the stairs. Mickey was on the step with a big smile on his face, expecting to hear good news.

Johnnie stared at him and held up a hand.

'Don't speak. Don't say a word.'

He nodded and years of habit kicked in as he stood and waited for instructions.

'Get the cleaner over here. I want the place cleaned from top to bottom. Got the van outside?'

Mickey nodded again.

'Go into the back bedroom and get rid of all the baby stuff. I don't care what you do with it but I want it gone, all of it, curtains an' all. Then get some emulsion and paint it all white, ceiling and walls, and get it done fast.'

Mickey nodded again but said nothing. Johnnie didn't notice his eyes were filled with tears. He'd assumed Alice's baby had died.

***

Sally

I could see from across the road there was something wrong, seriously wrong. Micky was slumped over the bonnet of the scruffy white van he used to run Marshall's errands. His body language screamed despair; head on crossed arms and legs buckling, his torso convulsed with what could only be sobs.

Although no longer so fast on my feet and the short distance seemed like a mile, I limped furiously over and put my hand gently on his back.

'Micky, Micky, it's Sally. What's up, what's the matter?'

There was no response but the sobs continued. I didn't know what to do. I'd never seen a man cry and it shook me. Mickey had taken many hard knocks during his short life and even as a kid, suffering torments at the hands of Johnnie Marshall, I'd never seen him do more than snivel a bit.

Leaning against the van to take the weight off my bad leg, I could do no more than keep up a rhythmic rubbing up and down his back. He smelled faintly of paint and turps. The sobs subsided and he lifted his head and turned to look at me. His red rimmed eyes were unfocussed and tears ran unashamedly down his pale face.

'Oh Sally,' he whispered. 'Oh my God, Sally.'

I opened the door of the van and pushed him into the front seat. He was like a rag doll.

'Mickey, what is it? What can be so bad?'

'It's Alice. Her baby died. I've to go over to their place and strip and repaint the nursery. He wants it all done today.'

It took minutes for his words to sink in. Poor Alice, How was she coping? What to do? What *could* I do in the face of such a tragedy?

'Stay there,' I said. 'I'm going to 'phone the hospital. Be straight back.'

Thank heavens, the 'phone box across the road was empty and though tattered, the directory was still on the shelf. Fumbling with the change, I dialled the hospital and asked to be put through to maternity.

'Are you a family member?' came the enquiry when I asked after Alice. No information could be given except to immediate family. I asked about visitors and was told the same; family members only.

Bugger that, I thought, I'm going down there. Alice was suffering. Back at the van, Mickey had pulled himself together and was loading up the back with cans of emulsion and painting gear. This wasn't for Johnnie but for Alice, he'd do anything to save her pain.

'Where is he now?' I asked'

'As far as I know, he's on his way down here to the shop.'

'He should be there, with her. Never mind, it suits me. I'm off to the hospital, I'll blag my way in. Meet me in the Queen's at six. I should know something then.'

I must have looked ridiculous limping at speed along the hospital corridors but I couldn't get there fast enough. It wasn't as difficult as expected. When I explained we'd been friends from childhood and I was worried about her, the matron relented.

'I wouldn't have let anyone in outside visiting hours if she'd been on the ward but the poor lassie is very distressed and could use a familiar face and a little comfort.'

She gestured towards the door of a single room facing her office.

'She's in there.'

Alice lay motionless on her side, eyes closed. Sunlight fell across the foot of the bed but her face was in shadow. There were none of the usual trappings of the maternity ward; no flowers, no cards and no cuddly toys. It must be true, I thought.

I pulled up a chair. Her face was drained of colour, dark rings under her eyes, her eyelids twitching slightly. My eyes filled with tears as I reached out and laid my hand over hers. I felt helpless for the second time that day, not a feeling I was familiar with.

She stirred and blinked and then opened her eyes. They were redder and even more swollen than Mickey's.

Registering it was me, she wailed. 'Oh, Sally,' and struggled across the bed and into my arms, shaking and sobbing. I held on to her, hugging and rocking and shushing gently into her ear.

Her hair needed washing and a slightly stale smell rose from the crumpled pink nightie. Under normal circumstances, she'd have been clamouring for soap and water.

There was no need to speak. She'd tell me what was going on in her own good time. Now, she needed comfort. Where was that bloody Marshall?

Exhausted, she pulled herself up and lay back on the pillows and heaved a sigh.

Her voice flat and expressionless, the horror story unfolded.

I breathed more easily as I realised the baby was alive but as she continued, doubted she would cope. Could it have been any worse if he'd died?

She'd seen the baby only once before the doctor had come to explain. The child was handicapped and would never live a normal life and 'it was best all round if he were taken away immediately.'

'It made no difference what I said, how I pleaded. Johnnie's already signed the papers and it's done. How could he? He never even asked me, never came to visit last night. I don't know what I'm going to do.'

Shoulders slumped, hands lying idle in her lap, she didn't raise her eyes to look at me. I could only wait for her to go on.

'This is what usually happens with mongol babies.'

It was the first time she had spoken the word and I winced.

'The doctor said I'll be able to see him whenever I want, be able to visit once I'm back on my feet. But Sally, I want him now, to look after him myself not put him in some institution where nobody will love him.'

Mother's milk leaked through the thin nightie but she didn't notice.

Her voice had risen and she was becoming agitated, bright spots of colour rising on her pale cheeks. None of this could be good for her but there was no remedy. Nobody could make the baby normal and only Johnnie could arrange for her to take the baby home. Where was that bastard anyway?

I held her hand and let her speak, going over the same ground over and over. Useless and helpless, I sat and listened, there was nothing else to do.

After an hour or so, the matron put her head round the door. My time was up and Alice needed to rest. I couldn't see any rest on Alice's horizon any time soon but I stood and leaned over Alice to give her a kiss and a final hug.

'I'll come again tomorrow afternoon.'

She couldn't even smile and who could blame her. As I turned to leave, she spoke,

'Will you let my mum know what's happened? She hasn't been and I'm not sure Johnnie will have thought to tell her. If she 'phones the house and there's no-one there, she'll be worried.'

Her voice became a thin wail with the age old cry of a body in despair,

'I want my mum.'

I promised to ring as soon I found a 'phone box. Closing the door gently behind me, I wandered along the long, bleak corridor. It hit me when I was half way to the exit. The lump in my throat turned to sobs and I ducked into the hospital chapel, fortunately empty, and cried my heart out.

There was no solace here, though the sun shone through the coloured glass in the window and a candle flickered in a holder. I don't know how long I sat there, tears coming hard and fast, muttering, 'poor Alice; poor, poor Alice,' devastated in the face of such tragedy.

Under control but still upset, I sat in the pub facing Mickey Smith. Alone in the main bar, we could hear a couple of guys playing darts in the vault, laughing and joking. The barmaid was watching them, leaning on the bar but she stirred herself to get our drinks and take the cash.

The paint splattered overalls were gone, replaced by a clean shirt and jeans but Mickey's face was ashen, the strain showing as I told him what had happened. The news hit him hard. For a man who normally had little to say for himself, the stream of invective was astounding. I'd never heard so many swear words strung together so constructively.

His voice had risen and was attracting attention from the vault and I gestured to him to keep it down.

Subsiding with a final, 'the bastard, the effing bastard,' he looked a bit shame faced at the language and muttered, 'Sorry, Sal.'

'It doesn't matter. All that matters is Alice. For the moment, don't say anything to anyone. The news will spread fast enough; bad news always does.'

Mickey shook his head.

'The baby's bedroom's cleared out and repainted. I don't know whether she'll be glad or not. Funny thing, I've seen Johnnie twice today and he doesn't look upset, he looks furious, you can see he's boiling.'

He'd always had a soft spot for Alice but I'd never realised the depth of his feelings.

'As soon as she's out of the hospital, you'll be able to drop round and see her,' I said. 'You usually know when Johnnie is in the shop and you can nip round for ten minutes. I'm sure she'd be glad to see you. She'll need all her friends now.'

Mickey looked unsure.

'I'm going to have to go sneaking round there myself. I can't take the risk of bumping into him and causing more bother for Alice. She'll be in the house on her own for most of the day. A friendly face could make all the difference.'

'Fancy another?' he asked as he upended his pint and poured what was left down his throat.

'Better not,' I said. 'Mum will be wondering where I am and I'll have to tell her, at least, what's going on. She's always been fond of Alice.'

'Right, then. See you Sal.'

I pulled over my battered black shoulder bag and rummaged around until I found a pen and an old envelope. Scribbling my 'phone number on the back, I pushed it over the table.

'Give me a call if you hear anything. I'll get in touch with you if I get any news.'

I was the last one Marshall would keep informed and it would never cross his mind Mickey might be worried.

'See you Mickey,' I said. 'Chin up.'

Glancing back I saw a picture of dejection, Mickey's shoulders slumped as he stared into his empty glass.

A bus was approaching as the pub door swung closed behind me. I couldn't manage the stairs to the top deck and I could hear the youngsters up there carrying on. It seemed only five minutes since Alice and I were sitting side by side without a care in the world. Now she had more worries than we'd ever dreamed of and I felt as though I were a close second.

Two women in head scarves in front of me, nattered and moaned about their respective husbands and the drone made it easy to filter them out.

I couldn't help beating myself up. I should have paid more attention, made the effort to keep in touch. Irrationally, guilt raised its ugly head. I'd always looked after Alice and had failed her. This was beyond help, Alice would struggle and suffer and I could only stand by and watch, offering feeble support from the side lines.

I'd been wrapped up in my own problems. I went over the past in my head. My recovery had been my overriding concern. The leg had healed, although not perfectly, and I'd been warned there would be a permanent limp.

My hand was another matter and with exercise, I could expect to regain dexterity. Constant practising with my stiffened fingers, loosened them up and I played the same few bars and the basic scales almost to the point of exhaustion. It took hours every day. Mum and Dad were so glad to have me home, they'd have put up with anything.

After an hour or so, Mum would pop her head round the door and say quietly,

'Time for a break, Sal. Come and have a cuppa. The piano will still be there in half an hour,' and I'd laugh and comply, knowing although my progress was slow, it was there.

Those weeks in hospital had seemed endless so to be home was a joy even though I spent long hours alone while Mum and Dad were at work.

Alice had continued to visit the hospital but after I was sent home, we saw less and less of each other. Our lives were on different paths. I was about to start my first year of teacher training and she was a housewife and hostess.

We met very occasionally for coffee. While she was busy furnishing the new house and buying clothes to attend various functions, I was studying hard or haunting the jazz clubs, hoping for a chance to play, if only for one number.

As uninterested in Alice's furnishing plans as I'd been in my mum's all those years before, she was as indifferent to modern jazz as she had been on our first visit to the Crown. We had no common ground and drifted apart. I felt the loss of her friendship keenly but knew I was no competition for the great Johnnie Marshall.

Chapter 21

Alice was discharged from the hospital two days later. Her mother had brought in some clothes and suppressed her tears as she helped Alice put them on, like a small child, who hadn't quite got the hang of buttons.

White faced and red eyed, Alice did as she was told, her voice flat and her gaze blank. Brenda despaired. Though she didn't make the connection, Alice was in much the same state as she herself had been when her husband died.

Johnnie was missing, pressure of business he'd said when he asked Brenda to collect Alice from the hospital. Brenda was relieved, the coldness apparent in Johnnie's voice had unsettled her.

She left Alice sitting on the edge of the bed and went to have a word with the Sister.

'Physically, she's in good condition. It wasn't a difficult birth but her mental state is a different matter. She needs good food and gentle exercise and above all, care and attention,' she said, eyes full of compassion. 'There's nothing more we can do for her here.'

Poor Alice, thought Brenda, she couldn't imagine much tea and sympathy coming from Johnnie but she nodded.

'Even mothers who have a normal delivery and go home with a baby can have difficulties in the early days and depression's not unusual. She'll need watching.'

'I'll do my best,' Brenda replied, wondering how on earth she was going to manage.

Alice was exactly as she'd left her; immobile, hands folded on her lap.

They walked down to the main entrance. Though the hospital was bustling with staff and patients, Alice registered nothing, leaning heavily on her mother's arm, putting one foot in front of the other. Brenda struggled with Alice's weight and the suitcase containing her belongings.

Brenda flagged down a taxi and eventually they pulled up outside the family home where Alice stood silently, impervious to her surroundings, and waited while her mother paid the fare.

'Come on, love. Let's get you inside,' she said, after rummaging in her bag for the key Johnnie had dropped off earlier.

Brenda got Alice undressed and back into bed and brought a cup of tea which lay untouched on the bedside table.

'I've left something in the oven for your tea. Perhaps you could sleep for a while?'

'Yes, I'll try. I'll get up later and have a bath. Thanks for everything, Mum.'

'I'm off then. I'll be back in the morning,' and she bent and kissed Alice's cheek, stroked her hair and finally dragged herself away, weeping gently as she made her way down the elegantly decorated staircase.

Alice dozed for an hour and then lay, trying to find the energy to get out of bed. The smell finally roused her. Her nightdress smelled of the hospital and as she picked up the clothes folded over a chair, they smelled of hospital too. She caught sight of herself in the full length mirror, formerly used to check her immaculate appearance before she left the house. Was that sad, lank haired ghost really her?

She piled everything in a heap on the landing and ran a bath, pouring in fragrant bath oil and putting out the shampoo and finally, sinking into comfort of the scented water. Her breasts, though still tender, had finally stopped oozing and the heat eased the ache. Relieved to be alone after the constant fussing of the last few days, she lingered in the bath until forced out by the cooling water.

A bit shaky, she pulled on a pair of loose trousers and a yellow tee shirt and thought she could make it downstairs to load the washing machine. The house was silent and she could hear herself breathing as she crossed the landing. Her own home felt unfamiliar to her. It all looked strange, like a stage set.

The door to the second bedroom was ajar and she pushed it open. She'd picked out the colours herself and it was a pleasant room, in shades of pale turquoise with matching curtains and bedspread. The bed was made up and a couple of Johnnie's dark suits were visible through the open doors of the wardrobe. He obviously intended to sleep in here tonight. The first spark of emotion for days flared up.

Good, she thought. I don't want him near me, not yet, if I ever will again.

She closed the door behind her and hesitated outside the baby's room. It contained all her hopes and all her unfulfilled dreams. Could she bear to look?

Bracing herself, she slowly opened the door. The starkness of the room stopped her in her tracks; white walls, white paintwork and bare windows. Gone was the teddy bear wallpaper she'd chosen so carefully, gone were the cuddly toys and the net curtains, gone was the pale yellow furniture and the cot with its soft blankets. All evidence of the expected child had been removed, as though he'd never existed.

It can't get any worse, she thought as she made her way back to her bedroom on shaking legs, one hand on the wall for support.

The dull ache of emptiness was beginning to fill with purpose. Away from the numbing atmosphere of the hospital, the stripped down baby's room had jolted her out of her apathy. She had to do something or she'd go crazy. Her baby, she had to focus on him, find out where he was, go and see him.

Platitudes from her mother, her grandma and even her Uncle Jim haunted her. If she heard even one more time it was 'all for the best', she'd scream. Even the doctor who'd come to see her before her discharge had said 'in time, she'd see it was the right thing to do.' What did they know? How could any of them know what she was going through?

She hadn't seen Johnnie since the baby had been taken and had no idea what he was thinking, what he was feeling. Was he as tormented as she was? Maybe he was trying to come to terms with it in his own way. The idea he might be blaming her never crossed her mind.

Determined to keep busy, she picked up the discarded clothes on the landing and made her way carefully downstairs. The kitchen was as she'd left it, pristine surfaces gleaming, the clock ticking away and a glimpse of fresh green from the willow tree at the end of the garden.

Clothes pushed into the washing machine, she wandered into the sitting room. It had been freshly dusted and vacuumed, she could see the tracks on the carpet. How strange, the large gold framed mirror which usually hung above the fireplace had disappeared. Where could it be?

Already tiring and back in the kitchen, she made herself some tea and sat at the table, nursing the bright red beaker, one of a set bought to bring a splash of colour into her all white kitchen.

The sound of a key in the door startled her. Johnnie was home at last.

'In here,' she called and heard his footsteps coming towards her and the door opened.

The cold expression on his face shocked her to silence.

'How are you?' he asked, his voice expressionless. No hug, no kiss and no warmth at all.

'I'm OK, a bit tired.'

'Is there anything to eat?' he asked, 'I'm starving.'

There was clearly to be no discussion. He was going to sweep all of it, their son included, firmly under the carpet.

Alice set the table, retrieved the casserole from the oven and served two portions. Johnnie tucked in without a word while she pushed hers around the plate, nauseated by the smell of the cooked meat.

Clearing the table and loading the dishwasher which had been her pride and joy, she turned to face him. She couldn't let it go. She had to know.

'Johnnie, where is he? Can I go and see him?'

'I knew you'd start this,' he said slowly, 'I knew yhere was no way you'd leave it alone.'

His voice was sharp, no touch of sympathy or understanding.

Reaching into his jacket for his wallet, he pulled out a card and tossed it on the table.

409

'It's in there,' he said. 'Go if you must but I don't want to hear about it. Right? I've got paperwork to catch up on, I'll be in there,' he said gesturing towards the dining room.

Alice stood, slack jawed, and watched him disappear, the door swinging closed behind him.

Dazed at his reaction, she gazed unseeingly at the framed Monet poster on the kitchen wall. Her lethargy had disappeared and her mind was whirling. She picked up the card, committing the number to memory before tucking it into her pocket. He might change his mind and tear it up.

Her loving, laughing Johnnie had disappeared and been replaced by this heartless monster. He'd let her down when she needed him most, his coldness like a smack in the face. Could she ever forgive him?

To hell with him, she thought, I'll concentrate on my baby. Go and see him tomorrow. Thank God for Sal, if I ring her, she'll come with me. In her despair, she was reaching out for the safety of the old, familiar friendship.

In the dining room, Johnnie threw the brief case onto the polished table. The subtle colours and polished surfaces which normally filled him with satisfaction failed to soothe. He was still teeth-grindingly angry.

His Alice, his beautiful Alice was gone and had been replaced by the drab in the kitchen. Pale faced and whining, the loose clothing failing to hide the slackness of her belly, she'd repelled him. He couldn't bear to look at her.

He wanted to escape. Escape from the house, escape from Alice and escape from the pitying looks he'd been subjected to for the last couple of days.

The news had spread, heaven knows how, but he'd been so obviously furious no-one had dared approach him with a word of sympathy. In fact, no-one dared approach him at all. He'd stormed through the shop and into the office and sat fuming for most of the day, unable to concentrate on anything except his outrage.

He had no close family and no friends, only 'contacts' and 'connections'. No-one except Alice cared about him and she'd failed him. Unable to keep still any longer, he strode back into the kitchen where Alice was still sitting in shock at the table, lifted his jacket from the back of the chair and his keys from the work top and without a word, stormed out, slamming the front door behind him.

Revving the engine, he backed out of the drive and scorched off down the road, not knowing where he was going but wanting to be away. He drove for an hour, furiously and dangerously, out into the Cheshire countryside miles from anywhere and pulled into a lay-by. The sky was darkening. A few cars passed and still he sat, staring blindly through the fly spattered windscreen, hands resting on the leather covered steering wheel.

At long last, his anger was subsiding. That level of rage couldn't be sustained. It was time to sort himself out, find a strategy.

First and foremost, what did he want? Easy answer, he wanted the golden couple with the golden child, living in the golden house.

Harder to face; he couldn't have them all but two out of three wasn't bad. He could still have Alice, the house and, of course, his growing business. He was making money hand over fist.

Ever the pragmatist, he faced the facts full on. Yes, he'd fathered an idiot. Folks would gossip for a while but the child would never be mentioned. Any questions from family, staff or acquaintances would be discouraged. No-one would ask twice.

Alice would come round. Even her mother sided with him. The best place for the child was out of sight and hopefully, he would gradually fade out of mind. He couldn't forbid Alice to visit but there'd be no encouragement, no questions and no discussion. The whole episode was a closed book.

He had a momentary twinge as he remembered Alice's face as he'd left the house. After all, she'd just had a baby but still, it wasn't an illness. Her looks would come back given time and attention and she'd lose the extra weight. After all, he knew plenty of women with kids and had bedded quite a few of them.

It was time to mend his fences. She'd see sense, she had everything she could wish for; her own home furnished the way she wanted, a car and a wardrobe full of expensive clothes. If it made her happy, they could move to a bigger place further out of town. The business was doing well and he could afford it. A new project might be what she needed. The only thing he wouldn't give her was a child and she'd have to come to terms with it.

He loved Alice in his own way but it was the love for a possession and not for a wife. She was his and would always be his.

Decisions made, he spotted a telephone box on the edge of the lay-by and, acting on impulse, he got out of the car and felt in his pocket for change. The box smelled a little musty but the telephone was intact and there were no tell-tale puddles or stains and no scribbling on the walls. Its miles from anywhere, he thought idly, no-one living round here would need a public telephone. It's probably not been used for weeks.

He dropped the coins in the box, dialled the well-remembered but long unused number and waited. In response to the voice at the other end of the 'phone, he said,

'Hello, Sandra, how've you been?'

Chapter 22

At twelve thirty, he pulled up outside his home; a pleasant, recently built three bedroomed detached, ten minutes' walk from Didsbury Village. The front of the house and the garden looked impressive in the soft glow of the street lights. The white of the roses in the border stood out in the dim light and their scent wafted in through the open window.

The place was in darkness. Alice must be in bed. He turned off the engine and the headlights and sat, hands on steering wheel, deep in thought. Calm for the first time in days and relaxed for the first time in weeks, he smiled wryly. Total abstinence was doing me no good at all, he thought, and Sandra had been as enthusiastic as ever.

There was a half-hearted pang of shame; not because of the way he'd treated Alice or because he'd rejected his own child and not because he'd been unfaithful for the first time but because he'd lost control.

The charm offensive would start tomorrow. She'd forgive him, he'd bring her round. He wanted Alice back, not the stricken figure he'd left at the kitchen table but the old Alice. The Alice who was beautiful and vibrant, laughing and compliant and a credit to him, his taste and his success. Anything less would be a crippling loss of face.

After a restless night, Alice had fallen into an exhausted, dreamless sleep in the early hours. She woke to the sounds of birds singing outside her window but no movement in the house. Rising slowly, she pushed her feet into her fluffy slippers and looked out of the window. The drive was empty; Johnnie had already left for the day. She'd heard him come in last night but had lain still, not wanting to see him or talk to him but he'd passed her door without pausing. He must have crept around getting ready for work and hadn't disturbed her and she was glad he was gone. She couldn't stand the sight of him.

There was a note lodged under the kettle on the work surface.

"Sorry about last night. I'll try and get home early. Love, Johnnie."

She crumpled the note and tossed in the bin. There were other things on her mind. The lingering smell of the hospital had finally disappeared and she was ravenous. There'd been nothing substantial inside her for days.

The card Johnnie had all but thrown at her now lay face up on the kitchen table. Nervously, she picked the receiver off the wall 'phone and dialled the number, throat dry and barely able to speak. Relief washed through her. Yes, she could visit today, any time after two. The voice at the end of the 'phone sounded pleasant and cheerful, a good sign surely.

She redialled and smiled for the first time in days. Sally would be only too glad to come with her and they arranged to meet later in the day. There was just the time between now and then to fill.

There was no doubt, she did feel better. Still in her peach flowered silk nightdress and matching dressing gown, she pottered around the house, wiping down the kitchen and clearing up.

She didn't notice the shirt Johnnie had been wearing the day before wasn't in the linen basket. It had been so scented with Sandra's perfume he'd taken it with him to dump on his way to work.

Her few chores finished, she made a coffee and took it out into the sunshine. The front garden was neat lawn and borders, Johnnie's idea. His only concession had been she could choose which roses were planted and even then, her instructions were to pick all the same colour. He wasn't interested in the garden, just how it looked, but she'd had free rein in the back. The planting was much more relaxed. The pale pinks, blues and lilacs she loved so much, the scent rising and insects buzzing soothed her. Her troubles momentarily forgotten, she closed her eyes and, raising her face to the sun, dozed for half an hour.

Waking with a start, she remembered her mother's promised visit and back in the house, she picked up the 'phone again.

'Hello, Mum. Yes I'm much better. Yes, the casserole was lovely, we enjoyed it.' A twinge of guilt rose at the thought of the plate she had scraped into the bin.

'Look, you don't need to come over today. You've been running around and need a rest as much as I do. Yes, there's plenty of food in the 'fridge, thanks to you. I can manage for a couple of days. I'm going to go for a little drive this afternoon and Sally said she might come over for an hour.'

Her mother's voice twittered in response, full of concern but fussing. Alice knew too much sympathy would undo her, reduce her to tears again, and her mother would pour it on. She was done with tears for the time being, she needed to be strong.

'No, I promise I won't overdo it. I'll put my feet up for an hour later on. Look, I'll ring you in the morning. If I manage the car OK, maybe we can go shopping later in the week, stock up on stuff. Things need to get back to normal and you need to get back to work.'

Though Brenda was still fussing, Alice could tell she was relieved, hopeful things would, indeed, get back to normal. For Alice, there would be a different 'normal' from now on but her mother wasn't to know.

'Yes, Mum. I'll take it easy. I'll ring you tomorrow. 'Bye now.'

No mention was made of the visit to see the baby'. It would unleash all sorts of new concerns, the 'do you think it's wise?' and 'are you well enough?' and possibly even 'does Johnnie know?' The least she knew the better. Alice wanted no interference and no good advice. Brenda never contacted Johnnie directly and never came to the house when she knew he'd be there.

Sally

More than happy there was something I could do and pleased Alice had turned to me, I waited in the arranged spot until the red mini pulled up.

She looked a far cry from the sobbing wretch I'd left in the hospital. The redness had faded from her eyes and she wore a touch of pale pink lipstick. She flashed me a quick smile and pulled away from the kerb. Her jaw was set and she looked straight ahead, determined and resolute.

'Thanks, Sal,' she said. 'I couldn't have faced it on my own.'

'Don't worry, I'm glad to help,' I said, patting her gently on the knee.

She drove in silence so I kept quiet. I didn't ask about Johnnie, but then again, I never did. With no idea where we were going, I watched the shops and houses pass until we stopped outside a large, well maintained detached house, more like a mansion, with smart black and white paintwork and the name 'Oak House' cut into the stone of the gate posts. I knew immediately this was the home set up by Mrs Hughes, our old head master's wife. I knew her well but she and Alice had never met. I decided to say nothing. Alice was so strung out, I doubt she'd have heard me.

'This is it,' she said and pulled into the parking area in front of the house.

Tense and nervous, she climbed the steps and rang the bell with me close behind. A smiling Mrs Hughes opened the door and asked,

'Mrs Marshall?'

Alice nodded and we were ushered into a large, beautifully proportioned hall. The moulded plasterwork on the ceiling and frieze, the polished wooden bannister and finial and the geometrically patterned tiled floor were obviously original to the house. Alice, of course, noticed nothing. From behind a closed door on the right, I could hear the racket of children playing and they sounded happy enough.

Mrs Hughes smiled at me too and shook her head warningly. There'd be time enough for explanations later. Alice was the prime concern.

'I'm Mrs Hughes, I run the place. You'll be wanting to see your baby. Come upstairs to the nursery, let's see if he's awake,' and she led the way up the carpeted staircase.

There were only two cots in the room with a baby in each; one asleep and one awake and kicking a bit. They looked the same to me but Alice didn't hesitate. Despite having held him for such a short time, she knew him immediately and hung over the cot, putting her finger against his fist until he gripped it.

'Can I pick him up?' she asked, looking pleadingly at Mrs Hughes.

'Of course, dear. Pick him up. He's due a feed any time. His bottle will be up soon, do you want to feed him?' and she gestured at a straight backed chair next to the cot.

'I'll leave you to it.'

Alice took the baby out of the cot, wrapping him in the soft blue blanket which had been covering him and sat down, face alight.

'Look at him, Sal, just look,' she said.

So I looked - but what did I know about babies? I'd never seen one close up, never been interested, and had never held one. He was very small but he was only four days old. Even with my lack of experience, I could see he wasn't right, something odd about his face. Alice was oblivious, cuddling him and crooning under her breath.

I was spared having to say anything by the arrival of the bottle, brought in by a young woman in a white nylon overall.

'I'm Mary, here you are, try him with this,' she said, passing the bottle to Alice, who put it to the baby's mouth as though she'd been doing it for years. He gripped it greedily and sucked like mad.

Fascinating for Alice but for me, standing propped against the wall, my leg aching, it was all a bit boring.

The room was bright and pleasant. Grey mottled lino covered the floor and pretty green and white curtains hung at the large window. Colourful Disney posters were tacked to the walls, contrasting with the elegance of the mouldings and the panelled oak door. From what I'd seen so far, the place was more like an affluent, upper class home than an institution. At the moment, Alice had eyes for nothing but the child in her arms.

Maybe I'd be able to work up some enthusiasm once he was a bit older and perhaps, doing something. I checked myself, would he do something? Would he learn to walk and talk like a normal kid? With no idea what to expect, I'd have to play it by ear. With Alice in such a precarious emotional state, I couldn't ask. She probably didn't know herself, clearly thinking no further than the moment.

Bottle empty, Alice put the baby over her shoulder and rubbed his back while Mary smiled approvingly, Alice was doing well. When he gave an enormous burp, I thought they were going to cheer, they looked so delighted.

Nappy instruction followed. The baby was laid on a towel covered table in the corner. Pin unfastened, the nappy was unfolded to reveal a god-awful mess. With the nurse at her side, murmuring advice, Alice wiped him clean, fastened on a fresh nappy and picked him up, walking up and down the room with him.

'He'll sleep for a while if you put him in his cot. Mrs Hughes would like a word. She's in her office, on the right off the hall as you go downstairs.'

Alice was reluctant to part with him but, with a kiss on the crown of his head, she laid him down and covered him with the blanket. Patting him gently on the bum, she turned away, her eyes filled with tears. She pulled a hankie out of her pocket, wiped her eyes and blew her nose vigorously.

'If I start to cry, I won't stop,' she whispered, 'and then I'll be no use to him or myself.'

So touched I had a lump in my own throat, I followed her downstairs.

In the office, we were offered seats and Mrs Hughes said,
'We have him down as Baby Marshall. What's his first name?'
Alice hesitated a moment,
'I'm calling him David, after a childhood hero,' she said, and smiled at me.

Although I was pleased, the unbidden thought rose; the rotten bastard couldn't even be bothered to give the poor kid a name.

Mrs Hughes continued,
'Both you and your husband are, of course, welcome to visit. We would ask you though to keep to a time frame, about two hours from two o'clock onwards. It's so much easier for us when we know when visitors may be arriving and avoids disruption of the routines.'

Alice nodded but I saw her slight grimace at the mention of Johnnie. I guessed no visits from him were to be expected.

'It isn't so important when he's so small, but it would be beneficial if you could keep to some kind of pattern, maybe three times a week and, if possible, always on the same day. Please don't come every day, we need him to be dependent on the staff who are here all the time.

Don't misunderstand, Mrs Marshall, these are guidelines and not hard and fast rules. You could, of course, come at any time and we wouldn't deny you access but we do have David's welfare at heart.'

'I understand, Mrs Hughes.'

'Try to remember, David's life will be here with us. I promise he'll be well cared for, loved even. Most of our staff have been with us since we opened and we encourage them to engage with the children, not just look after their physical needs. You'll soon get to know them.'

She paused briefly,

'Your life, however, will be on the other side of our front door. David is your child and I understand how much he means to you but it's important you carry on normally, as far as possible. Fill your time, keep busy. It would be a grave mistake to mark time, waiting only for the next visit. I promise it will get easier.'

Alice was on the verge of tears again but breathed deeply, refusing to weaken.

'Everything you say makes sense, acting on it may be a bit more difficult,' she said.

'If you're worried about anything, give me a ring and you can always pop in for a chat.'

'Thank you. You've been very understanding.'

'If there were any problems with David, health wise, we would inform you straight away. I promise, he's in safe hands.'

There was nothing else to say and Alice rose to her feet and I followed suit. She leaned over the desk to shake Mrs Hughes's hand and I did too. It seemed an odd gesture between women. I think Alice would rather have given her a hug but didn't know her well enough.

Back in the car, Alice sat stiff armed, gripping the steering wheel.

'I'm not going to blub,' she said. 'I'm going to get on with it.'

I'd never admired her more.

As we pulled out into the traffic she asked,

'Shall I drop you where I picked you up?'

I nodded. She had a lot to on her mind and we drove in silence. I didn't mind, there'd be time enough for me to fill in the blanks next time we spoke. Reassured the baby would be well looked after, she had some sort of structure to build on.

'Look, Alice. If you need me to come with you again, let me know. I'm still free most afternoons.'

'I'm grateful you got me through the first visit. I don't know what I would have done without you.'

I hadn't done anything but perhaps it was enough she hadn't had to face it alone.

'I'll be fine. I'll get myself organised, choose my days and stick to them and fill the time in between somehow. Perhaps I'll start dressmaking again, or painting even. There's a thought.'

I blew her a kiss as I got out of the car then leaned back in to say,

'I'll ring you in the morning.'

She waved as she pulled away. She didn't look good but better than the last time I saw her, some of the strain had gone from round her eyes.

Chapter 23

Sally

The smell of baked apple hit me when I opened the front door and I breathed deep. Mum was in the kitchen clearing away. The golden crusted pie had been placed to cool on the kitchen windowsill along with a wire rack covered in jam tarts. The emotional couple of hours I'd experienced had left me tired and hungry and a little confused.

There was tea in the earthenware pot that had been on our kitchen table ever since I could remember and I poured a cup for each of us and sat down at the grey Formica topped table.

'How was Alice?' she asked, concern clear in her voice.

It all came pouring out, Mrs Hughes, the home and the staff, Alice and the baby and my confusion about what was going on and how I felt about it.

Mum was quite clear what she thought.

'She'd be better off putting the whole thing behind her, trying again for another baby. There'll be no good purpose served by constant visiting. You know those children don't live very long and they're susceptible to all kinds of health problems. Did her mum know she was going visiting?'

I couldn't see what difference it made but had to say I didn't know.

'Please don't tell her, Mum. If Alice wants her to know she'll tell her herself.'

She nodded reluctantly. It was unlike Mum to sound so hard and to view anything Alice did with disapproval. Johnnie wasn't mentioned. She'd heard the rumours he'd brushed the whole thing under the carpet. There might never have been a baby as far as he was concerned.

'Honestly, Mum, I can't work out the rights and wrongs. If you'd seen her with the baby in her arms, your heart would have melted. I can't tell whether she'll suffer more if she goes to see him or more if she doesn't. It looks like heartache to me either way.'

'Poor Alice,' Mum's voice had softened. 'Poor girl, she's very young to have to deal with something like this.'

'She's stronger than we think. Look how she coped when her dad died. She'll do exactly what she wants. She's easy going as a rule but when she digs her heels in, there's no budging her.'

I felt a little guilty discussing Alice's affairs with a third party, even my mother, but she was fond of Alice and could be trusted. She'd never passed on gossip in her life.

There was nothing I could do except be there if she needed me. Little enough but it was all I *could* do. Unused to feeling inadequate, I didn't like it much.

***

So Alice started her double life. Three afternoons a week, she became what she wanted to be, a loving mother. More difficult now, was her role of loving wife.

In the early days, nothing fit her properly and her dusty sewing machine had been retrieved from under the stairs. Her maternity clothes hung on her slight frame but some of the weight she'd gained during pregnancy was still there.

Her mum had been only too happy to go shopping with her for fabric and patterns. Alice hadn't told her about the visits to the home and Brenda didn't ask about David. Like Johnnie, she hoped Alice had put it all behind her.

By the following afternoon, Alice had run up a pretty yellow dress to tide her over. Johnnie's approval, when he came home from work, had been clear and during the following week, she made two more in light, flattering pastels. There wasn't much point in making any more and once again, the days had to be filled.

House cleaning was a mindless occupation which suited her mood; every window gleamed, every polished surface buffed to a high shine, every carpet vacuumed. The garden also got its share of ruthless attention so when the gardener came, there was little for him to do except cut the lawns. Alice had weeded every inch of every border.

Spinning out her tasks became a challenge. She leafed through her cookery books, planning each meal for maximum nutrition and minimum weight gain, trying out time consuming and complicated recipes. Johnnie also looked better on the new regime although she knew he often snacked on bacon butties and pie and chips in the café near the shop.

Even when it rained, she walked through the park on her way to shops, a journey of about half an hour. Although the flower beds appeared to have been colour coded from a paint chart, regimented into orderly patterns and straight lines, the overall effect was easy on the eye and often cheered her. The major hazard was other young mothers pushing prams and she was torn between hanging over the pram to have a look at the baby and averting her face so she wouldn't have to.

It had been hard, the first time, to go into the local shops. She was faceless in the supermarket, just another customer. It had been a different story in the bread shop and in the butcher's. The people there knew her and had seen her developing pregnancy.

She'd been greeted by the butcher in his dark blue and white striped apron, with a broad smile and a 'nice to see you, love. How're you doing?' as he looked over her shoulder, expecting to see a pram parked outside. His face fell but he didn't ask any further except,

'What can I get you today then?'

The bread shop was even harder. The smell of fresh baking came to meet her and rows of golden scones and cream cakes filled the glass cases at the counter. She'd built up a rapport with Mavis, the elderly assistant, a jolly faced woman with rosy cheeks and a tight perm who often had time for a bit of a chat, following Alice's increasing girth with great interest. Now here she stood, bump gone, pale of face and no baby.

Alice smiled, a tremulous smile, but she managed it and said quietly, 'I'll have a small white cob and a couple of muffins, please.'

Mavis bustled to wrap the crusty bread in tissue paper while Alice fished in her purse and passed over a pound note. Dropping the change into Alice's hand, Mavis clasped it briefly but warmly, and whispered.

'Never mind, love. Have another one soon as you can. It's always the best way. Take care of yourself.'

Although it was meant kindly, it cut Alice to the quick and, eyes filling, she left the shop almost at a run. When she'd calmed down, she thought, well that's over and they won't mention it again.

As the days became shorter, Alice had difficulty filling her time. The walking, the housework and gardening had worked wonders. Her figure was as it had been, her colour good and her hair again soft and silky.

The summer bedding plants, thinning and leggy, had been pulled out of the borders and the weather, with autumn approaching, not always conducive to long walks or lingering in the park.

The days she visited David were easy enough to fill; housework in the morning, a quick bath and then a couple of hours feeding and changing and generally being with her baby. Satisfied her darling was in good hands, she still rarely left him without having a bit of a snivel on the way home.

One grey, drizzly morning with a long empty day stretching before her, she sat in the kitchen, fidgeting and drumming her fingers on the table. She cast about for something to do. Physical activity, she thought, and on impulse, decided to tackle the cupboard under the stairs.

She dragged everything out. Her sewing machine, now dusty again, was right at the front. Two pairs of wellingtons and a couple of boxes of various bits and pieces were stacked behind them and an old blue jacket she wore in the garden on chilly days hung behind the door. At the back, she found her easel, a sturdy affair knocked up by her Uncle Jim when she was still at school. Further excavation unearthed her water colours, brushes and the paint spattered palette her mum had bought her one Christmas. A small stack of paintings leaned against the wall and she pulled them out too. Sitting on the floor, she flipped through the stack. Some of them weren't half bad.

Studying the top picture, a landscape painted from a quick pencil sketch made on a trip to Lyme Park, she thought, why not?

Galvanised into action and laden with the painting gear, she struggled up the stairs and dumped the lot in what she always thought of as the baby's bedroom, closing the door behind her.

Fired up, the contents of the under stairs cupboard were quickly replaced, unsorted and undusted. She couldn't wait to get back upstairs.

There were still no curtains at the window but the room faced south and the stark white walls reflected what natural light there was. It would do very nicely. A cupboard and a chair and the room would be ideal. There'd possibly be something in the second hand shop in the village. Engrossed, she checked her paints and brushes.

Johnnie wouldn't be consulted. As far as she knew he hadn't opened the door to this room since she came home.

***

Their relationship had settled into an uneasy truce. He seemed the same as before; making her laugh, praising her newfound cooking skills and chatting about what went on in the shop. Nevertheless, occasionally she caught him looking at her speculatively and wondered what was going through his mind. Fairly sure he knew she visited on a regular basis, he never asked and she never volunteered information.

The complete trust of their early years was shaken. His coldness when David was born was never forgotten. Everyone who knew the situation, except for Sally, was determined to pretend he'd never existed. Even her mother and grandmother never asked about him so Johnnie could hardly be blamed. He couldn't help how he felt, she told herself repeatedly. What hurt most was his dismissal of her feelings, never acknowledging her sense of loss or her sadness. His view she should 'snap out of it' was hard to handle.

More isolated than ever, unable to talk about a huge chunk of her life with anyone but Sally, she battled on.

In the early days, she'd daydreamed about rescuing David and setting up home for the two of them. It couldn't happen. Johnnie would fight her all the way and she couldn't get a job and look after David too.

He was thriving at Oak House and as he grew, he'd be amongst children like himself. The outside world would be fairly cruel. The staff were not only efficient but evidently caring and the children were well and happy. It was her lot to be satisfied with three visits a week and know she hadn't lost him entirely.

A couple of weeks earlier, at her final post-natal examination, the doctor had said it would be possible 'to resume marital relations'. She hadn't told Johnnie and he'd never asked. Things could stay as they were for a while yet. 'Resumption of marital relations' was the last thing on her mind.

***

Sally

At a loose end one afternoon, I dropped in at Oak House to spend an hour with Alice. My face was familiar and I was waved upstairs to the nursery. Alice's voice was clear enough through the open door but the low rumble of a male voice surprised me. Surely it couldn't be Johnnie.

Hesitating, I peeped round the door. Alice was leaning against the cot and Mickey, of all people, was sitting in the low chair, holding the baby at eye level and rocking him gently from side to side.

'What's this David? Be a good boy for your Uncle Mickey.'

The baby hiccupped and beamed toothlessly.

Alice smiled broadly and waved me in when she saw me.

'I hadn't expected you but I'm glad you're here Sal. I have a great favour to ask you, both of you.'

There was nothing I wouldn't do for her so she could ask away. Mickey looked up and turned David so he was lying against his chest, facing his mother. You'd think he'd been handling babies for years.

'I want David to be christened and I'd like you both to be godparents. Nobody else is interested, so it will be the three of us, David and Mrs Hughes. The local vicar has agreed to come in and do it privately and he could do it on Thursday or Friday of next week. Will you do it?'

Mickey blushed with pleasure and nodded.

'Either day would suit me, Alice. Just let me know.'

'Me too,' I responded. 'More than happy either day.'

The day was set and Mickey turned up in a new-looking grey sweater, a pair of charcoal gabardine trousers, a white shirt with two toned blue striped tie, all bought for the occasion. His hair, no longer carrot coloured but a rich, warm auburn, was neatly combed, his nails scrubbed and his shoes polished. I hadn't looked at him closely for years, used to jeans or paint spattered overalls, but was surprised to notice he wasn't a bad looking chap.

Alice wore grey too; a pretty dress patterned with tiny pink flowers. I had made the effort and for once, was wearing a skirt and a new green jacket. Mrs Hughes looked like Mrs Hughes; twinset and pearls.

We were gathered in her office, the only room not overrun with kids. It had been tidied for the occasion and on the desk, next to a bunch of roses in a vase, the vicar had placed a crystal bowl of water, holy water, I supposed.

So David was christened, dressed in a pale blue jumper and pants. Thank heavens Alice had the sense to forego the full christening robe. He was sleeping and snuffling a little when the Reverend Porter cradled him in his left arm but left us in no doubt of the strength of his lungs when the water fell over his head and face.

He continued to whimper until he was back in Mickey's arms, being rocked and whispered to. Despite my growing affection for David, I knew I couldn't have managed half so well. Alice looked on and I read her mind. For a split second, she was wishing Mickey, not Johnnie, was the father of this little boy.

It could have been a sad little affair but the vicar, Reverend Porter, took control. Solemn during the short ceremony, he led us through the service, looking at each of us closely as we made our promises. Mickey was solemn but bursting with pride at the responsibility.

When it was over and the baby was officially David Jack Marshall, Alice poured from the bottle of sparkling wine she'd brought and cut the cake. Reverend Porter took David and danced him round the room, humming the tune of 'Old MacDonald' into his little ear while he gurgled in response. Alice was enchanted.

David still looked odd but I'd got used to him. He was responsive; laughing when you tickled him or talked nonsense at him but was otherwise a placid baby. He cried only when he was hungry, which was a great relief. Squawking, inconsolable babies were far beyond my capabilities. I was becoming fond of him despite my earlier misgivings.

We stayed only half an hour more then took our leave. Mickey was giving me a lift in his battered old van and Alice stood on the steps with David in her arms, waving us off. We were all relieved it had been such a cheerful affair. Johnnie wasn't mentioned and wasn't missed.

1970

Rhodesia severs its last tie with the UK, declaring itself a republic

Paul McCartney announces the Beatles have disbanded

Edward Heath becomes Prime Minister, ousting Labour's Harold Wilson after six years

Aswan High Dam in Egypt completed

Published: 'The Female Eunuch' – Germaine Greer
'Islands in the Stream' – Ernest Hemingway

Best Film Oscar: 'Patton' - George C Scott and Karl Malden

Popular Record: 'Bridge Over Troubled Water' – Simon and Garfunkel

Born in 1970:   Matt Damon, actor
Naomi Campbell, model
Louis Theroux, journalist and documentary maker

Chapter 24

Sally

The house was found and bought. I couldn't wait to get in. An old lady had lived there alone for years and it hadn't seen a coat of paint since before the war. The cream and green distemper on the wall and the dark brown doors and skirting boards would have to go. Mickey was roped in to help. A willing and reliable worker, he was always eager to earn extra cash.

After his mother died when he was about ten, he'd got scruffier and scruffier. His dad drank heavily and Mickey was left to fend for himself. My mum used to call him into our kitchen now and again, give him something David had outgrown and send him on his way clutching a piece of pie or a sandwich. I'd known him most of my life but we now had a common bond, much stronger than the links to our childhood.

We spent a lot of time together during those few weeks. He spoke to me more than to anyone, rarely volunteering information but loosening up as the days passed and the work on the house progressed. I'd settled for woodchip, walloped over with emulsion. He came whenever he could, getting the wallpaper up so I could carry on with the painting. His adoration of Alice was still there. That torch was still burning very bright.

He'd never had a 'proper job' after leaving school, picking up casual labouring work, a week here and a week there, drifting into working for Johnnie Marshall on a regular basis.

Intrigued, despite myself, by the workings of Johnnie's world, I asked him,

'What do you actually do, Mickey?'

The work didn't stop and he continued carefully lining up the pasted paper on the half covered wall. I didn't think he was going to answer.

'At first I ran errands, did a few odd jobs and cleaned up after closing. Then after I decorated the flat and he started buying houses, he put me in as a labourer. I was working with electricians, plasterers and plumbers and learned as I went along. I can do pretty well all of it now.'

A note of pride had crept into his voice and though he was facing the wall, the blush on the back of his neck showed over the collar of his open necked shirt. I thought he'd clam up but he carried on,

'I'm pretty much in charge. When he buys another house, I go and see what needs doing. I do some of the jobs, get people in to do the rest and generally keep an eye on things. Believe me, he watches every penny and still calls in now and again to make sure everyone's doing what they ought to be doing and checking he hasn't been charged for stuff that isn't there. We do a decent job, nothing fancy. He wants us in and out so he can make money.

I hardly go in the shop except for the odd repair or if someone's on holiday. They sometimes need someone to keep an eye on the punters, have a word if it looks like trouble brewing.

The puny, snotty nosed kid was now a strapping six footer and I could understand a word or even a look from him would discourage any kind of bother.

This was a long speech from our man of few words and I suspected only the link to Alice kept him at Johnnie's beck and call. I doubted I'd get any more out of him today and concentrated on the job at hand. Brushing out the bubbles under the paper he'd just hung, he turned and lifted the next piece which I'd already pasted. We worked well together and I watched carefully as he slid each piece into place and then swiftly smoothed it down. I'd be able to do this myself next time, once he'd shown me how to get round windows and light switches. At present, I didn't want to mess around, I wanted the job done so I could move in.

I'd known him all my life and found I didn't know him at all. The memories of that underfed, scruffy and inarticulate kid had clouded my judgement. In his element here, his organisational skills and workmanship were superb.

Through his contacts, everything we needed, from kitchen cupboards and bathroom fittings to paint and paper was bought at cost, saving me a fortune.

When all the walls had been papered, he left me to the painting and carried on with the rest of the work. The plumbing and tiling looked unhurried but each job was completed quickly and looked marvellous.

Paintwork was rubbed down until it was smooth as silk. When I'd said, 'that'll do,' he'd responded,

'Let's do the job properly, Sally. You'll see it'll be worth it. This isn't a quick job to sell the house on, this'll be your home.'

He was right, of course, so I picked up the sandpaper with a sigh.

If he was so particular about my place, I wondered what his own home looked like, wondered if it was done to the same high standard. I'd probably never know. I wondered too, if he had any kind of social life. Did he ever go out with girls? Nearly all his evenings seemed to be free to come round and help me and most of the weekend too.

One evening, I arrived a little early and as my radio was playing on the windowsill in the bathroom where he was tiling, he didn't hear me open the front door. I was about to shout up the stairs when he burst into song. I crept up and there he was, putting adhesive on the walls and singing his heart out. His voice, pure and clear, never wavered and he was word perfect. He sounded better than the singer he was accompanying, whoever it was. I wasn't too well up on popular music. When I said,

'Mickey, that's lovely,' he flushed, clearly embarrassed

It wouldn't do to push him so I went off to get the paint tins open and within ten minutes he was singing again, entirely for his own pleasure, the crystal clear notes floating down the stairs. Whoever would have thought it?

At the end of a couple of weeks, he was more relaxed with me and when we stopped for a break and a cuppa, he opened up a bit. It was fortunate I enjoyed the sound of my own voice as I did most of the talking but he responded, sometimes with a smart remark that had me in stitches. Another revelation, he had a quick wit and devilish sense of humour. He coped well enough with other men, I'd heard him laughing and joking in the pub and during deliveries but he was excruciatingly shy with women.

My sick fascination with Marshall raised its ugly head and I found myself asking,

'How do you get along with Johnnie these days?'

Mickey put down his mug of tea and produced a packet of cigarettes and a box of matches. Squinting through the smoke from the cigarette still between his lips and shaking out the match, he took a deep draw, plucked the cigarette from his lips and scowled.

'I hate the bloody sight of him and keep out of his way. He's in the office most of the time, counting his money, but comes out now and again throwing his weight about. I'm hardly there these days but everyone's scared of him.'

I got the impression Mickey wasn't as scared as the rest and wondered why he stayed. I hadn't the nerve to ask.

'He never turned a hair when his dad took ill or when he died. When David was born, he was cold as ice. He's as hard as nails, cares about nobody but himself.'

He paused.

'Do you remember when we were kids, you said one day I'd be big enough to thump him? I'm big enough now and believe me, I've been tempted.'

Alice wasn't mentioned but she was there all the same.

He finished his cigarette and crushed the remains on a paint tin lid he was using as an ashtray. Conversation over, I'd get no more out of him today.

'Come on, Sal. Let's get on with it. I want this job finished sometime this year.'

So I picked up my paintbrush and carried on.

Finally finished, my place was furnished, mainly with pieces from Gran's which Mum had been unable to part with and which had been stacked in our garage since the funeral. Mum ran up the curtains on her old machine and Dad came round to give us the benefit of his advice. We smiled and nodded. He was as useless at practical tasks as ever.

The house had been painted from top to bottom in white. Mum said it was too stark but I liked it and once we'd got the curtains up and a couple of prints on the wall it looked exactly the way I wanted. All those fussy patterns and contrasts weren't for me. The lingering smell of paint had disappeared too.

Pride of place over the fireplace hung a landscape Alice had painted when she was about fifteen. Though it lacked the assurance of her later work, it was easy on the eye. A long view of our local park with two girlish figures in the distance, the soft greens and browns were subtly applied and it evoked memories of our childhood.

Mum and Dad had gradually come to terms with my absence and I valued my freedom, freedom to come and go as I pleased.

In comparison to Alice's, my life was simple and straightforward; not the life I'd projected for myself in my early teens but satisfying enough.

***

Johnnie pushed open the door of the betting shop and was engulfed in cigarette smoke. The smell of stale fags, wet clothing and warm bodies engulfed him. This was the smell of money.

He caught the manager's eye and registered his nervous whisper to the rest of the staff.

'Johnnie's here,' he mouthed and the taking of bets and handing out of cash became a little brisker.

This was the first of his shops and round the corner from his old home. It had changed little in the seven years since Maurice had died.

Six months earlier he'd forked out a small fortune for heavy duty flooring but it was already damaged where cigarette ends had been dropped and ground out underfoot. The walls were painted a dull cream, with an overlay of nicotine. The windows were obscured to shoulder height cutting down the daylight and the stark strip lighting burned all day. It hardly mattered, people didn't come in to relax. They came in to place bets. There were very few women who braved the rough and ready atmosphere and the clientele was almost exclusively male although from many walks of life.

Betting shops were a great leveller. Men from local businesses in smart suits came in, placed their bets and left, as did many overalled workers who wanted a quick flutter. A hard core of inveterate gamblers could usually be found, chain smoking and leaning against the walls, waiting for the results of each race as it was run. Johnnie knew many of the customers by sight and nodded as he made his way into the back room, noting the overflowing ashtrays and discarded betting slips crumpled on the floor.

The manager followed him into the office, Johnnie always made him nervous. Johnnie made all his managers nervous and that was the way he liked it, it kept them on their toes. There were four betting shops under his control, spread around the inner city and within easy reach of each other.

Johnnie followed no routine and none of the employees knew when he would drop in so the books and takings had to be ready for inspection at any time. Draping his expensive leather jacket over the back of a chair and barely acknowledging the manager, Johnnie opened the safe and took out the day's takings so far. The betting slips and books showed entries for the last couple of days and he carted them over to the scarred desk in the middle of the room.

'Need anything else?' asked the manager.

'I'll let you know. The shop's full, better get back to it.' said Johnnie in dismissal and opened the first of the ledgers.

Breathing a sigh of relief, the manager left him to it, confident Johnnie would find nothing amiss. Only one of Johnnie's managers had been discovered with his hand in the till and he'd been found in a pub car park, unconscious and with a broken arm the following evening. The word had spread like wildfire although no charges were ever brought, the victim insisting he hadn't seen his assailants.

The manager himself was no light weight. In his early forties, stocky and well-muscled, he'd be round the counter at the first sign of a dispute and had physically ejected more than one trouble maker. The other employees were as wary of him as he was of Johnnie and he kept an eagle eye on the money changing hands. This was a good job and Johnnie paid well. He wasn't about to put his livelihood in jeopardy because one of the staff had sticky fingers. The flat over the shop was his home, which suited Johnnie too. Someone trustworthy lived on the premises and paid rent for the privilege.

The last race of the day was finished and the shop was emptying. There would be an odd punter straggling in to collect winnings but they'd be closing in an hour. Having seen Johnnie's look at the state of the shop, he sent someone out to sweep the floor and empty the ashtrays. The cleaner would be in later but Johnnie was here now and it paid to keep him sweet.

Johnnie leaned back in his chair. Not expecting to find any discrepancies, he'd still checked the books, counted the takings and added up the total bets. It didn't pay to get too complacent – or too trusting.

He ran his hands through his hair. A few fine strands of silver showed at the temples and it touched his collar at the back in the fashion of the day but the styling was crisp, expertly cut by one of the best barbers in town. The niggling pain in his chest had resurfaced and he reached into his pocket for the roll of indigestion tablets. Rubbing his knuckles up and down his breastbone helped and he rubbed until the pain eased.

'Bloody indigestion,' he muttered.

The dark suit and neat collar and tie of his early twenties had been abandoned in favour of more fashionable clothing. Although slightly overweight and pale of face, the slightly flared trousers and large collared, coloured shirts looked good on him. His aftershave was something French bought from Kendal's as a Christmas gift from Alice.

Only close examination would reveal the wrinkles around his eyes and the downturn of his mouth, the creasing between the nose and the corner of his mouth deepening with every year. Despite his increasing wealth, discontent and disappointment were etching their mark.

He still had control and although his employees displayed suitable apprehension when he was around, it no longer gave him the pleasure it once had.

With his elbows on the desk and his head in his hands, he tried to sort out what was wrong. Only a few years ago, he'd been 'Jack the Lad'. With Maurice's money behind him and Alice in his arms, he'd thought himself invincible.

Despite his obvious affluence, his standing in the business community and his beautiful wife, he felt empty and so did his life. The events of the last few years hung over him like a dark cloud.

The happiness of his marriage had foundered on the crisis of the kid's birth. When he did think of him, it was only to blame him for being born at all and by default, to blame Alice all over again.

She was still his although no longer the Alice of old. The sparkle had dimmed and her face, in repose, often looked a little sad.

'Marital relations' had resumed but never again held the joy of the early years, for either of them. The overwhelming tenderness had gone and his performance was mechanical and becoming more and more infrequent. They were having sex, no longer making love, and although Alice never rebuffed him, he often thought she was miles away and he was in bed with a total stranger.

At least with Sandra, he knew where he was up to. She wanted sex; vigorous and uninhibited sex and he was happy to oblige. That she cared for him was not in doubt, she'd put her life on hold for him yet again and was always available. Earthy and a touch flashy in dress and manner, Sandra would never be a substitute for his classy, beautiful wife, the wife who played her part so perfectly.

Alice was hostess to his dinner parties, providing beautifully cooked food, served in a tastefully decorated dining room, oiling the wheels of conversation and making everyone at the table feel they were special. Her presence on his arm at any event always turned heads. The men were full of admiration and their wives green with envy, knowing they were outclassed.

The clothes she bought were still subject to his approval and he wanted to know she was where she ought to be at given times of the day. She knows which side her bread's buttered, he thought. Alice didn't make a fuss and did what he wanted but sometimes he felt control was slipping through his fingers.

Some of the group of professional people he'd sought to impress had, on closer acquaintance, turned out to have feet of clay. Nevertheless, he was accepted amongst them and it still mattered. He had achieved his childhood ambition of 'being somebody' but it was an empty victory.

Chapter 25

Alice stood at the French windows of her detached home in Hale Barns, one of the wealthier suburbs of Manchester. Hugging herself, arms crossed and hands rubbing up and down above the elbow, she stared out across the beautifully tended lawn and borders. A look at her face would have shown she was seeing nothing; not the brave yellow of the forsythia or the clear blue of the crocus. She was deep in thought.

At the sound of the telephone, she stirred and crossed the room, looking briefly at her watch. It was ten thirty. That would be Johnnie. He rang every morning around this time and again around four and there'd be an inquest later if she wasn't there. After a short exchange, she replaced the receiver. Her time was her own until his next call.

Picking up the jacket and handbag which had been lying on the white leather sofa, she checked for her keys and went out to the front of the house, where her new Mini was parked on the drive.

At twenty eight, Alice was as pretty as ever. She still dressed stylishly, though considerably more expensively. This morning, designer jeans, crisp white shirt and a navy blazer completed the picture. Only a close examination of her eyes by someone who knew her well would reveal the pain beneath the surface.

As she pulled into the traffic, she smiled. A little shopping, a bite of lunch then Oak House; the highlight of her day, three times a week. She was on her way to see her son, her darling boy.

***

Sally

Relieved it was half term at last, I pulled on my old mac and went out to the car parked outside my home. There were kids playing in the spring sunshine, about the same age as the kids in my class, and a couple of them shouted 'Hiya, Miss' as I put the key in the lock.

The terraced streets had changed. The kids weren't as scruffy, most of the houses were smartly painted and many of them were owned by the people who lived in them. Some of them even had plants and garden furniture in the backyard. The days of block ownership by distant landlords were over. When I was a child, my dad's car was a novelty, now mine was only one of several parked along the street.

The cobbles had been covered by tarmac and there was a telephone in most of the houses. There were still a couple of curtain twitchers, anxious to keep track of my movements, my visitors and who else was coming and going in the street.

I was luckier than many women of my age and knew it. I didn't have a man under my feet, laying down the law, and was in the fortunate position of being able to please myself.

When I pulled up outside Oak House, Alice's car was already parked. The contrast between the two vehicles couldn't have been more pronounced. Hers was the latest, top of the range Mini, red paintwork shining in the sunshine. Mine was one of the oldest; maroon, a little battered and kept on the road by the kindness and ingenuity of a mechanic who lived at the end of my street.

It didn't bother me. I wouldn't have swapped my car for hers or my terraced house for her big detached if it meant taking on Alice's problems. She'd achieved our girlhood ambition of shopping in Kendal's and had had a team of well paid professionals to decorate her house. The place was a showcase of the latest ideas in furnishing; bold colours and contrasting patterns.

Alice was at the window with her arm round her four year old son, who was barely tall enough to see over the windowsill. His face lit up and I could see him pulling Alice towards the entrance.

Who could want for a better welcome? He flung his arms around the only part of me he could reach, hugging me round the legs and grinning up at me, his round, flat face, alight with joy. His voice, although without much tone, rose in excitement.

'Music, Sally, music. Come on Sally, music.'

Loosening his stranglehold and grabbing my hand, while his other hand reached for his mother's, he dragged us both towards the piano in the room at the front of the house. Usually at his best when I appeared, he could be a holy terror. I'd seen him lying on the floor, drumming his heels and screaming but with not a tear in sight. I might have been tempted to give him a quick slap but Alice had the patience of a saint.

Although the room was a little utilitarian; white painted walls and lino covered floor for easy mopping, it was brightened by the highly coloured artwork pinned to the walls, much of it enthusiastic daubs but some child's pride and joy.

There were several other children in the room, all with some kind of disability. One little boy was wedged in a corner strapped into a wheelchair. He felt safe there but kept up a continuous low moaning, mouth opening and closing and hands flapping uncontrollably. Initially, the noise had been distracting but I'd learned to play over it. It didn't bother anyone else, they were used to it.

A couple of other children were also marooned in wheelchairs and there were three more children like David. None of them were as bright as him but they had the extra fold in the eyelid, the flat features and slow movements of what were called Mongols, a term I found excruciatingly unkind. The great majority of these children never saw their parents from one month's end to another and had no contact with the outside world. They'd been forgotten by their families.

When I finally untangled myself from David's clutches, sat down at the piano and hit the first notes, the joy on most of their faces was reward enough. Despite the low keening from the corner and some pushing and shoving as they jockeyed for position, nobody could have had a more appreciative audience. They sat still when the music was quiet, the able bodied danced around when the tune was lively while the wheelchair bound rocked from side to side. Occasional scuffles broke out but they settled again quickly if I stopped playing. Alice was a dab hand at sorting them out and there was always a member of staff in the room to keep an eye on them.

This morning it was Janet who'd been one of the teachers at our junior school. Even at eleven, Alice and I had whispered we thought Mr Metcalfe was sweet on her. Now here she was, showing early signs of pregnancy and no longer Miss Marsden but a very contented looking Mrs Metcalfe. Another case of a childhood figure of authority turning into a friend years later.

Mrs Phillips put her head round the door, signalling it was almost time for tea. There was always a few minutes' warning so I could wind up and I launched into the first of two songs they could sing along with, simple songs with repetitive words. Although the erupting sound was far from choir quality and 'My Bonnie lies over the Ocean' was barely recognisable, what it lacked in tunefulness it made up for in enthusiasm

Those songs marked the end of the session and most of the kids were ready to eat at any time of day. After they were shuffled off to the dining room, Mrs Phillips came in with a tray with cups and saucers and a pot of tea. She sat with us for a minute and then said,

'I'll leave you to it, you must have a lot to catch up with.'

She smiled and, no doubt, went off to struggle with the endless paperwork and accounts involved in running the place.

Alice looked strained. The animation in her face had disappeared along with David. When he was around, her eyes shone and she smiled constantly. When he'd gone, she looked a little sad. Only David and her painting gave any meaning to her life.

We saw little of each other these days. I couldn't, or wouldn't, go to her place in case I bumped into Johnnie. The antagonism between us had strengthened over the years and we avoided each other like the plague. Fortunately, our social lives were worlds apart and it was unlikely our paths would cross.

She'd been to my place a time or two, flying visits on her way home from seeing David but was always on edge and eager to be away. I had no idea about the four o'clock 'phone call and often wondered at her scramble to be off.

Though I'd always pretended total disinterest when it came to Johnnie, I was secretly fascinated. What would he get up to next and what's more, who would be likely to pay for it?

Mum and Dad came back from their Friday evenings in the pub with the gossip; snippets of information passed round or gleaned from the workmen drinking in the pub. There was money to be made in property and Johnnie was getting more than his share. At least Alice had no worries on that count. There'd been whispers he'd been seen in town with 'some woman'. There may be nothing in it but I wondered if Alice knew.

We managed an occasional couple of hours during the school holidays and met in town, wandering round the shops as we had when we were younger. She had money in her pocket and bought stuff I couldn't even afford to look at but I didn't care.

It was clear all was not well but she couldn't confide in me and I understood why.

***

Johnnie's money couldn't buy what Alice wanted; for the closeness they had once had to be re-established and for him to acknowledge David. She'd be happy in a two bedroomed terrace if she had that. The big house, the new car and designer clothes and visiting David regularly had a price tag attached.

The house had to be immaculate and so did she. Her home-made clothes were a thing of the past, as were C & A and Marks and Spencer. Kendal's and King Street were her territory now.

The life they had led before David was born was resumed. They were out every weekend. When they were first married, it had been exciting and Johnnie's obsession with her appearance flattering. Her clothes, jewellery and hair were carefully examined before they left the house and his disapproval clear if she wore something he didn't like. More than once she'd had to return a dress or a jacket which hadn't met his high standards.

Most evenings, they sat in front of the television, speaking little. Johnnie drank his whisky and smoked incessantly; a mirror image of his father. Sometimes he went out alone and she was glad to see him leave. The 'hail fellow, well met' of their social life never appeared through their front door and he was frequently snappy and bad tempered.

She didn't know how he felt about anything these days, except David, of course. His feelings there were abundantly clear. There were times when she positively disliked him and briefly considered leaving him but was trapped in a vice with 'I've made my bed' on one side and David's welfare on the other.

The Johnnie she had known during their courtship and the early days of their marriage was gone. She was now acquainted with the Johnnie everybody else knew and came to understand Sally's antagonism.
She'd once asked if he ever heard from his mum and his response had been,
'I don't want to talk about it.'
She was unaware Christmas and birthday cards regularly arrived at the shop from Sussex and were dropped into the bin unopened.
'I don't want to talk about it,' was a standard reply and she'd heard him say it to friends who'd enquired about the baby and been instructed to say the same thing.
'I don't want anybody to know anything. They'll only ask more questions. The least said the better,' and for the sake of peace she'd acquiesced. He was making increasingly disparaging and sarcastic remarks about the people he'd been so keen to mix with only a few years earlier.

There was only so much shopping she could do, only so many times the vacuum cleaner could be pushed around the house and only so many hours spent working in the garden. She turned more and more frequently to her painting.

A south facing bedroom in the new house had been commandeered as a studio and though Johnnie had turned up his nose at her old equipment, it had been carried up the stairs and carefully arranged so her easel caught the maximum light. He had no idea how much time she spent in there and showed no interest in the results but it was a harmless enough hobby and a suitable occupation for his lovely wife; something else to brag about with his cronies.

Johnnie stood at the foot of the stairs, tapping his foot and jingling his keys.
'Come on, Alice. What's the hold up?'
She appeared on the landing in a floral summer dress in soft shades of pink and lilac, her little feet in low heeled white sandals and her shining hair swinging round her shoulders. The light dusting of freckles across her nose and shoulders heightened the effect. She still had the power to take his breath away.
He said nothing but grumpily turned on his heel and got into the car, fingers drumming on the steering wheel until she got in and closed the car behind her.
The garden party was at his solicitor's house in Knutsford, a more expensive place to live than even Hale where they lived now. Alice hadn't been keen but he'd insisted.
The host, installed behind a trestle table covered in a crisp white cloth, dispensed drinks and the hostess sat under an umbrella, talking to a good looking chap in his early thirties.
Like most of the men, he was dressed casually but with more flair. His streaked blonde hair with a central parting, flowed back over his pale blue shirt collar. He could have looked ridiculous but, in fact, looked elegant and classy. The gold watch and heavy signet ring added the finishing touches.
After collecting drinks and chatting briefly with the host, they went to say hello to their hostess.
'Do you know Jeremy?' she asked and when Johnnie shook his head, she went on,
'Jeremy, this is Johnnie and Alice Marshall, they live over in Hale. Alice is an art lover too. You'll have plenty in common.'
This last was said with a slight sneer, as though Alice's interests were beneath her notice.

They shook hands all round and Johnnie asked,

'What line of business are you in then?'

'I've opened a small gallery off King Street in Manchester. It's early days but things are looking good so far,' he drawled in a public school accent.

Johnnie had already dismissed him as too camp and too posh for words and suspected he might be of the other persuasion. In any event there was no benefit in the art world to him and he was ready to move on but Alice responded,

'What sort of work are you showing?' and listened intently to his response while Johnnie moved away to talk to someone else.

He kept an eye on Alice, he always did, and was surprised to see her still in deep conversation with that overdressed twit half an hour later. For once, she was smiling naturally, talking freely and looking as though she were enjoying herself.

Though she was often left to fend for herself on such occasions, he was quick to intervene if he thought someone was becoming too familiar. Not for one moment did he think Alice might be susceptible but he didn't want another predator moving into his territory. She looked safe enough, none of the body language suggested anything else and when he passed them with a smile and a nod to get another drink, they were still deep in the world of art.

The next time he looked for Alice, that Jeremy fellow had disappeared and she was walking through the beautifully landscaped garden with their host, who'd temporarily abandoned his role as bartender to show off his latest plant acquisitions. Borders of bright perennials lined the pathways, the scent of the pastel coloured sweet peas and crimson roses filled the air, the drone of insects barely audible. Johnnie noticed none of this, he saw only that Alice was in good hands. Charlie, approaching fifty, and besotted with his wife of twelve months, had only plants on his mind as he chatted and pointed and waved his arm around at the garden.

He turned and almost bumped into Charlie's wife who had come up behind him.

'They make a lovely couple, don't they? There's not much life in either of them - unlike us,' she said meaningfully in a low, sex charged voice, and laid her hand on Johnnie's arm and leaned towards him.

The woman's mad, thought Johnnie. As he stepped away, he saw Alice's head turn towards them. Had she noticed and put two and two together?

With a polite smile on his face, he muttered,

'Be careful. You know what this lot are like. They don't miss a thing and you've got as much to lose as I have. Better cool it for a while. I'm going for a top up, you want one?'

She looked as though she'd been slapped and looked away, back down the garden at her husband.

'No thanks,' she said icily as Johnnie walked off to get himself yet another drink.

Bloody woman, he thought. She's at least ten years older than me and should know better. God knows, it took her long enough to get Charlie to the altar. She's sitting pretty in the big house with plenty of money and putting it all at risk. I'll be giving her a wide a berth in the future.

Half an hour later as the party was breaking up, he collected Alice from a bench under a tree at the far end of the garden where she was sitting alone, nursing an orange juice turned warm in the sunshine and looking across the garden.

She said nothing in the car on the way home. Did she suspect? As usual, he attacked before he could be attacked.

'Jeremy seemed like "an awfully nice boy". D'you think he's queer? All that gold and powder blue.'

'I've no idea and don't much care.'

'Don't tell me he asked you over to see his etchings,' he sneered as he turned into their drive too fast, missing the gatepost by inches. He wasn't drunk but he wasn't sober either.

Alice didn't react to the near collision as she hadn't reacted to the interchange she'd seen in the garden. She didn't care much and had suspected Johnnie was playing away for some time but she did react to his sarcastic remark.

'You know, Johnnie, I can't remember when, if ever, you had a good word to say for anybody,' and she swept out of the car, into the house and straight up the stairs.

Johnnie locked the car and went into the lounge, slinging his jacket over the back of a chair and turning on the television. He thought he'd got away with it. When Alice came down half an hour later, he was sprawled on the settee, snoring gently.

At two in the morning he woke, chilled through, thick headed and with a sharp thirst. After two glasses of water at the kitchen sink, he stumbled up the stairs. Alice was sleeping peacefully so he undressed and, dropping his clothes on the floor, he slid into bed. Alice didn't wake but shrank away from the coldness of his body. He tugged the bed clothes around himself and quickly sank back into a drunken stupor.

Chapter 26

At the garden party, Jeremy's initial impression was she was too pretty to have a brain but as they talked, he realised she had a solid background in art and art history.

She had thought him a pretentious lightweight but revised her opinion too. He was well informed and knowledgeable. No dilettante, he was running a business and intended to make a go of it.

He'd suggested she bring a sample of her work down to the gallery for him to have a look at. Constantly on the lookout for suitable artists, it couldn't hurt to check her out and she *was* a looker.

A week later, Alice was walking down King Street, the best part of town. The few men around were in smart business suits and the women beautifully dressed, browsing in the expensive shops, spending their husbands' money. Alice could hold her own with any of them but she guessed none were as nervous as her, with butterflies in her stomach and a dry mouth. It had been years since anyone other than Sally and close family had looked at her work and naturally, they all thought it was wonderful.

The gallery was impressive, smartly painted on the outside with one picture displayed centrally in the window, over which the name 'Page Art' was written in gold on a dark green background. The interior was decorated in pale cream and the pictures displayed looked of a very high standard although mixed styles and sizes.

Jeremy, in a pin striped suit, came forward to meet her. Though they'd met only once, he kissed her on both cheeks and drew her into the centre of the space.

'What do you think?' he asked.

'It's wonderful, can I have a look?'

'First things first,' he said. This is my assistant, Jocasta.'

Jocasta, in her early twenties, in a severe black suit and hair scraped back into a bun, came forward, holding out a limp hand and greeting her with another cut glass accent.

Oh God, thought Alice. How can I keep my face straight? Jeremy and Jocasta, wait 'til I tell Sally.

'I'll show you round later, first let's have a look at what you've brought.' And he led her into his office at the back of the gallery.

He laid her battered old folder, the one she'd had since her student days, on his desk and untied the bows holding the folder together, exposing the first picture. He hadn't expected much, perhaps a competent still life or hillside landscape. Her artwork hadn't been the primary purpose of his invitation.

His sharp intake of breath startled her.

He hates it, she thought, I shouldn't have come. She was ready to grab the folder and run.

The dark red of Blackpool tower loomed against a grey sky and over a rain swept promenade. In the foreground, a couple of hardy souls braced coloured umbrellas against the wind, while the salt water crashed white over the sea walls. The subtlety of the washes and the delicacy of the strokes brought life to the picture, the splashes of colour lifting the effect. This was no wishy-washy hackneyed view but an accomplished piece of work.

'Alice, this is exquisite,' he said, walking over and placing the picture on an easel so he could see it from a distance. The overall effect had clearly bowled him over.

'It's fresh and vibrant and what's more, it's local. Have you any more?' he asked and she fumbled a little, fishing out another and placing it on the easel.

'Mmm, we can do something with these. I have to warn you, the market for water colours has shrunk in recent years. These days, customers, especially new buyers, want bright and vivid, something to make a statement. Nevertheless, there *are* discerning buyers still and some of them drop in from time to time. Local views are often snapped up. I think we can work out a deal, take a seat.'

Half an hour later, they'd hammered out the terms. The paintings would be left with Jeremy on a sale or return basis and he would arrange the framing. Later Alice realised he must be fairly confident or he wouldn't lay out cash up front. Would there be anything left, she wondered, after he deducted his commission and costs? The money wasn't the object. Her paintings would be displayed and seen, possibly by people who knew their art. She was excited and apprehensive at the same time.

'Shall we shake on it?' he asked and came round the desk to offer his hand.

'It's a deal,' she said.

'Let's hope this is the start of a profitable partnership.'

He held her hand a little too long, squeezing gently.

Crumbs, she thought. He's coming on to me. How do I get out of this?

She hadn't cared one way or the other about his sexual orientation but quickly realised Johnnie's evaluation couldn't be further from the truth. Although a little naive, she was far from stupid and saw the signs; the hand lingering on her arm, the unblinking look straight into her eyes, the step towards her. She could usually rely on Johnnie to extricate her or at least be in surroundings where she could escape to the powder room or into another conversation but not now. She was alone with him in the confines of a small office.

She gently withdrew her hand, panicking slightly. Not wanting to offend him, she didn't want to encourage him either.

'I'd better get going,' she said a little shakily.

He backed off. There was no point rushing her, she'd come round or she wouldn't and he didn't want to frighten her away. The paintings were worth having and would make a welcome addition to his stock.

'Of course, have you time for a quick look round the gallery?'

'Maybe next time,' she said. She would have loved to wander round but the need to get away was greater.

'One more thing, Jeremy. Johnnie doesn't know I'm here. Please don't tell anyone about this. If I sell a couple of paintings, that would be wonderful. I'd like to surprise him with the good news and if they don't sell, no-one need be any the wiser.'

'It will be our little secret,' he said, smiling.

He fastened the ties on her empty folder and passed it over.

'I'll walk you to the door,' he said. 'Let's see how we go with these two and if they sell, I would need to have a look at the rest. I'll give you a ring if anything happens.'

'Please don't ring in the evening or at the weekend.'

'No, I promise I'll be careful.'

'Thanks, Jeremy. I look forward to hearing from you.'

He watched her leave the gallery and head off across the road. There's more to that than meets the eye, he thought. Maybe she *is* ripe for a little extra marital activity if I play my cards right.

The first painting sold within two weeks and the second was framed and displayed alongside it. Jeremy was keen to have a look at the rest of her work and there was plenty of it. She'd been painting uninterruptedly for a couple of years.

Reluctantly, she had agreed Jeremy could come to the house to select the next candidates for sale. She kept the transaction as brief as possible, greeting him at the door and taking him straight upstairs to make his selection. It was unsettling to have him in the house, Johnnie would go crazy if he knew.

She didn't offer him a coffee, didn't invite him anywhere else in the house but escorted him to the front door with a folder under his arm, breathing a sigh of relief as he pulled out of the drive.

Sally

Alice had been excited when she 'phoned, anxious to meet and tell me her news.

'Can't you tell me now? The suspense is killing me.'

'No, when can I see you?'

The Kardomah café, the site of our early forays into the adult world, was long gone and these days, we met in the tearoom in Kendal Milne, the poshest store in Manchester. The clientele was predominantly female, many of them loaded with the characteristic dark green Kendal's bags and all looking extremely prosperous.

Leather shoes and handbags, tailored suits and expensively cut hair were the order of the day. Although I stuck out like a sore thumb in my worn old leather jacket and cropped hair, Alice completely filled the bill as she crossed the café towards me, a huge grin on her face.

'Come on,' I said. 'Spill the beans.'

She rummaged in her bag for a minute and pulled out an envelope.

'Take a look at that,' she said.

I looked, thick cream paper and obviously top drawer, and then pulled out the contents; a cheque for forty pounds made payable to Alice Marshall, stamped below with the firm's name, Page Galleries, and signed Jeremy Page-Johnson.

'I've sold a painting,' she said, with a broad grin.

Heads turned as I raised my voice almost to a shout.

'How fantastic, how bloody fantastic.'

If we'd been anywhere else, I'd have jumped up and thrown my arms around her but I'd already raised enough eyebrows in this refined, genteel atmosphere.

'So tell me all about it,' and I sat without speaking as the story unfolded; the garden party, the first visit to the gallery and Jeremy and Jocasta and by then we were both giggling.

'I honestly thought he was coming on to me but he's backed off, thank God. I couldn't have handled that.

But you know, Sally, I feel so good about it, as though I'm myself again; not only David's mum or Johnnie's wife. I've got something of my own.'

I nodded, delighted to see her so positive.

'Johnnie has no idea and I don't want him to know, not yet anyway. You can't tell anyone, not even your mum in case it gets back to him.'

I wondered at this but promised not to breathe a word.

'I'm going to the bank next.'

She waved the cheque in the air.

'This is going into a new account in my own name, something else that's just mine.'

Ten minutes later, we parted company. She was on her way to the bank and I was on my way up King Street, determined to have a look at this gallery.

I threaded my way through the shoppers and came to a halt in front of the window. As a result of Alice's influence over the years, I knew a fair bit about the art world and could only approve of the central display.

I pushed open the door and stepped inside.

Jocasta, who was everything Alice had said, came forward to meet me. Her opinion of my clothes, hair and battered handbag was written in the disdain on her disapproving face.

'Can I help you?' she asked and it occurred to me this particular posh accent didn't ring quite true but had been acquired somewhere along the way.

Unintimidated, I asked if I could look around. Naturally, there was only one thing I was looking for and spotted it over her shoulder.

I side stepped her and walked toward the back wall. I'd know Alice's work anywhere and there were two of her pictures hanging side by side, one of them with a tell-tale red dot in the right hand corner and I could feel the grin breaking out. I was so proud I could have burst.

Jocasta, bless her, was fuming when I turned back to face her, arms crossed and head back.

Coolly, I spoke softly so she had to lean forward to hear me.

'Thank you, I've seen what I came to see,' I said and made a dignified exit.

It was a pity the famous Jeremy wasn't around but at least I'd seen the pictures and was well pleased.

As I made my way up the side streets, lined with office buildings and fairly empty at this time of day, I reflected perhaps things were taking a turn for the better for both of us.

If Alice had sold one picture, she'd sell more and it had been great to see her so pleased with herself. It could only do her good to have something else on her mind besides David and, God help us, Johnnie.

Mum, particularly, wanted to see me settle down and couldn't understand that in my eyes, I was settled down. I had a job I loved, my own home and could come and go as I pleased.

There had been a few flirtations, some of which had led to something more but there was no-one I wanted to be with for more than a couple of months. Though I enjoyed the sex, the paraphernalia of a longer relationship was too much bother. Fine-tuned to any mention of events more than two or three weeks in the future, my internal lights flashed, the starter's flag waved in my head and I moved on. If I couldn't have what I wanted, there'd be no settling for less.

The damage to my leg was permanent and I'd come to terms with the fact I would always limp. However, my fingers were in good working order and though my earlier dreams of a career as a concert pianist were well behind me, I was playing on a regular basis with a jazz quartet in pubs and various clubs.

I'd recently progressed to singing a couple of numbers on each booking. My husky voice, though never suitable for classical music, melded into the jazz mood and my renditions of various standards were received with enthusiasm.

All four of the group had day jobs. The base player and the drummer played mainly for the money. The sax player, who led the group, was a truly accomplished musician. He'd recruited me in the first place whilst simultaneously making a pass at Alice and causing a rift between us.

He'd recently announced a job transfer to Birmingham, of all places, and I was seriously considering forming my own group. There were one or two good players who were looking for this kind of work. I wasn't in it for the money although the extra cash came in handy.

The whole package drew me; the hush when we played, the rapt attention of the audience, the interaction with the other musicians and the possibility and ability to take the tune wherever I wanted, creating a unique musical moment of improvisation. Of course, the enthusiastic applause at the end of a solo didn't hurt either. There were few women playing this kind of music in this kind of environment. Although in the early days, I'd been viewed with some scepticism, I was now accepted and welcomed even. The other musicians knew I could be trusted to support their solos and I was not just one of the group, I was 'one of the lads' too.

Alice had never come to terms with this kind of music but to my surprise, Mickey loved it and showed up fairly often to hear us play. He rarely spoke to anybody but stood at the back, pint in hand, nodding in time to the music. One or two of the girls obviously found him attractive but he didn't notice. Now and again, I watched him singing with me under his breath. I would have loved to invite him up on stage to join me, his voice was good enough, but I feared he'd die of embarrassment.

***

Fired with her initial success, Alice decided to try something different. For some time, the subtleties of the water colour palette had no longer entirely satisfied and after battling for several weeks to bring something new to her work, she came home with a bag of oil paints and brushes and a couple of large canvasses.

The artists' supply shop near the university was a delight; rows and racks of brightly coloured paints, stands displaying brushes, from the finest to the broadest and the cheapest to the most expensive. Stacks of canvasses stood against the back wall, sketch pads of all sizes sat in cubby holes. Anything an artist could need was in there somewhere and the prospective customer opening the door was engulfed in a heady scent; a mixture of paint, thinners and pastel chalks.

Alice had bought her supplies there since her student days and had been flattered to be greeted by name when she called in after an absence of several years, not expecting to be remembered, given the number of customers who crossed the threshold on a weekly basis

Though she was unaware, the elderly owner with his sharp brown eyes and pale face, dressed in a knee length buttoned up brown overall, was yet another member of the Alice 'fan club', one of a

number of people scattered across her acquaintances who were captivated by Alice's quiet charm and lovely smile.
When he was cashing up her purchases, he asked,
'Given up the water colours then?'
'I'm getting a bit stale. Thought I'd try something different.'
'Give it a go. What have you got to lose?'
'You're right,' she said and with her bag over her shoulder, a carrier bag in her right hand and the new canvasses under her left arm, she waited while he held the door for her and hurried to her car, anxious to get started.

She tried for weeks. It didn't work. She couldn't get the effect she wanted and everything looked stilted, even flat. The strong, vibrant colours were more appealing and suited her mood better but there was no flow and she was at a loss what to try next. With no-one to talk things over with, no-one to ask for advice, despair was hovering in the wings. Was she wasting her time? Perhaps she should give up the whole thing and stick to water colours?
She called in the shop again for a couple of new brushes and as there was no-one else there except the owner, they fell into conversation.
'How's it going? Are the oils working out for you?' he asked.
'Not really, the stuff I've done doesn't look too bad but there's no zip, if you know what I mean. I don't know whether to keep on going or whether I'm wasting my time.'
She was no longer an impoverished student, scraping through her purse for the cost of a paint brush. The small fortune recently spent indicated money wasn't a problem.
'Have you thought about trying acrylics? I'm selling more and more with every passing year. Customers say they are a dream to work with and very versatile. Some of the big names are using them; Bridget Riley and David Hockney for instance.'
'We tried most mediums in college and I always thought acrylics and oils were too bold for me. My best work was always with water colours but they're not working for me any more.'

Alice considered. The cost didn't matter. She didn't care how she spent Johnnie's money and he never asked where it went. Only the thought of another disappointment made her hesitate.

He waited, wanting to help, and another substantial sale to swell the week's takings couldn't be lightly dismissed.

She tapped her foot, played with the catch of her bag and stared into the distance. Should she? Shouldn't she?

'Let's have a look what you've got,' she said finally.

Yet another carrier bag of supplies was packed and ready to be carried out to the car.

Counting out the notes and waiting for her change, she felt a stirring of excitement.

'Heaven knows, I'm not a painter,' he said, 'but I've been round a fair few over the years. Sounds to me like you're trying too hard. Relax, throw the paint on, and see what it can do. Try a few things – you'll hit your stride, I'm sure.'

Carefully zipping her purse into her bag, she tossed her hair over her shoulder and flashed him a smile.

'If it's good enough for Hockney, it's good enough for me. See you soon.'

He came round the counter, held the door open and stood watching as she sauntered down the pavement, swinging the carrier and threading her way through the students coming from the direction of the art school.

He hoped he *would* see her soon, hoped she'd be in again for more supplies and hoped the acrylics would work for her. Only time would tell.

The first couple of days, she went back to the exercises they'd done at college, practising putting on the paint. Boxes, pyramids and spheres were painted and shaded and she stood back, head cocked and eyes squinting. There was something there which pleased her eye. Maybe this was the answer. Acrylics needed different techniques and she practised until she was getting somewhere near what she wanted.

The vague idea in the back of her mind was taking shape but she didn't push it. A picture was forming but she eased back and let it come, making a few preparatory sketches, lightly brushing the pencil over the paper.

Eventually, she could put it off no longer. The primed canvas was already on the easel, the paints laid out and the brush ready. She took a deep breath and made the first bold stroke on the blank surface.

When she next looked at her watch, two hours had passed but the painting on the easel in front of her looked as she'd seen it in her mind's eye. It was far from finished but despite her self-doubt, she thought she might have something.

Early the following morning, Alice picked up the receiver from the red, wall mounted telephone in her streamlined kitchen. Jeremy sounded enthusiastic but then again, he always did, and Alice took it with a pinch of salt.

'This isn't just another sale, Alice. This could lead to something big,' he'd said.

'This guy owns an exclusive London gallery and travels the country twice a year looking for talent. He's bought your second painting outright for an exhibition of new artists at the end of next month. If there's interest, and he's sure there will be, he wants another three, sale or return. For a London dealer, they're a snip at sixty pounds and you can bet he'll put on a good mark up.'

This was genuinely good news – the second sale in a month and the prospect of three more. The far off goal of being financially independent of Johnnie was a little closer.

'Jeremy, that's fantastic. Fingers crossed it comes off. I guess there's nothing we can do but sit back and wait.'

Faced flushed with pleasure, she tried not to get too excited. This could be a breakthrough.

The need to tell someone was overwhelming and she dialled Sally's number, tapping her foot impatiently but disappointingly, there was no reply. It would have to wait. She wouldn't tell Johnnie at all.

The potential for success spurred her on and she finished the picture in two days. She knew enough to leave it alone for a while and not tweak for tweaking's sake. The door of the room where she painted was left open during the day and she looked in every time she came upstairs, checking at the picture from first one angle and then another, working out if adjustments were needed and if so, where.

The door was closed well before Johnnie came home from work. It was nothing to do with him and she wanted to keep this piece to herself for a while, proud of what she'd produced but nervous of exposing it to anyone else. She was buoyed up, happier than she'd been for a long time and even Johnnie noticed.

'You seem cheerful, something happened?'

She brushed him off. She was hugging her secrets to herself and didn't want give him a chance to spoil them. He was getting grumpier with every passing day.

He can go to hell, she thought. I won't let him spoil this and went back into the kitchen.

The table laid and the food served, she called dinner was ready and as he sat down to eat, she noticed his face was drawn, almost haggard and felt a twinge of sympathy.

'Is everything all right?' she asked. 'Problems at work?'

'Nothing to concern you, and nothing you can help with,' he said dismissively.

He'd never talked to her about his business and wasn't about to confide in her now. Let him stew then, thought Alice.

His appetite had disappeared along with his good temper and even the carefully prepared chicken chasseur, wafting a hint of garlic around the kitchen and bubbling in a rich tomato sauce failed to tempt. He pushed a small portion around his plate, eating little and saying nothing.

Alice was relieved when he stood to leave the room, calling over his shoulder he had some paperwork to look at and he'd be in the dining room.

The routine was fairly well established. On the evenings he stayed at home, he'd spend an hour or so looking over whatever he looked over and then collapse in an armchair in front of the television, whisky and cigarettes to hand.

He occasionally went out alone without explanation except, perhaps, a muttered 'got to see someone' as he left, freshly showered and changed.

At the weekend, there was generally an outing of some kind, to a restaurant or club and Alice was expected to look her best and mix with his cronies and their wives. Not actively unhappy, she was discontented with her life but could see no way to change it.

She could escape during the day, either to Oak House or to stand in front of her easel, paintbrush in hand. Her previously buoyant mood deflated and with another lonely evening stretching in front of her, she did what she'd always done. She found something to do, briskly stacking the dishwasher and putting the remains of the chicken in the 'fridge. It would do for lunch tomorrow.

Her secateurs and the basket for cuttings were by the back door and she picked them up and went into the garden. The heady smell of the night scented stock rose to meet her, those tiny insignificant little flowers, easily overlooked during the day, which filled the evening air with fragrance. The murmur of Johnnie's voice on the telephone wafted through the open window as she worked her way along the borders, dead-heading the spent roses and pulling out the odd weed, stopping only when darkness was falling and she could barely see what she was doing.

There was no light in the dining room but she could see the flicker of the television through the patio doors and pictured Johnnie already sprawled in his armchair, whisky in hand and a pile of cigarette ends in the ashtray on the coffee table beside him.

She could either go and join him and sit mindlessly in front of some programme of his choice or go to bed early with the book she'd taken from the library that morning. 'Rich Man Poor Man' by Irwin Shaw had caught her eye and promised her another small escape. It wasn't much of a choice and she picked up the book and made her way upstairs.

Chapter 27

Summer was fading gently into autumn and Alice stood at the patio windows nursing a mug of coffee and watching the sparrows at the feeder in the garden. There was the slightest touch of gold in the leaves of the birch tree and, with the sun lower in the sky, the quality of the light had changed. The borders, which only a short time earlier had been bursting with colour, were losing their brightness, the lush growth of summer slipping away.

A long empty day stretched before Alice. It wasn't a day to visit David, Sally was back at work after the holiday and she wasn't yet ready to start a new painting. An idea was taking shape but she needed to let it settle. In the meantime, she was restless and fidgety. The housework was done. Her mother would always welcome a visit but she couldn't face the small talk. Maybe she'd drive out to one of the country parks, stretch her legs and look at the gardens. Nothing appealed. She recognised the feeling but didn't give it a name, she was lonely.

The ringing of the telephone was a welcome relief.

'Hi, Alice, Jeremy here. Thought I'd give you a quick ring to let you know your pictures have arrived safely in London and the gallery owner's confident they'll sell.'

'That *is* good news. Thanks for letting me know.'

'By the way, will you be calling in for your cheque or should I post it?'

She made a quick decision, this was a heaven sent solution to her problem.

'I'll come in. Would today be convenient?'

'Sure, I'll be here all day.'

'I'll be there around twelve and by the way, I've got something new to show you.'

'Look forward to it, see you soon.'

Alice raced upstairs and pulled open her wardrobe doors, scanning the clothes hanging neatly in rows, and pulled out a dark green trouser suit and a pale, jade blouse, patterned with a small diamonds. That would do nicely; smart and business like but still feminine. Fully dressed and wearing light make-up, with one last searching look at the new picture, she packed it into her folder and tied the tapes. She'd briefly considered going into town by train but the unwieldy folder might be difficult to handle if the train were crowded. The student days when it had been carted on and off buses and in and out of cafes and coffee bars were long gone.

Making her way through the traffic, thoughts of Johnnie were difficult to dismiss. She had no idea what was wrong with him. He was becoming more and more difficult to please and trying to keep the peace was becoming increasingly tiresome.

With a determined effort, she pushed him from her mind. More important was Jeremy's reaction to the new picture, so different to anything else she'd ever done. With some relief, she parked the mini, retrieved the folder from the back seat and set off towards the gallery, as nervous as she'd been on her first visit, hands a little clammy and heart racing.

Jocasta, still smart and still snooty, was in the gallery as she pushed open the door. She managed a stiff good morning before gesturing Alice to go through to the office.

Jeremy came round his desk to meet her, arms outstretched and gave her a peck on the cheek.

'How lovely to see you. You look stunning, as always.'

They chatted for a couple of minutes about mutual acquaintances, the weather and other inconsequentialities while Alice's nerves began to get the better of her. He still hadn't asked what was in the folder, was he purposely making her wait?

Finally, to Alice's relief, he said.

'Let's see what you've got.'

'It's different,' she said. 'Different from anything else I've done,' and she placed the picture on the easel where it caught the daylight.

'Hmm,' he murmured, putting his finger to his lips, his handsome face in a slight frown.

He hates it, she thought. He's going to tell me to stick to what I do best, stay with the water colours, at least they're selling. She waited, stomach churning. Didn't he know this was her baby he was judging? Finally, he spoke.

'Jocasta,' he called. 'Come and have a look at this.'

Oh God, was it that bad? What did Jocasta know about anything?

As Jocasta came through the door, she gasped and Alice put her hands together, gripping tightly, fearful of the response.

'It's amazing, just amazing,' she all but whispered, not noticing her accent had slipped. Was there the slightest whiff of 'Scouse'?

'It's a joy,' she said and for the first time she turned to Alice with some warmth and smiled.

'I'd hang it on my wall with the greatest of pleasure,' her accent back in place.

Alice breathed out, hardly realising she'd been holding her breath.

Jeremy was still studying the picture, moving around the room, viewing it first from one angle then another. Silent up to now, he finally spoke,

'Alice, you've excelled yourself. This is outstanding,' and he smiled broadly then paused.

'Wait a minute, I know this place. It's Charlie's garden, isn't it?'

The picture was vibrant with colour, much bolder than Alice's water colour style, not so defined. The outlines were slightly blurred, giving a softness to what could have been overpowering. At thirty inches by twenty five, it wasn't small but big enough to make an impact.

The borders looked almost alive but there was a darkness there too, in the shade beneath the trees at the far end. Two small figures in the distance, suggested total absorption, the grey haired man pointing towards the flowers and a young woman in a summer dress leaning forward to look and listen. In the foreground, bottom left, were two further figures with their backs to the viewer. They were stiffer and suggested conflict, heads half turned towards each other, faces indistinguishable, thrown into sharp shadow by the brightness of the sun. It was a picture that would provoke many interpretations.

Alice nodded.

'The idea came to me suddenly when I decided to try my hand with acrylics. It almost painted itself.'

Jeremy had an inkling of the emotion behind the picture but said no more about the content.

'There'll be no problem selling this. Let's celebrate, I'll buy you lunch. There's a good little Italian restaurant round the corner and we need to talk strategy.'

Why not, Alice thought. I deserve a treat. Her change of medium vindicated, and delighted with the response from Jeremy, she nodded.

'Mind the shop, Jocasta. I'll be gone about an hour,' he said as he shepherded Alice toward the door.

She stopped briefly and smiled at Jocasta. 'Thank you so much,' she whispered. 'I'm glad you like it.'

Welcomed by the waiter by name, Jeremy indicated a corner table and they were led across and settled with menus. Food ordered and a bottle of Chianti on the table, Jeremy chose his words carefully.

'I don't want to rush into anything. This picture could bring you double or more what you're getting for the water colours. We need to think carefully about how to introduce it and the best way to display it. Will you leave it with me for a few days?'

Alice took a sip of her wine. She couldn't help a smile breaking out, things were happening. She hoped Jeremy was right.

'Let me tell you something,' he said. 'I know Jocasta can be prickly and a little proprietorial but she has a terrific eye and an unerring instinct for what will sell. I trust her judgement implicitly.'

The food arrived, they'd both ordered lasagne, and Jeremy continued talking, telling amusing stories about some of his customers and the contemporary art scene. This talk of the art world was like food and drink to Alice. Someone was talking about the thing she loved, a proper conversation not sharp exchanges across the kitchen table.

Flirting gently, the unmistakeable look of admiration in his eyes made Alice blush a little but she was having a good time.

He put his hand gently over hers and looked her in the eye, more smitten than he cared to admit.

'You and I could go a long way together, Alice'

'Johnnie might have something to say about that,' she responded as she withdrew her hand, flattered despite herself but not wanting to encourage him.

Realising he might have overstepped the mark, he picked up his glass and said,

'Well you know where I am if you should change your mind.'

He raised the bottle to offer her more wine but she refused with a shake of her head.

'No more, I've got to drive home.'

Jeremy had called for the bill and suddenly said,

'Oh, damn. Isn't that Charlie's wife on her way out?'

Her eyes panicked, she clutched at her handbag and started to rise.

'Don't worry. She wasn't with Charlie, was she? She's got as much to lose as you. She can't say she's seen you here with me without having to account for what she's doing out to lunch with someone else; as frightened of you telling tales as you are of her.'

The moment was spoiled and Alice couldn't get away fast enough. Sick with worry, she knew Johnnie's reaction to this, however innocent, would be incandescent. Maybe Jeremy was right. It could be weeks before they saw Charlie and his wife again and maybe it would all be forgotten by then. She could only hope.

They parted outside the restaurant with a chaste peck on Alice's cheek. Jeremy went back to the gallery and Alice walked away. She needed to clear her head before she got behind the wheel. She had nothing to rush home for, Johnnie had said he was going out straight from work and didn't know what time he'd be in.

At least she'd be able to 'phone Sally for a good long chat and later watch what she wanted on television.

***

Johnnie slammed the 'phone down; aggravation after bloody aggravation all day. The lease being negotiated on yet another shop had hit a snag and one of the minions at his solicitor's office had been twittering on, should they do this or should they do that?

'Sort it out,' Johnnie had snarled, annoyed Charlie, who he regarded as his solicitor, had passed the job down the chain. Obviously, Johnnie's work wasn't important enough for the senior partner.

He was in the back room of the first shop he'd ever opened, going over the books and doing a spot check of the takings. Earlier in the day, his manager had come in with the news his mother had died and he needed a couple of days in Sheffield to sort out her affairs and arrange the funeral.

'Isn't there anyone else who can do it?' he'd asked, no sympathy and no condolences, only irritation. 'We'll be very shorthanded here. John's not back from holiday 'til the weekend.'

'Look, Johnnie. I've never asked for time off. I take my two weeks like everybody else. There *is* no-one else, my dad died ten years ago and I'm an only child. I'll go straight after work tonight and should be back the day after tomorrow.'

Johnnie sat back in his chair, twirling his pen.

'I suppose we'll have to manage,' he said grudgingly. 'Get back as soon as you can. I'll close up tomorrow night and get Micky round to do the bank run with me.'

It was standard practice for two male members of staff to walk to the bank to put the day's takings in the night safe. Occasionally, if any of the shops were shorthanded, Mickey was roped in.

There'd been some pilferage at one of the other shops; not much, a fiver here and a tenner there and not on a regular basis but it needed sorting. He'd threatened the manager with retribution if the culprit wasn't found.

'There's only three of you so it's got to be *one* of you. If it happens again, you'll be looking for another job.'

The stress was getting to him. The situation at home didn't help although Alice had seemed happier recently. Maybe they should get away for a few days, go down to Bournemouth or even to the Costa Brava, have a complete break. He hadn't had a holiday in years. As if that were going to happen, who could he possibly trust to leave in charge?

Slipping into his jacket, he passed the cash bag over and waited at the door while the manager locked up. They walked down to the bank on the corner without speaking, Johnnie mulling over the day's events, unaware the man next to him was near tears.

With the cash in the night safe, Johnnie muttered a quick goodnight and strode off briskly to retrieve his car. The manager watched him go with a shake of his head.

'Hard bastard,' he muttered.

***

He and Sandra had used this restaurant, a small curry house in one of the suburbs, several times over the last six months. With few customers this early in the evening and so far out of town, it was unlikely they'd see anyone they knew.

The brown skinned, neatly jacketed waiter came forward, white teeth gleaming, and gestured towards a table at the back where Sandra was looking over the menu. The décor, plenty of red flocked wallpaper and gold lights, left a lot to be desired but the food was excellent.

Bending to kiss her lightly on the cheek, Johnnie rubbed his hand over her shoulder and took a seat facing her. Her make-up was a bit too heavy, her neckline a bit too low but she looked good.

'How's it going then?' he asked.

Having loaned her the money to start her own beauty salon, he had a proprietary interest in the business.

'Takings are up again, not by much but up, nevertheless.'

She laughed.

'Don't worry, this month's payment will be on time.'

Johnnie never did anything for nothing and she was paying a good, if slightly reduced, interest on the loan.

The waiter approached and Johnnie placed the order; two beers, a chicken tikka masala and a rogan josh. The drinks arrived with a plate of poppadum and chutneys and as they started to eat, Sandra asked,
'How about you? You busy?'
She was hard headed and had a sharp business sense. She'd turned a run-down salon into a thriving concern, having worked for enough people who didn't know which end was up. Supplies were bought at negotiated discounts, two good stylists had been poached from other salons with a promise of higher wages while the juniors were paid peanuts. It would be no surprise if she sold the shop on at some stage in the future and moved to bigger, better premises.

Their relationship had shifted. She was no longer the empty-headed kid interested only in clothes, music and having a good time. He'd come to trust her judgement and talked to her about business affairs in a way he never could with Alice. This was no fairy princess who needed sheltering from the harsh realities of life.

Listening to his litany of complaints and looking up at him occasionally, she crumbled the poppadum on the plate in front of her, eating little but pushing the crumbs into a pile.
'Very inconsiderate of her,' she said.
'Who?'
'The woman in Sheffield who had the nerve to die while you were short staffed. Some people have no consideration.'
It wasn't often Johnnie laughed, especially at himself, but his face creased into a broad smile.
'You're right of course, right again.'
The food arrived and Johnnie tucked in while Sandra toyed with hers.
'What's the matter with it?' he asked.
'Nothing, it's fine. Just don't have much of an appetite.'
Johnnie lifted his glass to show the waiter it was empty and when his second beer arrived, he asked,
'Do you want anything else, ice cream maybe?'
'No thanks, I've had enough.'

He turned to the waiter, obsequious and smiling still, and said 'We'll have the bill then.'

He helped her into her jacket and followed her out of the restaurant. 'I'll see you there,' he said, walking towards his car.

Sandra was in her own car, a mini too. Unlike the brand new model Alice drove, it was several years old and she'd paid for it herself. Johnnie's tail lights disappeared and she followed at a more leisurely pace.

The rooms over the hairdresser's had, with Johnnie's help, been converted to a small flat and by the time she arrived, he was already upstairs, pouring himself a liberal scotch.

While the house in Hale was cool and elegant, these rooms were a jumble of colour, pink and green flowered curtains with a pile of cushions to match. The chimney breast was papered in a subtle matt gold paper and the mantelpiece dotted with the small china figures Sandra had started to collect a couple of years earlier. Alice wouldn't have given them house room.

Fleetingly, he thought this place looked more like a home than the big detached ever had. That was the home his self-projected image required; this was the place he felt most comfortable.

Shrugging off his jacket, he poured Sandra a drink and moved to sit next to her on the settee, putting his arm around her shoulders. She looked at him enquiringly.

'Television?' she asked.

'No, bed,' he said grinning wickedly, leaning in to kiss her.

Their love making was practised, like a well-rehearsed dance where each move called up a counter move, in complete harmony. Johnnie was lost in physical sensation, no conscious thought in his mind, responding to Sandra's responses, they pushed each other to the limit, increasingly demanding and vigorous. Johnnie felt the quiver of Sandra's oncoming climax and rushed to meet her but when he opened his eyes, was surprised to see tears leaking through her closed eyelids and coursing down her cheeks.

He lay on his back, Sandra tucked in with her head on his shoulder, her arm across him. The daylight had faded, there was a dim glow across the window from the street lamps outside and the faint sound of passing cars.

More relaxed than he'd been for days, Johnnie sighed gently and gave Sandra a gentle squeeze, about to sink into an easy doze.

'As good as ever,' he whispered.

She tensed a little before she spoke.

'Johnnie,' she whispered.

Sated and momentarily content, he asked,

'What?'

If she wanted something from him, now was the time she'd ask.

'I've got something to tell you.'

'What's that?'

'I'm pregnant.'

It took a moment for the words to register. She felt the rigidity in his muscles and he pushed her away, throwing the bedclothes aside and raising himself to a seated position on the side of the bed.

'What? How the bloody hell can you be pregnant? You're on the pill.'

'It must have happened after I had that upset stomach. A couple of days' sickness can play havoc with the pill.'

His voice was cold, devoid of feeling.

'Are you sure?'

'Yes, the doctor did a pregnancy test, I'm almost three months along.'

Silently, he rose to his feet and threw on his clothes, pulling on his socks and stuffing his feet into the shoes which lay side by side next to the bed.

Sandra lay and watched him, her hand, with the smell of him still on it, across her mouth.

'Say something,' she entreated.

He turned sharply, his face white with rage.

'I've only got one thing to say. Get rid of it.'

'Johnnie, can't we talk about it? I won't ask you for anything but I want this baby.'

'If you don't get rid of it, you'll never see me again,' he said, voice rising in anger.

He dragged his shirt off the back of the chair where he'd hung it so blithely only an hour earlier, and struggled into it, fumbling with the buttons. The spare he kept on a hanger in Sandra's wardrobe was the furthest thing from his mind.

'Let me know what it costs and call me when it's over,' he said, struggling for control. He didn't look at her again, didn't see the distress on her face and wouldn't have cared if he had.

The next moment he was gone, slamming the door behind him.

The screech of brakes roused Alice from a pleasant dream and she glanced at the clock. It was only eleven o'clock. Johnnie was home early and, by the sound of him, in no good mood. Their bedroom was at the front of the house and the thump of the car door and the low cursing as he searched for his house key carried clearly. The sound of the front door crashing into the frame would have roused a sounder sleeper than Alice. What on earth had happened to bring him home in this state?

She lay still, listening to his progress through the house, hoping he'd settle down before coming to bed. He'd come up sooner or later and, as usual, she'd pretend to be asleep. Dozing lightly, it was two o'clock when she next checked and there was still no sign, what was he doing down there?

Her answer came within half an hour. The bedroom door was flung open, the light from the landing falling across the bed, and he staggered in. Swaying and cursing, he struggled with his shoes and they hit the floor, one after the other. The shirt defeated him and after fumbling for a couple of minutes, he ripped it open and the buttons went flying. Alice watched through slitted eyes. She'd never seen him like this. Not only was he drunk, he was clearly furious. Lurching toward the bed, he banged his shins against the base, releasing a further string of obscenities.

Alice lay immobile, holding her breath. Would he make the bed before falling over? He finally hit the mattress, still in his underpants and socks, and pulled the covers around him, still swearing under his breath. Within seconds, he was out like a light and snoring fit to rattle the windows.

She wrinkled her nose, the smell was atrocious. The stench of curry and whisky was overpowering and lingering too, the smell of another woman on him. This was too much; he usually had the decency to wash before he came home.

She leapt out of bed and stormed into the spare bedroom, banging the door behind her. This was too much, she didn't know what she'd do but this was unbearable. After a restless, sleepless night, thoughts churning, she finally dropped off, waking with a start at eight o'clock.

There was no sign of life as she made her way downstairs. Let him stew, she thought. The sitting room was a shambles; cushions all over the place, the patio doors wide open, an open whisky bottle on the coffee table, a glass on its side and an overflowing ashtray. The table was ruined; stained and ringed from the slopped spirit with a cigarette burn on the edge. He could have burned the house down. Despite the open door, the place smelled like a brewery. No wonder, there was a huge stain across the settee, more whisky she supposed. Unable to face the mess, she closed the door in disgust. It would have to wait.

With no real plan formulated, she resolved to leave him. She'd manage. Like a light switched on in a darkened room, the realisation hit her. Her whole life had been controlled, first by her father and then by Johnnie; falling into line, not making waves and doing anything to keep the peace. Never again, she was done with it.

Chapter 28

Johnnie surfaced at ten, banging around in the bathroom and the bedroom, before making his way downstairs.

Alice was motionless on a bench in the garden, nursing yet another coffee. She didn't want to see him or speak to him, just wished he'd go, to hell if possible.

'Alice,' he called and when there was no response, he shouted again, voice rising.

'Alice, where the bloody hell are you?'

There'd be no peace until she answered and reluctantly, she went back into the kitchen.

As usual, his dress was immaculate although his face was a mess; blood shot eyes and pallid, slightly sweaty skin. Looked like the mother and father of a hangover.

'Where's the aspirin?' he croaked.

Without speaking, Alice opened a kitchen cupboard, pulled out the packet and tossed it to him, watching while he pushed two tablets out of the packing and threw them into his mouth, gulping down a glass of water he'd already drawn.

'Why didn't you wake me?' His voice was coarse and rasping.

'Why should I? I'm your wife, not your mother.'

She'd never spoken to him so defiantly, so coldly, and his rage of the previous evening was re-ignited.

'Bloody women, they drive you mad. Get out of my way.'

He pushed Alice violently to one side, heard her cry out but kept on going.

Shocked and frightened, Alice raised her hand. The steel trim on the open cupboard had caught her vertically down the side of the face and there was blood on her fingers. Her waist had collided with the counter and her hip with the handle on the cupboard below. It was hard to know what hurt most.

Still trembling she reached for the back of a chair for support and eased herself down, rocking backwards and forward, heaving sobs threatening to choke her. She'd never suffered violence in the whole of her life, never had a hand raised to her even as a child and she was shaken rigid.

There was no going back from this. She needed to get away and get away fast.

Painfully pushing herself to her feet, she climbed the stairs, holding tight to the handrail.

The damage to her face wasn't as bad as she'd feared. The skin was broken only at the high point of her cheekbone and the bleeding had already stopped but she suspected there would be some spectacular bruising and maybe even a black eye. Any other bruising would be under her clothes.

Sinking into a hot bath to try and relieve the pain at her waist and hip, she steadied. This is no time to panic. I'll go to Sally's, she thought, she'll put me up until I sort myself out. The first decision made, it was easier to make the rest.

Methodically packing the suitcase pulled from the top of the wardrobe in the spare room, she assembled enough clothing for a week or so. She lugged the suitcase down the stairs and parked it in the hall, gasping a little with the pain. Her clothes for the day were already laid out on the spare bed and she dressed awkwardly, favouring her left side. Her face would have to take care of itself, putting make-up over an open wound wasn't an option.

Despite the trauma, she was starving and made herself a sandwich and a coffee, washing the dishes and clearing up the kitchen when she'd finished. The patio doors locked and bolted, the chaos in the sitting room was left undisturbed. It's his mess, she thought, let him clear it up.

Her open handbag lay on the work surface in the kitchen. She found her cheque book and about twenty pounds in cash. Johnnie could be vindictive and may well block the joint account. He knew nothing about the new bank account with the painting money but still, it wouldn't hurt to be safe. With no conscience whatsoever, she raided Johnnie's hidden stash, taking three hundred of the five hundred pounds from the steel box at the back of the cabinet in the sitting room. It should tide her over for a while.

The struggle to lift the heavy suitcase into the boot of the mini left her holding her side and panting a little and she paused momentarily to get her breath back, leaning heavily against the car.

Crunching back across the gravel, she pulled the front door closed with a resounding crash. She reversed slowly out of the drive, looked at the house and wondered when she'd see the inside of it again.

The drive to Oak House passed quickly, she'd been on automatic pilot the whole way barely noticing the traffic, the pedestrians on the pavements or the shops and houses.

Mrs Phillips was in the hall talking to one of the staff as she came through the front door and Alice saw her register the damage to her face.

'What on earth happened, my dear,' she asked gently.

'I had a run in with a kitchen cupboard and came off second best,' Alice said. 'It looks worse than it is.'

This wasn't the first time Mrs Phillips had heard of married women walking into doors and she shook her head slowly, her eyes full of sympathy, but asked no more, only added,

'You know where I am if you want to talk. David's in the play room, he'll be pleased to see you.'

As usual, it was bedlam. For every child playing quietly, there were two with raised voices. The assistant in charge kept careful watch, ready to intervene if things got heated, as they often did, or step in to help a child who was in difficulties.

David, at four, didn't know the days of the week and didn't register exactly which days his mother visited. He accepted her arrival with shouts of joy, running up and tugging her along to see the towers of bricks he'd built, all sorted into colours, the red in one pile and the green in another. The yellow bricks were still under construction and she helped him separate them from the blue, trying to ignore her throbbing face.

Sitting on one of the low, tubular children's chairs, Alice watched him play, happy to be distracted from the thoughts spinning round in her head. Nothing held his attention for long and he was away, rummaging through the bookshelf against the wall, looking for his favourite book.

Flourishing a 'Noddy' book in its brightly coloured cover, he charged back, shouting,

'Story, Mummy, story.'

Alice moved to the shabby brown sofa against the back wall of the playroom and David climbed up on her knee, thrusting the book into her hands. She held him tight and for a moment, he relaxed against her, his arms round her neck. Overwhelmed, the tears dripped on to his shiny, clean smelling hair and she suppressed a sob.

He looked up into her eyes.

'Mummy hurt? Mummy sore face?' he asked, his expression sorrowful. His voice was, and always would be, flat and toneless but there was no doubting his sympathy.

'A little, I bumped myself.'

'Don't cry. Davie kiss it better,' he said pulling her head down and very gently kissing the bruise forming across her cheek.

'There. All better.'

'Much better, sweetheart, much better,' she whispered, struggling to keep control.

'Story now,' he said, turning to snuggle his back into her chest and turn the pages, wriggling to show she was holding him too tightly.

Story over, he was off again, pushing a sturdy red wooden truck across the floor in a race with another child pushing a similar blue one. The toys had to be robust, the children weren't destructive but some of them were clumsy and didn't know their own strength.

She didn't notice the door of the playroom open until David screeched,

'Mickey, Mickey!'

Mickey held out his arms and David launched himself into them, laughing and grabbing at Mickey's jacket.

Mickey spun him round to face Alice with a smile but as she turned, exposing her injury, he stood stock still and stared.

He often called in to see David, sometimes only for a few minutes, and often on the days when he thought Alice might be there.

Putting David firmly on his own two feet, he said gently, 'Go and play with Michael for a minute. I want to have a word with Mummy.'

'What happened?' he asked, gently putting his hand under Alice's chin and turning her averted face towards him.

'Not now,' she said. 'I need to make a 'phone call and then have a quick word with Mrs Phillips. I'll meet you in the car park in ten minutes. OK?'

A white faced Mickey sat on the old settee and watched Alice say goodbye to David. Saw too, the wince as she bent over to kiss him and the hand involuntarily move to her side. The bruise on her face was obviously not the only damage. His anger rising, he fought to keep calm while he played with David for the next few minutes, finally giving him a hug and saying he'd see him soon.

Alice was waiting, leaning on her car and gazing into space but she turned as he came towards her, tight lipped and tense.

'Well?' he asked, more abrupt than he'd intended.

'It was an accident.'

Mickey looked at her unbelievingly. There was no doubt in his mind she'd been beaten. He'd suffered enough at Johnnie's hands as a child to know what he was capable of.

Alice reached out and clutched at his sleeve, not wanting him to do something he might regret.

'It *was* an accident but it's an accident that won't happen again. I've left him, spoken to Sally and I'll be staying with her for a while. Please, Mickey, the last thing I need is to have you to worry about too. Don't do anything hasty, *please.*'

He was listening but not hearing, beyond furious, he wasn't about to make any promises. The bastard would pay for this.

He took in Alice's face; the red rimmed, haunted eyes, the pallor and the broken skin with its darkening bruise.

'Oh Mickey,' she wailed. 'It's all so awful.'

For the first time in his life, Alice reached out to him. He put his arms around her and pulled her against him, letting her sob quietly. For years, he'd imagined the bliss of any kind of physical contact with her but had never thought it would be like this.

Sobs subsiding, she pulled away, fumbling in her pocket for a hankie. Even distraught and distressed, she was as beautiful to him as ever, despite the sniffles and the running nose.

'Thanks for that,' she said quietly. 'I'd better get off, Sal will be waiting for me. Please don't do anything foolish.'

'I won't.'

It wasn't foolish to inflict just retribution, in fact he was looking forward to it, but Alice didn't need to know that.

***

Johnnie sat in the car outside the shop, one hand over his eyes, head screaming. He'd been drunker even than on the night the idiot was born. The idea of fathering another drifted in to haunt him and he pushed the thoughts away. There was a hangover to deal with first.

Roused by a tap on the window and through half closed eyes, he saw the face of one of the punters peering into the car. Wearily, he wound down the window.

'You OK, Johnnie?' and then a pause.

'Looks like it was a bit of a night. Get yourself over the road, have a good fry up. That'll put you right.'

Incapable of speech, he nodded and waited until the punter, smirking at his distress, had ambled off down the road. I'll remember that, he thought, next time most of his wages are in my cash box. See who's laughing then.

It wasn't bad advice though and he climbed cautiously out of the car and crossed the road to the café on the corner. As he pushed open the door the smell of frying eggs and greasy sausage met him full in the face and he backed away, on the point of gagging.

Some logical part of his mind told him he needed food; two aspirins on an empty stomach could never be a good idea. The shop door beckoned and he walked back, head pounding with every step.

The shop was empty apart from the staff, the two women looking nervously at each other when he appeared.

'I want two rounds of toast from over the road, a pack of paracetamol and tea, quick as you like,' and without stopping, he walked into the office at the back and closed the door behind him.

An hour later, the throbbing had eased although his stomach was still churning. Slouched back in his chair with his eyes closed, the coldness of Alice's tone and the distasteful look on her face crept in and out of his mind.

He'd never taken a day off sick since the first shop had opened but this was an emergency and in a sudden flurry, he jerked his jacket off the back of the chair. The accounts books were open on the desk but he'd achieved nothing, unable to focus on the blurred and floating figures. I can't function like this, he thought, I need more sleep.

'Back in an hour,' he shouted over his shoulder as the door banged closed behind him. It was fortunate he couldn't see the two women rolling their eyes and sniggering.

Alice's car wasn't on the drive and maybe it was as well. He couldn't have coped with her at present.

Straight through the front door and up the stairs, he pushed open the bedroom door. It hadn't registered through his hangover earlier but the place was a wreck. The bed was a tangle of crumpled cream sheets. His clothes from the previous night were strewn all over; trousers slung over the dressing table, shirt and tie on the floor and a scattering of white shirt buttons on the carpet. His stomach threatened to revolt against the sour smell of second hand booze and curry and he retreated to the spare bedroom.

Undressing to his underpants, he slid between the cool sheets and rested his head on the pillow. A faint scent, soothing and sweet, rose to meet him, the smell of Alice, and he drifted off.

He woke with a jerk two hours later, disorientated. It took a moment to register; he was in the spare bedroom. His watch showed quarter to four, later than he'd wanted but there was an improvement. His head thumped slightly as he rose, a warning not to move too quickly, and he realised he was starving.

There was no sound or movement in the house. To his relief, Alice wasn't home yet, there was time to pull himself together.

Washed and dressed and down in the kitchen, after rummaging around in the 'fridge and assembling a sandwich, he made some tea. There would clearly be some fallout from his behaviour this morning but he'd get round Alice, he always could. She should be home by now anyway, he always rang around this time. Her lateness and the state of the bedroom could be turned to his advantage, he might even turn out to be the injured party.

His major problem at present was Sandra. The thought of another child made his blood run cold. She would have to be dealt with first. She'd get the money for the abortion up front, today in fact. He'd take the cash round after closing the shop. He couldn't face another scene but it would be easy enough to put the cash in an envelope and push it through her door. She'd know exactly what it was for. There was cash in the sideboard he could use.

The bright, light and comfortably furnished sitting room was devastated, the smell of spilt whisky sharp in the air. Why wasn't it cleared up? What was Alice playing at?

The cupboard door was ajar, not a good sign, and he pulled out the cash box and lifted the lid; two packs of a hundred pounds, each in a paper band, and there should be five. His first thought was burglary and his second was Alice. What could she want with three hundred pounds in cash?

Despite his head, he pounded up the stairs and threw open the door to the spare room. The large suitcase had gone from the top of the wardrobe.

Into the master bedroom; Alice's make-up wasn't in its usual place on the dressing table. He flung open the door to the wardrobe. There was no way of knowing what was missing but there were lone hangers in the spaces where clothes had been removed.

He doubled over, holding his stomach as though he'd been thumped, fighting for breath. The feeling of abandonment was as sharp as it had been when Hettie had deserted all those years before. A note, perhaps she'd left a note.

As he kicked the clothes on the floor out of his way, the scent of 'Opium', the heavy musky scent Sandra wore, wafted upwards. My God, I *am* in trouble, he thought.

There was no note; not in the kitchen, which had been the logical place to look, not in the bedroom and not in the sitting room. He glanced at his watch; a quarter to five. There was nothing to be done and he had a business to run.

It was almost six when he pushed open the shop door and registered the relief on the faces of the two women behind the counter. Neither of them wanted the responsibility of closing for the day. All Johnnie's staff knew the consequences of mistakes.

'Any sign of Mickey?' he asked.

'He was in here about four thirty looking for you. He looked fighting mad but didn't say what about, only he'd be back later.'

'Any problems?' he asked.

'No, the cash is counted and the slip made out. It's all on your desk next to the bank bag.'

He often made a point of keeping them hanging around an extra ten minutes but couldn't be bothered tonight. Get rid of them as fast as possible. In minutes, they'd put on their coats, gathered their handbags and he was locking the door behind them.

The accounts ledgers were still open on his desk with the notes stacked on top. He all but collapsed into the chair. Disaster was staring him in the face and he realised he wanted Alice back more than he'd ever wanted anything.

She'd be at her mother's. Should he go round after he'd been to Sandra's and plead? He was even prepared to grovel. Would it be better to wait a couple of days, let the dust settle before he approached her?

The 'phone rang, harsh in the empty shop. It might be Alice, he thought, and snatched the receiver to his ear.//
'Yes,' he said.//
'Johnnie?'//
It was the unmistakable husky voice of his solicitor' wife.//
His rage was almost uncontrollable; another bloody woman giving him grief.//
'What do you want? I thought you understood it was over,' he said icily. 'Don't ring me again.'//
On the point of hanging up, he caught the amusement in her voice.//
'What?' he snapped.//
'In view of the fact your little angel is probably playing away too, I thought you might be interested in a re-match.'//
His heart pounded in his chest.//
'What do you mean?'//
'I'm not one to spread tales,' she paused. 'But .... a couple of weeks ago I saw that Page-Johnson chap pulling out of the end of your road. I didn't think anything of it at the time.'//
'That means nothing.'//
Johnnie's voice was unsteady. He didn't want to hear this.//
'Not on its own, it doesn't but lo and behold, I saw them yesterday in a restaurant in Manchester, around the corner from the gallery. Looked to me as though they were holding hands.'//
Johnnie held the receiver away from him and stared at it uncomprehendingly. He could almost see the malice dripping from the earpiece.//
On his feet and leaning heavily on the desk,//
'No,' he whispered and then again, louder this time, 'No.o.o.o' - almost a howl.

Motionless for a moment, the sweat broke out on his forehead and down his back. In one convulsive movement, he grabbed the telephone and yanked it violently until the cord left the socket. Half turning, he hurled it blindly across the room. It shattered the half glass in the office door and crashed to the floor.

***

As Mickey strode purposefully down the street, he saw the two women from the shop coming towards him.
Pausing momentarily, he asked abruptly.
'Is he in?'
'Oh yes, he's in all right,' said the older of the two. 'And he looks almost as mad as you.'
She started to smile but after a look at Mickey's face, thought better of it and nodded as they walked away.
'There's a spot of bother there,' he heard her say to her companion.
He reached the shop and pounded on the door. Although it was still broad daylight, the light in the back office was on but there was no sign of life. He banged again to no response.
'Bloody hell,' he muttered and pulled out his bunch of keys. Mickey had keys to all the shops and as he fumbled through the bunch, there was a muffled crack as the glass in the inner door shattered.
The earlier burning fury had gone, replaced with icy rage. He was about to administer the hiding of Johnnie's life. Alice's injuries would be paid for with a bonus for all the abuse he'd taken as a child.
As he came into the shop, he heard a strangled cry from the inner office, crossed the floor quickly and reached for the handle. Jagged points still adhered to the frame and the door grated over the smaller pieces of broken glass, pushing the larger pieces and the broken telephone aside.
'What the…..?'
Mickey stopped short. Johnnie was white faced and fighting for breath, his chest heaving. With one convulsive movement, he lurched

backwards and went down as though he'd taken a massive blow to the chest.

The chair broke his fall but his elbow caught the corner of the ledger protruding over the desk, tossing the stack of notes into the air. They fluttered and settled on him and around him while the ledger slid slowly at first and then faster to hit the floor beside him with a thud.

Jerking slightly, both hands clutching at his chest, his half open eyes looked up beseechingly, a clear plea for help.

Mickey stood and looked; no pity in his expression, just cold contempt.

'No more than you deserve, you bastard,' he said calmly. 'I suppose I'd better call an ambulance.'

Johnnie's head had fallen to the side. The last thing he saw was the lower half of Mickey's paint spattered jeans, his scuffed work shoes and the splintered glass. The last thing he heard was the crunch of Mickey's feet as he crossed worn lino and his voice, steady and unconcerned,

'I need an ambulance.'

Chapter 29

Mickey replaced the receiver and, leaning against the counter, lit a cigarette. As soon as possible, the impersonal voice at the other end of the 'phone had said.

His hands were shaking, reaction setting in. Full of adrenalin when he arrived and fully intending to knock seven bells out of Johnnie, he'd found him on the verge of what looked like a heart attack, lying helpless on the floor, ironically, covered in money. From first aid classes in the dim and distant past came remembered warnings not to move accident victims until help arrived. Did that count for heart attacks too? He had no idea but crossed the room to peer through the door, jammed open over the broken glass. Looking long and hard, he could discern no movement. The chest wasn't rising and falling when only minutes ago there'd been an obvious struggle to breathe. He looked like a broken doll.

The clamour of an ambulance broke the silence, followed by hectic activity. The attendants came through the shop and into the back office, grinding the slivers of glass into the lino and kneeling over Johnnie, brushing the notes to the floor. They tried chest compression and mouth to mouth but there was no movement, no resumption of breathing; nothing, a lifeless body, an empty shell. Mickey stood by and watched, unable to help and unable to look away.

'I'll get a brush and sweep that up,' said Mickey.

'Better leave it, sir. The police will want the scene undisturbed,' one of them responded.

After what seemed like hours, the activity ceased. They'd done all they could.

'Better get him to the hospital,' the driver said and turning to Mickey, 'you'd better come too, they'll want some details.'

He watched them put Johnnie onto a stretcher and roll him out to the ambulance. One arm fell and dangled, the signet ring catching the evening sun. The offending limb was tucked neatly back under the blanket as impersonally as cushions being straightened on a settee.

The thought of riding in an ambulance with a corpse, especially the corpse of someone he'd detested in life, was too much for him.

'I'll go and get the van and follow you down there,'

'Go into A&E, they'll put you right.'

The ambulance had attracted the usual complement of gawkers, the whispers going round. Is it Johnnie? Is he dead?

At Mickey's appearance, some wag at the back called out,

'Did you finally do him in then, Mickey?'

A remark which registered with the ambulance men.

Naively, Mickey had expected to fill in a form or two, give some information, and then be free to go and break the news to Alice.

Left in a waiting room for hours, wondering what was going on, he had time to mull over the events of the last couple of hours. God knows, he hated Johnnie's guts but he hadn't wished him dead. Despite everything, he suspected Alice would be devastated.

When a plain clothes policeman eventually appeared, he was rattled. He'd eaten nothing since lunchtime, could have murdered a cold drink. Anxious and shaken, he wanted to be away.

The copper, who'd introduced himself but whose name Mickey had already forgotten, led the way into a small, cluttered office off the main corridor. In his early forties and smartly dressed in a dark suit and white shirt, he sat down behind the desk and opened his notebook. He looked relaxed but his sharp brown eyes missed nothing.

'Now then, Mr Smith, if you can answer a few questions, we can get you on your way.'

The first had been easy enough, his name and address; then the name of the deceased, address and next of kin, the policeman writing everything down in his notebook.

'Tell me exactly what happened.'

Mickey told the officer how he'd arrived at the shop, seen the internal window break and then opened the door in time to see Johnnie fall, fighting for breath.

The questions gradually became more complex. What was his relationship to Johnnie? Did he know if anything was troubling him, did he have any enemies? What about Mrs Marshall, how well did he know her?

Mickey answered briefly and clearly without volunteering extra information, suddenly aware which way the wind was blowing.

'Am I suspected of something?' he finally asked.

'No, not at present. As far as we can tell, no crime has been committed but the circumstances are far from straightforward.'

Mickey was unaware the ambulance men and a doctor had made a preliminary report. There was no obvious physical injury; no knife wounds, no head trauma and no bruising. Nevertheless, it was still a suspicious death.

'Am I free to go? I need to go and tell Mrs Marshall. I'd rather it came from me than from a stranger knocking on the door.'

'Of course you're free to go. We know where to contact you if we need anything else.'

'What happens now?' Mickey asked.

'Of course there'll be an autopsy. This is an unexplained and unexpected death and we have to rule out foul play. The body can't be released before then.'

Mickey was grinding his teeth. If he says 'of course' one more time, I'll thump him, he thought.

'Where can we get in touch with Mrs Marshall? We'll need to ask her a few questions and we'll be along to see her in the morning and he waited, pen poised over the pad.

'In the meantime, if you'd be kind enough to leave me your keys, we'll want to have a good look at the premises. They'll be closed, of course, until we've concluded our enquiries.'

Mickey fished out his ring of keys, removed those for the West Gorton shop and placed them on the desk. With a nod at the policemen, he set off at high speed down the corridor.

Alice was with Sally at the kitchen table. She'd arrived on the step an hour earlier, suitcase in hand, tearful and worn out. The day had taken its toll and the worst was yet to come. The whole sorry affair had tumbled out and, for once, Sally was lost for words, shocked to the core at the injury to Alice's face.

The momentary silence was interrupted by a knocking at the front door which echoed down the hall and into the kitchen.

'It might be Mickey,' Sally said.

'And it might be Johnnie,' whispered Alice. 'If it is, I don't want to see him. Don't let him in. Tell him you don't know where I am.'

'Don't worry, I'll see him off.'

Alice heard the front door open, the gentle murmur of voices and two sets of footsteps approaching.

Mickey came through first with Sally on his heels.

Alice had risen to her feet when she'd heard his voice.

'Sit down, Alice,' he said. 'This isn't going to be easy.'

He looked terrible. His usual high colour was gone and even his red hair looked washed out. Alice knew it was going to be bad news, was it David?

'I don't know how else to say this except straight out – Johnnie's dead.'

'What?' whispered Alice. 'How can he be dead?'

Alice's eyes never left his face as he launched into the story for the second time in an hour. She sat motionless on the kitchen chair, one arm supporting her elbow and a hand unconsciously nursing the wound on her face.

She listened but was unable to take it in, couldn't grasp it; interrupting and asking again and again,

'Are you sure?'

Sally was silent, her arm around Alice.

The realisation it was true hit Alice like a sledge hammer. She started to rise, leaning heavily on the table and pushing herself to her feet, only to pass out cold and slide to the floor.

As she regained consciousness, she looked up into Sally's worried face.

'I can't take any more, Sal,' she whispered.

'You don't have to, not tonight anyway. You need to rest, get your strength back. It'll be time enough to face it in the morning. Let's get you into bed.'

Sally went up the narrow staircase first and Alice followed, leaning heavily on Mickey, who sat her on the bed and went back downstairs. She put on the nightdress Sally had fished out of her case and slid into the bed that had been swiftly made up. Her limbs felt rigid, barely able to move, her mind whirling.

Sally handed her a glass of water and a small pink pill and she looked up questioningly.

'What is it?'

'It's only a mild sedative, I take them now and then when I'm in pain. It won't do you any harm. Get it down you.'

'Don't leave me, Sal,' she whispered.

'I won't, I'll sit here 'til you drop off. Don't try to talk.'

Holding Sally's hand, she finally fell into a doze and then sank into a deeper sleep, unaware Sally sat and watched her for half an hour or more.

The following morning, Sally brought her breakfast in bed, hovering in the doorway and watching her eat.

'I'm so sorry, Alice. I can't take any time off. We're shorthanded at school already with someone on maternity leave and the headmaster's off with 'flu. I'll come straight home, should be here before four. Will you be OK?'

'I'll be fine, really I will. A few hours on my own might help me get things sorted in my mind. I need to 'phone a few people too, my mum especially. If she's trying to get hold of me she'll be worried sick.'

'Mickey will be at home all day. He'll ring you later but if you need anything or just some company, give him a ring. I hate to leave you.'
'Don't worry, I'll be fine. Go now, you don't want to be late.'
'Ok then, if you're sure.'
'I'm sure, see you later. I'll call Mickey if I need anything.'
With a final wave, Sally went downstairs leaving the bedroom door open and Alice heard the sound of the front door closing and the car starting up in the street.

Sadness lay like a weight on her chest. She was struggling with the reality of what had happened. Warm and comfortable, she wished she could go back to sleep and wake up to find it had all been a nightmare. No use wishing, the facts wouldn't go away, and she pushed back the covers and forced herself out of bed to face another grim day.

The 'phone call to her mother was far from easy. The story, as far as she knew it, was told and then repeated. The questions came quick and fast but she could answer very few of them. The concern in Brenda's voice was clear. What could she do, how she could help? Should she come and stay with Alice for a while? Although she sounded hurt, she acquiesced when Alice made it clear she wanted to stay where she was.

'Look, Mum, I'll be chasing round for the next few days. I've got 'phone calls to make and people to see, it makes no sense for you to be alone my place while I'm running around. I'll ring you as soon as I know anything else.' A slight pause, 'Yes, I promise.'

With one unpleasant task completed, she contemplated another, much worse. She couldn't rest until she saw the truth for herself.

She went to the hospital to see Johnnie. Either Sally or Mikey would have volunteered to go with her but it was something she needed to do alone.

At the main entrance, the memories flooded in. The long, final walk to see her beloved father and then, years later, the horror of the removal of her baby. The very walls of the place were steeped in misery. She barely registered the bustle along the corridors, nurses chatting and laughing with each other, white coated doctors striding along, and the odd, lost visitor looking around for one ward or another. Even the pervading smell of industrial strength disinfectant and overcooked food failed to register.

The mortuary attendant was brusque and business like, this was all in a day's work to him. He checked her name, asked her to wait and then led her into an inner room. It was cold. The walls were lined with old fashioned white tiles and heavy duty rubber flooring absorbed the sound of her footsteps.

Johnnie lay on a wheeled stretcher, covered to the shoulders in a white sheet with only his face exposed. He looked so young; skin unlined and face in repose. He was gone and for the first time, she truly accepted she'd never see him again. Unaware of the tears running down her cheeks, she pushed a stray lock of hair back from his forehead and leaned over to kiss his cheek.

She forgave him unreservedly for the pain he'd caused her; for the infidelities and the manipulation and general unhappiness of the last twelve months.

'Goodbye, Johnnie,' she whispered. 'Rest easy.'

As she left, she was handed a plastic bag. Her look of enquiry elicited the response, 'personal effects'. She opened it briefly; the clothing he'd been wearing and a large envelope containing the Swiss gold watch she'd bought him the Christmas before last, his heavy signet ring and wallet. Another, smaller envelope was pushed down the side.

The receipt form signed, she all but ran along the seemingly endless corridor and out on to the car park. Breathing deeply, she steadied. The bag went into the boot. It would have to wait until she could face dealing with it.

When the doorbell rang, she was staring unseeing into a rapidly cooling mug of coffee. Try as she might, she couldn't shake the image of Johnnie's poor dead face. The thought that his helpless body, the body she'd held and caressed, would be cut open, minutely examined and mutilated continued to haunt her. She didn't know how she would cope.

The insistent ringing of the bell finally roused her. She'd expected Mickey but it was a strange man, a policeman, who showed her a badge and asked if he could come in.

He said he realised this was a difficult time for her, could she answer a few questions?

She supposed she'd have to sooner or later and beckoned him in. The details came first, could she confirm full name, date of birth and address?

He was pleasant enough and asked sympathetically about the injury to her face. It was an accident, she told him. She'd banged into an open cupboard door. Technically, this was true. Nevertheless, like Mrs Hughes at Oak House, the sergeant looked sceptical. He too, was familiar with the concept of married women walking into doors.

The questions continued. When had she last seen Johnnie? How did they get along? Why was she in Sally's house and not at home? What exactly was her relationship with Mickey?

She finally protested, her voice sharp.

'This is too much. I can't see the point of what you're asking. My husband hasn't been dead twenty four hours and you're hounding me with all this. We don't even know what he died of yet?'

'Exactly, Mrs Marshall,' he replied. 'But that will do for now. Will you be still be here if we need to talk to you again?'

'Yes, yes I will, for the foreseeable future.'

'I'll see myself out' he said, putting away his notebook and heading for the front door.

Alice's hands were shaking. Surely not, she thought, they couldn't think Mickey was in some way responsible but the anger she'd seen in his face on that final day lingered in her memory, giving rise to thoughts she didn't dare put into words.

The police came looking for Mickey again later and he was invited down to the station to clear up one or two loose ends.

He waited in a dingy interview room furnished sparsely with four plastic chairs on tubular frames, two either side of a table scarred with cigarette burns. A battered metal ashtray, dark brown with burned on nicotine, was centrally placed for the convenience of coppers and suspects alike and there were bars over the grimy window. Half an hour passed before there was any sign of life and Mickey sat quietly and looked around him, breathing in the accumulated miasma of countless nervously smoked cigarettes.

His thoughts that he had nothing to fear and nothing to feel guilty about weren't helping much and by the time two detectives made their entrance, he was thoroughly on edge.

'Good afternoon, Mr Smith. You'll remember my name is Johnson and this is my colleague, Detective McAllister. Will you tell us again exactly what happened?'

Mickey went over the story, from standing outside the shop to the ambulance arriving.

'I understand Mr Marshall wasn't easy to get along with. Had you and he had a row?'

'No, I hadn't seen him that day until I saw him keel over.'

The questioning continued; was there bad feeling between them? What about Mrs Marshall, how well did he know her? Why was she not at home? Was he aware of any health problems, did Johnnie have enemies, why had he gone to the shop after closing? How had Mrs Marshall sustained the injury to her face?

It went on and on. Mickey answered each question as briefly as possible. He had nothing to hide, apart from his murderous intent. He hadn't actually done anything.

In a sudden change of tack, Detective Johnson asked,

'Are you sure you were outside the shop when the internal window broke?'

'Of course I'm sure. I heard the crack and saw the glass fall.'

'Mr Marshall didn't by any chance throw the telephone at you, did he? Had you threatened him? You're a big chap, you could inflict some damage if you'd a mind to.'

Suppressing his growing anger, Mickey sat back in the chair and stared the detective in the eye.

'That's enough. I want a solicitor. This is all guesswork. Whatever you think and wherever you're going with this, I never touched him and that's the truth.'

Detective Johnson looked at his colleague, who nodded. There was no evidence of any kind and the cause of death hadn't been established. Their efforts to unnerve Mickey into an early admission of some kind had proved fruitless.

'We're done for the moment,' replied Detective Johnson. You can go but we may want to speak to you again.'

'You know where to find me but remember, no more questions without a solicitor.'

Mickey left the police station. Johnnie had been a pain in the arse when he was alive and he was still a pain in the arse dead.

Chapter 30

Alice was close to defeat. She didn't know what to do next. She needed help. Charlie, she'd ring Charlie, he'd know what to do.

The news had spread like wildfire through the network of Johnnie's acquaintances and the telephone in Hale Barns had been constantly ringing in the empty house.

The relief in Charlie's voice was clear.

'Thank God you've 'phoned. I've been trying to get hold of you.'

'I'm staying with a friend for the time being,' she said, 'but I don't know what to do next.'

'What terrible news, I can hardly believe it. I'm so sorry, Alice, I can't imagine what you're going through but you can be sure you have my deepest sympathy. I'll help in any way I can.'

The kindness in his tone brought tears to her eyes yet again but she braced herself.

'Can you get down to my office? We need to speak. I know it's very soon but there are things that need dealing with.'

'Yes,' she said. 'I'll come whenever you say.'

'Leave it with me for half an hour. It would be a good idea if the accountant were here too. It could save time later on. I'll ring you back. Give me your number.'

She recited Sally's number and added,

'Please don't give it to anybody else. I couldn't face sympathy just now.'

'Don't worry, if anyone rings here, I'll take a message and you can deal with it when you're ready.'

A meeting was scheduled for the following morning.

Alice had dealt with the aftermath of her father's death but this was a whole different matter and she was out of her depth.

Dressed in the dark green suit she'd worn for her last trip into town only a couple of days earlier and under such different circumstances, she sat in the waiting room watching the receptionist pounding a typewriter and concentrated on holding herself together.

The intercom buzzed and a disembodied voice announced,

'Please send Mrs Marshall in.'

This was the inner sanctum, the meeting room where only the most important of clients were received. Her feet sank into the deep maroon carpet, the conference table shone with repeated polishing and the chairs were padded and comfortable. Heavy brocade curtains hung at the double windows, adding a distinct air of luxury to the room. The two impeccably dressed professional men came forward to meet her.

After an initial heartfelt hug from Charlie and a warm handshake from Roger, the accountant, they sat down either side of the table. Charlie began, brisk but reassuring.

'Johnnie's will has been lodged in this office since the day it was made. You know the terms; he left everything to you.'

Alice remembered the day clearly; they'd been married only a matter of weeks and Johnnie had been adamant. None of his hard earned cash should go either to his mother or his brother.

'I want you to have everything,' he'd said and Alice, in the first flush of married life, had simply acquiesced, eyes alight with affection, willing to do whatever he wanted. They'd thought they were indestructible, nothing bad could ever happen to them and love would insulate them from tragedy.

Was it only five years ago, Alice thought, it feels a lifetime away?

Charlie's voice pulled her back to the present.

'I'm the executor of the will and can deal with everything. However, nothing can be done until after the autopsy. I understand we're looking at a two or three week delay.'

Alice winced at the word with all it implied but she straightened. The grisly picture the word invoked haunted her but she tried to concentrate.

'What we can do, is start the ball rolling so we are ready to move as soon as the necessary documentation is available.'

He paused, pushing back his silver grey hair, and looking at her closely to see how she was coping.

'We have to apply for probate and it can be a complicated business. We need a complete list of assets. According to last year's accounts, the properties alone are worth around twenty thousand pounds.'

She was staggered and rocked back in her seat in shocked silence.

'Charlie and I have talked it over and unless you want to take over the running of the betting shops, our advice would be to sell them off. One of the big chains will snap them up.'

'Sell them, sell them all. I couldn't hope to run them properly.'

'Fine, we can set the ball in motion.'

Alice asked about the staff, sure they'd be worried about their jobs or even if their wages would be paid. Could it be made a condition of the sale that existing staff be kept on?

'I'll send my assistant round to all the shops to have a word with the managers, give them some assurances,' said Roger. 'We want them to be on the ball and not slacking off and if they're competent, the new owners would be foolish to lay them off. If they worked for Johnnie, they'll know their stuff, you can be sure.' he said with a wry smile.

Apart from their initial condolences, no mention had been made of Johnnie, the cause of his death or the funeral and Alice was grateful. She could only deal with one thing at a time.

'The housing stock is another matter. It will take care of itself for the time being. I understand there's a young man more or less in charge who knows what he's doing.'

'Yes, that's Mickey, Mickey Smith. He's worked with Johnnie since the beginning, both in the shops and on the building side.'

'I'll have a word with him. Put him in charge for the time being.'

There was no reason to mention he'd been closely questioned by the police. Surely her vague and shameful doubts were unfounded.

Charlie had always had a soft spot for her and she'd be guided by him. Trying to relax, her hands stopped shaking and the calm, controlled voice of the accountant made her feel she was in safe hands. They would start the proceedings and tell her what she needed to do and when she needed to do it.

'Alice, there's something we can't do for you,' said Charlie, 'something you need to do yourself.'

Alice stiffened and clasped her handbag tighter.

'What's that?' she said softly and in dread.

'Johnnie's personal assets need looking at. We have all the business figures but we need his private details too; bank accounts etc. and whether there was a life insurance policy. There may be stocks and shares or other investments and they'll all need to be declared. Do you know where they might be?'

'They'll be amongst his papers at home. I'll check and let you know.'

'Well then, we've done all we can at this stage,' said Charlie. 'Do I need to arrange for you to have access to some funds? All this is bad enough without you worrying about money.'

'No, no, I'm fine. There's quite a lot of cash in the house and we have, sorry had, a joint bank account. Can I still draw on that?'

'Of course, no problem there.'

Charlie took her hand between his warm palms and gave it a gentle squeeze, looking sympathetically into her eyes.

'Alice, if there's anything, anything at all I can do, please let me know.'

Sympathy undermined her defences and she fought back the tears.

'Thank you Charlie. I'll sort those figures out in the next couple of days. I promise I'll get in touch if I'm struggling,' she replied, her voice a little shaky.

'Please do.'

She shook hands with Roger and turned to leave. Charlie took her by the elbow and said,

'I'll walk you out,' and he accompanied her to the main entrance of the building, giving her bruised cheek a gentle kiss as she left.

'Try to keep busy, it's the best antidote to despair,' he said quietly.

The phrase 'life must go on,' came to mind as it had when her father had died and after David was born. She knew exactly what it meant. If she wanted to eat, she had to shop and cook. Beds didn't make themselves or bathrooms stay pristine by divine intervention.

By the time Sally arrived home from work, a light herby smell was wafting around the kitchen, the floor had been mopped and the sitting room carpet vacuumed.

'I hope you don't mind, Sal,' she said. 'I need to keep busy.'

'I don't mind at all, in fact I could get used to this.'

A brief smile crossed Alice's lips.

'Look, Alice, if you want to talk, I'm here. If you want to be left alone, that's fine too. Go your own speed, you've got a lot to deal with.'

'Thanks, Sal. Is it OK if I stay for a while, just 'til I get myself sorted out?'

'Stay as long as you like, you're more than welcome.'

'You don't know what that means to me. I have to go back to the house tomorrow anyway, there are papers to sort out.'

'If you wait until after school, I'll go with you.'

Alice considered the offer but then remembered the state of the house when she'd left. She'd be ashamed for Sally, or anyone else, to see it.

'Thanks but I'll manage. I can't hide forever and there's no point you hanging around while I'm shuffling paper.'

They spent the evening in front of the television although Alice registered little.

The sound of the front door closing woke Alice the following morning, Sally on her way to school.

An hour later, dressed in jeans and a loose pink sweater, she turned into the driveway of her home, got out of the car and stood for a moment, reluctant to go any further.

She sent a heavenward plea, 'Beam me up Scottie,' but it didn't happen and the smart black and white door still faced her, inviting no longer.

It had been only three days since she was last here but the place already smelled a little 'off.'

She walked through the house opening windows as she went. Only the dining room and the room she painted in were untouched, the rest of the house was in chaos.

In the kitchen, an opened and decidedly whiffy bottle of milk stood next to several slices of ham, open to the air, and curling at the edges. Half a dried up loaf lay on the breadboard, the butter was uncovered and oozing and crumbs speckled the black and white tiled floor and most of the work surface. The scum covered remains of a pot of tea sat festering in a beaker on the kitchen table. The 'fridge door hadn't been properly closed and a puddle had formed on the floor tiles.

The sitting room hadn't improved since she'd last seen it – rings and burns on the furniture and still a fairly strong smell of spilled whisky from the cushions of the tan leather settee which was drying out.

There were damp white towels on the bathroom floor, a ring round the bath and toothpaste on the mirror. Johnnie's shaved off black whiskers encrusted the sink, together with blobs of shaving cream.

Johnnie had clearly been home after she'd left. How could one person make this much mess?

More clothes littered the spare bedroom and the bed had been slept in but she knew the worst was still to come.

Her home, her beautiful home, reduced to a shambles. The mess was only superficial and could be cleared up but still, it cut her to the quick. It wasn't only how it looked, it was how it felt; grubby and soiled. He was the one who always insisted everything was perfect and not a thing out of place. She'd forgiven him all the other stuff but she wasn't sure she could forgive this.

Standing on the landing with her hand over her eyes, her mind churned. I could easily set fire to the whole place, she thought. I'd start in that bedroom and move through the house, torching something in every room and then stand outside and watch it burn.

There was no comfort and no peace for her here, only memories of the last awful morning, and though she'd vowed to keep control, broken sobs wracked her, wrenched from deep within and her whole body shook. She crumpled on to the top step, unsure her legs would hold her, and let it come.

Gradually, the sobs subsided and her mind wandered. Was this; Johnnie's death and her violated home, the worst thing that had ever happened to her? No, far from it, the worst thing was when Johnnie had signed the baby away.

Her anger rising, she jumped up, primed for action.

All the debris in the kitchen, including dishes, cutlery and the exquisite china butter dish were swept into a plastic bag. She refused to go round picking up pieces and tidying up. The bag was carried straight out to the dust bin.

She all but ran upstairs, waving a roll of refuse sacks like a sword, and flung open the door to her bedroom. Johnnie's discarded clothes were picked up between thumb and forefinger and dropped into a bag. The lingering smell of 'Opium' almost made her gag but she was unstoppable. She scooped up the loose buttons and they followed, the bag was tied up and slung through the open window.

The bed was stripped to the mattress. Duvet, pillows, and cream cotton sheets thrust into another bag which followed the first out into the garden. No matter the pillow cases were hand embroidered and had been a wedding present from her mother. She never wanted to see them again.

The spare bedroom suffered a similar fate; the suit, shirt and tie, underwear and shoes lying on the floor were thrust into a bag, closely followed by the bedding, and out they went.

The still damp towels lying in a heap on the bathroom floor were bagged, together with all the shaving paraphernalia cluttering the place, and went sailing through the bedroom window to land in the garden below. She did clean the toothpaste off the mirror and wipe the whiskers from round the sink, the mess was too disgusting to leave, but she'd do nothing else.

On the move, she ran downstairs and into the sitting room, looking objectively at the mess there. No, she wasn't about to shampoo the settee and rub down coffee tables. Her days of clearing up after Johnnie were done.

Back in the kitchen, she swept up the crumbs, wiped up the puddle from the half de-frosted refrigerator and picked up the 'phone.

'Mickey, I'm glad I caught you. Can you do something for me?'

His voice rumbled in response.

'I'm at the house, can you come round tomorrow with the van and move a settee and a coffee table for me. They can go to the tip.'

She waited and breathed a sigh of relief.

'What, now? Marvellous. Yes, I guess you and I can shift it between us.'

While she waited, she carried the plastic bags through from the garden and heaved them into the dustbin, now full to overflowing, and went to look in the garage for an empty box.

Mickey arrived within twenty minutes and although it was a bit of a struggle, they manoeuvred the furniture into the van, Mickey taking most of the weight.

'Do you want me to come with you,' Alice asked. 'You might need help at the other end.'

'There's always somebody there,' he said. 'In fact, I can guarantee it will disappear the minute it's unloaded. It's a nice bit of furniture.'

'One more thing, could you ask the cleaner from the shop to come round and give the place a thorough going over? I can't face it.'

'She'll jump at the chance. Better give me a key.'

Mickey asked no questions. Alice could do no wrong and whatever she wanted to do was fine with him.

'I'll let you know about the cleaner. I'll either ring or call in at Sally's when it's fixed up,' he said with a wave as he walked back to the van.

'Thanks, Mickey' she called after him. 'I don't know what I'd do without you.'

The remaining two hundred pounds had disappeared from the cash box. It didn't matter now but she wondered why he would need so much cash. She'd never know.

In one last effort, she loaded all Johnnie's papers and files into the box she'd found in the garage and carried them out to her car. They could be sorted out while Sally was at work.

Alice walked around the house closing all the windows. The place still didn't smell right and didn't feel right and never would again.

She stood on the drive and looked up at the house. It was unrealistic to think she could lock the door and walk away. Most of her clothes and personal belongings were still in her bedroom and Johnnie's wardrobes would need clearing and who knew what else there was to deal with.

One thing was sure, the house would go on the market as the earliest possible moment. She would never sleep under that roof again, whatever happened.

Chapter 31

Alice got through the next three weeks because there was no alternative. She wished the whole mess would disappear. Only her afternoon visits to Oak House kept her sane.
David sensed all was not well and was more than usually loving, giving her extra cuddles and saying, 'Smile, Mummy,' and kissing her until she did. Alice reflected he'd never met his father and now he never would. She'd harboured the faintest of hopes of Johnnie becoming reconciled someday. A miracle would occur and he would ask to see him. That door was closed forever.

Sally

The funeral was finally over and Johnnie was laid to rest, if he'd ever be at rest.
It had been truly awful. Alice, pale and composed at the church door, had shaken the hands of the mourners, one after another, fake sympathy expressed by the bucket load. I'd have taken a bet most of them hadn't even liked him.
I stood at the graveside, glad to see him gone. We'd grown up in the same streets and I'd known him since we were kids. He'd been a nasty piece of work as a kid and had only got worse. I was glad when people started throwing handfuls of earth onto the coffin. He was finally gone.
The only tears had come from Johnnie's mother, her gentle sobs almost inaudible as she leaned heavily on the arm of her eldest son. Tears had been shed too by the lone figure standing some distance away, not a member of the funeral party, but clearly a mourner. I recognised her as Johnnie's previous girlfriend, poor cow, and hoped Alice hadn't noticed.

The buffet that followed had been an even greater ordeal. I knew hardly anyone and couldn't help, couldn't deflect any of the attention from Alice. I could only stand by, trying to look discouraging and watching her cope with repeated insincere and empty sentiments.

Only Roger, the accountant, and Charlie, Alice's solicitor, had truly seemed to care about Alice. Charlie's wife, glamorous and dressed to the nines in a classic black dress, was unable to meet her eye and managed nothing beyond a vague mumble of sympathy.

As is the way with funerals, the atmosphere gradually eased with the appearance of food and drink and the buzz of conversation rose, interrupted by an odd burst of muffled laughter. Johnnie was already half forgotten. He'd had no real friends and would scarcely be missed. I'd expected the shop managers to make the most of drinking at Johnnie's expense but they were surprisingly subdued. Perhaps they'd realised one or other of the expensively suited men at the bar might turn out to be the new owner of the business and didn't want to make a bad impression.

Unlike the actual funeral, with a starting and finishing time, there was no definite end in sight. This lot could hang around for a couple of hours and Alice would be stuck there until they left.

Mrs Marshall came across the room, threading her way through the crowd at the bar to speak to Alice. It was ten or twelve years since I'd last seen her and I had to look twice to check it was the same woman. The head scarf, shabby coat and scrawny frame were gone. The well cut navy coat hadn't come cheap, nor had the matching shoes and bag and the light make-up made her look ten years younger than when I'd last seen her.

Alice and I were sitting as far from the bar as possible, nursing glasses of wine when she approached.

'Hello, Alice, mind if I sit down for a minute?'

'Of course not, I'm glad you could make it. It's a long way to come.'

She shrugged out of her coat and draped it over a chair, revealing a light grey sweater and pearls, and took seat facing Alice.

'This must be hard but I would like to know and Harry only ever has half a story. He said it was a heart attack, is that right?'

Alice, who'd spent two agonising weeks waiting for the result of the autopsy, was hard put to respond but this was Johnnie's mother, not some idle enquiry from someone looking for the latest gossip.

'No, not exactly a heart attack. The doctor called it cardiac arrest caused by congenital heart disease. There had always been something wrong with his heart but he never had any symptoms and it was never picked up. It could have happened at any time.'

Hettie sat back, hand over her mouth in shock.

'I should have known,' she whispered, 'I should have seen it.'

Alice reached out and touched her arm.

'You couldn't have. Nobody could. I never suspected anything either. There were no symptoms, nothing. The doctor told me the condition is fairly rare but not unheard of. There was no doubt at all.'

Answering the unspoken question, she said.

'The doctor said it would have been quick, very quick.'

Mrs Marshall, fighting back the tears, fumbled in her handbag for a hankie.

'I don't suppose it matters what it was. He's gone and no amount of talk will bring him back.'

For the first time, she focused closely on Alice's face then gently touched the faded bruise across her cheekbone.

'I've had one or two of those in my time,' she said softly. 'Never easy.'

This is getting worse, I thought, they'll both sobbing any minute, giving the assembled mourners something else to gossip about. Alice had kept her composure so far and she'd be mortified if she broke down. I gave Mrs Marshall a hard look, hoping she'd clear off.

To her credit, she saved the day. She couldn't have picked a surer way into Alice's heart.

'I believe I have another grandchild, a boy, David isn't it?'

'How did you know? Johnnie never told me he was in touch with you.'

She reached over and put her hand over Alice's, her expression sad and her voice low.

'He wasn't in touch, I never heard from him. I wrote to him regularly in the early days and have been sending birthday cards and Christmas cards ever since. My sister has always kept me up to date. That child was the worst kept secret in Manchester, everybody knew about him.'

Alice looked a little apprehensive, she was unaccustomed to speaking openly about David, always wary of an adverse reaction.

'You know about his condition?' she asked tentatively.

'Of course, but he's still my grandchild. Is there any chance I could meet him before I go home?'

The first real smile I'd seen on Alice's face since the day Johnnie died broke through, lighting up her eyes.

'Of course, I'll take you tomorrow.'

By this time, I was feeling like a spare part. These two were getting on like a house on fire, scarcely aware I was there. Alice was in safe hands. I was fairly sure no-one would interrupt this tete-a-tete.

I leaned over the table and said,

'Won't be long. Just going to have a quick word with Mickey.'

I was glad to escape for a while. The last three weeks had worn me down too and today had seemed endless. Mickey saw me coming and a drink appeared on the bar. We raised our glasses. Neither of us could drink to Johnnie. I'm not sure what we were toasting, maybe the fact that hopefully, the worst was over.

***

The room was all but empty, only a couple of stragglers lingering in the doorway, and we were finally able to beat a hasty retreat. Alice and I had gone to the cemetery in a cavernous black limo provided by the undertaker but Mickey had followed in Alice's mini. The three of us piled in, Mickey driving, all anxious to be away.

Despite the buffet, none of us had managed to eat much and Alice hardly anything at all. I raided the 'fridge as soon as we arrived at my place, piling the table with all sorts of fancy stuff Alice had bought, the likes of which the inside of my 'fridge had never seen; exotic pate, French cheeses, German sausage and ham and a huge rye loaf crusted with seeds. Tantalising smells filled the air as we unwrapped each package and within minutes, we each had a loaded plate and conversation ceased.

We were spread around my small sitting room on my gran's old dark green three piece, each with a glass in hand. It had seen more wear in the last two years than in all the time it had sat in state in my gran's front room.

Alice had changed out of the elegant black dress and court shoes she'd worn to the funeral into a pair of loose trousers and a bright red sweat shirt. She was sprawled on the settee, a revelation in itself, I hadn't seen her sprawl since we were teenagers.

Relief was in the air. The niggling worry of Mickey's repeated questioning by the police was gone, Alice's dealings with the legal stuff was under way and the funeral arrangements, a nightmare in themselves, were behind us.

Nobody mentioned the funeral. We talked about the past, about our school days and growing up in grim and grey post war Manchester. Neither Mickey nor I could have mustered a good word for Johnnie and even Alice would be hard pressed.

The alcohol was beginning to hit Alice. She'd never been much of a drinker and now the tension of the last couple of weeks was gone, she was like a slowly deflating balloon.

She waved her arm at the picture over the mantelpiece, the landscape of the park and the two girlish figures in the distance.

'It all seems such a long time ago. We were happy then, weren't we?'

She and I might have been happy but Mickey had been living a life of misery; scruffy, hungry most of the time and bullied mercilessly by the late departed. I let it pass.

'Any thoughts about what you'll do next?' Mickey asked in a low voice, rising to top up our glasses from the second bottle. Alice would be out for the count in no time and maybe that was what he intended.

'Sell the house, sell the shops but not the property. Buy a place near Oak House. You know, I could even bring David home for weekends.' The word 'now' hung in the air unspoken.

Her thoughts were wandering.

'Hettie's lovely, isn't she? We're going to see David tomorrow and she's even talked about me taking him down to meet his cousins. Too soon to make plans though, we'll see how it goes.'

Alice's glass was almost empty again, the last thing I wanted was for her to wake with a thick head.

Her voice was slurring badly.

'I don't know what I would have done without you two. I'd have gone out of my mind.'

She'll be blubbing in a minute, I thought and said firmly,

'Come on Alice, don't be maudlin. Thank us in the morning when you're sober. Let's get you into bed.'

I pulled her to her feet and though she wobbled a bit, she made it to the door.

'I can manage, I can manage,' she mumbled so I let her get on with it.

Mickey and I sat in silence as we listened to her pulling herself up the stairs and then banging around in the bedroom. Within minutes, all was quiet and we grinned at each other.

'She won't need a sleeping pill tonight,' Mickey said. 'Hope she's OK.'

He picked up the bottle, shaking it slightly to check the level.

'There's still a glass apiece in here. Shall we finish it off?'

'Why not?' I asked and held out my glass.

We sat for a moment, not speaking, as I swirled the wine in my glass, its ruby tones catching the light.

'Mickey,' I said. 'You love her, don't you?'

He looked at me, his eyes full of warmth and understanding.
'Yes, I do.'
His eyes said everything. He knew.
I loved her too. I'd loved her for years.

If you enjoyed this novel, try The Houses on the Green *by the same author. See details at www.eileensimkiss.co.uk*
: